THE BRIDGE ~~BOOK ONE~~

LOST
CONTACT

NATHAN HYSTAD

Cover art: J Caleb Design

Edited by: Christen Hystad

Edited by: Scarlett R Algee

Proofed and Formatted by: BZ Hercules

ISBN: 9798745357466

Also By Nathan Hystad

PROLOGUE

September 24th, 1989

Sweat clung to Dirk's forehead, and he wiped it off with a dusty sleeve. This was finally happening. The relic was heavy in his hands, even though it easily fit into one palm. He flipped the object around, ensuring each of the six hexagons was placed in the proper order.

"We can't do this," Clayton said, striding forward. The torches flickered as a breeze penetrated the cave, sending long dancing shadows across the far wall. Dirk watched them for a moment, almost expecting something to step out from the darkness.

"You know we have to. Are you telling me you don't want to see what happens, after all we've been through? We'll be the first people to solve the mystery. Our life's work." Dirk could have kept talking, but he saw the change in Clay's expression. His counterpart shoved round glasses up the bridge of his nose and frowned.

Clay held his hand out, hovering it above the artifact, and Dirk smiled at the man's tattoo. He had the same one on his shoulder. His thoughts drifted to his home, thousands of miles away. At this hour, his wife would just be waking up, preparing their children for the school day. He'd miss them fiercely.

"Are you sure we can trust them?" Clay asked, indicating the cave's exit. Dirk's gaze followed, pausing to look at the sketches from thousands of years ago.

"They'll do what we paid for. No sense in angering the gods," he told his friend, and Clay nodded absently.

Dirk walked to the cavern wall, running a finger across a rough etching. The creature was taller than the man depicted beside it, its head elongated, the eyes almond-shaped. It had been somebody's god centuries ago: an extraterrestrial from the stars. He turned the artifact over, seeing a matching shape on one of the sides. This was their final stop after procuring the sixth Token.

"We still don't know if the Bridge exists. Maybe we should check the…"

"No, Clay. We've been searching for years. This is the moment we've dreamt about."

Clay shifted on his feet, his dirty boots kicking up dust. "Things are different now. We have families, Dirk. We're not kids anymore."

Realization sparked in Dirk's mind, and he set the artifact on the stone pedestal, grabbing Clay by the collar as calmly as he could. "You didn't believe. You never thought we'd solve it."

"I wanted to, but… I can't go through with this," Clay muttered.

Dirk had to change tactics. He'd go alone if necessary, but provisions had been arranged, and he didn't trust Clay to disburse their findings properly. If anyone got wind of what they'd discovered, it would change everything, and Dirk didn't think it would be for the better. No. He needed to learn what lay beyond the Bridge. Hardy had so many theories, and if even one of them was true, they were going to need assistance from the other side.

"You're brilliant, Clay. I couldn't have solved these riddles alone. Your mapping abilities saved us on numerous occasions. Contrary to all of this, we have no idea what we're going to find, but I know one thing. We're a team. I can't do this without help. The entire human race needs us. They didn't leave these on our planet for fun. They want us to come to them. Now's our chance," Dirk said, letting go of Clay's shirt.

The other man wiped nervous palms on his pants and nodded with resolve. "Fine. We've worked hard on this. Believe me, I want to know if we're alone in the universe as much as you do."

It seemed like Clayton was back on board. "That's right, my friend. It's time." Dirk was nervous too, scared to death of what they might uncover, but he was more afraid that their dreams would shatter. That he'd have to return home empty-handed, with nothing but an old relic holding six hexagons they'd acquired from around the world over nearly two decades of exploring. He wasn't sure he could go on if that was the case. Not if what their previous benefactor had told them was true.

"Wait one moment. I need to give them something," Clay said, and Dirk saw the folded piece of paper in the man's front pocket.

He crossed the room, snatching it from the man's vest.

"It's nothing perilous, Dirk. Relax."

Dirk unfolded it, revealing coordinates and a series of numbers and letters. He passed it back. "What the hell is this?"

"Something for my daughter," Clay said. "I left her money in an account."

"Fine. But be quick," Dirk said, turning his attention to the artifact once again. It was ready. From the information he'd compiled on the Bridge, he was confident the hexagons had been placed correctly. All they needed to do was activate it. Hardy would be so proud of them. Hunter Madison would be furious.

Clay returned, white as a ghost and clearly terrified.

"We're about to uncover the truth," Dirk said, smiling widely despite his own apprehension.

The torches flickered again, though Dirk didn't feel any wind, and he lowered the artifact to the center of the stone podium. It was directly in the middle of the cave, and was twenty yards from any edge of the room. The ceiling was lofty; an opening overhead showcased the stars in a perfectly clear night sky.

Dirk stayed on one side of the podium, with Clay on the other as they'd practiced, and both set their hands to the device. It was made from an otherworldly material, a dense matte-black metal, and it was cool to the touch, even after spending most of the night in Dirk's clammy grip. He rotated it, ensuring the switch atop the cube faced up.

"Are you ready?" Dirk asked. The nerves he'd been ignoring surged forward, threatening to overtake his actions. He considered leaving. Maybe it was better not knowing what lay beyond the Bridge. He'd likely wasted the last seventeen years of his life on this fool's errand.

Clay watched patiently with eyes darting behind his spectacles, and Dirk waited for him to nod curtly before pressing the switch.

Nothing happened.

Relief flooded his mind, and his shoulders promptly relaxed. He laughed, unable to stop the feeling of joy.

Clay didn't join him. "The fifth Token. It's sideways."

Dirk turned it, realizing his mistake. "I was sure I had them in the proper placement." He stepped away from the stone lectern, hands shaking, but Clay took hold of his wrist and dragged him back.

"You're not going anywhere. Fix it, and try again. You spent all this time convincing me, and now you're too afraid?" Clay was angry.

Dirk planted his feet and only nodded in response. He corrected the Token, sliding it from its metal arms. He swiveled the hexagon, the peaks directing upward, and set it on the surface again.

"Here we go." The apprehension withdrew this time, and when he triggered the device, sparks ignited from the corners of the artifact. Neither of them let go as the specks of light grew in intensity, swirling around the cave. The wind tunnel blew out the torches, and a calmness overtook Dirk. Unabashed tears streamed down his cheeks as the brightness increased, and he craned his neck upwards, no longer able to see the same stars through the aperture in the cave's ceiling.

Blue light rushed from above, enveloping the pair of treasure hunters, and Dirk smiled as he was thrust to the sky.

He'd done it.

PART I
THE TRAIL

1

August 11th, 2025

I waved off the swarm of insects hovering in front of my face and stopped in my tracks. Angry welts burned on my arms, and at that moment, I hated myself for ever coming.

"This has to be it," I muttered, holding the GPS unit two feet from my eyes. The glow was bright under the dark canopy of heavy Ceiba tree leaves, which drooped ponderously with rainwater.

"You've been saying that for hours," Marcus responded. His forehead was covered in bites, and he tugged at his bandana, trying to conceal them.

"The main ruins are half a mile to our west, so the causeways ended around here. We know they built them for a reason," I told him.

"Rex, they wanted to relocate supplies around the swamps. It's the only reason for the roads." It was clear Marcus was losing his motivation for adventure, but I didn't blame him. The trek to El Mirador had taken three days on foot, thanks to the summer storms, and this wasn't his idea of a holiday.

I hunted for the stone path, noting it fifty yards to my

left. "There it is." My heart sped up at the sight of the crumbling square rocks. Just as I'd expected, the trail halted abruptly. My boots sank a good foot into the mud as I stepped closer, and Marcus stayed put on solid ground.

"You've got to be out of your mind. Tell me why I agreed to this again?" Marcus asked.

"Because you were my favorite student, and I've inspired you to leave your comfort zone," I suggested. My boots squelched with suction, but they landed on something stable again a moment later.

"You do know I'm not a student anymore, right? This is the third trip around the world, and it's always the same thing. We go home empty-handed, occasionally with some exotic disease," he mumbled, but I hardly heard him. "I can only imagine how many locals have come out here and robbed this temple clean of any artifacts since they discovered this place."

I glanced at the sky, seeing the glimmer of stars behind the thinning clouds. We'd already devoted two days to searching through the main complex, each of the three pyramids, and every abandoned structure, but my gut had led us to this spot. My father had always said to question the obvious route first, because it often led you in the right direction.

I took a step to the side, finding that the slab beneath my feet remained. This was the entrance. It was raining, but it had eased up, and a snapping twig caught my attention in the dense rainforest a short distance away. "Did you hear that?

Marcus tilted his head, setting a pack on the ground. "Hear what?"

I waited another minute, but finally ceased my worry. No one in their right mind would have followed us this far.

"This was a huge waste of time, Rex. I can't believe you

convinced me to join you. Come to Guatemala, you said. It'll be a hoot, you said. And there I was, hoping for a trip to the beach, chilling at a pool with a cerveza, but no…"

"Marcus, stop complaining." That silenced his ramblings. "Take the pack." I pointed at his heavy bag, and Marcus rolled his shoulders.

"Why?"

"Because you never leave your gear behind. Anything can—" I walked toward him and nearly tripped on something jabbing out from the slab hidden below the mud. The earth shook, vibrating deeply as the secreted entrance slid open, sending me into the swamp. Water rushed around me, and I was swept into the current, grasping at the air for purchase on anything stable.

I felt the hand clasp before seeing Marcus, his firm grip the only thing keeping me from plunging into the hole. The water was gone in a flash, and I scrambled to my knees, peering through the three-foot-wide opening into the ground.

"You were right," he whispered, slapping at a huge mosquito.

I was sore, sweaty, and soaked from the bog water, but I didn't care. We'd found our hidden entrance below El Mirador. "Grab the ropes."

A half-hour later, we had our rappelling gear locked and loaded, and Marcus started to move for the entry. I clutched his arm. "I go first. You know the rules." He was twenty-three and no longer my student, but I had a protective obligation to him. And truthfully, I owed him huge for all the effort and time he'd spent at my side during these ridiculous endeavors.

"Fine." Marcus turned his headlamp on and stared down. "It's a twenty-yard drop. I hope these aren't more tombs. I can't tell you how mad I'll be if some ancient mummy puts a curse on us again."

"Again?" I asked with a laugh.

"You didn't see the string of dates I went on after that last trip."

Ignoring his jokes, I shuffled to the edge and tugged on the rope, ensuring it was secured to the giant Ceiba trunk before starting my descent. I'd tracked this particular symbol for years, and it was inconclusive whether this was the right place or not. The sole artifact I'd seen at the Smithsonian, a golden moon on an eating utensil, was all I'd based this on, but it had looked so familiar. It was the same image drawn in the margins of my father's old journal.

I went slowly, one hand lowering to let go of the rope in my grip before the other grasped it, and in a few minutes, my wet boots hit the floor inside the underground ruins. The cave had remained intact over the centuries, huge chunks of stone piled atop one another, bracing the open excavation.

"Right behind you." Marcus started to drop as I detached my lanyard and drifted farther into the space. I turned on my lantern, the bright white light giving me a much better visual.

I glanced to the stone floor, seeing the water that had dropped from above rolling across the slanted stones. Marcus arrived, a huge smile on his face. "Rex, you're going to become a famous man!"

"It's not about that, and you know it," I told him quietly. The truth was, even if I discovered what I was seeking, no one would ever know I'd located it. I'd make sure of it.

"Sure, but imagine if you really come across something."

"Be cautious. Anything could be down here," I warned him, and he froze in place.

"What do you mean? Something worse than snakes or bats?"

"That would be the least of my concerns," I said, but I didn't elaborate. It wasn't common, but traps were still obstacles we had to contend with in well-concealed regions like this—although collapse was a more likely danger.

It was musty down here, years of mildew from rainstorms settled over the floor. The cave was empty, but I did notice two huge jaguar claws carved from stone above an exit, and moved for them, each step slow and deliberate. I listened for sounds of shifting rock but heard nothing out of the ordinary.

Marcus had his camera out, recording everything, the red light steady as he walked around the cave. I ran a finger over one of the claws and stepped through the arched opening, into the corridor beyond.

The symbols had baffled me my entire life. Six icons, repeatedly sketched in my dad's journal. He'd devoted his life to them, and one day had vanished. I'd been a little boy and could scarcely recall him now, but finding that book of his, stored with the few belongings Mom had managed to keep, had sparked something in me.

It hadn't been a coincidence that I'd studied archaeology, or that I was a professor now, just like he'd been at the start of his career. I figured that if I followed in his footsteps long enough, I'd learn what had happened to him.

My light seemed muted inside the hall, the lantern's beam cutting short in the cool caverns, but I didn't stop until I found the next room. It was on my left, the entrance up to my neck. Another emblem was carved in the stone mantel atop the doorway, and I smiled as I recognized the symbol for the moon. This was it.

"Marcus," I called, and he almost bumped into me as

he walked backwards through the corridor, getting a shot of the path behind him. Light reflected off his dark skin as he spun toward me.

"What is it?" he asked, aiming the camera at my face. I pushed his arm away and pointed at the carving. "Cool. The moon."

The room was dusty, the walls carved with intricate designs. A bench sat near a table, and I walked to it, lowering my palms onto the surface. Anticipation burned in my lungs, and my heart beat loudly in my ears. I blew on the table, sending motes of ancient dust adrift, revealing a single shape on the tabletop.

A hexagon.

I reached for it, but the shape was empty, devoid of the item I was searching for. "It's not here."

Marcus was closer, his camera jutting over my shoulder for the shot. "That's a bummer."

I turned, resting as I leaned against the table. Suddenly, I felt every bug bite, every mile we'd stalked through the treacherous journey here, and I ached for the lost funds to make this trip. It had been for nothing.

My sister was right. It was time to give up on these foolish dreams.

"What now?" Marcus asked, letting out air from his cheeks.

"We go home."

Marcus' shoulders slumped, and he'd started for the exit, when I heard the footsteps. I shoved my apprentice to the side, slapping my palm over his mouth. "Quiet," I hissed through my teeth. I pulled the old Beretta from its holster, acquired a few days ago from a seedy fellow a hundred miles from here. I flipped the safety off and kept one hand on Marcus, indicating he should stay put.

The corridor we'd entered had a single exit, and I

moved forward, Marcus trudging behind me while he continued filming. We'd left a lantern in the main room, and a shadow blocked the hall's entrance momentarily before stretching away from us.

Each breath felt far too loud as I listened to the muffled footsteps, and I had to turn to Marcus, pressing a finger to my lips. His eyes were wide with panic, and though I'd never shot someone, I was confident enough with a gun. My hand still trembled as I clutched the metal grip.

We returned to the circular open room, our ropes hanging from their secure mounts above ground level, and I motioned for Marcus to start the climb. He didn't hesitate. His compact camera slipped into his pocket as he darted for the exit. Whoever had followed us had gone into the adjacent archway, down another corridor. I wasn't going to wait for their imminent return.

Marcus was up the twenty-foot rise faster than I thought possible, and I clutched the ascender as the ground under my feet shook violently. Dirt and debris rattled loose from the ceiling, and long cracks formed in the stone walls and floor. The entire place was about to collapse.

Fear drove me up, my gun returned to its holster, and just before I arrived at the top of the hole, I saw the figure dash into the room. My abandoned lantern cast its glow over the black-clad man. He stared at me, but I couldn't make out a face in the shadows.

"Rex, time to hustle!" Marcus called, and I felt him clutch at my armpits, helping to hoist me above ground.

The earth shuddered, and I knew what was about to happen. Part of me felt terrible for doing it, but that man hadn't come to befriend us. "Cut the ropes."

Marcus did so without hesitation, and I pulled at him while rain poured over us from the storm. The stone slab cracked, and water rushed by our feet as we splashed from the causeway. I breathed heavily, my lungs aching from the effort by the time I let us take a pause, and we gaped at the location we'd emerged from, seeing the entire region buckle and drop.

"What the hell just happened?" Marcus shouted.

My gaze spun around, and I caught sight of the search-light. I heard voices heading for the opening. Whoever we'd left down there hadn't been alone.

"We need to hide," I told Marcus.

There were ten of them, and I yanked my binoculars from my pack, keeping most of my body behind a thick Ceiba trunk. I saw six men, all wearing black, and four locals holding assault rifles. Marcus must have seen the arsenal as well, because he was already running deeper into the trees.

It was going to be a long trek home, and we were leaving empty-handed, but at least we were alive.

2

Cassie's hand stuck in the air, her question spilling from her lips before I'd indicated she could ask it. "Professor Walker, are you suggesting a higher power called on them?"

I shook my head. "That's not what I said. I was only reminding you that each of the civilizations we're studying this semester showed proof of worshiping deities, many relating to the skies and beyond."

"Like heaven?" Luca asked. I saw a twinkle in his eyes. He loved to stir up debates in class, and tended to time the comments with the last five minutes remaining in the lecture. I appreciated his spirit.

"Sure. Kind of like heaven. As a people, no matter where we originated from, we always look to the stars for unanswered questions. All around the world, we have sun gods, or gods who ride dragons to Earth, visitors from afar. We have dozens of races paying homage to entities from space—or the heavens, if you will, Luca. We still do it to this day," I told them, crossing my arms as I leaned against my desk at the front of the classroom.

The seats were mostly full, which was a good sign. Many of the college classrooms would be missing forty percent of their students before Thanksgiving weekend, so I took pride that mine stayed engaged in my lessons.

Cassie's arm flew up again, and I smiled at her. She wore a sweatshirt, the college's acronym printed across the chest. Had I looked that young when I'd started post-secondary? It wasn't that long ago, only twenty years, but standing there, watching my students, it felt like a lifetime had passed.

I nodded at her. "Yes, Cassie."

"Do you believe in heaven?" she asked, and everyone regarded me with interest.

"I…" I didn't know how to answer them, but the bell rang, the clock striking three, and I shrugged as they started to rise. "I guess you'll have to wait until after the holidays to find out. Everyone stay safe and enjoy your time with your families. Don't forget that your paper is due when class resumes, so make sure you take a break from football and eating pie to comb through the assignment."

A few of them groaned at the news as they flipped laptops closed and slung packs over their shoulders. The rush to escape was on, and it only took a minute before I was alone in my classroom again. The silence was welcome.

My phone buzzed in my pocket, and I tugged it free, checking to see who it was. My sister was asking what time I'd be arriving. I sighed, sitting in my leather chair, and I spun around, stopping to gawk out the window. Most of the oak trees in the courtyard were bare-branched; a few desperate auburn leaves clung with hope.

I found myself regretting my decision to leave town for the holidays. It had been a year since Mom had passed away, and the wound was fresh in my mind. Seeing Beverly and the kids would only remind me of what I was missing.

The phone was heavy in my hand as I replied, *I'll be there by six.* I hit send and slipped it into the breast pocket of my tweed blazer. I'd accepted the role of classic professor with open arms: the loafers, elbow patches, complete with beige pants. I stifled a laugh, wondering what my dad would have thought of all this. From the pictures I'd seen of him at his college, he'd have told me to change into jeans and a t-shirt. Thinking of him made me check his old watch. The leather straps were cracked and had been repaired on numerous occasions, but the watch still ticked. I spun the mechanism around a dozen times, winding it, and slid my sleeve into place.

I flipped my laptop open, checking emails, and saw an incoming call from my old professor. With a smile, I accepted, tilting the screen until I was in the center of the video chat window. "Doctor Klein, to what do I owe the pleasure?"

"Are we using titles now, Doctor Walker?" the man asked. He was nearing sixty, but to me, he still seemed like the forty-year-old man that had mentored me from a young age. His hair had more gray in it, and his neatly-trimmed beard was whiter than ever, but he'd always taken exceptional care of himself.

I've never cared to be called a doctor. I'm proud of my achievements, but at the end of the day, I study old relics and teach anthropology classes. "Let's skip the formalities, Richard."

"Good. I heard you were in Mexico." Richard leaned away, picking up a cup with *Harvard* written on it.

I lifted an eyebrow. I hadn't told anyone where my true destination had been, instead opting to pretend I'd left for some rest and relaxation. "A few months ago. I can't believe we haven't spoken since then."

"That's how life gets. I've been busy, and you, with the new job…"

So that was what this was really about. "Richard, the job is going well. I think I'm getting through to these students."

The older man sipped his drink and set the cup down, steepling his fingers. "You were my best student. Your father would want you here, teaching in my department at Harvard, not for some two-bit college…"

I cleared my throat, speaking low. "I know what I'm doing. I get that you're trying to protect me and my career, but I won't work there. I've told you a hundred times."

"I understand, but please consider it at least. I've had some issues with the new Method and Theory professor, and I've already suggested the perfect replacement." Doctor Richard Klein knew how to push the right buttons.

I tapped my desk, seeing someone approach my office door. She looked through the glass, and I lifted a finger. "Richard, I have to go. I hope you have a great Thanksgiving. Say hi to Janelle and the kids for me."

My mentor rubbed his chin and nodded. "You heading home?"

"I am."

"Tell me you'll contemplate taking the position."

I sighed and smiled at him, not wanting to argue. I'd only make myself late for dinner. "I'll call you soon."

"Splendid. Take care of yourself, Rex."

The call ended, and I shut the laptop, waving Jessica inside.

"Do you mind if we speak for a moment?" the president of the college asked. She looked as professional as ever, her curly black hair dropping to her shoulders, barely skimming her jacket. She was part of the reason for my wardrobe change since I'd started here. A strict dress code was mandatory for the professors at this college, and I was happy to oblige.

"Sure, Jessica. Come in." I stood, coming to sit on the desk, and she took the first-row seat Luca had occupied.

"Rex, I know this wasn't your first choice of

schools…" she began.

"I love this job." I couldn't help but cut her off, and I zipped it, sealing my lips. I wondered if she'd overheard any of my conversation with Richard.

"Regardless, with your father's tenure at Harvard and your subsequent graduation there, I assume you had your sights set on teaching in his footsteps. I just wanted to say how delighted we are with your performance so far, and that we're thrilled to see you thriving in our administration." Jessica smiled, and I returned it.

"I'm glad to hear that. I know what you said makes sense, but I'm ready to carve my own path. Hopefully, that involves teaching here for as long as you'll have me," I assured her. She got to her feet, reaching her hand out. We shook, and her grip lingered a few seconds longer than I expected.

"Are you doing anything for the holidays?" she asked.

"Leaving town to visit my sister and her husband," I told her, and she nodded. "How about you? You and Mr. Hansen doing anything special?"

Jessica cleared her throat. "There is no Mr. Hansen." She walked to the doorway and turned before exiting. "See you in a few days, Rex."

What was that? I snapped out of it. If I was going to make it to my hometown by six, I'd have to put a move on.

An hour later, I was driving west in my five-year-old SUV, the heated seat on low as the temperature had dropped substantially. Growing up in the bedroom community north of Springfield had been boring as a kid, but once I was out of Boston's traffic, I appreciated the open air and the quiet roads. It was still busier than normal, even though it was mid-week. The holidays always created a mad rush to and from the big cities, but it didn't seem as bad today as previous years.

My music was interrupted as someone called me. I glanced at the screen, seeing Marcus' name, so I tapped the phone button on my steering wheel. "Marcus, what's up?"

"You have to be kidding me. Didn't you see my text?" he demanded, his voice high-pitched. It tended to do that when he was excited.

"No. I'm driving to my sister's. What did it say?" I asked.

"Turn on the radio," he said.

I went to do so, but he was on the Bluetooth. "I'll have to hang up first."

"Fine. Call me back. This could be it," he said ominously.

"Could be what?" I questioned out loud as I scanned through the radio stations. I used my satellite radio to pick up what I thought to be the most reputable news feed, and waited for an advertisement to stop.

"*Welcome back to* Across This Great Nation *with Bill McReary. Today, we're with astronomist Dr. Lisa Bronte. Lisa, what can you tell us about the anomaly discovered last night?*" My interest was piqued, and I shifted in my seat, waiting for her reply.

"*Well, Bill, we don't know much. The image only shows a small dark object against Pluto, so this will be speculation and conjecture, but there is a chance it's not just a hunk of asteroid from the Kuiper Belt.*"

"*What makes you say that, Dr. Bronte?*" Bill asked.

"*This is early days, but it doesn't appear to be moving.*"

"*Which means?*"

"*If it broke free from something, it would have a trajectory. You need reverse thrust to completely stop out there.*"

"*What are you saying, Doctor? That this is a vessel from outer space?*" Bill asked, and I cracked a smile.

"*Doubtful, but we'll be keeping a close eye on it,*" Lisa told him.

They went on to discuss what it most likely was, and that ranged from a distortion of gas to a large meteoroid. I turned it off and returned Marcus' call.

"You can't be serious," I said as soon as he answered.

"I thought you were looking for proof?" he asked.

"Proof? That's not what this is about," I told him.

"Then why are you searching for these strange artifacts from your dad's book? You want evidence of visitors from another world, don't you?" he asked.

I stared forward, staying within my lane as I cruised down the highway. I saw the signs for my hometown, and the familiar local shops' billboards along the ditches, advertising a couple of businesses I used to frequent as a kid. "Marcus, I told you I'm done with all of that. My days of dragging you into underground chambers are over." I cringed as I recalled the man killed in the cavern's collapse. I still didn't know who'd been chasing after us.

"But what if there's more?" he asked, and I could picture his face: sullen and withdrawn, as it always had been when he'd first been a student of mine. I knew he'd come from a tough background and had been looking for a real future when we'd met.

"There is, but I can't spend my life in pursuit of the invisible. It's time to let this rest."

My tone had a sense of finality to it that Marcus seemed to pick up on. "Okay. I'll keep an eye on this anyway. Just in case," he said.

"Fine. You do that. What are you up to for the holidays?" I asked him, and the pause explained the upcoming answer.

"Catching up with some friends. Enjoy your sister's house. Say hi for me," Marcus told me.

"I'll get you a piece of pie. I'll be home Sunday. Want

to stop by for dinner?" I asked him.

"Sure. I'll bring the beer. Talk soon," he said, ending the call.

Everything tended to feel smaller when I returned home, and this experience was no different. Except that for the first time, my mom wasn't here. The welcome sign was convivial: stark white, with our town's name painted in red. I drove through Main Street, slowing as I did so, and pulled over, deciding I shouldn't arrive empty-handed. The little market my sister and I used to frequent as kids with our mother was gone, replaced with a gym.

"Rex? Rex Walker?" someone asked from the sidewalk. Cool air rolled through my half-cracked open window, and I squinted toward the friendly-voiced man. I climbed out of the SUV, tilting my head, trying to recall his name.

"It's me, Turner Denworth," he said, grinning ear to ear. His teeth were straight and too white, his hair perfectly styled, and he wore an oversized trench and an obviously expensive suit.

"Of course, Turner." I shook his hand, squeezing tighter than I'd intended.

"What brings you to town?" he asked.

"Completely random. Nothing to do with the fact that it's Thanksgiving and my sister lives here," I told him with a smile.

"Always were a sarcastic one, weren't you? How is Beverly?" he asked.

"I thought you'd know everything about your community."

I'd seen his re-election posters plastered on the billboards as I'd driven into town. He ignored my jab. "Do you mind asking if I can count on her for her vote?"

"No problem, Turner. It was good catching up," I lied. I'd never liked the guy, not since he'd dumped my sister for some cheerleader in Springfield twenty something years ago. I thought he was smarmy then, and he hadn't changed a bit.

"Oh, I'm sorry about your mother. Must be difficult coming home," he said before getting into his BMW. He backed out, leaving without a wave. I watched him go, wondering if it was a mistake to visit here. I could be at my townhouse in Boston, listening to Bach and stoking my fireplace over a glass of red wine. Instead, I was looking for a grocery store in a town I barely recognized.

Five minutes later, I pulled into a giant chain store a few blocks away, one where you could buy a tent, shoes, and lettuce all in one transaction. I'd always hated this kind of place. I tried to picture my dad shopping somewhere like this, but couldn't imagine it.

I kept my head down, careful not to run into anymore familiar faces, and I managed to escape with a bottle of wine, a fresh-baked loaf, and coloring books for the kids. Were they too old for that? I hoped not.

Beverly's house was a place I'd never forget, since it was our childhood home, willed to her by Mom. I had no animosity about the inheritance, but I couldn't believe she'd actually chosen to uproot her family and move into it.

The sun had set by the time I approached her place, and I paused at the two-way stop signs, contemplating turning around. Instead, I flipped the blinker on and went right, driving the last few blocks faster than I should have so I didn't change my mind.

The streetlights were the old kind, with outdated low-pressure sodium lamps, casting an orange glow across the tar-patched street. Massive trees overhung the road, blocking out the night sky, and I parked in front of the house instead of using the driveway. I watched through the living room window, seeing Beverly and Fred inside, bustling around the dining room table. The kids sat on the couch, the lights of the TV flickering over their blank stares.

With a deep breath, I lifted my paper bag and small suitcase, and strode up the cobblestone sidewalk centering the yard. I remembered Dad putting those in himself. I'd been too young to help much, but I'd stayed with him the entire weekend while he labored, sweating in the summer sun.

His best friend Clay had come for the second day. Uncle Clay. I hadn't thought about him in years.

"You going to come in or admire the pavement for a few more minutes?" Beverly asked from the front door. A golden retriever ran through her legs, barking once before circling me.

I petted Roger while he sniffed the grocery bag. "Hey, sis. Good to see you."

The kids hardly looked up as I set my bags on the old hardwood floors, but Fred entered, wiping his hands on a stained apron before shaking my hand.

"Something smells wonderful," I told them, and Beverly's eyes lit up at the compliment.

"I didn't think you'd make it," she said softly, hugging me. "Come on, kids, say hello to your Uncle Rex."

Carson was five, and he sauntered toward me, eyeing me suspiciously. I hadn't visited since the funeral, and I didn't blame them for being cautious. I was practically a stranger. "Hey, fella. I brought coloring books."

"Thank you," Edith said, coming in for a hesitant embrace. I patted her back and handed her the goods. She was seven and was a spitting image of Beverly at that age.

The two ran off, returning to the couch, discarding the books on the coffee table. Beverly shrugged and motioned for me to follow her inside. "I made up Carson's room for you."

My old room. This was too strange. The house didn't feel the same, yet nothing had changed but the people inside it. The walls were still a tired beige, the cabinets sturdy but worn.

"I know what you're thinking. We're going to do some work on it, but…"

"It's too soon," I said, and she nodded.

"You always could read my mind. How have you been?" she asked. "Didn't you take a trip this summer?"

"I did."

Fred opened the oven, and I spied a ham inside. "Where did you go? A relaxing tropical vacation?"

I glanced at Beverly, and her face grew long. "Don't tell me you're still doing that."

"Doing what?" Fred asked, setting the roasting pan on two cork boards.

"Jeez, Rex. You want to end up like Dad did? What the hell are you doing?" Beverly asked, her teeth clenched together. I hadn't seen her this angry since we were kids.

"Okay, what's going on?" Fred asked, stepping between us.

"He thinks he can track down Dad. Stupid me actually believed he'd grow out of it. You're dreaming, Rex. He's gone, and there's no bringing him home." Beverly's shoulders stooped.

"I'm not trying to bring anyone back from the dead. I just want to know what he was after. Why would he abandon his family? We were kids!" I said it too loudly and leaned against the sink cabinet. "Look at us. Two minutes together and we're already fighting. Maybe this was a mistake."

Fred frowned. "Nonsense. You're family, and there's no shame in wanting answers."

"Great, take his side," Beverly said.

"Side? He's a grown man… an archaeologist by trade. One needs an inquisitive mind to do something like that. I don't blame you one bit for being curious about your father. Did you tell him about the box we found?" Fred asked.

My skin flushed as he spoke. "Box?"

"I should have told you to forget about that, Fred. Now he's going to obsess over it until he leaves."

I barely heard Beverly's words. "Where it is?" I asked.

"Can we discuss this later? Dinner is ready."

I glanced at my sister, seeing the girl I used to spend so much time with as a kid. She was still in there somewhere, buried behind twenty years of life, two childbirths, and a job she hated. I let it go. She was right. Whatever box of Dad's stuff they'd uncovered wasn't as important as me visiting with my family.

I walked over to her, pulling her into a real hug, one without pretention or obligation. I held Beverly, her arms wrapping tightly around me, and we laughed at the same time. I kissed the top of her head and let go. "I love you, Bev."

"You know I'm only mad because I love you too," she admitted.

I pulled the wine from the brown bag. It was the best I could scrounge up at the chain store, and Fred passed me a bottle opener. Soon we were all sitting around the table, the food plated, the wine poured, our hands washed. Beverly had some casual easy listening playing, and it reminded me of our mother. She'd always played music while we ate, something she'd done since I could remember.

"How's the new job?" Fred asked.

"Pretty great. The students are receptive. It's nice teaching somewhere and being taken seriously. I have a few bright minds that have some potential, and that makes it worth the effort," I told them. "How about you?"

Fred took this one, since he wasn't mid-bite, and he told me about his landscaping company. He'd expanded the previous summer in Springfield, but since they'd relocated here, he commuted two days a week, alternating from his home office in the basement.

The food was delicious, far better than whatever I would have scavenged, and even the cheap wine went down nicely with their company. The kids asked to be excused, and Fred took a phone call, leaving Beverly and me alone in the kitchen, cleaning up.

There was something on her mind, and I wanted to know what it was. "Everything okay?"

She paused, holding a plate of scraps above an organic bin. "It's tough living here. There are so many memories."

"Then sell it and go somewhere else," I told her.

She seemed shocked. "Mom wanted me to move in. To stay here with the kids."

"Bev, she wanted you to be happy. Plus, she's not around anymore. No one's going to be upset if you sell." Selfishly, I didn't want to have to return again, if I could help it.

"Are you sure? Fred was saying the same thing. He puts on a supportive face, but I can tell he never wanted to leave Springfield." Bev continued cleaning up, and I washed the table. "I'm going there tomorrow, if you want to join me."

"Where?"

"The cemetery," she replied.

The last thing I wanted to do was visit a gravestone for my father and mother, but it might be good to put some closure on this chapter of my life. I was done searching for a ghost. He was gone, and I wasn't going to find him. I needed to accept that he was dead once and for all. "I'm there."

Her eyes teared up, and she dabbed at them with the dishtowel.

"But promise me something," I said.

"Anything."

"We grab lunch at the diner after." I smiled, making her laugh.

"It's a deal."

3

Carson's bed was tiny, and my feet draped over the wooden ledge at the end. The pillow was lumpy; the sheets were freshly washed and smelled of fabric softener. His nightlight was the silhouette of a UFO, and I grinned as I stared at the dimly glowing device. When I was his age, I'd been into the same things. He had posters of dinosaurs on his wall, a T-Rex traipsing through a forest. Given my name, it had always been my favorite too.

The box sat on his desk under the window, and I'd left it there untouched. There were a few leather-bound books inside; a second, smaller box and a couple of miscellaneous shirts, holes in each of them from insects in the attic.

I'd promised myself I wouldn't look at the contents until I brought it home with me, but as I stared at the glow-in-the-dark solar system on Carson's popcorn ceiling, I knew that wasn't going to happen. The room was far cleaner than mine had ever been, and I climbed from the bed, hoping there weren't any building blocks on the old carpet to hinder my path. Carson had a rocket-ship-shaped lamp on the desk, and I flicked it on, the orange light spilling onto the box.

"What did you leave, Dad?" I whispered, taking the first book. It was dark leather, the edges curled from water damage, and had a band wrapped and tied around it, keeping it closed. I attempted to untie the knot but failed. The bind was old, maybe thirty-five years, and I reached for my folded pants on the chair, pulling free the pocketknife I always carried. I slid the blade through the strap and opened the book, seeing my father's familiar penmanship.

A thrill coursed through me as I noticed the icon. I knew this one. It had five stars forming a circle, with a streaking dash between them. There was no explanation for it, and I overturned the page.

Bridge. A single word underlined ten times, the strikes of the pen seeming to be erratic and deep.

I flipped to the next page, but it was blank. What was the bridge?

The next book was dated, and I noticed the writing was slightly more faded. I read the first journal entry.

March 2ⁿᵈ, 1973.

Clay and I did it. The trip to Mozambique went without a hitch, if you don't count the twenty-four-hour layover in Cape Town. The locals have been friendlier than we expected, and Clay was right to bring offerings for their village leaders. The bus ride took us as far as it could, and we found them a day's hike from the last stop. If Hardy's theory is correct, we're going to locate the symbol on-site tomorrow. Our hosts prepared us a delicious meal of seafood and piri piri sauce, and Clay is regretting going in for seconds. It's late now, and we have an early morning, so I'll be signing off.

Mozambique. I'd been there twelve years ago, after finding it was one of my father's many stops during his expeditions, but this was remarkable. The village he referred to here was gone by the time I visited, and I'd found nothing but overgrown trees and a crumbled stone wall.

I went to the next page.

March 3rd, 1973

Clay wanted to abandon the mission. He felt like someone was watching us, but I assured him he was foolish. Perhaps he wasn't. We found it, though. I don't know what it means yet. The piece is roughly the size of my palm, hexagonal in shape, and black. The symbol is etched inside the center, not protruding like Hardy had anticipated.

The locals have asked us to leave the site intact. They went so far as to search us, but I hid the artifact as well as I could. I'm lucky they didn't peruse below the belt, because I have a feeling they might have done something rash if they knew the truth. Now I feel the same eyes on me as Clay had, and I am regretting coming. This Token could be special, but I fear danger may follow it.

If Hardy is correct, there will be five more of these. The Bridge awaits.

There it was again. The Bridge. It was capitalized. It was a name. "The Bridge." I tested it on my tongue, and the hair on my arms stood. A light flashed in my periphery, and I peered outside, seeing bright stars in the distance, casting their glow from so far away. One of them flickered, and I assumed it was a satellite. I blinked, and it was gone.

The room I'd grown up in felt cold suddenly, and I was uneasy being here. The walls were closing in on me, and I gaped at the closet, as if expecting the monster I'd imagined in my youth to walk out and bite my toes.

I shut the book, gathering my pillow and blanket, and quietly crept down the hallway, the old hardwood creaking at the late disturbance.

I found the couch and knew sleep would evade me for some time.

———————

"*B*ed too small?" Fred's voice woke me from a restless sleep, and I opened my blurry eyes to the dull morning light seeping past the living room curtains.

I groaned, sitting up while rubbing my face. "Something like that."

"Look, I'm sorry about Bev last night," Fred said, sitting on the chair across from me. The kids' coloring books were on the coffee table, untouched.

"You have nothing to apologize for. We're good," I assured him.

"I know… she's been under a lot of stress. Would you believe it took her a month to even sleep one night in her parents' old bedroom?" Fred asked. He was dressed already, his hair damp from a shower. He'd shaven, and I spotted a tiny piece of tissue stuck to his chin, a red circle in the center of it.

"Would *you* want to sleep in your parents' room?" I asked with a laugh.

"Not for a second," Fred said. "Coffee's on. Can I get you a cup?"

"Sure. Shower free?" I asked, and he nodded.

"Kids are in the basement watching cartoons. Bev usually sleeps in when she can," Fred said, and I nodded in understanding. The Bev I knew was always up before dawn, ready to take on the day. Time heals all wounds, but tends to leave a scar.

Ten minutes later, I was drying off, dressing in dark jeans, a light blue shirt, and a brown blazer. I left my stubble and styled my hair as formally as I could. I was used to letting it air dry, then attempting a reasonable look befitting a professor of archaeology. With a dash of cologne, my transformation was complete.

Bev was in the hallway, wearing a bathrobe and

drinking a cup of coffee. "Happy Thanksgiving, Rex."

"You too. Sleep okay?" I asked her, but her face said it all. She hadn't.

"Fine. And you?"

"Perfect." We both lied to each other. They were the kind of white lies that meant no harm, but when you added them up, you struggled to recall what the truth was to begin with.

"Fred's making bacon and eggs. I'll be there soon." And with that, my sister was gone.

True to her word, I joined Fred and the kids for a delicious breakfast and a thick cup of coffee before Bev came in. She wore a long black dress, a simple gold chain, her hair pinned at the sides. She looked great, and I told her so.

"Thanksgiving comes once a year." She smiled, bringing back the young girl I used to know.

"Are you coming today?" I asked Fred, glancing at the kids.

He shook his head. "I think this is better suited for you two. We'll stay home and prep dinner, won't we?"

"I don't want to stuff a turkey's butt," Carson said.

"Then you can remove the gizzard," Fred joked, and Carson stuck his tongue out.

"Gross."

We all laughed, and I wondered if this was what I was missing out on. I was over forty, single, and living alone in a brownstone.

"Time to go," Bev said, still grinning.

We took my SUV and let the radio fill the silence between us. Outside, it was cold, thin gray clouds threatening to release precipitation that could turn to snow. We listened to a local forecast saying the same prediction, and it switched to the scheduled program. Usually, Thanksgiving

Day would have nothing but pre-recorded programming, with the news automated on the national holiday, so I was surprised to hear the familiar voice mentioning the date.

"*Welcome back to a special live edition of* Across This Great Nation *with Bill McReary this beautiful Thanksgiving Thursday. We're discussing the possibility of life from other worlds, and what that might mean for humans if we established contact.*

"We've been studying the stars forever, and many argue there is significant proof of visitations to the ancient civilizations on earth. Have we been visited, and when? My first guest is…"

"What are you listening to?" Bev asked after turning the radio off.

"The news. Marcus mentioned they found a mysterious object near Pluto yesterday. I guess it's bringing the crazies out of the woodwork," I told her.

"You don't believe in this crap, do you?" she asked, her tone friendly rather than confrontational.

"Are you saying you don't?"

"Aliens? Why would I? There's no proof, and there never will be. Because we're truly alone," she said.

"Isn't that a little far-fetched?" I asked her. I'd studied every ancient culture and still didn't feel like I had any concrete answers.

"More of a leap than aliens visiting the Mayans?"

I drove further, the quiet town's streets all but empty on a holiday at ten in the morning. The cemetery was north, and we came upon our old high school. We talked about our teachers for a moment, and I kept driving past the football field, toward the older part of town. The lots grew larger, and soon we were near the golf course. It was closed for the year, and I continued until the merge for the highway. The road swerved left, and I followed it as it turned to gravel, leading to the cemetery.

Snow started to fall the second we crossed Sleepy

Grove Cemetery's boundary, almost like an omen. A white blanket for a new start, or a reminder of how cold and dark death truly was. I didn't know which one I preferred.

"You come out here often?" I asked Bev, and she broke her stare through the windshield.

"I did, at the start. But now I feel more of Mom at home than I ever could here. You know how I get with this kind of thing. This is a grave. It's not Mom… or Dad. It's a symbol, but they're not really at this cemetery," Bev said, and I nodded along, agreeing with the sentiment.

I held nothing against people visiting their loved ones, bringing flowers and talking to gravestones. It just wasn't how I operated. "I hate that I feel guilty."

"For what?" Bev asked as I drove to the parking lot. I would never forget where their graves were located. I used to visit Dad's site every week when I was a little boy.

"I should have been here at the end."

"Mom knew how much you loved her," Bev said, as if that one phrase would atone for my sins.

"Sure." I parked, not quite ready to leave the warmth of the car. I hadn't added a jacket over my blazer and was quickly regretting my decision.

Bev rested a hand on mine. "Remember how angry she used to get with you?"

"Which time?" I laughed.

"She always told you to stay away from this place, but you'd hop on your bike and come regardless. I used to think you were so brave, going to a cemetery by yourself. I was scared. As stupid as it sounds, I still am, a little." Bev's gaze drifted to the falling snow, and I finally built up the nerve to exit the SUV.

"Mom was mad because she never believed Dad was dead," I told Bev.

"She did at the end," she replied.

This was news to me. "Is that so?"

"She had some pretty frank conversations with me about him. She admitted there was a time she considered that he'd run off to start a new family somewhere, but that didn't add up because of Clayton Belvedere's disappearance too." Bev started forward, her flats grinding against the parking lot gravel.

Clay. I tried to recall the man but struggled. They'd been thick as thieves, constantly setting out on adventures, but I couldn't really picture him. He'd had a daughter a couple years younger than me, a tiny blonde thing. What had she looked like? I'd just been a little boy, and my memories were foggy at best. Even my recollections of Dad were glimpses of emotions and feelings, rather than distinct images.

"What else?" I asked as we strolled down the stone walkway, heading for our parents' resting spot.

"In the end, she thinks he either got into trouble with some locals, sticking his nose where it didn't belong, or the pair of them were trapped underground, left to die. Even if their remains had been found, no one would ever send word," she said.

"Did she finally tell you where he went… that last trip?" I asked.

Bev shook her head, and I smiled as a snowflake landed on the bridge of her nose. *Bridge.* The name from the journal. I needed to read more of it, to discover who this Hardy was, and what Dad was truly searching for. I'd been ready to give it all up, but I doubted I could, given this new information.

"Rex, you have that look again. I thought you were done," she said, her voice full of disappointment.

"I'm not sure I can stop, Bev." I paused, trying to familiarize myself with where I was. The eagle statue stood twenty yards away, and I swept my gaze toward the angel guarding her quadrant. That was where I would start. "What if he was right?"

"About what? Aliens?" she asked, unable to suppress her disbelief.

"Yeah. What if it's true?" I asked.

"You're an educated man, with science backing everything you've been taught. How could Dad have stumbled on anything important?" she asked. "He was so…"

"Normal?"

Bev kept walking. "Dad never wanted to be with us, Rex. Don't you understand that? He made things up to give himself excuses for never being home. Not only that, but he's also ruined your life because of it. Mom's too. You think even if he didn't die back then, that it's worth finding him? After what he did to us?"

She pulled her jacket tight, blinking quickly as she stared at me.

"You're right. He didn't want to be with us, but only because there was something greater than his family to deal with," I said, maybe for my own benefit.

She didn't buy it. "That's a bunch of crap. I'm a parent, and there's nothing I wouldn't do for those kids. Nothing. You wouldn't understand," she said.

There it was again. The inevitable dig at my lifestyle choice. The perpetual bachelor. "No, I guess I wouldn't."

Snow fell harder, already coating the entire cemetery with a fresh sheet as far as the eye could see. The land flattened within the cemetery, rolling hills lining the back acres. The town, as I thought of it, technically was a city, but the cemetery was far larger than the population should have demanded. The township had been formed over one hundred and fifty years ago, making the dates on some of these crumbling gravestones well past a century old.

Most of those were in the far corner, near the vast oak trees and the duck pond. Those trees were bereft of leaves, and a few blew by me as we stopped. Dad's gravestone didn't match Mom's. His was from the late eighties, sometime after he'd gone missing. We'd held out as long as we could.

Dirk Allan Walker. Father. Husband. Dreamer.
05.18.48 – 09.24.89

He'd been almost the same age as I was now when he'd gone missing. It made me feel unaccomplished. Professionally, I was right where I should be. I'd done the schooling, worked for one of the world's largest museums, and now I was teaching in Boston with a doctorate under my belt. I'd met many of my goals, but I still felt like a fraud every time I threw that tweed jacket on.

I yearned to be chasing his journal entries, learning what my old man had been after. It was almost ironic. He'd had the family, the house with the white picket fence, the job and friends, and a doting wife, but all he'd wanted to do was the same thing as me. Adventure was in my blood, and the idea of never feeling that thrill again made me squirm.

In contrast, my mother's stone had ornate roses—her favorite flower—carved over the top ridges. There was gold etched on it, and I still couldn't believe she was gone.

Bev didn't speak as she gawked between the two markers like she was in a trance, and I stepped away. Something was bothering me from the book I'd found the night before, an avenue I'd failed to explore.

Clayton Belvedere. My father's best friend. They'd been sewn at the hips since childhood, and when Dad had first started his freelance treasure-hunting business in the early seventies, Clay had been there, leaving his job at the auto mechanic shop.

His tombstone had to be here too, somewhere among the thousands of markers. I peered over my shoulder, seeing the chapel a half-mile further, and decided to leave Bev for a spell. She didn't seem to notice me abandoning her, and I hugged my arms around myself, the chill of the morning seeping past the thin layer of my blazer.

A narrow river ran across the land, and I stepped onto a ten-foot-long arched wooden bridge, my feet slipping over the damp snow. *Bridge.* What had my dad been referring to? The name sounded familiar, but not distinct. It was like trying to think of the name of a band from your youth, knowing it, but unable to withdraw it from the recesses of your memory. It nagged at me, tugging at my brain.

The chapel wasn't large, its spire holding a rusted cross on top. It was Thanksgiving and snowing, so I wasn't surprised to see that the cemetery was empty and the building was closed. I knew this chapel also held their administrative offices, and I walked the perimeter, scanning for CCTV cameras. Nothing. I presumed they didn't run into many issues.

The walls were stucco, bits of glass and rock plastered to the exterior, and I touched one right under the window. The window was an old lift-style, single-pane, with a twist lock latching it along the bottom edge of the frame. In my occupation, I'd had to break in to a few unsavory places. Sometimes out of a few too.

My knife was in my hand a second later, the blade flipped open, and I dug it under the window. Snow had begun accumulating, and I blew at it, revealing the crack I was hoping for. The latch turned easier than I'd expected. The maintenance crew must be on top of the facility, greasing them to keep them from corroding.

I glanced around, ensuring no one was watching, and pushed up on the wooden window. It slid halfway open, and I judged that enough space to crawl through. I hopped, using my hands to lift me inside. I rotated as I entered, landing on a desk full of plastic containers holding pamphlets about death and upgraded mahogany coffins.

I was in. The lights were off, and I listened for any sounds of life. It was quiet, with the exception of an old cherry-wood grandfather clock near the coat rack loudly ticking the seconds away. Bev would be wondering where I'd gotten to, and I hurried, seeing the entrance to the chapel to my right. The offices were to the left.

I jogged past the bathrooms and found the door unlocked. There were three desks, along with four filing cabinets. I searched the tags on the fronts, finding they were filed in alphabetical order. A place like this might have the files all stored in the cloud these days, but I didn't have time to mess with electronics or password protection. Plus Clay had been missing since eighty-nine, long before they kept digital records of things at small-town cemeteries.

The B's were precisely where I expected them, and again I had to use the knife to pick the cheap barrel lock. It opened easily, and I began flipping through the files, combing for *Belvedere*. I found four, and assumed they were related to Clay. Parents or relatives. I retrieved his second and pulled it free. There was an address, and a next of kin listed. Ronnie Belvedere. His daughter. I hadn't seen her for thirty-something years, not since her mother had dragged her off after Clay's disappearance. She'd always blamed my father for losing Clay, and she was probably right to condemn him.

Each person was given a map when their loved one made their eternal resting place at Sleepy Grove Cemetery, and it looked like the office had added a copy to the resident's paperwork. I snatched it, returning everything to its original location. I crept from the offices and went to the window, which I'd left wide open. I exited, shutting the pane behind me. All that would be left of my visit would be melted snow on the desk.

I peered at the map and followed the dotted line from the chapel toward the duck pond. Clay's family must have purchased a plot for him prematurely, and I could tell from the quality of the gravestones that we were entering a different era.

Bev was still nowhere in sight, and I knew she was going to be pissed with me for leaving her out there alone. She'd just admitted she was scared of this place, and I'd run off.

I counted the ticks on the map. One. Two. Three. Four. Five. I walked as gracefully as I could over the plots, trying to be respectful, until I reached the proper markings. *Clayton M. Belvedere.* It was a simple stone. My heart hammered in my chest as I spotted the symbol. It was almost like a P overlapping over a capital T. The tattoo. My dad and Clay each had the marks on them, and the very same image was inked on my chest.

There were dates, and I crouched, noticing something else etched over the surface near the bottom left.

"Rex, what the hell are you doing?" Bev asked. I'd been so enthralled that I hadn't heard her approaching.

"Give me a minute," I said.

The digits weren't painted in; rather, they were carvings less than a quarter-inch high. I yanked the phone from my pocket and snapped a couple of shots, zooming to see if I'd captured it well. I didn't.

"Bev, do you have a pencil in there?" I asked.

"Pencil? Let's get out of here… wait, is that Clayton's?" she asked, the anger vanquished from her voice.

"Pencil. Do you have a pen? Something to write with?" I held a palm out, and she rifled through her purse. I'd seen the inside of my sister's bag before, and it carried enough survival equipment to make it through an apocalypse.

"No pen, but I have lipstick," she told me, holding out a golden tube.

"It'll do." I popped the top, twisting the base, and used the map in my other hand, flipping it over so I was looking at the blank side. I ran the lipstick across it aggressively, ultimately ruining the tube. "I'll buy you another one."

Bev was beside me, resting fingers on my back. "What are you doing?"

"Taking a rubbing. Usually, I'd use charcoal and a better-quality paper, but this'll have to work." I finished, and scanned the stone for any other markings. When I was convinced there were no more, I stood back, looking at the image I'd recorded.

It was a series of numbers. From a quick glance, they didn't make sense. Maybe they were coordinates, but something was off about them. This was Marcus' area of expertise, and I needed to share this with him.

"What are you hoping to find?" Bev asked me, her expression exhausted.

"I don't know, but aren't you curious what really happened?"

She started walking away. "I thought I could have a normal holiday with my brother. We'd catch up, you could spend some time with the kids and bond with Fred over a football game. And here you are, up to your old games."

"My career isn't a game."

"It sure seems like it. Give me the keys, I'll be at the car."

I glanced at the paper before folding it evenly, making sure the lipstick didn't smudge, and set it into my breast pocket. "Let's get some lunch." Whatever I'd just discovered could wait. It already had, for thirty-five years.

4

I said my goodbyes with mixed feelings about leaving. The past few days had been great once I'd let go and immersed myself into visiting with my family. I was stuffed, having eaten more in four days than I usually did in two weeks. Bev seemed better as she stood on our childhood home's front step with her lovely family, waving as I drove off. I had the box of Dad's belongings in the back seat, along with the rubbing from Clayton's grave, and I dialed Marcus the moment I was out of Bev's range.

I peered through the rear view mirror, noticing a dark-tinted BMW emerge from across the street, failing to signal as it ran a stop sign.

Marcus answered on the second ring. "Rex, you have to be thinking what I am, right?"

I laughed, imagining his goofy expression. From the tone in his voice, it was obvious he was excited, probably pacing around his small apartment. "About what?"

"The object near Pluto. This is it."

"I've been off the grid for a couple days. You're going to have to fill me in." I drove from town, happy to be on my way home. It had been nice to reconnect with my sister, but I was on the brink of a major breakthrough. I was sure of it.

"It's doubled. There are two of them."

"Two? How is that possible?"

"No idea. They split like a cell. Like mitosis."

"More likely, there were always two sections, stacked together to appear as one. It's too far out to see clear enough," I guessed.

"Maybe. You're going home?" Marcus asked.

"Yeah, be there in a couple of hours. I need you to come over."

"I already was. Remember, you invited me for dinner. Said there'd be pie," Marcus reminded me.

"Sorry, buddy. Forgot the pie, but we can order take-out. Even from that crappy noodle place you keep mentioning." I wanted to share the news about what I'd discovered, but held back. My foot pressed firmly to the pedal, and I had to ease off. The state troopers were out on the Sunday after a holiday, waiting for low-hanging fruit.

"You must have something really good, then. I'll be there." Marcus paused, and I could sense more coming. "Rex. What if they *are* heading for Earth?"

"The objects near Pluto?"

"Sure. What if they've decided now's the time?"

I prided myself in the evidence of facts, and I'd never openly admitted my belief in aliens in a professional setting. I'd followed the careers of some of the top people in my field, and anyone that remotely accepted the role of extraterrestrials in the shaping of our ancient cultures was quickly lambasted and kicked out of all social circles.

There may not have been enough actual proof for me to straight-up say without a shred of uncertainty that I knew aliens had visited us. On the other hand, I was certain my father, Dirk Walker, had believed, and that kept me open-minded.

Traffic was heavier, and I glanced in the mirror as I attempted to lane-change around a particularly slow semi-trailer. The dark BMW was still trailing me. *It's nothing. Just someone from the big city visiting relatives.*

"Meet me at my place at five. We'll chat then." I hung up before Marcus could ask any more questions, and instead of listening to talk radio for the duration of the trip, I set it to some soothing classic rock. I drummed my fingers to the beat of an old Journey song, and kept an eye on my speed as I anxiously drove for Boston. By the time I'd entered the city limits, there was no sign of the other car, and I breathed a sigh of relief. Something really had me on edge.

Marcus was already waiting for me as I pulled in front of my brownstone. Amazingly, there was an open parking spot three units down, a benefit of everyone leaving town for the weekend. Marcus sat on my front steps, scrolling on his cell phone, and I shoved the box at his chest. "Do you mind?"

He grunted, and I retrieved my keys from my pocket, unlocking the townhouse door. I loved everything about my home, and had lived here for the past decade, long before I'd even considered a job in the city. My parents had met in Boston and spent their first five years struggling in a small apartment downtown while Mom worked two jobs, Dad finishing his final dissertation at Harvard.

The place was stuffy when I entered, and I kicked off my shoes. The snow hadn't hit Boston yet, but it would only be a matter of time. I opened the front window, cool air passing by the white curtains, and I dropped my keys in the bowl on the foyer table.

"What's in this?" Marcus asked, setting the box on the kitchen table.

"Shoes," I reminded him.

He rolled his eyes and took off the laced boots, tossing them to the entrance. He ditched his jacket near the door, and I groaned at his taste in attire. It was nearly impossible to see Marcus in something other than a comic book or science fiction t-shirt.

Marcus was digging into the books, flipping through the empty one. "What's a Bridge?"

"That's what we're going to find out. I need you to locate someone named Hardy." I sloughed my jacket off and rolled up my sleeves.

"Hardy? Never heard of him. Where do I start?" Marcus opened his laptop and starting making quick work of the search.

"My dad mentions it in his journal. Hardy had theories about a Bridge. Something with a symbol. They found the first Token, and it mentions five more in existence," I told him.

"We know there are six. We've chased down every angle from your dad's records and come up empty-handed each time. Do you remember this summer?" he asked. "The AK-47s ring a bell?"

I placed the food order on the app and cracked a couple of beers, passing one to Marcus. "Here's what we have. Dad and Clay knew there were six of these Tokens. What if they collected all six? Used them to create this… Bridge."

"Then what?" Marcus asked.

"Your guess is as good as mine. That's why we have to find Hardy. He was ahead of them, so he had more details than Dad did. They were using his leads, which tells us he had a theory on the Bridge." I took a sip of the IPA, my tongue tingling at the hops.

"Locate Hardy, find out what the Bridge is and where it leads." Marcus smiled, fingers flying across the keyboard. "Not seeing much on Hardy. But I'll run it through my database; should get a hit if there's ever been mention of him in any collegiate-published papers or museum archives."

Nathan Hystad

Marcus was a genius at information gathering, and he held more research details on his personal server than anyone else I'd ever heard of. He liked to keep it low-key, not often sharing the resource with anyone but me.

By the time the noodle delivery guy arrived, we'd drunk the first beer, and his program beeped, indicating there were over two hundred hits. Most of them were references to a man from the eighteen hundreds, Jeffery A. Hardy. His work had revolved around the study of migrating Neanderthals, and that didn't seem like a match.

"How's the food?" Marcus asked, slurping a noodle. It spilled on his keyboard, and he wiped at it with a napkin, shrugging.

"It's not the worst thing I've ever had. Who's next?" I asked. "Anyone from the sixties or seventies?"

Marcus' eyes grew, and he clicked over a search result. "Brian Hardy. He worked at Columbia for a few years in the late sixties. Says he was let go after an incident, but the file was redacted."

"You got all that from your server?" I was surprised at the level of detail this kid was able to access.

"You think I half-ass anything? It's why I was your favorite student," he told me.

"'Favorite' might be a stretch. How about 'most determined'?" I smiled at his frown.

"Same thing. Brian Hardy. This has to be the guy."

I leaned over his shoulder, staring at the screen. There was noodle slop dripping from the top of it, and I used a sleeve to wipe it. "For someone so invested in his computers, you might want to take better care of them. Where's Brian now? And don't tell me he's dead."

"You're not going to believe this," Marcus said.

He paused, wagging his eyebrows for suspense. "Cut it out. What's so special about him?"

"Him? Not a lot. Looks like he never took another teaching job after Columbia, but he's done work for some pretty powerful collectors." Marcus switched browsers, pointing to the website.

"Hunter Madison…" The man was a billionaire eccentric who was into collecting anything and everything involving ancient cultures, particularly those centered on visitors from the stars. Not many people outside the circle knew of it. On paper, he was an investor, owning majority shares in at least seven Venture 500 firms. I was aware of him because my father had worked for the man. From what I could gather, most of his expeditions had been funded by Madison.

"You know this guy, right?" Marcus asked.

To say I knew him was a stretch. I knew he'd been at my father's funeral service, and apparently had a heated conversation with my mother. I heard my uncle had intervened, and Madison had left in a flurry, tearing away in a black Lincoln limousine. "We met when I was a kid. Where's he living?" I asked.

"Last known address is in New York. Once a New Yorker, always a New Yorker," Marcus said.

I laughed and went to the fridge, taking out two more beers. "Didn't you used to live there?"

"I'm the outlier," he replied.

"Ain't that the truth. Mark it down. We're making a road trip," I told him.

"Now?"

I glanced at the clock. I was beat after the weekend, not to mention, I'd had a drink, and the holiday traffic was going to be insane. "Tomorrow."

"I think you're forgetting something." Marcus started cleaning up the Styrofoam containers, tossing them into the empty garbage can under my sink.

"What's that?"

"You know, that thing you do during the week. You wear patches on your jacket, probably chew a pipe, try not to gawk at the hot third-year students twirling their hair around their fingers, asking you for some 'personal attentive at-home studying'." He said the last making air quotes with his fingers.

My job. He was right. "Damn it. Finals are soon." I couldn't wait two weeks. "See if you can reach this Brian Hardy and make the appointment for Friday. I have class in the morning. We'll go after."

"What if I have plans?" Marcus asked. He was a freelance research assistant, and from the sounds of things, work was skinny these days.

"Do you?"

He lost his grin. "I'll set it up. What if he won't talk to me?"

"Then he'll have to turn us down in person. Either way, we're going to New York this Friday."

"There was something else, right? An important discovery you couldn't wait to share with me? Now would be a good time."

"The rubbing," I said, slapping a palm against the table. I couldn't believe I'd forgotten it.

Marcus turned to face me, raising his hands. "Rubbing? I don't like the sounds of this…"

"Quit kidding around." I went to the box, picking out the folded paper cemetery map, and opened it, smoothing it on the table beside Marcus. "I found this on Clayton Belvedere's gravestone. They're numbers."

"I can see that. Why haven't you ever thought of this before?" he asked, his lips moving as he recited the digits at a whisper.

"I haven't gone looking. How was I to know there

would be some secret message engraved on the tombstone?"

Marcus shook his head and shrugged. "They don't make sense. There are no degrees or directions listed."

"Wait, what about decimal degrees?" I asked, and he frowned while sipping his beer.

"The decimal is near the end. I don't think that's it."

Puzzles. Why did everything have to be secretive and hidden from plain sight? Who else would have been desperate for coordinates on some obscure treasure hunter's gravestone in a nowhere city a couple of hours from Boston, unless it was meant to be a message for someone?

"That's it!" I stood up, bumping into the table. My bottle fell over, spilling on the map. I picked the paper up by the corner, the liquid running over the rubbing. It was fine.

"Now who's the messy one?" Marcus asked before grabbing the paper towel. He dabbed it gently. "What has you channeling Archimedes?"

"He must have set this up before he went missing. Clayton knew the message would eventually be put on his grave's marker. They're coordinates, Marcus. This is the big break we've been waiting for!"

I could hardly contain myself. I'd been chasing ghosts for so long without the hint of a real trail, always coming out with less money and fewer answers. This could be the moment everything changed.

"They're not. I'm telling you…" Marcus stopped and stared at the sheet. "Unless the numbers are reversed." He opened the computer again. Clicking on the mapping app, he keyed in the digits as they were. It didn't work. He started with the first string, adding the last number at the beginning, then a decimal, and the next six numbers from right to left. He repeated it with the second string on the rubbing, and his finger hovered over the search button.

"Would you quit being so dramatic? Hit it," I told him, and he obeyed.

I slunk to the chair as the map displayed the location. It was the middle of nowhere in Venezuela, four hundred miles south of Caracas. From what little I knew of the region, I wasn't overly keen on making the trek.

"What the hell are we going to find there?" Marcus asked me, but I really had absolutely no idea.

"I couldn't begin to guess."

"I'm sure you have a few theories."

I considered the statement. "Why was it on Clay's grave? That implies my father didn't want anyone revisiting his trail. Maybe Clay did this without my dad's knowledge. He hoped to leave the breadcrumbs for his daughter or someone willing to follow. It was his out. Or maybe he just wanted someone to eventually learn what happened."

"You don't think they died in a collapse on an underground site, do you?" Marcus leaned away in his chair, and we both stared at the satellite image of Venezuela.

I shook my head and tapped my finger on the table. "I know that's the widely acknowledged hypothesis, but there wasn't proof to corroborate that. We think they were brought to Portugal by boat, but that's where the line runs dry."

Of course, no one had truly put a real investigation into their disappearance, not to the level that would have been necessary to track them. I'd done my best when I'd graduated college, spending a summer backpacking every site possible in Portugal and Spain, attempting to learn any bit of information that might help. I'd returned with my tail between my legs and zero job prospects.

Marcus' eyes had that excited glint in them, and he finished his beer. "When do we go?"

"To South America? I don't have the money to fund

an expedition like this," I admitted. "Do you have any idea how much it's cost me this last decade? Not to mention paying you for your time."

"A man has to eat, even if it is noodles." Marcus patted the screen. "This could be the answer you've been waiting for. There's no way you can ignore it."

I was at a precipice. My career was going well, and I loved teaching. This school was becoming prestigious, a real step up for my resume. If I stayed long enough, did a great job, gained tenure, I could teach on panels, publish a few more papers, and build up my name in the community. No one knew who I was, since almost everything I'd done so far had been self-serving. There was also the offer to teach at Harvard, and despite my misgivings about the nepotism, I had to take Richard seriously.

But this was important. My dad had traveled to all these locations. He'd gathered the six Tokens, and one day, when I was five years old, he'd vanished. What was the Bridge he'd spoken of? Brian Hardy was our lead.

I made the decision on a stomach full of ramen and beer. I glanced outside, seeing the window cracked open. Snow had begun falling, and I closed it, staring across the street at the park. A father and son walked by, wearing matching jackets, their English bulldog sniffing a No Parking signpost.

"We're going to New York Friday. We'll figure the rest out later," I told Marcus, and could almost hear his smile from across the room.

"You need funding? I think I know someone interested in this kind of venture," Marcus said.

He didn't have to tell me who he was referring to.

5

"*W*ill this be on the final?" Luca asked. I glanced at the clock, trying not to make it obvious I was ready to escape the school week.

"Luca, assume everything will be on the final," I told him.

This elicited a petrified gasp from Cassie. "Professor Walker, are you suggesting there won't be a study guide?"

Study guide. I almost snorted, thinking of my Ancient Civilizations professor's expression when I'd asked the same question of him all those years ago. He'd nearly had a heart attack at the mere idea of making a final exam easier on his students. It was a good thing for Cassie and the others that I wasn't a bitter old divorced man with a gambling problem.

"I'll have it ready next Wednesday," I assured her, and the class made an audible sigh of relief. The bell rang, and I sat on my desk, saying goodbyes to the students, wishing them a good weekend. It was gloomy out, the sky shrouded in thick gray clouds, and it had drizzled rain instead of snow since the temperatures had climbed just enough to avoid winter weather. I preferred snow over the incessant icy dampness the winter rainstorms carried with them.

I wandered into the halls, exiting the building and moving toward the professors' lounge. It was lunch time for most of them, and I spotted Jessica near the coffee maker, heating up leftovers.

"Rex, how are you doing?" she asked.

"About as good as you can on a rainy December Friday. And you?" I wanted to cut the banter and make a direct line to my SUV. Marcus was probably at my place, waiting for me already. He was a lot of things, but tardy wasn't one of them.

Jessica smiled, and under different circumstances, I might have been persuaded by her charm. "I'm fine. Any plans tonight?"

"I…"

Her hand settled on my forearm, and she stepped closer. "I have tickets to the Boston Pops. I know how much you like Bach. They're playing his most memorable sonatas, and I happen to have an extra seat."

She was coming on to me. I hadn't expected this, and my response would seal my fate. The last thing I wanted was a scorned boss. I had to assume there was an important human resources rule she was sidestepping. "I'd love to, but I'm actually off to visit my uncle in New York. I'll be staying the weekend."

Her hand lifted, and she had the grace to keep smiling. "Another time, perhaps."

"That would be great," I told her, not elaborating. I exited as quickly as I could. I must have been crazy. She was definitely attractive. Marcus would harass me for weeks if he ever heard I turned a date down. I needed new friends.

As expected, Marcus was on my front step when I pulled up, a backpack slung over his shoulders as he hid near the door from the downpour. "About time. You know, I could have driven us. Grabbed you from the school."

I reached for the door handle and found it opened

without my key. "Marcus, were you inside?"

"No. If I knew it was unlocked, I wouldn't have been standing in the rain."

I pressed the door open and stepped slowly, lifting a hand to keep Marcus on the front steps. I listened for signs of any intruders and found silence. "Stay here," I whispered to Marcus, and he nodded, finally cluing in that I might have an unwanted visitor. He took his phone out, ready to make an emergency call.

My shoes clipped against the hardwood as I strode for the office to the right, just before the staircase. Using a code, I tugged open the locked desk drawer, gripping my P229 Sig Sauer. I walked through the entire condo, finding no traces of an invader. Five minutes later, I returned to the entryway and motioned Marcus into my home.

"What the hell are you doing with a gun? You know that most people get shot by…"

"Save me the dramatics. It's for my protection. *Our* protection." I ensured the safety was on and considered bringing the weapon with me on the road trip.

"Maybe you forgot to lock the doors. Tell you what, I'm going to hook you up with one of those smart locks, so you can secure it with your phone," Marcus told me.

I hardly heard him. There was no chance I'd forgotten to lock my house. I thought about the armed men tracking us in El Mirador and the black car trailing me from my sister's. Now this. Was someone really after me? All of my dad's notes and possessions were hidden beneath the floorboards in a secret safe beneath my office desk, and I checked it, ensuring nothing had been taken. I hesitantly returned the gun to its lockbox.

"Rex, are we going to New York?" Marcus asked, already holding my luggage.

"Sure." There was no sense in worrying the guy.

"You're probably right. I forgot to lock it."

He grimaced as he carried my bags to the SUV. "What's in this? You know we're only going for a couple days, right?"

"My suit jackets weigh more than your Spider-Man underwear, Marcus," I joked, trying to deflect from the possible invasion. Maybe he was correct, and I was overanalyzing things. I clicked the deadbolt shut, and we were off for the four-hour drive to Manhattan.

"What did you learn about Hardy?" I asked Marcus once I was outside of Boston, heading south.

"I tracked him to an upscale townhouse near the Park. He's ancient. Like, ninety-two years old."

"But he's alive?" We'd been through this earlier in the week, but I liked to comb the details with Marcus to make sure we had everything in a neat row. He knew this about me and had given up arguing the merits of my ways.

"As far as I can tell. No R.O.D. or memorial in the papers."

"Good. Were you able to make an appointment?" I asked.

Marcus shook his head and flipped open his laptop. It shone brightly against his face. "He doesn't have a business to call, and there was absolutely no number listed in his name."

"I was hoping to visit him tonight, but by the time we arrive and check into our hotel, it's going to be too late, especially for a man that age. We'll regroup and head over first thing in the morning." I imagined Brian Hardy would wake up with the crack of dawn, probably reading the newspaper with a cup of coffee and a hodgepodge of medication.

By the time I veered off Henry Hudson Parkway, Marcus had been asleep for a good hour, and I stopped a little too abruptly at a red light, jerking the car to a halt.

Marcus' eyes sprang open, and he wiped a string of drool from his lips. He peered around slowly. "We almost there?"

"We'll be at the hotel in five minutes." The light went green, and I urged the SUV forward, dreading the parking cost alone. I did all right as a professor, but my recent expedition had drained most of my savings. Financially, I wasn't where I'd wanted to be at this stage of my career, penny-pinching and worrying about paying the bills.

Instead of staying somewhere fancy, I'd opted for a basic room at a hotel near the museum. When the valet took our bags and car, Marcus smiled, inhaling deeply. "I love New York."

It was dark, but not too late. The sidewalks were still busy, with diners laughing and talking loudly from al fresco restaurants across the street. I did love the energy of this area. A taxi honked, and I glanced up, seeing a dark BMW attempting to change lanes. The windows were tinted, and I tried to get a look at the driver but couldn't with the streetlight's reflection off the glass.

"Come on, Rex. Let's unpack and find something to eat." Marcus left me on the street, walking past the doorman and into the hotel lobby.

I saw another BMW drive by, a similar model, then another a moment later. "Get it together, Rex," I whispered to myself.

"*D*id we have to wake up so early? I thought this was a vacation," Marcus complained as we walked down Central Park West, a bagel and coffee in our hands. "Speaking of which, when is the last time you took a real vacation?"

"I don't know. For pleasure?" I asked, making Marcus laugh.

"Yes, for pleasure. You know, hit the beach? Hike to a Vermont lake? Not to mention bringing a woman. Seriously, Rex, you need to get on a dating app before you forget what goes where."

We sat at a bench on the west end of the museum, and I popped the top off my coffee. It steamed in the cool morning air. It was late in the year, but the city wasn't showing any signs of snow quite yet. A lot of the stores were adorned with Christmas ornaments, and the museum had decorations draped over ancient trees. Everything was turned off now, as the place wouldn't be open for another few hours. Marcus held his cup with both hands, trying to get warmth from it. I knew he'd rather have eaten indoors, but he didn't complain as he started munching his bagel.

"I haven't seen you making any proposals lately, kid," I told him.

"Believe me, all the ladies I've been seeing aren't into the long-term kind of thing." He crumpled up the paper his bagel had been nested in and tossed it perfectly into the center of a cast-iron wastebasket.

A woman strolled by with two dogs, and she was so bundled up from the cold, I couldn't even see her face. One of the mutts stopped at me, sniffing my leg, and I fed it a piece of my bagel without the woman knowing. Then they were off.

"Any game plan we need to abide by today?" Marcus asked.

I examined the building behind us. It was where Brian Hardy lived. I wore a trench coat, with my finest suit underneath. I had to look a certain part. Even Marcus had a blazer covering a t-shirt, the best I could get him to do on short notice.

"You know the drill. We have to make it inside so we can speak with him." I had a feeling Hardy would want to talk to me once he heard what I had to say. A breeze carried through the courtyard, rustling more leaves, and I cringed against the chilly air. "Let's go."

"You sure he'll be up?" Marcus asked, dropping his mostly-empty cup into the trash.

I peered at the watch, the same one my father had left in my care before his final trip. It was like he had known he wouldn't be returning. I wondered what he'd given my sister. Bev had never mentioned anything of the sort, but then again, I hadn't thought to ask.

"It's after seven. He'll be up." The dawn was only beginning this late in the year, and we hiked the cobblestone sidewalk to the museum grounds exit. I didn't bother going to the crosswalk, and waited until there was no traffic coming before jogging across the street. Marcus beat me to the other side, and we strode with purpose toward the building's entrance.

"This guy must have done well for himself," Marcus whispered as we neared the doors.

He was right. This building was gorgeous. Old money nice. I admired the ornate stone carving above the awning, and a hefty doorman opened the doors at our arrival.

"Can I help you?" he asked. He smelled like cigarettes and coffee, and I noticed the frayed sleeves and scuffed shoes.

"We're here to see one of your residents. Mr. Brian Hardy. Suite nine-seventeen." I dropped a hint of Bostonian culture into my voice, mimicking some of my old professors.

"Mr. Hardy rarely has visitors. Is he expecting you?"

I glanced at the man's nametag without him noticing.

"Darrel, we're with the Committee of Archaeology and couldn't reach Mr. Hardy by email or phone. He's won an award for a study previously unpublished until someone found it in the archives two years prior. It is an article worthy of so much more than our mediocre award, but Mr. Hardy should be notified nonetheless."

"I'll have to call up, see if he's better today."

"Better?" I asked, furrowing my brow for added concern.

Darrel seemed like he'd said too much and lifted a finger, walking to the desk, where a pack of cigarettes lay beside an unread newspaper. I saw a key ring hanging on a nail stuck into the side of the desk, with a bellhop's hat on the floor underneath. He returned a minute later, shaking his head.

"Sorry, sir. No answer. If you'd like to leave a message, I can…"

"No worries. Marcus, give the man something for his troubles." I waved for the door, and Marcus seemed to comprehend my motivation.

"Thank you, Darrel. We appreciate your time…" Marcus walked to the exit, pulling a twenty from his wallet, and I moved as fast as I could, silently pilfering the key ring from its resting place. It was tight in my pocket, and I clutched my trench to keep the keys from ringing.

"Cold morning out there. Take care." I stepped past Darrel, who was none the wiser, and hurried down the sidewalk with Marcus in tow.

"What was that all about?" he asked.

When we were around the block, I stopped and pulled the key ring from my pocket, two dozen keys jangling as I waved them.

"Professor Walker. I didn't know you were so sneaky."

With one glance at the building's entrance, I waved

Marcus into the alley. "Time to find our own way up."

"Fine. But you owe me twenty bucks."

6

*A*fter testing my patience searching for the loading zone entrance key, we were inside and jogging up the stairwell. It was dimly lit, and I doubted any of these well-off tenants used them often. By the time we made it to the ninth story, I was sweating under my suit and jacket. Marcus seemed unfazed by the workout.

"Getting too old for this, Prof?" he asked, holding the door open for me.

I huffed a bit and bumped him with my shoulder as I passed by. "I'm fine."

"What are we going to do, break in?" Marcus asked. The carpets were a dark green, old but well maintained, and we walked by five suite doors before arriving at Hardy's. Nine-seventeen.

I lifted a hand to knock but held back.

"What's the matter?"

"What are we even doing here?" I asked. "I should be at home, working on my final exam study guide."

"Don't give up on me now, Rex. I had to break a date."

I peered at Marcus, and he stared back eagerly with his dark brown eyes, a smirk on his face. He was right. I knocked three times and let my arms dangle by my sides.

No one answered. I went to knock again, and the door opened just enough for me to see a middle-aged woman through the crack.

"Can I help you?" she asked with a Filipino accent.

"We're here to speak with Brian Hardy. He's won an award…"

"How did you get up here?" she asked, glancing at Marcus.

"Darrel said he wouldn't mind some visitors." She started to shut the door, and I acted quickly, shoving my foot in the jamb. "Please. We've come a long way. Just tell Hardy that Dirk Walker's kid is here to discuss the Bridge."

She clearly had no idea what I was talking about, but nodded and opened the door wider. I didn't enter yet, and we waited for a lengthy five minutes while she was gone. The décor inside the foyer was dated, but in pristine condition. There was a stack of papers near an umbrella stand, and a long mat covering the oak floor.

"Mr. Hardy will see you." She seemed surprised by this.

"We're sorry for interrupting," Marcus told her, and she gave him a muted smile.

"Follow me."

The hallway was short, the walls empty and devoid of anything personal. We passed a clean but dated kitchen, and I saw the living room was tidy, with a little TV mounted on the wall. The furniture looked unused.

There were two bedrooms, one with a cross on the door, and Hardy's aide led us to the master. She leaned toward me and whispered words of caution. "He is having a good day, but it might not last. If he starts to lose focus, please come and tell me, and you'll have to leave."

I nodded as she opened the door. Everything changed. Gone were the neatly-washed hardwood floors and the uncluttered living space. This was the room of a madman. Books were everywhere, numerous stacks of them behind a huge wooden desk.

"Whoa." Marcus walked toward the hundreds of papers across the room, where clippings were taped, thumbtacked, and glued to the surface of the wall.

Brian Hardy sat in a recliner, oxygen feeding through a tube into his nose. His left hand was clutching the arm of the chair, and his fingers twitched as I approached him. He was a skeletal man, with only a few white wisps of hair remaining on his liver-spotted pate. His eyes could have been blue once, but they were so clouded with cataracts that I couldn't tell for sure.

"Hello, Mr. Hardy. I'm Rex Walker."

"I met you once. Did you know that?" His voice was oddly deep, powerful despite his diminished frame.

I sat on the bed, noting the mattress was rock hard. "I didn't. When was this?"

"You weren't much more than a baby. Your father and I were good friends."

My arms tingled at his words. "Do you know what happened to him?" I couldn't believe my mother hadn't mentioned Hardy before, or that his missing journals had been hidden so well, I'd never found them.

"Who?" he asked, his glance settling on Marcus.

"My dad."

"Right. Dirk. He was a good man. Who's the kid?" Hardy seemed cautious of the young black man reading his clippings.

"He's my research partner," I said.

Hardy nodded slowly. "You look just like him."

"My dad?"

"Yep. Same nose. Penetrating eyes. Have you found him yet?"

I froze. "How could I find him?"

"The Bridge."

"Tell me about it," I said, my words so quiet, I wasn't sure he'd heard at first.

"They exist." He lifted a scrawny arm, pointing

upwards. "They're real. Everyone thought I was a lunatic, but I was right. Your dad saw that too."

"Aliens?" Marcus asked, coming over to crouch near Hardy. "You've seen them?"

"I don't need to *see* them, son. I gave everything I had to your father and that sidekick of his. They weren't supposed to leave without me…" His hand trembled, and he set it in his lap. All I could hear was the beating of my own heart and the hiss of his oxygen tank.

"What did you give my dad?" I asked, louder this time.

"The signs were there. It just took solving the clues. I was always good at puzzles. Not so much anymore," he grumbled, sending himself into a coughing fit.

His aide came to the door, poking her head in, and he waved her away. "I'm fine, Phoebe." She disappeared, and he glared at the hallway. "Damned woman. Thinks every little hiccup is the end. Wouldn't she like that? Probably rob me blind and vanish before I hit the floor."

"Can we return to this puzzle you're speaking of?" I asked.

He wore a dress shirt, but the sleeve wasn't buttoned at the cuff. I spotted the matching tattoo on his skin, the same one I'd duplicated on my chest in homage to my father. I motioned to it. "What does it mean?"

He lifted his arm, glancing at the marking. "We were brothers. The four of us."

"The four?" I asked. "Who? Dirk, Clayton, you, and who?"

He blinked quickly, and his breathing grew more labored.

"Mr. Hardy, what is the Bridge?"

He didn't answer, and I peered at Marcus. "Look for a journal. Something that looks old."

Marcus stood, and Hardy disregarded the young man

as he rifled through his stacks of books.

"What is the Bridge?" I asked, louder this time.

He met my gaze, smiling widely. "I was supposed to go with them. Now look at me."

I needed to change tactics, to uncover something valuable. "Where did they go? Where did my father and Clay go in 1989, when they vanished?"

"Estrelas," he said, pointing up to the ceiling.

I didn't know Portuguese, but it sounded familiar. "Can you be more specific?"

He started coughing again, his face turning bright red. I rose quickly, panicking, and Phoebe ran in, adjusting the dial on the machine. She wiped his mouth and turned to us. "Time for Mr. Hardy to get some rest."

I ignored her as she helped the old man to his bed. "Hardy, where did they go? What is the Bridge?"

Phoebe recoiled in fear, and Hardy only laughed gruffly as his head settled on the pillow. "Estrelas. Don't you see, Dirk? You better not leave without me."

Marcus arrived, breaking my hypnotized state. "I found something." His voice was quiet.

"I'm sorry, Phoebe. Maybe we can return when he's…"

"I don't think that's a good idea. Please go." She spoke with authority, and I let Marcus lead me into the hallway.

I was shaken by the whole experience, and Marcus paced the corridor, running his hands over his short black hair. "What the hell was that? He knows about the Bridge! The tattoo! This is like some real-life mystery stuff right here."

"What did you get?" I asked, and he smiled again as he pulled a notebook from under his shirt.

We returned to the stairwell, me clutching the book tightly as I tried to read the first page under the half-burnt out light fixture. There was a drawing of the five stars with the streak between them. "This is in my father's journal. Let's go to the hotel. We have some reading to do."

"Where are they now?" a voice asked, and I pressed the stairwell exit open a smidge to see the doorman's big body standing by Hardy's suite.

I left the keys on the stairs and ran. We made quick work of the steps, taking two or three at a time, and rushed through the exit into the alley, out of breath, a minute later. Marcus kept moving, turning to face me as he walked backwards. "That was awesome. Remind me to go on these trips with you more often, Rex."

Tires screeched as a black luxury sedan slid to a halt, nearly striking Marcus as he stepped into the middle of the back alley. He patted himself on the legs, then his chest, and moved toward me without saying a word.

The tinted rear window slid down, revealing an older man in an expensive suit. "I was wondering when you'd show up. Hop in."

I groaned as I recognized his face. "Marcus, meet Hunter Madison, the billionaire."

---

*M*arcus was asked to occupy the front seat with the driver, and Hunter motioned me into the back-passenger side. "What are the odds?" I asked him, but of course, he offered no reasoning to how he'd conveniently found us in an alley behind Brian Hardy's complex.

"Mr. Walker, it's been a long time." He stuck his hand out, but I ignored it.

"Cut the crap, Madison. I want to know what you're up to right this instant." I gave him my best stare-down, but the gray-bearded man didn't flinch.

"I want the same things as you, Mr. Walker."

Lavish cologne clung to the man like a cape, and I rolled my window down, feeling suffocated. "And what's that?"

"The truth. You refused to accept my assistance before, but now… I have something you're going to be interested in." His green eyes crinkled as he showcased a veneered smile.

"Come on, Marcus. That's our cue to leave." I tested the door, finding it locked. "Driver. Unlock the doors. We're going to the hotel."

"I've taken the liberty of checking you out already. Your luggage is in the trunk." He jabbed a thumb behind him.

Before I could think, I had his collar firm in my grip. "What do you have? And don't play games." I knew Hunter Madison had funded my father's ventures, and that my mother had hated the man, and it was enough for me to blame him for Dad's disappearance. When I'd come knocking twenty years ago, he'd claimed to know nothing about it. Of course, a decade later, after I'd begun my own investigating, he'd found me, offered me money to continue the mission Dirk and Clay had begun.

To the old man's credit, he remained calm as he lifted his hands in the air. "Mr. Walker, we're professionals. Let's act like it."

I released him, the fury burning away from me like gasoline with a flame. "How could you even check us out?" I heard someone shout, and I saw Darrel exiting the building, anger in his eyes. "Before you answer that, drive!"

The car sped up, racing through the alley, and turned onto Central Park West, heading north.

"I own the corporation that retains your little hotel.

Nice spot. Very budget friendly." He wiggled his eyebrows as he made the dig.

"Driver, pull over. Let us out." I tested the door handle again as he drove, but it remained locked.

"Mr. Walker, all I ask is for a few hours of your time. You two can stay at my house for the night, and then make up your minds." I noticed how he used the plural version, and Marcus craned his neck around from the front seat.

"Rex, this could be our lead, and you've been grasping at straws. If he knows something about this whole thing, we should talk to him. It's worth a shot," Marcus told me.

I didn't see a way out, and I hated that Marcus was right. After hearing Hardy recall being part of my dad's team, and the mysterious Bridge, I had to know more. I'd never be able to return home and pretend this information hadn't found my ears. I owed it to my family and to myself to discover just what had happened to Dirk Walker.

"Fine. But don't get any ideas, Madison. This is a conversation, not a contract. I know how your type operates."

He fixed his ruffled collar and jutted his hand out again. This time, I relented and shook it.

"Alberto. Take us home." Hunter Madison smiled as classical music softly played through the car's speakers.

The conversation remained civil for the duration of the trip, but when Marcus or I asked the billionaire anything relating to my goals or his association with my father, he changed the subject, refusing to answer until we were in his study. I noticed him checking behind the car more than once, and wondered if he had any issues with being tailed, or if it was a natural instinct to look over your shoulder when you were so wealthy.

"Any stock tips?" Marcus asked as the car hit a freeway, the Manhattan bridges far behind us. I had an idea where he was taking us, though I'd never been this far east on

Long Island.

Hunter Madison actually laughed and nodded. "Kid, you team up with me, and you won't have to stay in my crappy hotels ever again."

"I'm listening," Marcus said.

"Where are we going?" I asked, slightly annoyed. We'd already been in the car for over an hour, and I had to use the bathroom.

"Take a guess," Madison said.

Marcus waited a second before answering. "East Hampton. You have one of the largest ocean-front properties in the area, not to mention that behemoth of a yacht in the marina. Do you think we could go for a ride?"

I didn't know how he knew this, but since Marcus loved doing research, I was sure there was a lot of public information on the rich man accessible from online magazines alone.

"Bingo. Mr. Walker, it seems you've found a good one here."

"I taught him in his local college before he was smart enough to realize there was no money in anthropology."

"Isn't there?" Madison asked. "I know all about you, Marcus Wells. Parents live in Sarasota, Florida. Dad works maintenance for the school division, Mom checks out books at the local library. You aced every test in your senior year. Scholarships to any institution, but given your slightly disappointing SAT scores, you ended up in Boston, at Dr. Rex Walker's school. Stayed the full four years, despite having the grades to transfer elsewhere. You two must have really hit it off."

The car went silent. The only noise was the humming of the tires treading down the interstate. "You're not the only one who does his research, I'm afraid." Hunter stared at Marcus, and my sidekick started laughing.

"Good one, Hunter. I think I'm going to like you."

I shook my head. Water off a duck's back with this kid. "He got part of it wrong, though, didn't he?" I asked.

"I'll say." Marcus laughed.

Hunter lifted an eyebrow, curious what he could possibly have overlooked. "What is it?"

"He finished his degree in three years." The fact that Hunter Madison had missed something was enough to make me feel like we were on even ground again, and I took solace in that fact as we veered off the highway, merging onto an exit. The driver slowed, and the scent of the salty ocean hit my nostrils. We were close to the shore.

"Rex, do you see the size of these places?" Marcus gawked at the mansions as we drove past the massive lots. Some were extremely private, with huge fences and trees lining the road; others presented enormous pools and well-manicured lawns. All were far beyond any kind of wealth I could ever aspire to.

"Friends of yours?" I asked Hunter, and he grinned.

"I think you'll find that most of these people don't have friends, Rex. They have allies, business partners, and acquaintances, but rarely friends." The billionaire lost his smile as he said this, and I wondered how true a statement it was.

"And you?"

Hunter didn't answer as the driver came to a stop a few houses down. I watched as the dark iron fence slowly swung inward, and a moment later, we were entering Madison's estate.

We waited while the fence closed behind us, sealing us in, and the second it clicked shut, my heart pounded harder in my chest. There was a sense of finality to the action, as if my life had changed as the latch connected.

"This is insane." Marcus had his window open, and I

appreciated his excitement but wished he'd rein it in a little bit. Hunter didn't seem to mind; he just smiled as Marcus asked him about the house and its lineage.

"This house was built in 1919 by an architect who intended on staying. His wife fell ill five years later, and when the market crashed in the twenties, he lost the home and his love in the same year. But in that tragedy, the next owner named the gardens after her, and I kept the dedication when I purchased it." The car went past the most opulent flower garden I'd ever seen, and I noticed the sign. "Lily's" was painted in a light green on an old white sign, likely restored many times over the years. "I've lived here for thirty years… on and off."

It had the charm of the region, with shutters and cedar shingles, but the sheer size of the mansion was off-putting. I couldn't imagine living somewhere like this, so far from anything and anyone.

"If you ever need a house sitter…" Marcus climbed out of the car, and I rolled my eyes at him. "What? I'm good for it."

The rounded driveway ran directly by the house's main entrance, and I glanced up the three steps, past the two pillars that braced the awning over the front porch. Potted plants stood in perfect symmetry on either edge of the stairs, and it was obvious that Hunter liked everything neat and in its place. It was something we had in common.

"Come on in." Hunter waved at the car, dismissing Alberto, and he drove off, disappearing around the house.

The door opened, and a man in a dark navy suit greeted his boss. His hair was slicked back, his expression grim.

"Gentlemen, this is Francois. If you need anything, just ask. Your bags will be brought to your rooms."

The front door closed, and I stared around the luxurious foyer, wondering what I'd gotten us into.

7

*I*t was far too early for a drink, but when Francois offered after bringing Hunter three fingers of Scotch, I nodded, accepting the tumbler of amber liquid. Marcus took one too, glancing at me with doubt in his eyes. As far as I knew, he'd never drank Scotch, and before I could tell him to sip it, he'd downed the contents. Hunter was considerate enough to pretend not to notice Marcus coughing, his eyes watering.

When the billionaire raised his glass, I did the same, sipping from mine. It was smooth and full. The bottle probably cost more than my entire bank account currently held.

"How did you find us?" I asked.

"There'll be time for that later," Hunter said, mischief in his eyes.

"You said once we were in your study…" I glanced around, admiring the man's taste. He had an assortment of fine pieces from around the world, adorned and showcased from stunning dark wood shelves. I thought it might be African blackwood, but couldn't be sure.

The lights were dim, and we sat in the softest leather chairs I'd ever parked on, with a round table complete with a crystal ashtray centering it. An envelope sat precariously on the edge of the table, closer to Madison than to me, and he must have noticed my inquisitive stare.

"What is it that gets you up in the mornings?" Hunter Madison asked, his voice low and growly. He took a long sip of his Scotch and sat back, crossing his left leg over his right. His free hand fidgeted, playing with a thick white-gold ring on his pointer finger.

The question was a little esoteric for me. "Are you going to ask me what my sign is next?"

He set his glass on the table and leaned closer to me. "Rex. You have an opportunity. You wouldn't have come to see Hardy after all these years if you hadn't learned something new. What is it?"

I fought the urge to stand up and walk away. Fire burned in Hunter's eyes: an intensity I'd only ever seen in my own father. "You want to know what I'm after?"

He nodded.

"How about you mind your business," I told him.

"Rex… your father was a great man. Don't ruin his legacy by turning me down today. If you have new information, I'll be here to support you. I need to learn what happened to Dirk Walker as much as you do."

"I doubt that," I muttered.

He stretched his arm out, and his cuff slid up his wrist. I gawked at it, checking for any tattoo markings, but didn't see one. "Did he ever tell you about our trip to the Galapagos?"

I shook my head.

"It was eighty-six, and he had a lead to… an artifact. I demanded to come, since I'd been funding his ventures for so many years but had never tagged along. Clayton was against it, but Dirk, he was much more amiable to the hand that feeds. We flew in my private jet, which loosened his sidekick up a bit." At the mention of my father's working partner, he glanced at Marcus. "The islands were even more remote than they are today, and we shored on Isla

Isabela, paying a couple of local kids to watch our boat. We got what we were after in only two days of searching." Hunter stood from his seat, striding over to a display case across the study.

"What was it?" Marcus asked, following Hunter.

I finally joined them, knowing he must have a point to the story. The item beneath the glass covering was small, the size of an old silver dollar. But the markings on it were almost familiar, in a vague sense.

"This was smuggled from ruins in southern Ecuador. The entire site was rumored to be haunted by the villagers found murdered there seven hundred years ago. It sat empty for most of that time, until an archaeologist from Spain braved the trek through the thick jungle to see what kind of credence the speculations held."

Hunter was a natural storyteller, and I was immersed in his tale. I leaned closer, trying to read the etchings on the metallic artifact. "And what did he discover?"

"This. There were countless other items that are still displayed around the world. He would have been rich if he'd lived long enough to sell them." Hunter smiled and turned to face me. "Your father tracked his movements to the Galapagos. It was really quite the thing to observe. He was like a bloodhound, that one."

"What is the coin?" My voice cracked.

Hunter's voice lowered. "It's not of this earth."

"No way. You're trying to tell me this is from…" Marcus looked to the ceiling. "Up there."

Hunter nodded. "I've had it tested on numerous occasions, and yes, as I said, many components are familiar, but not in the exact combinations."

I laughed. I tried to stop, but couldn't. "You can't be serious. No wonder my mother warned me never to trust you. Alien coins? What's next? Are you going to tell us you have a little green man frozen in your basement? Maybe a UFO in the garage?"

Hunter set his hands on my shoulders so calmly that I didn't flinch. "Your father believed, Rex, and so do you. I know that to be true."

I coughed, irritated that the focus was on me again. "What I believe isn't in question." I walked away, gazing into the next display case. It was familiar, since I'd seen pictures of it in old articles. The metal carving had been found in a remote region of Egypt, far from any known villages. "How did you locate this?"

"I told you, I'm resourceful. More proof they exist," he said.

My mouth felt dry. Everywhere I looked, I spotted small artifacts that anyone in the business would claim represented otherworldly beings. Some I knew of; others were unfamiliar, and I judged, like the coin, that not many people had laid eyes on them before. "How many of these did my father bring you?"

"Most. As you can see, I've been without my best treasure hunter for too long. I'd hoped you'd join me a decade ago, but that didn't pan out. Look at these, Rex. Aliens have been to Earth."

Marcus seemed uneasy, and he kept quiet as I returned to my seat. "What is the Bridge?" The words were sticky on my tongue, and I grabbed my Scotch, taking a heavy drink.

"The Bridge is the answer. Hardy claimed there was a route to another world. He suggested there were six objects hidden here on Earth, and when they were combined in the proper order, a gateway would connect the two places."

I drained the glass, setting the tumbler on the table. "What are you implying? That my father and Clayton found these items and what… took a rollercoaster ride to

Alpha Centauri?"

He shook his head. "I don't think it's anywhere near Alpha Centauri."

Marcus stood behind his seat, hands clutching the chair. "Wait, Rex. Madison isn't kidding. I told you this was real! What about this discovery near Pluto? Is it related?"

Hunter grinned at my friend, but it wasn't a pleasant expression. His eyes deceived him. "I fear that is something else entirely."

My hands were sweating, my pulse erratic as I tried to absorb the half-truths and conjecture. One thing at a time. "Where did my dad go?"

Hunter sat again, and as if on cue, Francois returned with a remote and a decanter of liquor. He set both on the coffee table and departed without a word. Our host poured himself another drink and refilled our cups with a shaky grip.

"I've told you all I know. Dirk was on his own mission with Clayton. They left me out of it. When I threatened to pull his funding, he walked away, telling me it didn't matter anymore. I tried to follow them, but they evaded me in England. He was a wily one," Hunter said.

I contemplated the coordinates I'd found on Clayton's gravestone, leading me to Venezuela. Were they a hint to these artifacts? Had Clay left a trail for his daughter or perhaps Hardy to find? If so, maybe someone had already done their research, and I'd be wasting my time regardless.

"He… my father was in Portugal." I gave the detail up in good faith.

Hunter went rigid. "Portugal. Of course. Where?"

"I don't know. Everything came up empty for me. I spent months there."

"Wait, Rex. Didn't Hardy say something in Portuguese?" Marcus asked.

He had. I repeated the word. "Estrelas. He said it twice. Then something about how Dirk can't leave without him."

"Interesting," Hunter said, tapping his neatly-trimmed beard.

Marcus was on his phone, and I knew what he was doing. In all the excitement, we'd forgotten to check what the word meant.

"You don't need that. It means *stars*. And also a site few are aware of." Hunter Madison took another drink and lifted the remote from the table.

"I assume you're one of the few?" I asked.

"I may have visited the location," Hunter whispered as he pressed a button on the control. A discreet screen on the dark wall flashed on, momentarily blinding me. A video played, showing rough footage in black and white. "Ever heard of the Believers?"

"Isn't that a band or something?" Marcus asked.

"No. It's a cult," I answered. "An old one. They don't still exist?"

Hunter smiled, showing teeth. "Life would be much simpler if that were the case. No, the Believers are around, though perhaps with fewer members than before. Or perhaps many more. It's difficult to tell."

I watched the video, seeing over a hundred people as they marched through a stone corridor, each wearing a dark cloak, their faces obscured by heavy cowls.

"I don't like the looks of this," Marcus said.

"They used to be harmless, a group of people fascinated with the stars, like so many have been since the dawn of time. They began as scientists, explorers, doctors, and"—Hunter pointed at me—"archaeologists, like yourself."

"What happened to them?" Marcus asked as the camera tracked the last cloaked person into a circular room.

Unrecognizable symbols were painted in a dark color on the floors and walls of the cavern, and the Believers circled a center pedestal where a shiny item lay unmoving.

"A man named Thomas Rembrandt joined. He was an unconventional millionaire from the south of France, carrying with him a lot of ideologies about what the Believers should be, and many followed him because of his wealth. Believe me, once you have money, it's easy to get what you want." He glanced at me while he said this, and I returned my gaze to the screen. There was no audio accompanying the footage, but I could almost hear the synchronous chanting as their bodies swayed back and forth.

I'd heard some of the stories from my old professor, though he always made it sound like they were seeking facts, not grasping hands and singing to old relics. This looked like something from a movie, and for a second, I wondered if Hunter Madison was having fun with us.

Marcus was freaked out. "What are they doing?"

"This item was rumored to be a link to the beings they worship. Apparently, it had nothing to do with them and was merely a depiction of an Incan god," Hunter told him.

"How do you know so much?" I asked curiously.

His eyes shone again, but he didn't smile as he set the remote down. "I was there. I used to be one of them."

The video ended, and I could only gape at Hunter as he waited for me to speak. "You were one of the Believers? Did my father know that?"

He shook his head firmly. "I left them in the late seventies, a few years after Dirk and I got into business with each other. Rembrandt died, and I didn't like the direction the group was taking. Things were growing... desperate."

"And you think they're still around?" I asked.

"They are... and they're much more threatening than ever."

I considered the men outside of El Mirador… my townhouse being broken into… the car that might be following me. "Do they know who I am?"

Marcus laughed nervously. "Why would they care who you are? You're a prof in Boston."

"They know you, Rex. That's why you must accept my help. We need to find the Bridge." Hunter's hand continued to tremble as he reached for his drink, and I passed it to him.

"Why the urgency? If you've been searching for this long, what's the rush?" I asked him. "Plus, you say you've visited this Estrelas before."

"If I explain, will you consider my offer?" came his reply.

Marcus was on the edge of his seat, clearly invested in our conversation. I could tell he wanted to join forces with this rich man, if only for the romantic idea of an adventure, but seeing the chanting cloaked Believers in that footage had me worried. "I'll contemplate it."

"There are two reasons why I must reach the Bridge," he started. "The Believers foretold of an age where we'd encounter visitors from another planet. They'd come from the outer reaches of the solar system and arrive at Earth: not to meet us peacefully, but to rule our kind."

"And they encourage this?" Marcus barked.

"They'll welcome them as part of their demented fantasy. Their minds are brainwashed, and they actually believe they'll be rewarded for their faith and patience."

"And you think this is related to what? The shapes near Pluto?" I asked, trying to determine if Hunter Madison was as mad as the cult he spoke against.

"It doesn't matter if I believe the object is related, but that they do. Things are in motion here, Rex, things that will be dire to our planet if we don't act on it." Hunter spoke with so much passion, I instantly found myself trusting him.

"You said there were two reasons why it was imperative," I reminded him. "That's only one."

"The other is my own selfish motivation."

"Which is?"

The screen flipped off, leaving the room darker. Shadows creased his face as he leaned closer. "I'm dying."

8

"*W*hat do you make of this?" Marcus asked when we were alone.

I paced around the study, scanning each priceless artifact Hunter had collected over the decades, and tried to piece together, everything we'd heard. It was still early afternoon, but I felt like the sun should be descending any moment.

"He seems to believe what he's telling us, and he had my father's trust, enough to partner with him for a few years. But… Dad did cut Madison out at the end. He didn't tell him everything about the Bridge or the clues he and Clayton found. That speaks volumes to me," I admitted.

"We don't have any evidence about why Dirk stopped working with him. There could have been extraneous factors we're not accounting for," Marcus said with a sideways grin. "Are you going to look at the envelope?"

I peered around the room, confident there was surveillance in here. I stepped closer to Marcus and lowered my voice. "Don't discuss the coordinates we found."

He nodded, glancing at the corners of the study. "No problem."

I returned to the chairs and stared at the circular table. The stark white envelope was out of place on the rich wood, and I snatched it up.

The check inside was printed on thick paper stock,

golden edges outlining it. I read the details.

Paid to the order of: Rexford Walker.

In the amount of: One hundred thousand dollars

Hunter Madison's signature was sprawling and illegible, but I knew it was his. I'd come across stubs left over from payments to my father, stored at my mom's for years.

Marcus grabbed the check, pumping a fist in the air. "Rex, imagine what we could do with this money."

I stuck my hand out, palm up, and he hesitantly returned it to me. I slid it back inside the envelope and dropped it onto the table. "We can't take his money."

"You heard what he said. If this Bridge is real, we have to look for it. And what about these Believers? What if this is the end, and we can help prevent it?"

I appraised the young man, the clever student I'd taught in college and had been close friends with ever since. "Marcus, you don't really buy in to all of this, do you?"

"Why the hell not? We've discussed the possibility of life on other planets enough for me to know you believe in aliens too. Man, this is crazy." Marcus paced the study, but my eyes remained fixed on the envelope.

"If we say yes, we have to make a deal. This is the only venture with Madison's money. We check out our lead, and if it doesn't take us anywhere, we return the leftover money and go home—"

"Imagine if we find something."

"Deal?" I asked, ready to shake on it.

"Rex, this could be…"

"Marcus, I need you here with me. Do we have a deal?" I offered my grip, and he nodded, shaking my hand.

"Deal."

The door opened, and in walked Hunter. His eyes were droopy, his voice slightly slurred when he spoke, but the fire had returned. "I take it you're accepting my offer?"

"Consider it a loan," I told him.

"Nonsense. I know you're holding your cards close to your chest, but, Rex, if you find what you're hoping for, I'll be here to assist your search for the Bridge. And your father." Adding in the last bit was a dirty trick, but it was obvious the older man was desperate.

"Okay, but don't hold your breath."

"Francois will show you to your chambers." Hunter picked up the check and passed it over. "I'll join you for dinner in a couple of hours. Perhaps you'll be more forthcoming after the chef's Paella Valenciana."

He sat down as Francois appeared at the study's doorway, waiting for us. I trailed after him, glancing back to Hunter before leaving. His eyes were closed, and I noticed him clenching his fist, lips moving ever so slightly.

"I can't wait to check out this house," Marcus said. Today had started off with a longshot, and suddenly, I'd been thrown into a scenario bigger than I'd ever imagined.

We climbed a flight of stairs, ending in a landing that overlooked a massive living space and the front foyer. The hallway led to a series of bedrooms, and Francois motioned for Marcus to enter one on the left. The servant had yet to speak, and I considered asking him a question but held back. Instead, I allowed him to show me to the room across the hall, and I told Marcus I'd see him in a few minutes. I needed some alone time.

With Francois gone and Marcus in his own quarters, I studied my surroundings. It was finer than any hotel I'd ever stayed in. With its own bathroom and gas fireplace, the space was fit for a king. I found my suitcase at the corner of the bed, and I pulled out my laptop, opening my email. I didn't know his wi-fi, and couldn't trust that Hunter wasn't spying, so I used my phone as a hotspot and linked up, retrieving a handful of emails.

They were mostly from students, and I replied, letting the work distract me. My sister had texted me, wondering about the Christmas holidays, and when I started to flip my laptop closed, a message from Richard Klein appeared.

Subject: Gathering

Hello, Rex. I was hoping you'd be able to attend a dinner party at my house next Friday. I have some friends from the board coming and thought you might be interested in meeting them. Please let me know at your earliest convenience. I was in your neighborhood earlier, but you weren't home. Hope to hear from you soon.

Your friend,

Doctor Richard Klein

I let out a frustrated breath of air. I'd stated numerous times that I wasn't leaving my job, but I also appreciated his intensity. He was a mentor of mine, and I was honored that he thought so highly of my teaching ability.

I hit "Reply" and started typing a message.

Richard, as you know, I'm comfortable where I am, but I might be able to come by. I have much to prepare for finals, but maybe I can sneak away for dinner.

Be in touch,

Rex

I hit send before I could talk myself out of it. My father's words from his journal rang though my mind as I closed the computer. *If life gives you an opportunity, say yes. No one has lived to the fullest overusing the word no.*

The younger me hadn't understood the exact meaning of his words, but now it felt like he was trying to tell me something. A lesson from the past.

Someone knocked on my door, and a second later, Marcus' head was poking into the room. "Rex, time to ditch the tie. There's tennis courts in the back."

I laughed and waved him inside. "It's November. Not

really tennis weather." My jacket sat near the door, and I recognized the book we'd pilfered from Hardy's place. In all the excitement, we'd forgotten about it altogether. "Marcus, Hardy's journal."

He raised an eyebrow and snatched it up. Lacking any grace, he bounded onto the bed and opened the cover. "This is bizarre."

The book was covered in symbols and writing, but not in a language I'd ever seen before. "See if you can scan something and cross-reference it with your database. It could be a primitive dialect." I flipped through it, seeing more of the same squiggly lines. From this vantage point, it appeared to be the ramblings of a madman, but judging by the age of the binding and the cracks in the leather spine, Hardy had written it when he was much younger.

I closed the journal and handed it to Marcus. "It's always another mystery. Why can't anything ever be simple?"

———————————

*D*inner was incredible, and I dropped the napkin on my empty plate. The food had been spicy, and I already knew I'd be desperate for an antacid before bed, but at the moment, I thought it might be the best paella I'd ever had. Marcus was onto seconds, but Hunter had barely touched his food.

The dining room was ridiculously large, but his décor was simple and tasteful. White wainscoting; tray ceilings holding fixtures with minimalistic medallions. It was less distracting than I'd expect from such a mansion, and it told me a few things about the billionaire beside me.

"Why have you never been married, Rex?" Hunter asked out of the blue.

I sipped from a stemmed glass, enjoying the smoothest red Spanish wine I'd ever tasted. "It hasn't happened."

"It's because he's too closed off to let anyone in," Marcus said from across the table. "I've been trying to convince him to do some dating for years, but he rarely goes on a second one. It's kind of sick."

I frowned at him, wondering why he'd tell Hunter any of that. "I haven't met the right woman, that's all."

Hunter set his fork down and dabbed at his lips with a napkin. "This life isn't for everyone. It's difficult to keep a partner who understands our obsessions. I had one, once…" His voice drifted with his gaze. "She was everything I ever wanted, but…"

"What happened?" Marcus asked.

"She left years ago. We weren't copacetic, so it seems."

"Was it mutual?" I found myself intrigued. I'd expected the wealthy collector to be more difficult to hold a conversation with. My experiences with him as a younger man had been rushed and short-lived, but now, I hated how much I was appreciating the dialogue. Here was a man that had legitimately known my father for years. It was a connection I'd never sought before.

"I have to say that almost any decision in life, when made by two people, is rarely mutual, Rex. Sometimes one person is for or against one side, and the other is leaning that way, but it's not the same as being equal in the outcome."

"Meaning you had reservations, but she did the walking," Marcus offered, making Hunter laugh.

Hunter turned his attention to Marcus. "Yes, Marcus, you've read the situation correctly. And you?"

"What about me?"

"Do you wish for a long and healthy existence? Perhaps with a wife, offspring tearing up the carpets and drawing dinosaurs on the wallpaper?" Hunter asked.

Marcus paused eating, his fork hovering with a piece of sausage near his lips. "Nope. No kids for me. I prefer the bachelor lifestyle at this point anyhow. I mean, I couldn't leave for Venezuela if I was tied down."

And there it was. I'd asked Marcus to keep our destination a secret, but the moment it leaked, I understood exactly what the old man had been doing. He'd been lulling us into complacency, confident we'd slip about our mission.

To his credit, Hunter didn't comment on the error. "Children can be far more rewarding than that. It's one of my biggest regrets."

Francois was there to clean up our dishes, and he refilled our wine glasses, even though I shook my head when he drifted behind my shoulder. "Look, Hunter, we're going to take the money, but I'd prefer to keep the details between Marcus and me for the time being."

He raised an eyebrow. "Wouldn't want to get a dying man's hopes up, would we?"

"It's not going to work. I think I may have found something that can lead us to the Bridge, but if it falls flat, I'm hanging up my hat. You'll have to dangle your money in front of someone else," I told him.

Marcus raised a hand, his index finger lifted. "I could always—"

I amended my statement. "Marcus and I will be done if we don't discover the next clue."

"Very well. It's getting late, and I have to be leaving." Hunter Madison rose, still in his expensive suit, and smoothed his tie with his palm.

I was in jeans and a sweater, opting for more comfort, and I peered at an old grandfather clock just as the hands struck ten PM, a chime ringing as many times. "See you in the morning."

"I'm afraid I have some business to attend to. The driver will return you to the city. Be ready at nine in the morning. Francois will see to your breakfast." Hunter stepped over, his arm extended. I rose from the chair, shaking it, and he tugged me closer, his breath smelling like wine. "I have the utmost faith in you, Rex Walker. I know you don't believe everything I've said today, but I want to leave you with a few questions. What if it's all real? What if your father found this Bridge and traveled somewhere? What if the Believers are right? Keep an eye on the sky."

And with that, he was gone, abandoning us in the expansive dining room. I waited until the clipping of Hunter's heels on the hardwood had dissipated, and downed the glass of wine.

"This wasn't how I expected things to go," I told Marcus.

"Are you kidding me? Best day of my life," he said, grinning as he finished his own drink.

We exited the dining room, and I noticed the trees in the backyard bending sideways. I expected to find a raucous storm blowing in from the ocean, but spotted the blades of a helicopter instead. It landed on a concrete pad, and we watched through the sprawling living room windows as Hunter pulled his jacket tight, crossing the yard with Francois directly behind, carrying his bag. The copter lifted a few minutes later, and Hunter's servant glanced up toward us from the landing pad.

"Good luck sleeping tonight," Marcus whispered.

We drove most of the way in silence, with our

uncertainty vacant from the bits of conversation we did share. It was mid-afternoon on Sunday when we entered Boston's city limits, and a few snowflakes stuck to my windshield. It was finals week, and I had far too much to prepare for, not to mention booking flights and details for our visit to Venezuela. I hadn't looked into the country's current political standings for a while, and asked Marcus to do some research before jumping in blindly. In the end, I assumed we'd be entering from Mexico under the guise of a humanitarian venture. I was lucky to have an acquaintance who didn't mind me using her foundation as a cover on my more delicate trips.

As I travelled to Marcus' apartment complex, I saw a group of volunteers decorating a giant Christmas tree in the park. "Are you heading home for the holidays?"

"To Florida? Man, I hate leaving all this for the sunny beaches. I never thought I'd love the season so much until I came up here. Snow, trees, sled rides. I know, you wouldn't expect it from me, right?" Marcus asked.

"You seem to forget that I saw those pictures of you singing carols in an elf costume," I reminded him. The roads were busy coming into town, but near Marcus' place, traffic had eased off, providing a clear line of sight through my rear view mirror.

"That was for a girl, and she was…"

I slammed on the brakes, catching the same black-tinted car tailing us for the last ten minutes or so.

"What are you doing?" Marcus asked, but I was already running from the driver's side, my flashers on.

"What the hell do you want?" I shouted at the car, my heart racing as I dashed for the BMW.

It had stopped twenty yards behind, and instead of confronting me, the driver opted to speed off, nearly clipping me in the process. A minivan coming in the opposite direction swerved to avoid a collision and rolled his window down, shouting obscenities. I lifted a shaky hand, expressing my apologies, and he tore away, honking loudly.

"Did you get the plate?" I shouted to Marcus, who stood recording the incident with his cell phone.

He didn't reply for a second, and I saw him zooming on the image. A moment later, he shook his head. "Sorry, Rex."

Someone had a lot of interest in my whereabouts these days, and if it had nothing to do with Hunter Madison, it had to be a connection to the Believers.

9

"*T*ime is complete," I told the class, walking through the rows of seats toward the door. "Please hand in the tests on my desk in a neat pile, and enjoy the holidays."

Luca was the first to stand, cockily crossing the room and setting his exam down. "Nailed it."

I smirked, watching as the rest of the students dropped their tests, some obviously more confident than others. "I'm sure you all did well. It's been a pleasure teaching you this semester, and I know I'll be seeing many of you in January for Linguistic Anthropology." I hadn't taught the course before, but it was part of the curriculum I was responsible for now. I wouldn't have to spread myself as thin at Harvard, but this was the price I'd paid for my freedom.

Cassie was the last one to my desk, and she lingered, watching the door as the other students filed from the class, saying their goodbyes to me. I replied half-heartedly to them, sensing Cassie had something to say.

When it was just the two of us, I stood and crossed my arms. "What is it, Cassie?"

"I know the material, but with my class load… I'm having problems with my roommate, and my parents can't send me money until January." Her posture was slack, and tears formed in her eyes. I'd heard all kinds of excuses from many types of students over the years. Hell, I'd had to embellish a bit when I was younger in order to get a grade-point bump, but everything about her composure told me she was telling the truth.

Her hair was pulled into a tight ponytail, her eyes dark and puffy. "Cassie, if there's anything going on, you can tell me."

I stepped closer, and she glanced up. "It's nothing I can't handle, but… if there's a chance you can go easy on me, I'd appreciate it. I'll work extra hard in Linguistics next term."

I nodded slowly, but my words weren't as reassuring. "I'll do my best, Cassie, but I can't treat any of my students preferentially. You understand."

A fat tear slipped over her cheek, and she glanced at the door, then to her smart watch, which flashed as she received a message. She wiped at her face and pushed past me without so much as a thank you.

I sighed as she sped from the exit, and sat on my desk beside the uneven stack of tests.

"How did it go?" Jessica asked from the hallway.

"You know. Some of the kids looked pleased with themselves; others were willing to make a sacrifice to the ancient star gods in an effort to pass. The usual," I joked.

Jessica walked in, her high heels clacking on the floor. She was in a red pantsuit, and it made her look like a high-priced lawyer. Her eyes gleamed as she closed the door behind her. "Rex, I need you to stick around next week. We have a scheduling issue with the main exam supervisors, and I'm asking the professors to step in."

I raised my hands at my chest. "Jessica, I won't be in town."

An eyebrow raised. "Is that so? Where are you going so soon after exams and before the holidays?"

I swallowed, wishing I'd practiced the lie before I'd arrived. I hadn't thought this through, but my tickets to

South America had already been purchased by Marcus. We were leaving in two days.

"There's been a find near Fiji. Small island, and something that might significantly change that region's history. I've been hired to join the crew... for a few days." I pursed my lips, wondering if the lie would stick. I had read a blog from a contemporary of mine seeking evidence of a thousand-year-old migration through that area, and she might be able to track the proof down if she searched.

"I thought you were working for me, Rex." Jessica frowned, and her tone spoke volumes.

"I am. I didn't think it was against my contract to operate on the side, if it didn't interfere with my teaching," I said, knowing what my deal had been when I'd signed the papers. Richard Klein had been sure to read over the verbiage before I'd added my signature.

Jessica stepped closer, and I could smell her perfume. It was probably French. "Professor Walker, I'm telling you it does interfere. You're expected to assist us around exam time, like the rest of the faculty."

I glanced at the clock, and she noticed. "Somewhere more important to be?"

"Look, Jessica, I—"

"Save it. You go to Fiji, but I want your full attention when you return. Am I understood?"

I put on my best smile and reached out, gently shaking her hand. "I'm sorry about the mix-up. I won't let it happen again."

This seemed to break the ice, and she relaxed. She turned, slowly walking away, and I did my best to not stare after her as she did so. She paused at the door and returned my smile. "Maybe we can go for dinner when you're back. You can tell me about the trip."

"It's a date," I replied, and she was gone. I was in a load

of trouble with that woman, and knew I'd be walking on eggshells with her from now on.

I had three hours before I needed to be at Richard's house, and Marcus would be waiting for me. My phone buzzed, and I pulled it from my jacket pocket, seeing his initials on a text message.

Dr. W. I'm outside.

I laughed as I gathered the tests and my things, tossing them into the leather satchel. Marcus hadn't called me that in years, not since I was his professor.

As I stepped from the classroom, I hesitated for a moment. What if that wasn't him?

I grabbed the phone, dialing Marcus' number. He answered on the second ring. "Rexford, you old bean. What is taking you so long?" He put on his best Bostonian accent, mimicking the wealthy elitists he so often admired. In the background, I heard sounds of the pub we'd planned to meet at.

"You're not outside to pick me up?" I asked.

"What do you mean?" he retorted, no longer goofing around with accents.

"Damn it. I'll be right there. Watch your back," I warned him, and ended the conversation.

The phone buzzed again, but I ignored Marcus' call. I probably should have explained myself better.

I walked through the hallways, nervously checking over my shoulder, but nothing felt out of place. The students were louder than usual, chatting happily, as some had finished their last exam. Others gathered books, studying along common-area tables in groups. I walked by the registrar's offices and the cafeteria as I headed for the front doors.

There it was. The same blacked-out car, parked in the loading zone.

"Professor, great test. The study guide really helped," Luca said, jogging over to me.

I plucked a flyer for a Christmas party off a bulletin board, and handed it to Luca. "Would you do me a favor?"

"Sure." Luca was always quick to a debate, and even quicker to please those around him. I hated that it could be dangerous, but I doubted the driver would do anything to a student with a piece of paper.

"See that BMW?"

"Yeah, 7 Series. It's sick."

"Can you knock on the passenger window and invite them to join this party?" I pointed at the flyer in his hand.

"Uhm, friend of yours?"

"Something like that. Just don't mention my name. If he asks, you don't know me."

Luca shrugged and pressed through the doors. I waited until a group of students were leaving and followed behind them, ducking low as Luca approached the car. I caught him banging on the glass, and I dodged away, racing for the staff parking lot.

By the time I was in my car, driving the opposite direction, Luca was walking from the BMW, hands up, shouting something. The car remained there, waiting for me to exit the building, and I turned my attention off the rear view mirror.

I drove, making quick work of the twenty blocks between my college and the bar, and decided to park past it, in a local auto shop's lot. There were ten or so vehicles in various stages of body work, and no one would notice my SUV among them on a Friday at closing time. I left my bag and checked the streets before dashing for the bar.

The spot was close enough to downtown to catch the blue-shirts crowd, and a few of them were already loudly arguing the merits of their investment plans when I entered. Marcus was at the same booth we always occupied, his laptop open. When he spotted me, he frowned, shaking his head.

"I'm sorry about that." I plopped into the seat, the cracked leather bench pinching my leg.

"What the hell, man? You scared the crap out of me," he said loudly.

"I know." I explained what had happened, leaving out the issues and subsequent planned date with my boss, and he listened without a word until I was done.

"Damn it. Good thing we're leaving town. Let's lay low until Sunday," he advised.

"I wish I could. I'm going to Klein's for a dinner party tonight." The waitress brought over a beer, sliding it across the dark wooden table.

"Rex, the last thing you should be doing is walking around in the open. Everyone knows you and Klein are close. If someone's after you, they'll be at that party."

"I'd hope they weren't on the guest list." I sighed, wishing I could rewind things. How long had they been following me? Was it after I'd visited my sister, or well before?

I took a sip and stared at his computer. "What have you found?"

"These Believers are no joke if half of what I'm reading is true. Lots of speculation on some conspiracy sites, but nothing substantiated. They're ghosts, Rex."

"And what do the internet whackos think of them?" I asked.

He leaned closer, glancing around. Two gruff men sat in the booth beside us, wearing Red Sox hats and sharing a pitcher of beer.

"One guy, a reputable source as far as the internet goes, says they worship beings from outer space. He claims they mirror the coming of Christ, but instead of Judgment Day, we'll be visited by aliens."

"So Hunter Madison wasn't lying."

"Nope. And if Hunter was one, I wonder how he escaped," Marcus said, making a good observation.

"You know cults. Easy to get in, impossible to leave. If he actually did break away, I bet it cost him a pretty penny."

Marcus flipped the computer around, showing a picture. It was a symbol, one I thought I'd seen somewhere before. It looked like the top half of a star with three points only, bending at their tips.

"Do you know it?" I asked.

"No. Can't find much on it, either These guys are covert, Rex. Like, clean as a whistle." Marcus sipped at an iced tea, and I had an idea.

"Can you give me a ride tonight?"

"Oh man, I have a date. She's meeting me here in an hour," Marcus pleaded.

"Fine. But if I'm driven off the road and shot before I get to Klein's, you'll have to live with that," I told him, keeping my voice low.

"Damn it. Rex, you owe me for this."

———————————

*D*octor Richard Klein came from money, and I suspected he'd also done well for himself along the way. He owned a few properties near Harvard and rented them out to students who were used to the life of luxury. The type that wouldn't stoop to residing in a dorm. Those alone probably earned him more annually than my salary, and every time I visited his home, I was reminded of how different our social classes were. The estate houses off Hammond Street continually impressed me, and while they weren't quite on par with Madison's East Hampton mansion, they were closing the gap quicky.

Klein's home was a large brick colonial, with four dormers topping the roof and a guest house at the end of the yard, a pool between them. It was shut down for the year and covered, and I walked toward the house, avoiding the main entrance. If someone was watching for us, they likely would have missed Marcus parking his hatchback several blocks away and our ensuing trail across Klein's neighbor's land.

Klein's two golden retrievers were in a large outdoor kennel, and they barked excitedly as they spotted Marcus and me. A motion sensor light flickered on at our movement, and a second later, the back door opened, revealing Janelle Klein. "Rex, is that you? What are you doing out here?" She wore a knee-length dress, an olive green number that made her look like a youthful fifty-seven.

I stammered out an excuse. "I… I wanted to show Marcus the yard. Isn't it incredible?"

"Sure is. I like how the… trees line the…" Marcus stopped as Richard arrived, peering over his wife's shoulder.

She turned to him and smiled, her eyes twinkling. "Look. Rex brought a guest."

Richard frowned but waved us inside. "Marcus, good to see you again."

"Likewise." They shook hands, and I kissed Janelle's cheek, entering their warm and inviting abode.

Richard's wife slid her arm into Marcus' and led him off toward the living room, and Richard came over. "What are you doing? You're late, and you brought Marcus? This could be a real push for your career, Rex."

"I know, but my car broke down, and I needed a lift," I said.

"Too good for a taxi?"

"We were at the bar…"

"When are you going to grow up, Rex? You're over forty, and you're hanging out with this kid. Doing what? Chasing apparitions? I owe it to your parents to ensure you're successful, and I'll not let you throw your life away."

It had been some time since I'd been chastised by a parental figure, and I clenched my jaw, taking the brunt of it without response.

"Did you hear me?" he asked, moving closer. Richard was wearing an Armani suit, the same one he'd worn to my mother's funeral, and for a second, I closed my eyes, picturing the event. I'd walked around like a zombie for a week when I'd heard the news, and being reminded of that time firmed my resolve.

With a glance to ensure none of the guests overheard, I tapped his chest with a finger, stepping directly in front of him. "No one asked you to butt into my life, Richard. I appreciate everything you've done for me over the years, helping my admission into school and providing references when necessary, but it's gone on long enough. You're right. I'm not a child, yet you feel this innate need to treat me like one. I like my job, and I'm not throwing anything away, let alone my life." He was right about some things. I was still chasing after Dirk Walker, but I wouldn't give him the satisfaction of admitting it.

Richard relaxed, smiling widely, his teeth white and perfect. "Maybe I have been pushing you a little too much. Why don't you come in, have a drink, eat some dinner, and enjoy the company of contemporaries for an evening?"

There was something about his tone that had me searching for Marcus over his shoulder. "Fine, but I can't stay late. Lots of loose ends to tie up." I realized I hadn't mentioned going away to Venezuela to him, and at this moment, it was the last thing I wanted to do.

We entered his living room, and I couldn't believe how many people were in attendance. I should have known by the volume of cars lining the usually quiet street, but I had been more concerned with sneaking in than watching the road. I quickly estimated there were over thirty guests, and our quiet dinner party had turned into something much more.

Jazz music echoed through his wireless speaker system, and I spied at least three servers wearing white dress shirts with black bow ties. One of them arrived with a tray of three-quarter-full champagne glasses, and I gladly took one.

"Would you like some introductions?" Richard asked, but I'd met a few of them before, at summer barbecues or Harvard alumni events he'd dragged me to.

I was about to wave him off when a man I didn't recognize captured Richard's attention. I caught the hard stare, the frown, and the puckered lips of a man desperate for a discussion. "I'll be back shortly, Rex. Don't forget to meet Genevieve Belcourte. She's the one…"

He must have noticed my expression firming again, and he stopped midsentence, walking toward the bald man across the room. I watched them as I sipped the champagne. Richard leaned in while the man whispered something to him, and they both turned, exiting the room, heading toward Richard's staircase.

"Quite the place." Marcus startled me.

"Sure. He's the definitive host," I muttered.

"Did you try the crab puffs? And this bubbly is killer," Marcus said.

I glanced at his t shirt, with its obscure joke about computer coding half-covered by the sport coat I'd made him bring. "I think we should go."

Being here felt fake, and all I could concentrate on was the car trailing me for the last while and how badly I wanted to fly to Venezuela to investigate our lead. Even if it turned out to be nothing, I had to know, and it was being funded by a man who could afford the loss.

"We just got here," Marcus protested.

I was curious what had caused Richard to rush out of the room, leaving his guests, but his wife didn't seem to notice, casually conversing with her friends, floating from one to another like a feather in the wind. She ended up approaching as I set my glass on a curio cabinet. A woman lingered behind her, and our gazes met. Her silky auburn hair was captivating, and she stepped around Janelle, jutting her small hand out.

"I've heard so much about you," she said in a rush. "Terri. Terri Prophet."

I didn't know the name. "Pleased to meet you." I shook her hand, finding it warm, like she'd just been cradling a cup of coffee.

"I read your paper on the Bering Land Bridge when I was in my senior year. It changed my understanding of migration patterns," she said.

"Oh, *you* were the one that read it," I joked, catching a glint in her eyes.

"I'll leave you to talk," Janelle said, and a moment later, she was gone, chatting with the next guest.

The room was sizable, tall ceilings with enormous windows overlooking the backyard, and wood crackled in the giant fireplace centering the room. A couch faced it, and no one was seated there, leaving it open. Terri motioned for us to sit, and I watched Marcus wiggle his eyebrows and take off, holding another champagne flute.

"Do you have a moment to chat? I'd love to pick your brain," she said.

She was striking, her dark blue eyes widening as if awaiting my response. "Sure. That would be nice." The sofa was firm and uncomfortable, like everything in a formal living space, but the heat from the fireplace made up for it. "What do you do, Terri?"

Color rose in her neck, but I pretended not to notice. "I'm a TA, working in Doctor Klein's department."

"And how do you like it there?" I asked.

"It's great. I'm hoping to teach at Harvard one day, after I earn my doctorate."

My attention was drawn to the opposite edge of the room, where the shorter bald man had returned without Richard. He peered around the living space, his eyes glazing over the guests, and when he saw me, his head stopped turning. He continued on, feigning the action, but I sensed he'd been looking for me. Something was off. He lifted his arm, taking a drink from a server, his suit jacket sleeve sliding up his wrist. Even from this far away, I could make out the symbol: a three-pointed half-star. This man belonged to the Believers.

"Terri, it's been lovely, but I have to be going." I stood, but not so quickly as to draw attention to myself.

"Oh. I'm sorry to hear that."

Marcus was near the dining room, sampling more food, and I walked over, clutching his elbow. "Time to make our exit," I whispered.

He didn't object, and we wound our way past the guests with a few muttered apologies and pressed through the front door. I scanned for any signs of the tinted vehicle, and when I didn't see it, we jogged for Marcus' car.

"What has you so worked up?" He started the engine.

"The cult… the one Madison was so ramped up about. One of them was with Klein."

"You don't think…"

"No, but I'm not sticking around to find out. Richard can take care of himself, but if I was to guess, they're using him to get to me. Let's see if we can't book an earlier flight." I glanced behind us, but the road was quiet, the streetlights casting unfamiliar shadows beyond the parked cars.

10

"*I* can't believe that cult is after you." Marcus entered my townhouse, shaking snow from his jacket. It had cooled down, a storm moving in with little warning.

"Us. They're after *us*," I reminded him.

He appeared to contemplate this but gave me a shrug of his shoulders. "Whatever. We're a team. Don't think for a second I'm going to let some old white cultists mess me up."

I admired his confidence but didn't mirror it. "Take the computer. We're heading to the airport." I hadn't started to pack for our trip yet, and I pulled a duffel bag from the closet under my stairs. "We'll stop at your place on the way."

"No need. Already have my stuff in the car." Marcus didn't look away from the laptop. He was perched on my island, fingers quickly flying over his keyboard.

"Of course you do. Always prepared for anything."

"Nah. I just saw how on edge you were lately and knew you'd want to leave early." I heard him as I dashed up the stairs, heading to my bedroom.

I flicked the lights on and looked around the room. It was so plain, bland in its bachelor stylings. Everything was dark wood, gray paint and bedding. My closet was full of suit jackets and dress shirts, and I plucked a pair of cargo shorts, jeans, and short-sleeved plaid shirts, along with some plain tees. It was snowing here, but down in South America, it would be another story.

Once I had enough to carry me through a few days away, I added the toiletries and stopped, watching myself in the mirror. My eyes were heavy, tilted down in a way that only age and exhaustion could muster. I leaned into the sink, washing my face, and dabbed it dry on a hand towel. I had to do this. If I stayed, these lunatics could do something drastic.

But what if I came back empty-handed? I'd have to deal with them in some fashion. I contemplated going to the police, but that wouldn't help, not now. Not when I needed to skip town and follow our one lead.

Why had Clayton left the coordinates on his grave marker? What were we going to find in the jungles of Venezuela? I had too many questions and none of the answers.

"You coming?" Marcus shouted from downstairs.

I didn't reply, just zipped up the bag, hoisting it over my shoulder. Marcus was already by the front door, grinning at me.

"You changed the flights?" I asked.

"Done."

"And we can leave soon?"

"We can."

"What aren't you telling me?" He was oddly quiet as we exited my place. I locked the door, hoping that no one would break in while I was gone. I should have added the security system Marcus suggested but hadn't made time.

"There may be a couple of layovers," he finally spouted as he lifted my bag, tossing it into his hatchback. He fired up his car, tires slipping on the wet pavement as we lurched forward.

I watched behind us but found nothing. "Take the long way," I suggested, hoping it would throw off anyone

Part of me thought I might have been fabricating danger: the fact my door was unlocked, even spotting the three-tipped tattoo across the room. Maybe I'd been seeing things, giving into the paranoia since Hunter Madison had revealed the truth about the Believers. He had a lot to gain from us acquiring the links to this Bridge he was so anxious to locate. Fueling my panic and fears was a tactic a man like him would use to get me on his side. I'd need his protection, his funding too. His friendship. I shook my head as we drove on, feeling like a fool who'd been had by a man far more experienced in the game than I was.

I remembered what Marcus had said, and circled back. "A *couple* of layovers?"

He flashed me a grin. "We'll be there in no time."

———————

Dust covered every inch of my body, sticking to my sweaty skin. I wiped my face with my bandana and glanced at the ever-present sweltering sun.

"Did someone forget to tell them it was December?" Marcus asked. His words came out like a man on his last breath, and I passed him my canteen. He took a greedy swig, water dripping down his chin, and I did the same.

"This is a nightmare." The bench in the back of the ancient pickup was uncomfortable on the main roads. Out here, in no man's land, my spine protested every small bump and hop of the vehicle.

After connecting in Pittsburgh, then to Mexico City, we'd landed in Caracas on Saturday morning. It had taken three hours to vacate the airport, and finding someone to bring us south had proven more difficult than anticipated.

This was our third local hire, and I suspected he was being paid a month's salary just to drive the last hundred miles to our destination.

It was Sunday morning, and we'd been lucky enough to be dropped off in a village a few hours north of here the night prior. After sleeping on squeaky cots in what passed for a hotel, we were both a little on edge.

"How much longer?" Marcus asked me, and I stared ahead.

The driver was with his son, maybe twelve years old, and the kid kept staring at us in the truck bed. I knocked on the window, and he unlatched it. "*Cuánto tiempo más?*"

"*Unos minutos,*" the boy replied. *A few minutes.*

The window stayed open, and I leaned my elbows on my knees. "Almost there."

Sweat covered Marcus' forehead, but he was acclimating well. For a kid who'd never traveled growing up, he'd sure adapted to the hardships of adventure, even better than I did.

It made me wonder if my dad had ever come here, to this town. How had Dirk Walker dealt with muggy weather, mosquito bites, and sleeping on the ground? These were things I'd never had the chance to learn.

The landscape was oddly level, with a few ranges of low-lying mountains some miles in the distance. We'd passed the main river that bisected the country an hour ago, and now it was drier, the lush jungle giving way to thinner tree cover and hard-packed soil.

Five minutes passed, and I finally spotted a farm. A trickle of goats lazily trotted across a fenced field, and children kicked a ball in the street as we drove by. I lifted a hand in greeting, but the kids only regarded me with suspicion. "Friendly place," I muttered, but Marcus didn't seem to hear.

The truck lurched to a stop, nearly knocking me from my seat, and the driver hopped out, tapping his palm on the side of the vehicle. This was it: the end of the line.

My legs protested as I climbed to my feet, and I descended from the truck bed, swinging my pack over my arm. "Pay him, Marcus."

My sidekick had half of our money, and he slipped our agreed-upon amount from his bag, shoving it toward the tanned man. He didn't say a word as he headed to his seat and turned the truck around, driving the way he'd come.

This was it. Our destination. Marcus had his cell phone out, and he shook his head. "This isn't it, Rex."

"What do you mean?" I asked, trying to catch a glimpse of his screen.

"The coordinates are still several miles away." He waved farther down the road, and I sighed. There was a scattering of buildings in this godforsaken town, all of them constructed at least a hundred years ago, and they'd been neglected since then.

I'd visited a lot of places like this over the years, and at some point, they all blended together into one miserable pit stop you didn't want to linger at. The air of poverty was heavy, and I wondered how they got up every day.

Still, as we walked across the rough and bumpy road centering the village, the inhabitants seemed happy. Maybe this was far enough from the oppressive government. They got by with what little they needed, and that carried them through the days.

Some of the structures were solid, with white plaster and thatched roofs, while others were no more than shacks. A pair of men sat outside what looked to be the local watering hole, each smoking cigarettes and clutching sweating bottles of beer. "Let's ask." I walked past them, feeling both of their stares on me as I entered.

A fan circled precariously from a low ceiling, and I heard soft music playing from an old stereo behind the bar. It was early in the day, and there were only a handful of people inside, including us. The barkeep was in his fifties, wearing a white short-sleeved shirt and dark pants. His moustache was too large for his face, but he seemed friendly as I crossed the room, sitting at the bar.

"*Dos cervezas,*" I said, making the peace sign with my left hand. He nodded, popping the tops off two brown bottles and sliding them to us.

Marcus flipped his phone and turned it to face the man. "Do you know where this is?" he asked, and I translated.

The man's eyes narrowed slightly, but he just shook his head. "*No hay nada ahí fuera.*"

Marcus glanced at me, and I relayed, "Says there's nothing out that way."

"Are you sure?" I asked him in Spanish.

"*Antigua cantera de rocas.*" The man flipped a towel over his shoulder and turned around, cleaning a glass.

"Rock quarry." I tapped the bar, sipping the beer. What I really needed was more water, and I asked for some. The man started to pour some from a tap, and I shook my head, sliding ten US dollars' worth of bolivars at him. He smiled, snatching it quickly, and brought two bottles of water from a refrigerator.

"What do you think? Walk the rest of the way?" Marcus asked, and I nodded.

"Unless you want to ask those guys out front for a ride."

Marcus swallowed half his beer in one chug and made a refreshed sound when he was done. "Not on your life, Rex. I've seen this movie before, and I'm not ending up in the bottom of the quarry with my computer in their hands."

We had a few hours before dark settled, and I wanted to keep moving. I didn't know if we were going to uncover buried secrets in this rock quarry, or what we'd find, but I definitely didn't want to be out there at night.

I finished the beer and slipped the barkeep another note, thanking him.

The two patrons were gone when we exited, but I smelled their lingering body odor mixed with cigarette smoke. Two miles wasn't far, but after a day of traveling across the tumultuous landscape in the back of trucks, the hike would be a strain.

The sun was high as we left town. Only a few people remained in the streets, and I guessed the population of this place had to be under three hundred. Little more than a blip on the map.

We kicked up dust as we walked, and within ten minutes, my shirt was stuck to my chest. The ground ascended as we went, and as we crested a hill, we spotted the quarry from this vantage point. The rocky opening was massive, with a set of giant dump trucks parked near the entrance. They weren't much more than rusted-out hunks of metal, and I wondered how long the place had been abandoned.

"This doesn't look promising," Marcus said, licking his lips. "Dammit, Rex. Why would that guy send us here, of all places? Are we supposed to find something hidden? Because if that's the case, it seems like we're missing a clue."

He was right, but I didn't say so. "It's okay. We're almost there." I felt a renewed energy upon seeing the quarry, and my legs picked up speed. I stopped at the edge of the opening, where the roads circled down, ending with pieces of old machinery. I assumed whoever owned this land had cleared out anything of value years ago, abandoning whatever they couldn't salvage or sell.

A house stood off to the right, across the opening, and I laughed as I spotted the van beside it. "Marcus, someone's here."

"Is that a good thing?" he asked.

"We're about to find out." I'd considered attempting to buy a gun along the way, but didn't want to risk being caught with a firearm in Venezuela. I'd heard plenty of horror stories from other archaeologists to know better. I hated being unprotected out in the open like this.

We arrived at the house in less than five minutes, and I peered into a dusty window, unable to see inside. The door wasn't latched, and I knocked on it loudly.

"*¿Quién es?*" a woman's voice called.

I struggled for a minute to think of the words, but they eventually came out. "We're looking for some information," I said in Spanish. When the door didn't open, I added, "We can pay."

Her feet shifted behind the wooden slab, but the door finally pressed wide. A short dark-haired woman stepped onto the front step, looking in both directions past us. "What is it you seek?" she asked in English, her accent thick.

"May we come in?" I asked, nodding toward the living room.

"You can pay?" she asked, making the universal sign for money by rubbing her fingers over her thumb.

Marcus pulled another wad of bills and gave her a reasonable sum, returning the rest. Her eyes lingered on the money in his shirt, but she stepped aside, letting us enter.

The home was welcoming and neat, and she motioned to the couch, taking a chair across from it. I dragged in some dirt onto her white tile floor and gave her an apologetic look. She didn't seem to notice or care.

"What's your name?" I asked.

"Marta," she replied, still frowning.

"Lovely name. I'm Rex, and this is Marcus."

"What are you needing?" She was around my age, but had heavy lines in her forehead. I reasoned living beside a rock quarry wasn't ideal, but her eyes were bright and carried a spark in them.

"Does the name Dirk Walker mean anything to you?" I asked.

She shook her head.

My heartbeat quickened. If she knew nothing, we were at the end of the trail. "What about Clayton Belvedere?"

Her expression changed instantly. She stood up, speaking in hurried Spanish. I could only pick up a few words, but she wasn't happy to see us.

"What is it? How do you know him?" I asked, and she sat down again, her hands shaking.

"My *padre*. Father used to do work. Out of country." She made the sign of the cross, starting at her forehead, and I looked at Marcus. This was it.

"Where is your father? Can we speak with him?" She looked confused, and I tried again. "Your *padre*. Is he here?"

She lowered her head. "Father is dead."

The wind blew out of my sails at the words, and I slumped into the couch, my energy suddenly sapped.

"You said he was employed out of country? Where, exactly?" Marcus asked.

Marta crossed her hands over her lap and looked at my sidekick. "He went to other places. He was an excellent rock climber, and strong. He was hired by some men. Did jobs for them for ten years. I was just a child. I recall him gone for weeks at a time."

"Was one of these men Clayton?" I pressed.

She nodded. "I think so. Mister Clayton."

"What was his last trip? Working for them?"

She sat still, her gaze shifting to her kitchen. "I was a little one. Thirty years or so."

"Thirty years." That was close enough to my timeline. "Where was he?"

Marta brightened. "I remember. He came home with gifts. He told my mother that he was done leaving after one more job."

I smiled at Marcus. This meant he'd been there with my father on their final trip. "Where was he?" I asked again, my voice low.

"Portugal. Then he was gone again. For a month."

Her answer confirmed my suspicions over the years.

"How does this help us?" Marcus sighed, rubbing his face with a palm.

"Maybe we can pick up the trail again. There has to be something I missed." I tried to think about it, going over the details I'd weighed countless times throughout my life.

"You want to find Mister Clayton?"

"Can you tell us where he went?" My lips almost stuck together as everything went dry.

"No, but I know that Father kept something from him. He hid it, but I was a curious child." Marta smirked, and I saw a glimpse of the troublemaking girl she could have once been.

I was fighting my desire to climb to my feet and shake the answer out of her. "Where is it?"

"Across the mine." Marta peered at Marcus again, toward his shirt pocket, and I nodded at him.

"Give her the money," I said calmly.

"All of it?" he asked.

"If this is what I think it might be, it's worth every penny."

11

*T*he sun had fallen past the rolling rocky hills to the east, creating silhouettes across the pit before us. Marta lived alone, now that her parents were deceased. Her husband had vanished on her five years ago, gone without so much as a note.

Remembering the armed men near El Mirador, I wondered if the Believers had caused the man's disappearance. It could have been as simple as him abandoning his wife, but my gut was telling me otherwise.

"Be careful," Marta warned as we began to descend choppy steps cut into the wall of the quarry.

"Did your family own this?" I asked.

She laughed, as if that was the most ridiculous question in the world. "No. My *abuelo* was the…" She searched for the word, finding it after a few steps. "Supervisor of the quarry."

"How did you learn English?" Marcus inquired.

"It was owned by a British man. Father worked with English people like Mister Clayton, and teach me to speak." She continued down, her footsteps sure and faster than mine.

Soon we were at the bottom of the quarry, and I peered up, witnessing nothing but a sheer cliff face greeting me. "When did it close?"

Marta waved us on, striding for the opposite edge.

"Two decades. The owner left Father in charge, giving him the house. Now it's mine. The owner never come back."

It was over a mile wide, and we walked the next section in silence, my mind reeling from what we were potentially about to encounter. Marcus went ahead, chatting with Marta as I stayed a few steps behind, wondering how my dad had found Marta's father in the first place. This woman and I were connected in a strange way by the relationship of our parents.

The sun had vacated the quarry, the last of the light climbing up the west cliff until we were in the dusk. Already it felt cooler, and I billowed my shirt, tugging it near my chest. A doorway came into view as we neared the rocky wall, a wooden entrance with supporting beams across the top.

"In there?" I asked, and she nodded.

Marta held a flashlight, and she flicked it on, the incandescent beam hitting the ground. A thick old padlock hung on a rusted hinge, and Marta pulled a key from a leather strap around her neck, using it to click the lock open. She removed it and tried to push the door but failed. "It is stuck."

Marcus tried, and it shifted an inch.

We set our packs down, and I helped him, our hands close as we pulled with all our strength. It finally shifted enough for us to enter.

"If this door was that sticky, the entire room could be compromised," Marcus warned me.

Marta shone her light into the dark space, and entered without hesitation. Marcus gaped at me, and I could only shrug, stepping into the cliffside room.

"They stored supplies," Marta said, and I saw what she was referring to as the flashlight showcased the wall. There were a dozen shovels, pickaxes, and other various tools lined on hooks, but she kept moving past them all, heading for a secondary door. "The quarry had tunnels under it. Father say they are natural."

I peered into the corridor, seeing dust fall from wooden braces. It looked like the bowels of a mine, and I cringed at the thought of walking under so many tons of rock. "Is it safe?"

"I think this here for millions of years." She patted the wood with a palm and grinned. "These were added too." She moved on, but I noticed Marcus hadn't entered with me.

"Rex, I'll stay. Guard the exit," he said, picking up a shovel.

"Fine, but the next time we go into an abandoned quarry mine, it's your turn."

Marcus nodded noncommittally, and Marta was already far ahead; the only sign of her was the bobbing of the flashlight beam. I rushed to catch up, hoping to be in and out in a few minutes. That wasn't the case. The corridor went on for a half-mile, and rocks blocked part of our path near the end.

Marta didn't seem to care. She set the light on the floor and started moving boulders. I joined her, nervously gawking at the ceiling, and she climbed effortlessly, maneuvering the flashlight when we'd cleared a route. With a sigh, I landed across the pile where the corridor opened up.

The smell changed. It was damp, with heavy notes of metal. "What is this?"

"A lake." She exited the tunnel and stopped, aiming her light at the water. It was calmly flowing, and I glanced up to find bats on the roof. I hated bats. Which was detrimental in my line of work, since they seemed to exist in every cave, cavern, and crawlspace I'd ever worked in.

The walls held an assortment of minerals, and they

sparkled under the light. "I used to love it here. I was not allowed in, but I followed Father when he returned from his trip." She paused, staring at the lake. "He walked into there. I heard him say a prayer, and I hid." She motioned to an outcropping near the cavern wall behind us. "I had never seen him so afraid."

"What is it? What did he dump here?" I asked Marta.

She shrugged. "I didn't check. Don't like water. Think there might be snakes."

I flinched at the words, staring at the underground lake. "Your father put something in there? How far?"

"Not very. Ten feet."

Ten feet. I could do that. "Where?" I started for the edge of the water, looking at the murky depths. I had no way of knowing how deep it was, and Marta helped with the flashlight, glancing at the tunnel entrance and back to the lake.

"Around here," she said, pointing at the ground.

The last thing I wanted was to go in, but I didn't have a choice. I slipped from my boots, removing my socks, and set my possessions on the rocky ground. "You're certain of this?"

Marta nodded twice.

The water was warmer than I'd expected, but I still recoiled as my foot entered it. The rocks were slick below, and I nearly slid the moment both feet were in the lake. With a wave of my arms, I stayed balanced and took another step, then another.

I tentatively walked a few more yards and stopped, craning my neck to see Marta. It felt like something might have brushed by my leg, but I couldn't be certain.

"There. Or close."

I crouched, sticking my hands under the surface. It was past my knees, soaking the bottom hem of my shorts, and

I felt around, gripping more stones.

I was about to give up when my finger snagged something. I grabbed hold of it and lifted, hefting a burlap sack from the water. The bag dripped, making a hundred small ripples as I stared at it.

I exited the lake in a hurry. What had been so important as to hide all the way out here?

I set it to the rocky ground, tugging my shoes on, and suddenly being in the cavern with the bats high above was too much. Taking the prize, we returned abruptly, jogging the short distance to the storage room.

"What's inside?" Marcus whispered as we stepped outside. A constant insect chirping carried across the entire quarry now that the sun had set, and I clutched the bag in my grip. I didn't know if I wanted Marta to see the contents, but I couldn't delay any longer.

I pulled my pocketknife out, carefully slicing the top of the bag, and reached inside. The object was chilly. Metal. It was six-sided, like a cube, with a two-inch-thick frame. Along each edge was an opening, five inches tall and wide. I ran my finger through the hole, smiling as I understood what I was seeing.

"This is it," I muttered.

"That shape. The hex. It's like the empty holder in El Mirador," Marcus said reverently. Marta just stared at us, probably not understanding what we were so excited about.

"Do you think this is it? The thing that creates the Bridge?" Marcus asked, and I frowned at him, shaking my head curtly while turned from Marta. We'd said we wouldn't speak of it in front of anyone, and he'd just broken the cardinal rule.

I returned it to the bag and beamed at our guide. We were still missing a piece, and I had to know. "Marta, did your father keep any books? Journals? Something that might be of use?"

She shifted uncomfortably on her feet. "I have some of his things. Jose repaired the house after he passed. Found some stuff."

I raised an eyebrow but refused to let myself get too far ahead. "Can we see it?"

———————

"*T*his is intense. Six coordinates, Rex. Six slots in that… whatever you found." Marcus paced the room Marta had offered us for the night.

There was no cell reception, so we couldn't check the locations on a map. I held the single sheet of paper in my grip, careful not to smudge the old ink. I was certain it was my father's handwriting, and it brought even more questions. Were these the coordinates of the spots where he'd found the six Tokens, or was it something else?

"We should take her van," I said, peering at the door.

"Madison gave us enough cash. We can offer to buy it," Marcus said.

"We need some cell service, and that's probably a few miles from here, at least. I doubt that town even had internet, but I could be wrong. I forgot to check when we passed through." I sat on the bed, the springs protesting.

"Are we going to tell Madison?" Marcus asked. I was used to flippant easygoing banter, but his expression was grave. This was serious, the real thing, and neither of us knew exactly what to do.

"I don't think so. Not yet." I stared at the door, trying to listen for Marta's footsteps. "I guess it depends on what Marta has from her father."

I waited silently, thinking over the few details we knew. My father had disappeared with Clayton Belvedere in 1989. Hunter Madison had funded their initial expeditions, but something happened that caused my dad to cut him out of the deal. The Bridge. Hunter admitted that he'd been part of the Believers at one point, but bailed on them due to differences in principles.

Dirk and Clayton hired Marta's father, Luis, after meeting him in Venezuela, and this meant he'd been with them in Portugal, the day they vanished. Did her father have something to do with their disappearance? Could he have killed them, stolen their things? Or had it been as Marta indicated: Luis had been a loyal employee, and they'd paid him well to hide this article somewhere it wouldn't be found?

This was bothering me. "Marcus."

He stopped pacing long enough to glare at me. "What?"

"Why?"

"Why what? Why are we here?"

"Why were these coordinates on Clayton's gravestone?" I asked.

He plopped onto the bed beside me with a huff. "Man, I've been wondering the same thing."

I didn't know my father well. I'd been a little boy when he'd gone, so to me, he was a distant memory with rough stubble, magnetic brown eyes, and a smirk that when you saw it, you knew everything was going to be all right. Only it hadn't ended up that way. I could remember him picking me up and placing me on his shoulders, the smell of his musky cologne stuck to his collar.

The more I'd learned about him later in life, the more I understood his passion for adventure. My mother had claimed she got more than she'd bargained for when they met, and there were days when I thought she considered marrying him was the biggest regret of her existence. Then I remembered her in her bedroom after he'd gone for the last time, staring at a picture of their wedding and crying. Near the end, she'd admitted to me that she loved his spirit, but that he wasn't meant to have a family.

I glanced at the watch he'd given me and ran a finger along the fractured leather strap.

"What did you come up with, Rex?" Marcus asked me, and I forgot I'd even started a discussion.

"My dad. He wouldn't have left loose ends. He was so particular with what he added into his journals and the clear lack of evidence of his trips, that this couldn't be his work. Dirk Walker didn't want us to locate this artifact." I picked up the metal Token holder, hefting it in my grip.

Marcus' eyes went wide at the revelation. "So it was all Clayton. He set this up with Marta's dad."

I nodded, lowering the item into my pack. "That's why she didn't know who Dirk was, just Mister Clayton."

"That makes sense. Okay, Clayton wanted someone to find this. There has to be a reason." Marcus stopped talking as we heard the creak of the floorboards down the hallway. A soft knock clicked on the door, and I asked Marta to enter.

She had a box in her hands, water-stained and torn at the edges. "Here. Jose wanted to throw it out, but I kept it in the attic." She smiled sadly and passed it to me.

I accepted the box. She stood there watching me, then seemed to realize I was waiting for privacy. She could have asked to stay, since it was her father's possessions I was about to rifle through, but she stepped to the door, resting her hand on the knob. "Would you like some *batidos*? Uhm, fruit smoothie?"

Marcus said we would, and she left us in the spare

room.

"There has to be a clue." Marcus picked up the first item, a picture of a man. It had to be Marta's father. Luis was smiling at a girl beside him, who I guessed to be his daughter. The beam of pride in his eyes was unmistakable.

An address book was next, and I flipped through it, checking if there was anything remarkable about the names or locations. Nothing seemed out of place, but Marcus took photos of each one regardless. Perhaps it was written in a cipher. We couldn't be too careful.

A faded t-shirt, a belt buckle, and an old pistol rounded out the collection. I eyed the gun but kept it where it sat in the box. "Damn it. No leads."

Marcus took the box, careful to return the possessions in it, and I heard something slip along the bottom. "What was that?" I asked.

He dug his hand in, moving the gun, and pulled out a key. "This is it. It has to be. There was a number stamped on it, and a ring."

I retrieved the key from him and shoved the box at Marcus, rushing for the hallway. Marta was pouring us the fruity beverages when we entered the kitchen, and I slammed the key down on the countertop, startling her. "What does this open?"

She shrugged noncommittally. "He always carried it. When I asked him, he said it was a key to the stars."

My heart raced, and Marcus grabbed the key. "To the stars."

"Nothing else?" I pressed, but she only shook her head, sliding a cup to me. I took it with a thank you as Marcus inspected the ring.

"I think I recognize this name. What does it mean?" he asked me. There was Spanish writing on it, and the logo for a restaurant located at the Caracas airport.

"The airport," I whispered. "This must open a locker."

"What if we're wrong?" Marcus was nervous, and so was I.

"If Marta is certain there's no lock here, it's our only lead. We'll have to try it. Marta, what are the chances we can buy your van?" I wanted to get moving, but it was very late, and I didn't love the idea of cruising around these foreign back roads in the dark.

She appeared distraught by the idea and muttered a few quiet words in her native tongue. "I cannot sell it."

"Are you sure? We'll pay far more than…" Marcus was cut off by her hard stare.

"It was his. My father's, and I won't give it up." She was determined, so I didn't want to argue. Her expression softened, despite our intrusion on her day. "But I will take you to the airport."

"To Caracas? That's a long drive." I appreciated it but didn't expect it from her.

"Not a problem. I've been wanting to see the city for some time. This is a good excuse." She smiled, and it was settled. "But we leave in the morning. I won't drive at night."

I downed my cold beverage in seconds, providing slight relief from the lingering heat of the day. As badly as I wanted to leave, a night of rest would do us a favor. We settled in, and soon I was in bed, dozing off and dreaming of coordinates and a key to the stars.

12

Compared to the trip south, sitting in Marta's van's passenger seat while Marcus slept in the back was a pleasure. The slightest breeze rustled from the old AC unit, and I stared at the landscape through a heavily cracked windshield. She told me about her people and described the terrain as she drove. She had a passion for her country, and I enjoyed the company. The object in my bag was never far from my mind, and the key in my pocket was heavy on my spirit.

We arrived at the airport, and Marcus had already secured our seats on a flight in five hours, giving us what we hoped was enough time to locate the proper locker. With our bags in our hands, we took turns hugging Marta, and Marcus slipped her another envelope of cash.

"I cannot take this," she said, shaking her head.

I grasped her hands, closing her fingers around the money. "Look, either you take it or I return it to a man who doesn't need it. Trust me."

This sold her, and she averted her gaze, staring at her shoes. "I hope you find what you're after." Her words were kind, and I smiled at her as I backed away. Someone honked behind her, wanting her parking spot, and she turned, calling out to the driver before hopping into her van. And she was off.

"Nice lady. Not everyone would have helped us,"

Marcus said.

"I can see why Clayton trusted her dad. They're good people." I eyed the key, and we entered the international airport.

An hour later, we realized there were no lockers here. "Damn." I'd asked every employee I'd found about them, and they'd all given the same response: *There are none.* One woman thought they used to exist but hadn't seen them in some time.

We'd avoided passing through security so far, and the airport was growing extremely busy, with long, slow-moving lines at every corner. "What if they had them and they're gone now?" Marcus asked as we sat on a bench, the endless cycle of stressed-out fliers walking by, the noise of luggage rollers a main part of the soundtrack.

A man mopped the floor, whistling as he wrung the bucket lever. "I have an idea."

Marcus followed me as I approached the older man. He wore headphones, his hips swaying as he cleaned the tiles. I tapped him on the shoulder, and he seemed surprised someone had noticed him.

"Yes. Can I help you?" he asked in his native tongue.

I told him that we were looking for a locker, and that they must have stored them somewhere on the grounds.

I translated his words as he spoke them. "Yes. We remodeled a few years ago. I think they're stowed away."

"How can I get to them?" I asked, and he glanced around, as if searching for signs of a superior in the area.

"You don't." He started to mop again, placing an earpiece back in.

I set a hand on the mop handle. "We can pay you. Do you know where they are?"

"I don't want to lose my job," he said in Spanish. "It's not allowed."

"Are they on the premises?"

He shrugged, playing it casual. "I might know where they are."

"Maybe your mop bucket has a faulty spring. What if you were looking for a spare…"

He smacked his lips and glanced at Marcus suspiciously. "How much?"

Marcus grabbed my arm and leaned in. "Rex. We give this guy a few bucks, he'll go to the break room and call security on us."

"What choice do we have?"

The man was getting tired of this charade, and he started to drift away from us. I named the price, casually saying it, and he stopped in his tracks, turning with a grin on his face. "Show me the money."

I had some on me, in case a situation arose like this. Money speaks, and this man was listening. I passed it over discreetly, and to his credit, he didn't even look at it, just folded it into his shirt pocket. I reasoned counting money in public would be a mistake you only made once.

"What locker number?"

I hated giving him my only copy but didn't have a choice. "3B19."

The number was stamped on the key, and he slid it into his pants. "Espera aquí." *Wait here.*

We watched him take off, rolling his bucket of murky water, and I felt like we'd never see him again. Marcus bought us coffees, and I picked at a muffin while we waited. My duffel bag between my feet, and I kept glancing at it, wondering if customs would give me any issues with the cube we'd acquired. I'd been through enough security stations around the world to know that the level of scrutiny varied. This didn't look valuable, and I doubted it would end up being a dilemma.

An hour later, Marcus started to grow restless. "Check out the line. It's getting out of hand, and this guy hasn't come back. I bet he's laughing about the gullible tourists and drinking a beer with his pals."

He was probably right, but I didn't want to give up quite yet. The second I started to consider joining the security queue, I saw the janitor strolling across the tiled floor, pushing a cart with cleaning supplies on it. He whistled, his eyebrows lifting as he spotted us.

"Did you find it?" I asked him in Spanish.

"Si."

"Well?"

He returned the key first, and I shoved it away shakily. What had he found? The janitor pulled out his phone, flipping it toward us. The first image showed a locker, stacked in the corner of a dark room, and I noticed the embedded number on the open door. 3B19.

He flipped to another but pulled the phone away. "I think you'll pay more for this."

Marcus didn't speak Spanish, but he seemed to pick up the man's tone. "Tell this guy to show us already. We're running low on time. And patience."

"Show us and I'll pay, if it's what we're after."

He shrugged, offering the picture. The locker was empty.

"Damn it." My shoulders slumped, and Marcus snatched the man's phone before he could react.

"Wait." He zoomed in, and I leaned closer. There were numbers scratched into the door. Coordinates.

The janitor reached for his phone, but Marcus side-stepped. A minute later, he tossed it to the man and pulled a few bucks from his pocket, handing it over. "I've taken a copy and removed it from your cloud. Go to the locker and scratch those details from the door. Lock the door and chuck the key." I translated for Marcus, and the guy stared at the money and nodded, licking his lips. He took off as Marcus reached for his own phone, clicking the new message. "I wiped my deets from his phone too. We were never here." He glanced at the ceiling. "You know, unless someone has access to their surveillance."

"These are coordinates," I whispered, staring at the phone.

He clicked it off and started for the line-up. "They are. And there are six of them."

My heart pounded as we maneuvered through the airport. I couldn't wait to return home and see what we learned from a blurry photo taken in a dark storage room.

I glanced at the clock, realizing only ten minutes had passed since I'd checked. I'd made it home in time for Tuesday's final exams, so I'd decided to offer my services to Jessica. She'd been angry with me, and the last thing I needed was an irate boss.

Plus, Marcus was struggling at my place to locate the sixth destination. The first five had been simple, the numbers clearly identified by Marta's father's crisp knifework on the inside of the locker. The lowest one had been the sloppiest, whether he was rushed, or whether he couldn't find the proper angle from a standing position. Either way, we didn't have the coordinates for the sixth Token, and without it, what use was looking for the other five?

I thought about the boxy metal holder and imagined my father grasping it as he placed the artifacts into the slots along its sides.

A paper dropped to the desk I sat behind, and I looked

up to see an unfamiliar student walking away, heading for the gymnasium's exit. There were five different exams going on simultaneously, with the students spaced apart to mitigate any risk of cheating.

I had two hours before the buzzer would ring, ending the students' time with their final test for the semester. Many of the young adults were struggling, nervously tapping their feet, chewing the end of their pencils, playing with their bangs. I remembered what it was like feeling the strain of college at a time like this, mixed with the anxiety of going home for the holidays, with the ever-present vacant seat at the end of the table where Dad used to sit. Meals were always quiet, with Christmas music playing in the background and Mom drinking white wine.

Another student walked up, and she smiled at me as she set her test on the desk. Economics. I'd always hated courses like that. They were too mundane for me. I wanted adventure, mysteries explained, history to show us where we came from. Researching GDP and graphs with theoretical dollar values and calculations had never been my forte.

It was snowing outside again, and I stared at the dark midday through the window, feeling like I hadn't seen the sun since we'd returned from Venezuela. Snow blanketed the courtyard outside the gym.

My phone buzzed in my pocket, and I pulled it out.

Beverly: *Rex, are you coming for Christmas or not?*

I bristled. It was a couple weeks away yet, and she was pressing for an answer. There were other messages, and I scrolled through them.

Hunter Madison: *You owe me an explanation. What did you find?*

I'd ignored every communication from Hunter so far. I knew he'd be pissed, but I had to figure out just what precise details I wanted to share.

Richard: *You okay? I don't like that you left so abruptly the other night. Call me.*

Doctor Richard Klein had already left three voicemails since my disappearance from his dinner party, and I wasn't in the mood to tell him why I'd vanished, or that I was tired of his endless attempts to convert me to Harvard.

I rubbed my temples, the pressure building up. It was like the nervous energy of the two hundred students was encapsulating me, threatening to burst. I took a deep inhale, hearing the scratching of pencils across stapled pages, and replied to my sister.

Rex: *I hate to do this to you, but I can't commit. The school has decided to send me on an expedition, and I don't know how long it'll last.*

I stared at it for a few moments before hitting send. I didn't enjoy lying to her, but if she had any inclination of my plans, she'd drive to my house and handcuff me to the radiator.

I waited for a response, but none came. I could picture her cheeks growing red in anger, her lips pursing as she hastily typed a furious reply. Then her better judgment would take hold, and she'd delete it, returning the phone to her purse.

Before I put the cell away, I sent one note to Marcus. I'd left him alone for hours, but curiosity and dread forced me to contact him.

Rex: *Any luck?*

Marcus: …

I watched the screen, impatiently wanting a positive response. The dots vanished, and I slumped in the seat as a thickset bearded man set his completed exam on the desk.

The two hours passed with the slowness one could only experience in a doctor's waiting room or at a traditional Italian orthodox wedding. The seconds dripped away, one tick at a time, until the buzzer finally sounded. Only a dozen students remained scattered among the empty desks, and I smirked as one set his head on the exam paper, his pencil rolling onto the floor.

"Time's up. Please bring your exams to the front. I hope you have a well-deserved break." I stood, feeling the stiffness in my back, and saw Jessica waiting at the gym's exit.

The students shuffled out, and Jessica entered, her heels clicking on the wooden planks. "Thank you for stepping in today. I don't know what I would have done without you."

"It was no problem at all," I assured her.

"That's it. The last of the exams. School is officially out of session."

"What are you doing for the holidays?" I asked her, gathering the tests. There were five piles, and I spun them around, making sure not to mix them up.

"Nothing much. My parents have decided to go for a cruise again this year, and after much insisting, I had to decline."

"Why's that?" I asked.

"I've never been one for confined spaces with hundreds of other people. Plus, I don't have the best sea legs." She grinned as she said it, and if her intention had been for me to peek at her long, stocking-covered legs, it worked.

I really didn't need a distraction at the moment. I was about to walk past her when she set a hand on my chest. "You owe me a dinner. Remember?"

I checked the clock, seeing it was four. "Rain check?"

"If I didn't know better, I'd say you were blowing me off. It's okay, I don't expect you to drop everything and make the time." She lowered her hand, stepping back a few feet. "I may have come on a little strong, and dating isn't permitted. Especially in my position, but there's something about you that intrigues me."

I hadn't seen anyone following me since we'd returned, and suddenly, I had the urge to check her wrist for a tattoo. I was being rash. Jessica had an exemplary record and was the youngest president in the college's history, not to mention a woman, which was also a first for this establishment. I doubted she was overly interested in beings from another planet.

My phone buzzed, and she glanced at my pocket. "Go ahead."

I gave an apologetic smile and grabbed it, tapping on a reply from Marcus.

Marcus: *Still trying. Gonna be an all-nighter.*

I frowned and sent a quick message. *I'll be a while. Dinner with Jessica.*

Marcus: *You dirty old dog… I hope you…*

I exited the program, not finishing his response. "Dinner would be great."

She started away, and despite my anxiety to go home and begin planning our next move, I had to admit, she was going to be a nice distraction.

———————

*J*essica had picked a quiet spot, not what I expected from someone of her stature. I guessed Jessica came from money, with a large colonial to match, so her choice of a quaint Lebanese place didn't quite fit with my image of her.

We were still in our formal work attire, her in a smart black pencil skirt and white blouse. I had a navy blazer with a salmon shirt underneath, and jeans. Since it was just exam babysitting, I'd opted out of the tie today, and I was glad as I glanced around the half-empty restaurant.

"Are you good with this?" she asked as the waitress led us to our table. The middle-aged woman had a smile only an owner could muster at work as she passed our menus out.

"It's perfect. I've been meaning to try it after work one day, but haven't yet."

The waitress asked if we wanted any drinks.

"Turkish coffee for me," Jessica said, and I was relieved she hadn't suggested wine.

I didn't know if this was a real date or something Jessica liked to do with the newer staff members, even after her earlier comment. "I'll have the same."

The woman wandered off, stopping at the table two down to remove empty plates.

Jessica looked relaxed, more so than I'd ever seen her. "Do you live near the college?" I asked.

"No. I drive in, but I like the commute. As much as I feel married to my work, I prefer to be able to turn it off when I need to. Being too close to the office reminds me of how much I could be doing. My first year, I decided to rent an apartment within walking distance, and I couldn't pull myself out of there most nights. After a run-in with burnout, I thought it best to give up the second home and make the drive." Jessica lowered her hand from the table as the coffees came, and I was greeted with the rich aroma of the unfiltered grounds. It was a good thing Marcus had said we'd be up for hours, because I'd be bouncing off the walls by the time I got to the townhouse.

"What about you?" she asked. "Where are you at?"

"Had the same townhouse for years. Can't seem to part with it."

"Does it ever get lonely?" she asked, her focus shifting to her cup as she sipped from it.

133

"Living alone?" It was a little bit of a probing question, but I didn't mind. "Sure. Who doesn't? And you?"

"I was married for a time," Jessica admitted.

"Has it been a while?"

"Donovan and I were too young. Fresh out of college, and full of dreams and aspirations. He was in law school, and... things fell apart." Jessica ran a finger over the menu, and I browsed as well. When the waitress arrived, I nodded at Jessica.

"I'm going to let the lady choose the meal tonight."

Jessica was used to taking charge, so I didn't think she'd mind. She ordered what seemed like far too much food, but I kept that to myself.

"And you?" she asked. "Why is Rexford Walker single?"

"Me? Not much to tell. I've had some relationships—some close calls, if you will—but nothing quite so drastic as love."

"I heard rumors about you before I hired you, Rex," she told me with a smirk.

"Is that so?" I took a drink, the caffeine seeming to hit me straight away.

"That you were bullheaded and opinionated. Challenging to work with, and not much for following the rules." She said it quietly, and I watched her, trying to understand where she was going with this. "But what I see is a smart man with passion for his craft. It's been so long since we had a real archaeologist on staff, with dirt under his nails and sweat on his brow. This school is my passion, Rex, so I can understand why you're always looking to the next thing."

"Why do I sense a 'but' coming?"

She didn't smile, just leaned in slightly. "You *are* perceptive. Are the rumors true?"

"The ones about Professor Hughes and that student?" I joked, trying to change the topic.

"See, there it is. The disregard for authority I mentioned."

This was taking a hard turn in the wrong direction. "I thought we were two contemporaries having a nice dinner together." I went to stand up, but her grip wrapped around my wrist, urging me into my seat.

"We are, Rex. Stay put. I didn't mean anything by it." She said it so casually that I let it go.

Jessica's smile returned, and she ripped a piece of the pita. "You have to try this hummus."

"I will when you tell me what you were talking about," I said.

"Whatever happened with Fiji?"

"It fell through," I replied.

"That's funny, because I had my secretary do some investigating, and there don't seem to be any active petitions in their system." Jessica dipped more of the pita into the creamy hummus.

I relaxed a little. It didn't sound like she knew anything about my real purpose, just that I'd been lying about Fiji in the first place.

"I'm sorry about that. I made it up. I've been dealing with a family issue, and didn't want to air my dirty laundry. I was there for the exams regardless," I reminded her, and she nodded. "You don't have to worry about me, Jessica. I won't let it happen again."

"Anything I should be worried about?"

"Huh?

"The family issue," she said.

"No. It's settled."

"Good. That's a relief. Despite how this appears, I *have* been wanting to spend some time with you outside the office. Can we start over?" She looked so innocent, her voice like honey, and I nodded against my better judgment.

I tried the hummus, and it was as wonderful as advertised. I attempted to put the stress of what was forming in my mind for a while but couldn't shake the feeling that this was my last supper.

———————————

I set the keys on the side table near my door, and Marcus glanced up from the glow of his laptop. He was at the island, in his usual spot, and he closed the computer. He looked as tired as I felt.

"Anything?" I asked. I knew he'd been out of luck; otherwise, he would have texted me earlier.

"Nope. Let's face it. It's impossible to decipher that sixth coordinate. We have five, though. I mean, we're far closer to the truth than before," he told me. I peered at his shirt, seeing an old comic book dog sleeping on his house.

I took off my jacket, draping it across the couch, and sat beside him. "What's next? Hunter's getting impatient. If we're going to do this, we need his funding."

Marcus gave me a sly grin. "More importantly, how was your date?"

I laughed. Marcus always found a way to ease the tension in a room. "It was… good. She's quite the woman, but I don't have time for that."

"I've seen Jessica. She's…" Marcus stopped himself when he saw my expression.

"Let's focus. Anything strange go on today?" I asked, not wanting to recall the bizarre date I'd just experienced.

"Like, did any black-suited G-man types knock on the door, flashing fake badges? No. But the pizza guy did forget to charge me for the breadsticks." Marcus glanced to the half-empty pizza box on the table.

"Good."

Someone banged loudly on the door, a muffled voice calling through the dense wood. "It's after ten. Who the hell…?"

I walked over slowly, wondering if I should take my gun. I pressed my eye to the door viewer and saw Hunter Madison's distorted face.

I unlocked the deadbolt and stepped aside, letting him in. His expensive jacket was blanketed in snowflakes, and more sat on his gray hair. He was animated as he dashed inside, shaking flakes from his sleeves. "Rex, you've been holding out on me. Let me see it."

I froze. "See what?"

"I know you have it. Don't be silly." The billionaire was alone, and I peered out the door to see his driver parked in the luxury sedan, the engine still running. I closed the door as Hunter strode through my townhouse, his gaze lingering curiously on my few possessions. "How quaint."

I suspected he didn't spend much time in regular people's houses, and I dismissed the insult quickly. "What do you want?"

He shifted to Marcus' side, looking at the computer. "You found the Case."

"Case? You'll have to be more…" I started to say, but he moved with a speed defying his age and health.

"Listen here, Rexford Walker. I paid for your little adventure, and you're going to tell me what you found now, or you'll regret it." Hunter was serious, his gaze murky and cold, his hands clutching my shirt.

"How did you know?" I asked calmly.

"You had to have the bags scanned at security, didn't you?" He pulled his cell phone out and flipped it to face me. My duffel bag showed on the screen, the scan showing the shape of the cube inside it.

He let go, and I nodded, impressed that he'd been able to access the Caracas airport scans like that. "Fine. If it's any consolation, I was about to call you."

"Is that so?" he asked.

"Sure," I lied. I would have had to tell him something if I wanted to continue the search, but how much information I shared was up in the air. "Be right back."

I left him with Marcus while I went to my hiding spot under the office floor. I returned shortly after, and Marcus had three glasses of whiskey poured. Hunter held his, sniffing it as I brought the object in the original burlap sack. He stared at the bag as he downed the drink and set the glass on the island.

"This is it?"

I opened the drawstring, pulling the cube out. He stumbled toward me, his hands clasping it firmly. "This is the Case. Hardy explained his theory well."

"He knew this existed?" I asked. So far, I'd had little to go on. Marcus hadn't been able to translate the book yet, and I feared we never would.

"There are six Tokens and one Case. Once combined in the proper order, the Bridge will appear."

"In the right location," I finished.

"That's right. Portugal. *Estrelas.*"

"Stars. You know the spot now?" I asked.

"I always have, and I've been there, as I've said. Many times. But it's barren. Nothing to indicate your father or Clayton ever visited. It's an empty cavern, with a hole in the ceiling and a pedestal directly under it."

My hands flexed with extra energy as he spoke of it. "That has to be the Bridge access point."

Marcus' expression was grim. "This is real?"

"You didn't believe before, son?" Hunter asked.

"I dunno. I mean, Rex is a little pragmatic about this stuff, but now, with hired guns chasing us and unidentified objects arriving in our solar system... I kind of wish it weren't true. How can we go back after knowing all of this?" His question was simple, and it sounded hypothetical, but that didn't prevent Hunter from answering.

He sat at the island, clutching the Case. "You don't, son. Once you've seen Pandora's Box, you come to be obsessed. Everything becomes futile, because if there *is* so much more to this existence than the monotony of life, we're driven to obtain it. Can you imagine what it was like to live five thousand years ago? With no means to travel, no knowledge of anything outside your own plains, or valley, or island, or whatever you lived nearby?

"Picture that, and suddenly, you see a boat crash on the shore, or a plane land among the fields. Then it leaves before you've had a chance to investigate. Would you be able to return to tending the crops, to hunting for food, to building your hut?"

"I'd probably need to eat, so yeah," Marcus joked, but Hunter wasn't fazed by the comment.

"I've known about the Bridge for years, and suspected that aliens existed since before the Believers showed me proof," he told us. Hunter's eyes were watery, his knuckles white as he held the Case.

Something he said stuck in my brain. "Proof? What's your evidence of alien life?"

He seemed to notice his blunder, but he dismissed it. "Never mind. This is important, Rex. Humanity has been waiting for this moment for ages. Since every culture has looked to the sky for answers, now we must do the same and find them."

I expected him to say more, but he went silent.

"We need more money," I said quietly.

Hunter's rheumy glazed-over stare met my gaze, and he smirked. "Where are they? You found the Tokens, didn't you? You Walkers are brilliant; I've always said it."

"I haven't found them, but I think I know where they're hidden," I admitted.

The change in his expression caused me to step away, trying not to make the motion obvious. "Where?"

I glanced at Marcus, and he protectively placed a hand on his laptop. Hunter noticed.

"I'm not ready to tell you that. It's… I want to be the one to gather them. If I offer my only bargaining chip to you, I could be left in the dust."

Hunter made a tsking sound with his lips and relinquished the Case over to me. "You have two options, Rex. You can give me this Case, along with the coordinates for the Tokens. Right now. I'll pay you one million dollars, and your friend here half of that. It'll become common knowledge that you botched your task, and that I'm disappointed in your failure. The Believers will give up, and you'll return to life as you know it."

Marcus had a hard time retaining his poise, and I had to admit, the idea of stopping and taking the cash was enticing. "These sightings. The ones near Pluto. What are they?"

"The Believers will say it's their saviors, returning to Earth."

"But not to give us the answers to life?" Marcus asked.

"Quite the opposite. I suspect, as they do, that destruction is more likely," Hunter said.

I considered this and downed my whiskey with a quick tilt of my hand. "What's my other option?"

Hunter flashed another look, one that betrayed his emotions. He knew I was going to continue, and his answer came in a hurry. "We make a very small team and spend the next two weeks gathering each of the six Tokens. You can hold on to the coordinates if you please, but I will be a part of this. You run the team, but I run the show. Understood?"

I saw the dying man, his desperation seeping through his composed speech.

"Marcus, you have a stake in this." I didn't keep a lot of friends, not ones I could trust with my life. "What do you want to do?"

He waited a minute, clearly deep in thought as he contemplated the money versus the adventure. If aliens were coming to destroy us, as Hunter suggested, he might not have a lot of time to enjoy the cash, and I could see him evaluating these very facts as I waited for his answer.

"What the hell. If there's a Bridge, we're going to find it," he said, standing up.

The three of us were close together, and Hunter stuck his arm out, palm facing the floor. "What do you say, boys? All for one?"

I hesitated but added my hand after Marcus did. "I'm in."

PART II
THE TEAM

1

December 12th, 2025

I thumbed through the journal for the tenth time that morning, unable to determine where the Bridge cavern was located. Hunter wouldn't tell us, and with the Believers searching for it too, I didn't blame him. He'd been there, and so had my father, but Dad had abandoned Hunter, leaving him behind and out of the loop. It was probably a good thing for the wealthy entrepreneur; otherwise, he'd be dead like my dad and Clayton.

"Dead." I said the word out loud as I set the book on the desk, and wondered if he wasn't really gone. Maybe he existed somewhere. A bridge, by definition, was a structure that carried across an obstacle. They connected two places. By this logic, Dirk Walker could have taken this Bridge and arrived elsewhere.

But why had he never returned?

I glanced out of my office, seeing my luggage beside the kitchen table. The car would be here shortly, but I didn't feel ready. While everyone in town was settling into the holiday season, thinking about their final days of work before their families came to visit and Santa rolled into their chimneys, I was prepared to embark on the journey of a lifetime.

I flipped my computer open and scrolled to the saved bookmark. The syndicated radio show played on the app after I clicked on the latest episode.

"*Welcome to* Across This Great Nation *with Bill McReary. As most of you are aware, I've been keeping a close eye on the mysterious shapes continuing toward Earth. One first appeared near Pluto almost a month ago, and shortly after, we discovered there were two of them. Identical in size and shape as far as we can tell, and I've been told they have increased velocity. Scientists are baffled, and we've had various professionals on the show to speculate, but no one seems to have the answers we're seeking.*

"*Today, we're speaking with Isabella, and she claims to have been part of an organization that centered their beliefs on this moment in our history.*"

I stopped fidgeting with the computer and leaned back, listening closely. This sounded revealing, and even though I'd been ignoring the whole "mysterious objects in space" for the most part, I felt confident there was a connection to the mission I was participating in.

"*Thank you for having me, Bill.*"

"*Isabella, tell me about this group you were referring to.*"

"*They've been around for decades. I was brought in young, because of my boyfriend. He was older, successful, but caustic. I found out what he was actually doing when I suspected him of cheating on me; he only laughed and invited me to join their meeting.*"

"*And where were you, Isabella?*" Bill asked.

"*I lived in Chicago at the time. If I told you his name, you wouldn't believe me,*" she said.

"*I've heard a lot of implausible things in my life, and more often than not, it's the really unfathomable ones that have come true. You can keep him anonymous if you like.*"

"*The Believers don't let just anyone leave their fold. Once you're in, you're in. It's… I've feared for my life for the last eight years, Bill. Every day.*" Isabella's voice wavered as she spoke.

"*I've heard of this group, the Believers. You were involved with them?*"

"*Yes. As I said, it wasn't by choice. Once they had their claws in me, I couldn't escape. I saw… too much. But their main focus was preparing for the return of their redeemers.*"

"*And by this, we're not talking about Jesus or Judgment Day?*" Bill asked.

"*We will be judged, according to the Believers, but not by God. By them.*"

"*Them?*"

"*Alien beings. I didn't trust them at the time, Bill, but… have you seen these things? Their trajectory is leading them to one place. Earth.*"

There was a slight pause: dead air as the host contemplated what he'd heard. If what she said was true, how had Hunter Madison gotten out of this cult?

"*Isabella, was this a cult? What kinds of things were done behind closed doors?*"

I waited, leaning closer to the laptop's speaker.

"*Sacrifices, prayer, and attuning.*"

Somehow Bill managed to avoid asking about the sacrifice comment, and he went for the easier question. "*What is attuning?*"

"*The Believers await the return of these aliens. They speak their language, or think they do. Attuning is an ancient meditation, meant to link them to their masters when they arrive.*"

I had never heard of such a thing and decided to interrogate Hunter further when we were next together.

"*Did you practice this? Do you speak their language?*" Bill's voice was low, his excitement palpable through the speakers.

"*I tried to. I didn't attune. I wasn't high enough. I catered to the leaders."*

"So there's a ranking system?"

"In a manner of speaking."

"Can you offer anything in the alien tongue?" Bill asked calmly.

Isabella's voice changed, her words thick and heavy. *"Dreen allono reespenlen."*

"And what does that mean?"

A pause. *"Prepare for arrival."*

My skin itched at her words. It reminded me of the scrawling in Hardy's book, and I decided to ask Hunter about the language. He'd failed to mention that to us.

"You heard it here first, folks. The language of the incoming savior aliens. Take a break, grab a stiff drink, we'll be right back with more from the former cult member Isabella."

It cut to an ad, and my buzzer sounded.

I closed the laptop, wondering how much of what the guest had said was true. Were there really aliens coming to Earth, or was it as most of the scientific world thought? Asteroids from deep space. They predicted the twin objects would avoid Earth and head past, using the Sun's gravitational orbit to loop around, shooting them far away forever.

Marcus waited outside in a thick winter jacket, gloves on his hands. Snow fell, and I shivered, recalling one of our destinations. "You ready?"

"All set." It had been two days since Hunter had visited, and they'd gone very slowly. With my exams marked and sent to the college, I was done until the end of the year, when I'd have to go in for a few meetings. That didn't leave us a lot of time, especially during the holiday season. We still had to build our team, and that wasn't going to be as simple as Hunter thought it would be.

Marcus collected one of my bags and I took the other,

glancing at my place before closing the door and locking it. With any luck, I'd be home before I knew it. Over the last couple of days, I'd realized how impossible all of this sounded. A Bridge to another world.

But even if there was no such thing as aliens, I was going to end up where my father was last known to have visited, and I wanted closure on that part of my life so I could focus on my career and maybe settle down eventually. My mind was always wandering, trying to take me to the next thing, the next clue, the trail left by Dirk Walker over thirty years ago. It wasn't healthy.

I considered what Isabella had said, about some man bringing her into the fold without a choice, and I stopped near Madison's town car. "Marcus, you know you don't have to do this, right?"

The driver came around, taking my luggage. He stowed it in the trunk while Marcus stared at me with a confused expression. "What are you saying, Rex?"

"This… it could be dangerous. I don't necessarily believe everything, but there *is* an alien cult after us. We've seen the cars, the tails, the guns in El Mirador. Even if it's all in their heads, they will harm us. The trek, the stops around the world… this is not safe and predictable."

"Rex, are you forgetting I've followed you to five continents already, searching for these Tokens? I want to do this. I *need* to." Marcus' voice was low, and I set a hand on his shoulder.

"I just don't want things to get out of hand. I feel like I'm dragging you into the crosshairs, and I don't like it. You should go home to Florida for the holidays. See your family."

"And leave you with no one guarding your back? I don't think so," Marcus told me firmly. "Besides, how are you going to get anything done without me around? You'd be lost." He opened the car door and slid into the idling vehicle.

Snow melted on the warm hood as it fell, and I glanced around the street, finding it quiet in the early morning. Everything was covered in a fresh layer of flakes, and the streetlights were on despite the hour. The thick clouds were low, making the day darker than usual.

I entered the vehicle and shuffled in beside Marcus. Once the door closed, we started to drive, marking the official start of our adventure.

---

*T*he helicopter landed at Hunter Madison's East Hampton mansion, and the pilot confirmed we could disembark. Francois arrived, his slicked hair unaffected by the gust the rotor sent across the yard.

"This way, sirs," he said, and grabbed our two heaviest bags without issue. Marcus just shrugged, taking his carry-on, and the helicopter lifted, the noise finally growing quieter by the time we'd crossed the grounds to the house's rear patio.

Hunter stood inside, eyeing the sky as if he anticipated a tornado to appear. His expression was cautious, even fearful.

I followed after Francois, passing over the extremely detailed cobblestone courtyard. The entire area was strung with Christmas lights, surprising me. "Hunter, I expected more of an Ebenezer vibe from you," I told him, and the billionaire's gaze lowered, as if he'd only then realized we'd entered his home.

He looked older, his cheeks a little sallower, his hair whiter, if that was possible. "Welcome back, Rex. Hello,

Marcus." He held out his hand, and we took turns shaking it.

I reached for my bag and pulled out my laptop. "I have some ideas on the team."

"Straight to business?" Hunter asked. "Marcus, tell me, is he always this anxious to work?"

"Sure is. The guy's wound tighter than a…"

I lifted a finger. "If you want to wait until after the holidays, we can reschedule everything." The anger in Hunter's eyes at the mention of delay told me he was even more ready than I was to begin our endeavor.

"There is something I'd like to speak with you two about. Care to join me in the study?" Hunter started away, and I removed my wet shoes. It was damp outside, rain spitting on and off, but no snow yet: a common East Coast December day.

We walked through the mansion, and I slowed to check what the wonderful smell was in the kitchen. A man stood near the island, chatting with the chef.

"Any chance I can have a snack?" My stomach growled at the scent of his cooking. I'd been too worked up earlier, too worried about this mission to eat this morning, but being at Hunter's relaxed my anxious nerves.

"Sure thing, Mr. Walker." The chef was a formidable man with a white apron and a friendly smile. "We have tomato bisque and a scattering of hors d'oeuvres. Help yourself. Mr. Madison requested lunch in a half hour."

"Excuse me," I said, striding past the man who stood between me and the cooling food. He hesitantly shifted on his feet and stepped aside.

"Mr. Walker, is it?" The man had a tough visage and was out of place among the opulence of Hunter's home.

"That's what it says on my driver's licence. How about yours?"

"Tripp. Tripp Davis." He didn't offer his hand, and neither did I. I knew who he was, although we'd never formally been introduced. It was difficult to do so when you were being hijacked in the middle of the jungle.

"No way." I left the finger foods behind, stalking for Hunter's study with expedience. "Hunter, this wasn't part of the deal!"

Hunter was seated, talking with Marcus when I barged in, and he lifted his hands defensively. "I see you've met Tripp. Calm yourself, Rex. We can discuss this like adults, can we not?"

"Wait, *the* Tripp? That jerk that took your loot and left you high and dry in the rain forest?" Marcus rose, coming to join me in my posturing.

"I'll have you know that what we did was within our rights according to local…" The man was behind me, and I clenched my jaw, using all my reserved strength to stop myself from decking him.

"You screwed me over and took the prizes I'd committed months of research and weeks of scouring to locate." I pictured the carved figure, with red jewels embedded as eyes in the black onyx statue. "Not to mention the investment I failed to return to the museum funding my expedition."

"Tripp always gets the job done, Rex. That's why I'm insisting he join the crew." Hunter stayed seated, and Tripp gave me a satisfied smirk as he watched me, arms crossed over his chest.

"It's off. I won't work with this man," I said, and started for the exit. Francois arrived, and he blocked the doorway. I could feel the tension rise in the study, and I glanced at Marcus. He moved closer to me. This was a real make-or-break moment. A man like Hunter, who claimed to have been part of an alien cult at some point, hadn't gotten this rich and stayed wealthy by being a nice person. I had no doubt he'd done many unscrupulous things.

Everything inside the study looked the same, but it was the opposite of the inviting space it had been the first time we'd visited. It was hostile. Angry. Hunter Madison finally stood, his hands clutching his chair arm to assist the motion.

"I'm dying, Rex. I've spent far too long on this to give up or lose it now. Tripp is devious, yes, but he's working for me. You're in charge of this expedition, so by every account, he answers to you. Is that understood, Tripp?" Hunter asked.

The man picked at his nails, avoiding eye contact with me as I stared daggers at him. "Fine by me." He smiled. "As long as I get paid, we're aces."

Francois stepped aside and disappeared into the corridor. I had to keep an eye on that one. He was dangerous despite his stuffiness and reluctance to be seen.

I stood my ground, the adrenaline in my body giving me a boost of energy. "I'm hiring the guide. We need a pilot who we can trust. I know just the guy." The sooner we started, the faster my time with Tripp would come to an end.

Hunter nodded. "See, we can work together on this. Let's eat and discuss how to proceed in a timely fashion. You can contact your guide, and we'll make the offer. Sound good?"

Castro was going to be thrilled to join our crew. The last time I'd talked with him, his tour business in the outback had been suffering.

"Fine." I reluctantly let Marcus past me, and he jogged ahead of Tripp, both of them advancing toward the dining room.

Hunter's grip held me back, and he stumbled, almost

falling over. "Are you okay?" I asked him.

He grunted and righted himself on my shoulder. "I'm terribly sorry. The medication… It throws me for a loop on occasion. Do you mind staying close in case it happens again?"

He still hadn't told me what he was dying from, but now wasn't the time to ask. "Tripp Davis. You sure this is the right call?"

"Tripp is tougher than nails. He's been deployed to the world's darkest corners and returned without a scratch."

I doubted that. The man had been a Navy SEAL, but doing whatever clandestine missions he'd accomplished under the orders of the US government would have left marks. Maybe not on his skin, but in more unpredictable recesses of the mind—not that I felt sorry for him. "If he so much as screws us in the slightest, he's done. Understood?"

"We won't have to worry about that. He's being… compensated well."

I halted before we entered the dining room, and turned to face Hunter. "If this Bridge is real—and I still have reservations, of course—there's no amount of money to keep our secret. Tripp will use the knowledge to his benefit. I believe that."

"Dirk…" Hunter's eyes narrowed. "Sorry. You're acting just like he used to. Your resemblance is uncanny. Your voice… Rex, the Bridge isn't a lie. Your father found the Tokens, and he used them in the Case. I know this without a shadow of a doubt. He departed. And I have to find the Bridge."

"What do you expect on the other side?" I asked him.

"Contact."

2

The tires kicked up plumes of sand behind us as we drove from the local airport toward Castro's home. It had been over five years since I'd visited, and I'd almost forgotten how remote he was. I admired the man for taking the plunge. He spent his days guiding tourists on exotic and adventurous treks through the main sights of Australia's outback.

The air conditioning raged from the clunky 4X4's vents, and Marcus played with the air, trying to make it colder. "It's ninety degrees in December. This is wrong on so many levels."

"If it helps any, it's cooler in July." I wiped sweat from my forehead and steered the rented car on the rough roadway. There was little in the way of traffic, and I raced down the street, hoping to catch Castro at his house.

"How do we know he's even there?" It had been an ongoing complaint from Marcus after I couldn't reach Castro on his phone.

"His reception is terrible. We're going to find him drinking a beer on his deck." The drive was over an hour but went by quickly as Marcus and I discussed our next steps.

"From here to Madagascar. Will Hunter join us there?" Marcus asked. A huge white two-ton truck barreled down the road, and I had to slow, craning the wheel to the left to avoid being creamed. "I'll never get used to driving on the wrong side of the road."

I watched the truck continue on, speeding even faster as it swerved in the middle. "It's a little arrogant to assume driving on the right is the correct way, isn't it?" I smiled at Marcus, but he didn't return it.

"Sure, Rex, whatever you say." He grabbed his phone, tapping the screen. "Should be a fork soon. We're staying left. Looks like five minutes."

At first, I expected to greet an envoy of vehicles, judging by the volume of dirt in the air, but with my window cracked, I began to smell the smoke. We were at a higher elevation, with Castro's tour company at the far end of the valley. It became obvious that was the origin of the smoke. So far, there were no emergency responders on the scene. "Call 112!"

I pressed on the gas pedal, hoping the fire wasn't as bad as the smoke it had created, but I was sorely disappointed. The flames were higher by the time we neared the structure. His house hadn't been much more than a cabin, hidden from the sun by a rocky hill wall that helped to keep it cool. The entire building was engulfed in flames.

Marcus frantically tried to explain our location to a dispatcher, but it would take anyone a long time to respond all this way into the wilderness. There was nothing but dune fields and mesa for miles in every direction.

I clambered out of the vehicle, leaving it running, and ran toward the home. The sign near the turnoff had his business name, *Tours by Castro*, and I coughed from the thick smoke.

"Castro!" I shouted his name. I tried to see if his truck was there, and spotted it, along with a newer van closer to the home. "Castro!"

The fire was spreading to his garage, and within minutes, the flames jumped toward Castro's truck, which was parked near the open door. The explosion rang out loudly through the valley, and Marcus rushed beside me, staring at the destruction as pieces of the truck landed on the shale-colored ground.

"Was it those guys in the white truck?" Marcus asked. "I gave the description to the dispatcher."

"It probably was. I hope Castro wasn't home." I had a sinking feeling someone had known we were coming to offer him a job, and now he was dead.

———————

*F*our hours later, after being grilled by the police, we were allowed to return to the airport for a quick hop back to Sydney in Hunter's hired bush plane. By the time we arrived at the hotel, Marcus and I were exhausted, ready to call it a night.

"Where's Castro?" Tripp asked as I stepped toward the elevator.

"How long were you waiting there?" Marcus demanded after jumping in shock.

"Long enough." Tripp wore beige cargo pants and a short-sleeved white top, mostly unbuttoned. I noticed both arms were covered in tattoo sleeves.

"Castro won't be joining us," I advised him. By the time we'd returned to the airport, both of our phones were out of juice, and I hadn't wanted to give Hunter the heads-up anyway. He would have just gone ahead and hired someone else without my input.

"Why's that?" Tripp asked.

"He's dead."

This elicited the reaction I wanted. "Dead? Are you sure?"

"I saw him after his house fire finally burned out. I'm certain he's gone," I told him as I walked on and pressed the elevator button. Hunter had set us up in a nice hotel near the Opera House, and all I wanted to do was hit the shower and get a nap in before we figured out what came next.

"He's going to want to talk to you," Tripp said.

"Are you his personal secretary?" I asked, and the man only grunted.

"I'll let him know you'll join us in the bar for dinner in two hours," Tripp said.

"Fine. But can you do me a favor?"

"That depends." The elevator dinged and opened. Marcus stepped aside to let a young couple by. "Just don't tell Hunter about the… incident."

"A man's dead and you call it an incident? You're harder than I'd expected." Tripp said it like this was a good thing in his books.

"Can you do that?" I asked again.

"You have two hours."

I gave Tripp a nod, and he locked gazes with me. He had the look of a military man or a lifelong police officer. He'd seen too much during his tenure with the SEALs and carried it with him everywhere he went. It was in his posture, his tone, and his gait as he walked.

"See you then."

The doors closed with Marcus and me inside, and my friend exhaled. "Rex, we haven't even started yet and we're already behind."

Castro was dead, and it might have been my fault. The guy always had a problem with gambling, and I'd guessed that was part of the reason he'd ended up isolating himself in the middle of the outback. The fact that someone had burned down his business might have had no connection with the search for the Bridge.

I clung to that hope as we entered our floor. Marcus stopped at his room, beside mine.

"Two hours?" he asked.

"I guess so."

"I'll come get you." With that, my sidekick was gone. For someone who hadn't grown up in the field, he had sure taken well to the difficult adventure. I was proud of him.

I went into my suite, shaking my head at the lavish surroundings. This was my first time being catered to in my life. I'd had expense accounts allocated for artifact hunts before, but they were always limited, and usually just kept me from the worst hotels—definitely not in the top resorts.

Hunter had had an air of excitement surrounding him the last couple days, and he was going to be disconsolate that my choice for a pilot was no longer available. Any delays would really set back our timeline. I sat on the bed and plugged my phone in. The red light flashed on the top right corner, and I headed into the bathroom.

The water did its best to wash the sweat, smoke, and dirt from my skin, but the image of Castro's burned corpse on a gurney didn't rinse off quite so easily. I stayed under the scalding heat for some time, and when I emerged from the shower ten minutes later, the entire room was fogged up.

My phone held a few messages.

Jessica – *Rex. Was hoping we could get together again. Maybe Sunday?*

I'd deceived her at dinner about not leaving town. I scrolled to the next one.

Richard – *You have to stop avoiding me. Please, I have some information you might find useful. Call me.*

I stared at the screen, wondering why he always felt the need to be so cryptic. Why couldn't he just come out and say it? It was his way of trying to ensure I'd contact him, but it wasn't going to work this time.

With nothing but a towel wrapped around my waist, I lay on the bed, my eyes closing as my head hit the pillow. I needed to source another pilot. Someone I trusted. Someone on my team, so I wasn't overpowered in every decision by Hunter and Tripp.

There was only one person left in my mind. I sent a message to her, knowing she might not want to hear from me, since I hadn't called her back after our fling in Germany. I sat still, waiting for a response, and saw three dots appear. They flashed for what felt like five minutes, and vanished. When she did reply, the message was short and to the point.

Elise – *Nope*

I ran my hands through my wet hair and rolled onto my side. There had to be someone else. All I needed to do was think. What was the name of the guy who'd airlifted us out of Nepal that one time? He was willing to go the extra mile, but I thought he might have had a drug problem.

I set the phone down and closed my eyes as I considered my options.

A hurried knock woke me some time later, and I checked my phone, seeing no more messages from Elise. That was a burned bridge.

More knocks. "I'm coming!" I called. My mind was blurry, but even a short nap was better than nothing. I did feel slightly more focused as I strode across the suite, finding Marcus the culprit.

"Rex, better get dressed."

He looked at my towel, and I secured it. "Sorry. I dozed off. Come in."

"Did you have any luck hiring someone else?" Marcus

asked.

"Sadly, no."

"What about that one from Germany... what's her name?"

"Elise... and she's a hard no."

"I remember Elise. She was quite the..." Marcus smiled, and I threw a throw pillow at him.

"This isn't a joke. We're supposed to be leaving for Madagascar tomorrow, and we're missing our pilot." I climbed into a pair of jeans and tossed on a short-sleeved shirt, buttoning it up.

"Hunter has cash. He can hire locals—"

"Locals can be bought by the cultists. This mystery is running deep. I can't help but think Castro would have been safe if it wasn't for us," I said.

Marcus shook his head, as if trying to convince himself that wasn't true. "They couldn't have known. It was last minute, the bush plane pilot paid in cash. He must have been tied up in something else."

"You know what, he was always smoking cigars. He probably had a few too many beers and lit his porch on fire."

Marcus' eyes blinked wider. "Is that why you called him Castro? The cigars?"

"The very same reason." After adding some deodorant and a splash of cologne, I moved for the exit. "Let's find out what Hunter wants to do."

And we were back in the elevator after too short of a sleep. "Did you get any rest?" I asked Marcus.

We were alone, and he leaned against the wall. "Barely. This whole thing has me wound up. How do you do it?"

"It's new to me too. Usually, we're investigating one site, and we have a far larger team of professionals. This worries me. Tripp is a concern."

"What's the guy's deal?" Marcus asked, and I glanced at the numbers, seeing we had six floors to go.

"Navy SEAL. Single. Never married. He's a killer, Marcus. That's why Hunter brought him on. He knows his way around a vast array of weapons, and he understands how to stalk and evade better than ninety-nine percent of the population."

The doors opened, and Marcus held still for a moment. "Is he on our side?"

"Let's hope so."

The place was busier in the late hour, and I checked the time, wondering if it was the next day yet. It was almost eleven. The bar was loud, filled with well-dressed patrons drinking heavily as music played from unseen speakers. I scanned the room, spotting Tripp with Hunter Madison at a private table apart from the action.

We walked toward them, and I tried to avoid getting a spilled martini dumped on my shirt while Marcus stopped at a table, chatting with three clearly intoxicated ladies. I reached for his arm, leading him away. "Not the time."

He shrugged an apology and followed me through the busy lounge.

Hunter looked annoyed as we arrived, and he craned his neck to see around me. "Where's the pilot?"

I swallowed and explained the recent events. All of them.

He coughed and sank into his seat. "Then we're at a disadvantage. They know. But how?"

"Who's *they?*" Tripp asked.

"The Believers."

"That cult? Do we really think a group of nutcases could have beaten us to the remote outback? They'd have to be…" Tripp paused and glanced at Hunter as he nodded.

"Tripp, they'll be on our heels this entire time," our benefactor said slowly.

"But why?" Marcus asked. "I thought they were into these redeemers, not the Bridge."

"They are connected, just not in the way you might assume. One thing you should know is that they want the Bridge; not to open it, but to destroy it," Hunter said.

A waiter appeared, wearing all black, his expression telling me he was ready to close this place down and go home. "What'll you have?"

"Coffee."

"Make that two," Marcus said, sliding in beside Tripp. I went next to Hunter, and we waited until the guy was out of ear's reach before speaking again.

"You can't be too careful. I fear they're in this very room. They're always listening." Hunter sounded slightly ridiculous, but he might have been right. I found myself looking around as inconspicuously as I could. A woman and a man bumbled their way to the booth behind us, the man slurring loudly as he shouted for another drink.

Hunter frowned and lowered his voice. "If we don't finish this team off by tomorrow, our window to the stone forest narrows. My contact is expecting us, and I don't know if we can slip in otherwise."

The woman behind us spun around, kneeling on the bench to face us. "I hear Tsingy is beautiful this time of year."

The man with her started complaining, and she waved him away dismissively. "I think you should head out, love."

This angered him, and he stood, stumbling over to her. "I bought you dinner. The least you could do is—"

I jumped from my seat and stepped between them. "You heard the lady. Time to exit."

The waiter arrived with the coffees, and he set them on

our table. "Everything okay?"

I tilted my chin, waiting for this drunk buffoon to answer. He lifted his hands and walked away, returning to the bar in search of easier prey.

"You really didn't need to do that," the blonde woman said. She was smiling, her cheeks just slightly ruddy. "I can take care of myself."

"Do you mind? We're having a private conversation," Hunter advised her.

She wasn't dressed like the other guests at the hotel. She had on high-waisted jeans, the legs faded, and hiking boots with a black tee. "Veronica Jones at your disposal." She walked closer, attempting to shake Hunter's hand.

He didn't oblige. "As I was saying, we're—"

"I know who you are, Mr. Madison. And I also know this gentleman." She indicated me.

"And what, pray tell, do you want?" Hunter asked angrily.

"You have a problem, and I want in."

"You're a pilot?" Tripp asked, eyeing her up and down like a predator on the hunt for a kill.

"Sure. Fly pretty much any type of birds, mostly Chinooks and Hawks, but I've tried 'em all. Planes too. There's nothing like the loud, cramped, and sweaty cockpit of a Cessna zooming across the Indian Ocean."

Hunter's lips pursed, and he crossed his arms defiantly. "I'll take your word on it."

"Wait, how did you know we were here?" I asked her. Hunter's warning about the Believers rang in my mind.

She lost her smile, and her cocky stance shifted into something different. "I'll be honest. I was here with my plane, running a few tours in the area. You see, I have a bit of a niche business. Hauling snotty trust-fund kids around to remote regions so they can show off to their friends.

The latest brought me to Sydney, and I advertised on social, picking up a couple more jobs. But I saw you…" She flipped her phone around. It was Hunter Madison in the same suit he wore now, walking behind some vapid-looking duck-lipped woman taking a selfie in the hotel lobby.

"I was checking out hashtags for this place, trying to see if anyone wealthy enough to take a private charter might be in the area. And as luck had it, I saw you, Mr. Madison."

"What do you want?" he asked.

"I heard you say you need a pilot. That's me. I'm the woman for the job." She placed her hands on her hips and smiled widely.

I had to admit her energy was electric, and we did need someone. "You said you had a plane? How big?" Marcus asked her.

"Six-seater."

"Then you're wasting our time. We can't take a bush plane across the Indian Ocean. It's thousands of miles."

Veronica only smiled wider. "Then it's a good thing I have another one on the coast of Mozambique. Assuming you can charter a flight out of Sydney."

"Why should we trust you?" Tripp asked.

"You shouldn't, but I'll tell you what. You don't have to pay me until we get to the stone forest. We'll discuss the payment—"

Hunter rubbed his forehead and cut her off. "Fifty thousand if we find what we're after in Madagascar. I'll pay you the same for each of our stops." I was confident he'd do some digging on the woman when he returned to his room, but for this moment, he was desperate. Hunter was dying, and the Tokens were within his grasp.

My jaw dropped, but to Veronica's credit, she didn't flinch at the sum. "When do we leave?"

3

*T*o my surprise, there were something like fifteen airports spread out on the African island country. Unfortunately, I didn't see any of them from our current vantage point.

The engines sputtered as we neared land, and Veronica grinned as she lowered toward the bare ground. Seated beside the pilot, I listened as the dash alarms chimed out repeatedly. The gauge dials were pushed to their limits, but none of it seemed to discourage Veronica.

"What the hell were we thinking?" Hunter shouted, and I peered at him. He was whiter than a ghost and clutched the seatbelt tightly. The plane was a stark contrast to the ones he was used to traveling in. The seats were cracked, the paint chipped, but so far, they'd managed to cross the gulf between Mozambique and Madagascar, if only by a hair.

"You worry too much," Veronica said into her headset. Tripp had remained quiet, and Marcus seemed pensive, his eyes pressed closed as his lips moved silently. I suspected he'd just found religion.

A voice carried through her radio, speaking in crackling French. She responded and gave me a thumbs-up as she steered the plane south. "We're cleared for landing. What, you didn't think I was going to touch down on the rocks, did you? They do have laws, Rex."

The plane jerked to the side, sending me into Veronica.

"Hands to yourself." She smirked, and I found myself liking the woman more and more with each quip. She was easy to look at, not to mention carefree in a way I'd never managed in my life.

The airport looked like a few others I'd stopped in over the years: a single ratty tower, a lone runway with a few rusted-out planes parked outside a chain-link fence. There was a narrow road between the water and the tarmac, and she headed for it, descending faster than any of us liked.

We each sat in a kind of petrified state as the wheels touched the pavement, bouncing up, then screeching on the strip as she leveled it out. We jerked sideways several times and finally slowed, the engines cutting out as she directed the plane toward a man in an orange vest, waving his batons.

"Told you. Smooth sailing," Veronica said as she powered off the plane.

"I've never—" Hunter started, but I cut him off.

"You got us here. Thank you." I unstrapped, and she gave me an appreciative grin.

Tripp opened the exit, and Marcus was the first out, landing on wobbly feet. "I'm never getting in there again."

"Maybe not, but I bet it won't be your last hectic ride," I told him.

The air was humid, but a far cry from being as hot as the harsh terrain in the outback, and I took the offered bags from Tripp. I hadn't asked him what was inside his, but judging by the heaviness of it, there were a few guns and God knows what else.

"*Bonjour, bienvenue à Madagascar*," a man said in fluent French.

"Thank you," I replied.

"This way," he said in English. A few men watched us from the main building, leaning in the shade and staring with curiosity at our strange group.

Hunter Madison was the last to disembark, and he looked like he was on death's doorstep. "You sure you can do this?" I asked quietly. Tripp and Veronica were ahead, with Marcus a few feet behind, lugging another pack.

Hunter's eyes were lively, and he managed a smile. "Rex, I've been waiting to see a Token for thirty years. If it's where those coordinates say it is, I'd make that flight fifty times over." He took off, moving spryly, and I jogged after him.

We followed the local airport attendant to the fence, and I watched as a white truck drove by, exhaust billowing from the tailpipe. The town was across the street. It spread across the beige landscape, a few baobab trees jutting from the ground around the region. An animal screamed, and I spotted a lemur on a tree branch, his ringed tail drooping behind him.

"How do you know the guide?" I asked Hunter, and he motioned to a truck across the road as we exited the airport. He didn't respond.

Tripp stopped near the first escort and slipped him some currency before grabbing his pack again and crossing the road.

There were two men at the truck, one with a green shirt, the other in an orange one; each wore black shorts. "*Bonjour*," Hunter said. "Is everything prepared?"

Green shirt nodded. He set a hand on his chest. "I am Haja. This is Hasin."

"Well met," Hunter said, and gave them our names. Their eyes lingered on Marcus for a moment, then on Veronica.

"There's no time like the present. Let's make a move," I said, chucking the packs in the back of the truck.

"Would you like to ride up front with me?" Haja asked

Veronica, and she was quick to respond.

"Hunter, it would be much more comfortable for you up there."

"Right. Then it's settled." Hunter started for the door and stopped. "Marcus, give Haja the coordinates."

Marcus glanced at me, seeking guidance, and I answered for him. "Get us near the northern region. You can do that, right?"

Haja nodded cockily. "Not a problem."

I climbed into the back of the truck, sitting on the wooden bench. I tucked my pack under it, and Veronica came beside me. "You'll get the last coordinates when we arrive safely," I told them. I couldn't risk giving away the location of our first Token, not to strangers. For all I knew, they'd relay the information to friends already waiting at the stone forest. To activate the Bridge, we needed all six of the relics, though we currently only had the accurate locations of five of them.

Tripp was the last to climb in, and he sat heavily, putting himself between Marcus and Hasin. The engine cranked, shaking the entire truck, and Haja started forward, easing his foot on the pedal. "This might be a little bumpy," he said through the open window between us.

The sun was high and hot, and Hasin opened a cooler, kicking it across the truck bed toward the center. There were six bottles of water, along with a bunch of green-bottled beers. Tripp took one of those and snapped the cap off on the edge of the old truck. He offered it to me, and I shook my head.

"I'll have one," Veronica said, and took it from Tripp. He found another, while Marcus and I settled for water.

"How long is the drive?" Tripp asked Hasin.

"Three hours," he said.

"Damn. I'll admit I've been on worse roads than

Madagascar, but not many. But rarely did we have refreshments like this." Tripp lifted the beer and gulped from it.

I hadn't been here before, so I didn't know what to expect, but I learned quickly enough. We drove through town, and I watched as a group of children were let out of school. They shouted and ran from the whitewashed building, dashing for their daily dose of freedom. Ten minutes later, houses became exceedingly sparse along the roads, and the trees grew thicker.

We passed only a handful of cars on the road, fewer the farther inland we went. Judging by the sun and the maps Marcus and I had reviewed, we were heading southeast toward the stone forest. I'd seen pictures before, but we weren't going to the tourist location, with public washrooms and guided tours.

"Have you seen Madagascar before?" I asked Veronica.

"Sure. Couple times. Stone forest is quite the sight, but not for everyone. Tends to be dangerous. Between the suspension bridge and the rock climbing, it can be a bit of a test," she said. "What can you tell me about our prize?"

I glanced at Hasin, but he and Tripp were in conversation and on their second beer. I kept my voice quiet. "There's an artifact located inside. Something valuable."

"It would have to be, with Hunter Madison chasing after it. I didn't think anyone lived out there in the forest. Are you suggesting there's an ancient village?" she asked.

"I can't know for sure, but... this isn't the original location of the artifact," I admitted.

This piqued her interest. "How interesting. So these six stops we're planning on making... did someone spread out a collection or something?"

She was smart; I had to give her that. "Along those lines."

The truck lurched, and I peered over the front of the vehicle. The sun was bright, and I struggled to see why Haja would stop in the middle of nowhere.

Hasin rose, jumping from the truck, and Tripp followed him.

"I sense trouble," Marcus said, pointing down the road, and then I saw the other vehicles. The lead one stopped a hundred yards away, pulled sideways to block the road. Three men hopped out, hardly more than boys, but I didn't like the look of them.

"Toss my pack," Tripp called from the rear of our truck, and I threw it over, the bag landing with a hefty thump. He unzipped it, shoving a handgun into his belt behind his back.

"What's going on?" I asked Haja through the window.

"Stay put. I will deal with this. Mr. Madison, do you have any ariary?" he asked Hunter.

It took me a second to remember that was their local currency. "Some. What do you need? Who are these men?"

Haja sighed. "They control the passes. Any hunting is done so with their permission."

"Hunting?" I whispered, and it all clicked. I opened a crate near the window and found three long rifles, along with sacks. "They're poachers. What do you hunt?"

Haja shrugged, and told me, "Lemurs."

"You hired poachers to bring us in?" I asked Hunter, and he frowned at me.

"How else did you expect to get to the illegal passes of the conservation region? We do what's necessary to complete our mission," he stated firmly.

Haja opened his door and climbed out, taking the envelope with ariary bills with him.

"I can't believe this," Marcus said. "Do you see the heat they're packing?"

I did now. Two of the men opposite us were carrying submachine guns, and I flinched, picturing this ending in a shoot-out. I glanced into Tripp's pack and spotted an M240. I quickly closed it and caught Veronica eyeing it suspiciously.

"Some friends you have, Rex," she whispered.

"You're telling me."

Haja and Hasin met a skinny older man halfway, the two machine guns close behind him. I noted how Tripp stood beside Hunter's door protectively. It was clear who he was hired to shield, not that I blamed him. The team was being paid handsomely for this mission, even if they didn't understand what the end goal was.

Haja handed the other guy the bills, and he smiled, sniffing the cash. He barked an order, and his escorts turned around, lowering their weapons. I relaxed, glad the meeting hadn't ended in violence, but the old guy didn't follow his friends. He was staring at the truck. He asked something else in a clipped dialect I couldn't quite hear from my position. He pointed at us and started walking forward. Judging by Haja's expression, he was worried about something.

"Tripp, what do we do?" Marcus asked him.

Tripp didn't take his eyes off the incoming man. "Have you ever fired a gun?"

"No. Well, yes, but only at the range with Rex…"

"Rex, in my pack. There's two P226s. Take one, give Marcus—"

Veronica already had one in her hand. She released the magazine and slapped her palm on the end, clicking it back in place. She spun the other around and passed it to me. "Don't worry. I won't shoot myself in the foot."

This was a weapon I was familiar with, and it gave me confidence as I waited, still sitting in the box of the truck.

The skinny guy Haja had paid off was closer, and he whistled, catching the attention of his armed escorts. They both turned around, lifting their guns, and I saw Tripp stand straighter. He was prepared for anything.

He started to reach for his gun when I overheard the man speaking in French. "One of their tires is low. Give them a hand." I translated it in my head, but Tripp clearly didn't speak the language. I climbed past Marcus and hopped to the ground, leaving the Sig behind.

I was right on time. I told him what they said as Tripp started to swing his arm around, and he stopped, turning to face me. "Are you sure?"

"They're changing the tire."

Hunter was still inside the truck, and at my words, he exited, stretching his back. "As good a time as any for a quick break, don't you think?" he asked, dabbing sweat with his handkerchief.

The armed guards set their weapons on the dirt track and glanced at their boss, who nodded and pointed to the low tire. He grunted something about earning their share and laughed with Haja. Our escorts seemed nervous at first but were warming up.

They pulled a tire from beside the bench Veronica and I had been seated on, and made quick work of the swap. Once the jack was lowered, the skinny man whispered something to Hasin and walked off, whistling while his two companions shuffled after him. Haja returned to the driver's seat and waited while the two vehicles drove by us with a honk of the horn.

"How close was that?" I asked Hasin as he sat across from me.

"You never know with him. But he's interested in money, and we give him good business." That was the end of it, and the truck started up. We continued on, toward the ever-thickening jungle ahead.

———————

*B*y five o'clock, the sun was behind the canopy of trees, and we drove on for another hour, until it was almost impossible to make out the rough jungle passing. I wondered if this trail had been physically cut by local poachers over the years, or if some part of it was natural.

Lemurs called out everywhere, and they were an eerie soundtrack to the journey. I'd never seen so many as they sat in treetops, nimbly moving between branches with ease. Their voices intermingled with bird songs, and I searched the surroundings for the source, unable to spot any feathered friends in the dark.

Marcus stared at the lemurs, his interest in the exotic animals waning after hours seated on the uncomfortable wooden bench. I felt his pain and banged a palm against the truck as Haja began pulling off the road. "What's the plan? I thought we were getting there today."

"No. We cannot go on without light. Too dangerous."

"Great," Marcus mumbled.

"Buck up. A night in the jungle never killed…" Tripp stopped. "Well, that's not true, but if you're stuck outside, there are worse places in the world to be. I was in Mosquitia twenty years ago, looking for the White City with some foolhardy intellectual type."

"And what happened?"

"Damn snake killed our doctor. Can you believe it?" Tripp grinned, and Marcus glanced at the nearby bushes.

We hauled out of the truck, retrieving our supplies. The trees opened up to a clearing, and I stared at the darkening sky, watching the pinpricks of light blink to life.

"What happened after the snake bite?" Veronica asked him.

"I never did reach the city. Only a complete lunatic would bother—" Tripp glanced at a skittering sound from the trees.

"You have to be *slightly* mad to scour a jungle in search of a lost city, don't you?" Veronica prodded.

"Sure, I'd agree with that."

"And the expedition?"

"The man that hired us died two weeks in. We warned him to wear his snake gaiters, but he whined that they chafed his ankles." Tripp didn't have to finish the story. I glanced at my feet and into the jungle, and hurried after the two locals as they led us into the clearing.

"We stay here. Put the tents close together," Hasin said.

"Can we have a fire?" Marcus asked.

"Yes. There are predators, but we don't have much to worry from the fossa." Haja started to unroll a tarp.

"What's a fossa?"

Hunter surprised me by answering, "Kind of a cross between a cat and a hyena. They mainly eat lemurs, which means they're in direct competition with our guides, aren't they?"

It was a passive-aggressive dig at their choice of career paths, but he was the one who'd hired them knowing that.

"And snakes?" Veronica asked as she built her pup tent.

"There are lots, but don't fear, pretty lady," Haja said. "They don't like people much."

"Good, because I don't like them," Marcus replied.

We were experienced with our equipment, and camp was erected within minutes. Hasin had the fire going soon after, and we rolled a set of fallen logs over, making seats as the flames licked the sky. It was peaceful, with the sounds of the region shifting from daytime to those of night. It was a different world in the dark, like a shift change on a factory floor.

Tripp brought out a supply of dried meat and nuts, and we ate. Hasin left, and I eyed him suspiciously, but he returned in a few minutes with the cooler from the back of the truck. He'd refilled it with more beer from somewhere, and now I accepted his offering. The nights were cooler, and I was thankful for the heat of the fire as I sipped the bitter brew.

"Tomorrow." Hunter's gaze was affixed to the sky. "How far?"

"The edge of the forest is near. Two hours, maybe," Haja answered as he poked the burning logs with a stick. Ashes shot into the air, and the fire crackled. "From there... that depends on the location."

"Marcus, I think we can share that with them now, don't you?" Hunter asked my sidekick.

Only the two of us held the actual coordinates, as part of our deal, and when Marcus looked to me for leadership, I nodded.

He pulled his phone out and handed it to Haja beside him on the log. "This is in a restricted region."

"We already assumed that. We can make it, right?" Hunter asked, finally breaking his game of chicken with the stars.

"It's accessible," Hasin chimed in after peering over his friend's shoulder. "There is nothing, though. Why would this thing you seek be out in the forest?"

"Someone left it there by accident," I lied.

Haja nodded, but his stare didn't waver from my face. I sipped my beer. A mutual understanding.

"I think it's time to check out for the night, Hunter,"

Tripp said. He was sharing a tent with our financer and helped him to his feet. Hunter groaned and clutched at his stomach. I didn't expect Hunter to be along for the entire duration of our expedition around the world, not after he realized he was too old and too sick to sleep outdoors and sweat in foreign countries. He wore matching white linen pants and a short-sleeved shirt. I'd never known anyone to use a handkerchief, but Hunter's hadn't left his grip in hours. He dabbed his face with it and finally shoved it away.

Tripp nodded to me before entering the tent after Hunter. I imagined he slept lightly, with one or maybe both eyes open.

Haja and Hasin did the same, retiring to their canvas tent, and Marcus yawned, finishing his beer. "I'm going to call it too, Rex."

I noticed Veronica was still up, and I decided to keep her company for the time being. "I'll be there shortly." It was early, but we had a long day ahead of us, and I was beat after the last few days of travel.

"He's a good kid," she said, indicating Marcus.

"Smart too. One of the best students I've had."

"He was your student?" she asked.

"Yep, until he decided he couldn't make a career in the field. He transferred to something more… sensible."

"Are you saying archaeology isn't as romantic as it's cracked up to be?" Veronica asked, shifting closer to the fire. We sat inches apart, and she wiggled her knees, bumping my leg every few seconds.

"I wouldn't say that. There are times. Entering a site for the first time, brushing the cobwebs from the stone archways, and carefully treading on the floor, hoping you're not about to set off some ancient burial guardian system. Then there's the bats…"

She laughed, her blue eyes bright in the firelight. It was a nice sound amidst the jungle noises. "Bats? You're scared of them?"

"What's there not to be afraid of? Wings... those little faces. Not to mention the movies," I said, feeling a little foolish.

"Don't tell me you believe in vampires," she said.

"No. I wouldn't go that far."

"How about aliens?" Her voice dipped lower, and I saw her glance toward Hunter's tent.

"Aliens?"

"You know... beings from another planet."

"I don't know what to believe. I do think it's awfully arrogant of us to assume we're the only world with intelligent life."

"Are you certain we're speaking of the same planet? In my experience, the aliens would keep flying by... we're waving a sign... nothing to see here." She smiled again, making me join her.

"Why do you ask?" She wasn't privy to our mission details yet, but she wasn't naive. She knew more than she was letting on.

"Everyone's heard about Madison the billionaire's obsession with the unknown. I heard he has quite the collection." Her lips were close to my ear, her voice barely a whisper.

"It is impressive."

"You've seen it?" she asked too loudly, and slid a palm to her mouth.

"I have. Briefly, at least." I thought of the last time Marcus and I had been in Hunter's study, and the threat of violence from Tripp and Francois.

"That's the real reason, isn't it?" she asked me.

"I'm not—"

"Don't lie, just tell me. I have a right to know if I'm going to be part of the team," she said, sitting up straighter.

"Someone spread out these artifacts years ago. Hunter wants to gather them. It will complete a collection of his," I said. It was only a half-truth, but that would have to be enough for tonight.

That seemed to slow her inquiries on the subject. "Was it hard growing up without a father?"

The question came out of nowhere, and I sat still, staring at the dwindling fire.

"I'm sorry, was that too far? I've read up on you, and I know that your father was Dirk Walker. A legend in certain fields, if my research was correct," Veronica told me.

"My dad's been gone a long time. It's a wonder why I didn't become a grocery store manager instead of this, but I'm not my father. I'm a professor." Saying it didn't make it real, because at this moment, I felt just like him, and I liked it. I was connected to a great puzzle, the same one he'd gone to great lengths to hide. Why had they paid Marta's father to disperse the Tokens in these bizarre and remote areas? To what end? Had he been that afraid of someone following him? Had he really wanted to leave us behind, with no hopes of reconnecting?

"Molding the minds of the young. If Marcus is any proof of your skill set, you should be proud of your teachings."

"Marcus was already a special kid. I can't take any credit."

"But he's here with you now, on this wild adventure," she said.

"He is, but I wish he'd stayed home. I feel like I'm bringing him into something he shouldn't be part of," I admitted.

Veronica rose, waving a fly away, and headed toward

her tent. "He wants to be here. I only hope you find what you're looking for, Rex."

"And you?" I asked, watching her crouch near her tent's entrance.

"I'm in it for the cash."

4

The first sight of the stone forest was awe-inspiring. The rocky razor-edge tree-like formations were like nothing I'd ever witnessed before, and it took a while to comprehend what we were seeing. The trees were thick, the lemurs plentiful, but the wild species darted off at the sound of the trucks' engine carrying through the dense forest.

"How did the forest come to be?" Hunter asked Hasin as we gathered our supplies. The Token's coordinates were three miles away, and our guides suspected it might take us all day to traverse the distance.

Hasin shrugged. "God created it."

The elevation increased beyond our location, rising with the stone trees. That was exactly what they looked like: rough gray trees, almost like a forest of spruce that had been frozen into stone by Medusa. It also appeared deadly and impossible to navigate.

"We should have brought a copter in," Veronica said.

"Nowhere to land," Haja told her.

"We don't need to land. I could have lowered our buddy Tripp." Veronica hefted her pack onto her shoulders and added an elastic to her long blonde hair, pulling it tightly into a tail.

"We'll keep that in mind for next time," Tripp said with a smirk. He was in a good mood today, and I guessed the layer of caution around him was lowering. We were becoming his squad, and now that we'd shared a meal around a fire and slept in tents on-site, he considered us more of a team than he had the night before.

"This area looks unique," Marcus told me.

"Madagascar is much different. Islands often bring completely radical ecosystems with them," Veronica said. "Deciduous trees here will give way to wet limestone slabs farther into the valleys."

I glanced at Hasin, and he nodded his agreement. "She is right. This is Tsingy de Bemarah, and *Tsingy* means *where one cannot walk barefoot.*"

My boots were broken in; they'd been on numerous adventures with me, and I hoped they'd stand up to the harsh hike we were about to endure.

"Mr. Madison, you should stay with Haja," Hasin said, leaning against the side of the truck.

Hunter looked at Tripp. "I think he might be right. I'll only slow you down, and my lungs..."

"I know you want to reclaim this hidden article, but do you trust this man?" Tripp asked.

"I'll be fine." Hunter seemed older today, and I wondered just what was wrong with his health. His handkerchief was out again, and he wiped his brow with the embroidered cloth.

"Someone else should stay put," Tripp said. "Keep you company." It was obvious that he was thinking we would have safety in numbers, but the two local guides didn't seem to care one way or the other. "I vote for Veronica."

"No way." She crossed her arms, stepping toward the ex-SEAL. "I'm fit and can do this hike in my sleep. My suggestion is the kid stays."

All eyes fell on Marcus, and he visibly relaxed. "I'll hang here with Hunter, Rex. You guys get what we came for, and I'll see you soon."

I reached into the back of Tripp's pack and pulled out a handgun, giving it to Marcus. I stared at Haja to see his reaction, but he just shrugged.

"There will be no one to shoot with that, but if it helps you feel better, go for it." Haja lit a thin, brown-papered cigar and smiled at me as he puffed it.

"Then it's settled. Time to go." Hasin was the thinner of the two, but his size betrayed a certain evident strength. He pulled out an assortment of climbing gear and tossed shin guards at Tripp, Veronica, and me. "Put these on. A slip and your leg will be mangled."

We did as ordered, and I patted Marcus on the shoulder before taking the GPS.

"Good luck, team," Hunter said from the tailgate. His eyes were haunted, his posture rigid. There was so much riding on our mission, perhaps even farther-reaching than my initial speculations. Selfishly, I wanted to see what had happened to my father, and the rest were invested for financial reasons. Hunter, on the other hand, wanted to see if his life's passion was real. Did aliens exist, and if so, did we really have the means on Earth to travel to another place to meet them?

We might find out in a couple of weeks, if everything went according to plan. The only issue was the last location that we'd found in the locker at the Caracas airport. Hunter's team was working on analyzing the skewed digits from the photograph, and while he was optimistic, I was more doubtful.

With my backpack secured, and my legs already warmer with the shin protection wrapped around my calves, I headed after Tripp and Hasin, who'd taken the lead.

"I've always wanted to come to this region of the forest," Veronica said from beside me. Her cheeks were red from the heat, her forehead locked in a frown. "I even went so far as to request a private tour from a local, but it was definitely not in his comfort zone. No one wants to be caught trespassing out here."

"Neither do I. It's funny. I've seen a lot of sites, mostly digs and previously explored ancient cultures' civilizations, but there's something special about places like the stone forest. Mysteries that seem to be created by the majestic Mother Earth. But in the long run, it's just lots of water, time, and erosion." I shielded my eyes from the sun as I stared toward the valley beyond. We could view some of the region ahead, but a few minutes later, once we crested the coverage of the forest around us, the area spread out beyond, wowing my every sense.

"I see what you mean. Where are we going next?" Veronica asked casually. She'd taken the job without anyone sharing the details of the entire mission with her, and I assumed there was no real harm in revealing the location.

"Japan," I said.

"Where?" Her voice lifted in excitement. "I miss good sushi."

"I don't think there'll be time for that. But we'll finally get to see your helicopter skills in action," I told her, and she walked faster, trying to bridge the gap between Hasin and us.

The ground began to grow exceedingly uneven as we started our descent into the park. This area was off limits, and there were none of the permanent steel rock-climbing ropes present. There would be no suspension bridges helping us across dangerous areas. The three-mile hike looked like a hundred from here. I saw the destination on the GPS and peered west to the target zone. A hundred-foot-tall limestone cliff stood between us and it, but Hasin didn't seem to care.

There were still a few trees, most holding a lemur or two watching us cautiously with their big eyes, occasionally calling a warning to their nearby friends. The entire area was dark gray, and as we lowered into the stone forest, the rocky ground became slicker with moisture. Veronica almost slipped as we rounded a bend, but I was there to catch her.

"My hero," she muttered sarcastically.

"Hurry up," Tripp shouted from ahead.

We found them stopped at the end of a flat walkway ten minutes later, and Hasin muttered something in French that I didn't understand.

"What's the issue?" Veronica asked.

"The wall. There's an entrance up to the right, but the climb is steep, and the locals are picky about who they let inside," Hasin told us.

"The locals?" I asked.

One of the ring-tailed lemurs stood at the entrance, running away as Tripp walked closer to it. They were rarely a threat to harm a human, unless given cause.

"Come on. Let's get this over with." Tripp started up the cliffside, and I saw what Hasin meant. The fissure ran along the limestone wall, but it had natural footholds in the edges, meaning we were able to move up the face in relative safety.

"There's no other way?" I asked.

Hasin shook his head and strapped a harness around his shoulders. He gave us each one and attached a link between himself and Tripp, then to Veronica, with me at the tail end.

"Won't this just pull us all to our deaths?" Veronica asked with a laugh.

"It's safer this way," he said. "Something happens, stop and plant your feet."

With that said, we began the ascent after I checked the GPS to see we were halfway to our target.

———————

I accepted Tripp's extended hand as we exited the crack in the limestone wall, and I lay on my back a moment, letting my heartrate slow with a few deep breaths.

"That was incredible," Veronica said. She was bent over, resting her hands on her thighs, and she smiled at me.

I climbed to my feet and looked back in the direction we'd just emerged from. The stone forest covered a vast area, and I peered past the rocks to the forest, where Marcus would be waiting with Hunter and Haja.

"Any chance we'll be able to return before nightfall?" I asked Hasin, and he nodded, surprising me.

"Maybe. We have made good time." The Malagasy man stretched his back and cracked his neck. "The trail is easier before it grows more difficult."

"You've been here before?" I asked.

"Once."

I didn't press him. We took a brief break, and I drank deeply from my canteen before stowing it. My protein bar went down quickly, and soon we were on the trail, only a mile from the final destination.

Tripp lingered behind the guide, and Veronica switched positions, chatting amiably with Hasin.

"She's quite the piece of work, isn't she?"

Tripp's comment could have been rhetorical, but I answered anyway. "She sure is. How can someone be so chipper after a climb like that?" My own legs were tired, but the thought of obtaining a Token fueled my motivation.

Tripp stared forward, his steps like robotic marches. "I

don't trust her."

"Why?"

"She just happened to be at the hotel, and she conveniently had an airplane secured on the coast? It doesn't add up," he said.

"Why didn't you say anything?" Marcus and I had discussed this exact thing, but it wasn't like we'd had time. I had a job to go home to, and Hunter was adamant we locate the Tokens soon. I thought about the Believers tracking me and remembered the dangers that awaited us if we failed.

"Hunter wouldn't have listened. He's so hell-bent on finding this Bridge, whatever that is. When this is done, and you all realize it's been a huge waste of time and resources, let me buy you a beer and tell you where it went wrong," he told me.

"Then why are you here?"

"I'm forty-nine, Rex."

Tripp looked older and younger at the same time. "What does that have to do with anything?"

"Everything. I've never slowed down, and Hunter has made it clear that if this mission is a success, I won't have to work another day in my life," Tripp told me.

"And what does the future hold for Tripp Davis?" I asked, genuinely curious. A thick white cloud slowly moved above us, giving us reprieve from the midday sunlight.

"I'm gonna buy a place along the Baltic sea. Fish and grow a garden. Maybe meet a nice woman."

"Sounds pretty great," I admitted.

"What about you?"

"I have a job."

"No plans for retirement? I've spent my entire existence taking orders from other people, and I finally want some freedom of choice. And maybe the odd nap on a hammock overlooking the ocean." He laughed, the sound a little off-putting from the grizzled veteran.

I wanted to know where my dad had gone off to, and after that, the future was wide open. "I wouldn't mind tenure at a reputable school. Maybe lecture on a circuit some day. But I'm also not finished with the thrill of the hunt."

"You really love this stuff, don't you? Digging up lost artifacts."

"Only when someone doesn't chase you down and steal your goods," I said, remembering who I was dealing with.

"I thought that was water under the bridge. For the record, I didn't do anything illegal," he told me.

"You paid off my guides and stole months of my life." I tried to maintain my composure, but dragging out our history was angering me.

"As I said, it wasn't illegal there." Tripp chuckled. "Besides, it turned out that stuff was useless. My backer wasn't very pleased with me."

"We found tools. That statue. Coins, even," I said, dumbfounded.

"Then the guides you hired scammed you. They must have swapped the goods without you noticing. I looked like a fool, and you went home empty-handed. If it means anything, I *am* sorry. I've learned a lot in the last eight years." Tripp stuck out his hand, and I peered at the callused palm.

"Fine." I shook it, gripping it tightly. "But you definitely owe me a beer when this is finished."

"Done."

"If you two boys are done, I think you'd better see this," Veronica said from ahead, and we arrived, staring into a dip in the rocky outcropping.

A single dwarfed tree sat amidst the sharp, pointed limestone, a beacon to our destination. A gecko ran in front of my feet, and I watched as it headed for the open vegetation in the area. With a look at the GPS to confirm what I already knew, I smirked. "We're here."

Hasin slowed, apparently not wanting to get any closer, and I went first, deliberately traversing the uneven slope. It was slick, and I saw water funneling from higher up the ridge. It rolled across the rocks in a steady stream toward the tree.

I stared at the sky, silently asking my father or Clayton why they'd chosen this location to have Luis hide the Token. It was remote and extremely difficult to locate, and I doubted anyone would ever stumble across this exact tree, considering it was far from the public park. Only poachers, and a few of them at that, would have ever trod anywhere close.

The tree was maybe eight feet tall, with thin branches, the leaves light green. The gecko sat atop a branch, trying to stay frozen as I crouched near the trunk, searching for a sign of the Token. I was surprised to see the tree growing from the stone, and noticed the limestone crumbling around it. I dug a finger near the trunk and felt damp dirt. Life always found a way, especially when there was a water source.

Perhaps Luis had hidden this here and planted the tree. If it had been thirty-something years, that would account for the small size. Stunted growth in the infertile stone forest.

Then Tripp was beside me, his shadow blocking the sun from my face as I peered up at him. "Anything?" he asked, but there was nowhere to hide an object.

"It's not here," I muttered, finding a seated position.

"Damn it," Veronica said, sitting on the opposite side

of the tree. "Hunter's going to be upset. He'll pay still, right? Will he want to continue on to the next site?"

Her questions washed over me, but I had no answers as I observed the water flowing from the limestone peaks. It moved for the trunk and dripped into an opening. The gecko started to shift, and I lifted a hand slowly, indicating for Tripp to stop fidgeting. The small creature's head tilted toward the sun, then it darted down the trunk, disappearing into the ground.

"There's an opening!" I exclaimed, shifting on my knees in front of the tree. The space was small, and my hand didn't fit inside.

"Want me to bust it out?" Tripp had his rifle poised, holding it as if to bash the ground with the butt end, but Veronica set a palm on it.

"You boys, always trying to beat the answer out of things. Allow me." Her sleeves were already rolled up, and she stuck her tongue out the corner of her mouth as she stretched her fist into the opening.

"Be careful. There could be rats or snakes." I held my breath as her arm entered a foot or so into the ground, and her expression suggested it was empty. Then a smile broke, showcasing perfect teeth.

She pulled her arm up and held a sack. It was beige burlap, like the one we'd found the Case inside. Surprisingly, she handed it to me without looking, a satisfied *harumph* escaping her lips.

I was speechless and clutched the bag in my palm. It was heavier than I'd expected.

"Go on with it. What's inside?" Tripp asked, annoyed.

The bag was cinched at the top, and I used a knife in my pocket to slice the sack, sliding the Token out. It was hexagonal, as we'd known, the symbol embedded in its center, just as my father had mentioned in his journal. I stared at the dark metallic shape, remembering the entry of this particular find in the book Beverly had given me a few weeks ago.

September 17ᵗʰ, 1977

After four years, we've discovered the second piece. The trail grew cold for many months, but we managed to trace it to El Mirador. Its icon is strange: three circles within one another. Hardy still doesn't know how the objects were distributed by the celestial beings, only that they were placed on six different land masses. This one comes with more relief than the first, from Mozambique, but also more trepidation. One item implied something... a mystery. But two... it makes it real. Hardy's theory of the Bridge is genuine; that much is evident.

Clayton grows weary of the mission and talks of starting a family with his wife. I will continue with or without him, and reinforce that with the funding of Hunter Madison, his children will never want for anything. I think I can convince him to side with me and to continue the search for the third article. There are times I wish S hadn't left our team, but it was necessary.

We'll be departing the jungles of Guatemala posthaste, but one thing is clear. The Bridge awaits.

The three circles were as he'd described them. Three rings, each smaller than the previous. "The Bridge awaits," I mumbled.

"What? What's the Bridge?" Tripp asked.

"Never mind." I clutched the Token and slipped it into my breast pocket, where I could feel the weight of it against my chest. "Let's move. Hunter won't want to delay any longer."

We had another piece of the puzzle, but I couldn't help but mirror my father's apprehension at the discovery.

5

I walked outside, feeling the crisp air brush against my face. Coming from Australia, then to Madagascar, then to Japan in December was a reminder that it was winter in a lot of the world. Japan always felt slightly more like home than most countries. The people were quiet and friendly, the streets clean, and a sense of pride emanated in everything they accomplished.

"Alone time?" Veronica asked from the hotel entrance. I stared into the distance, toward the enormous snow-capped peaks of Mount Fuji in the setting sun.

"Something like that."

She came outside, wrapping her arms around herself. There was a dusting of snow on the ground, but most of it melted as it hit the pavement. "Hunter seems pleased."

"He has what he's been after for a long time."

"The Token?" she asked.

"Validation."

"You like him, don't you?"

"I respect him. He believes in a cause greater than himself, and he's trying to ensure its detection."

"Mount Fuji. Seems like an odd location to hide something, doesn't it?"

I watched her looking at the famous peaks, and smiled. "They didn't hide it there, but it's kind of brilliant if you think about it. It's actually thirty kilometers from here, and twenty from Fuji." I pointed left of the majestic mountain.

"So if anyone discovered the Token might be near Fuji, they'd start there instead? Why this elaborate ruse? Why not dump them at the bottom of the ocean?" A snowflake landed on her nose. She looked at it cross-eyed and blew it away with a puff of breath.

"I don't have the answers. I can only assume they wanted someone to find them." Why else leave a trail at all? I had to think it was something Clayton had done. His gravestone had led the way to Venezuela and the Case, as well as the locker, etched with the remaining coordinates. "I'm just following the breadcrumbs."

"You're doing a good job. Care for a drink?" Veronica pointed to the doors, and I joined her inside. The lobby was warm. The hotel was probably the finest in Fujino-yama, with clean white tile and ambient lighting.

"Where are the others?" I asked.

"Hunter and Tripp are securing a permit. I haven't seen Marcus," she told me.

Neither had I, and that was concerning. He was probably just sleeping off his jetlag after the last week of hectic travel. "Shall we?"

The hostess spoke English and ushered us into the bar. It was a weekday, and the bar was quiet in the late afternoon. A couple of businessmen in suits sat talking quietly to one another over beers, and they stopped as we walked by.

We took seats at the marble bar near the far end, where no one could sit behind us. We hadn't seen any signs of the Believers for a while, but I had a feeling they were out there, still searching for me.

I was underdressed even for this bar, wearing a plain long-sleeved t-shirt and jeans, but Veronica wore a hoodie with dark leggings, so we made an equal pair. The bartender approached, a serious expression on his face as he awaited our drink orders. We opted for local beers, and he poured them, setting the glasses on coasters before leaving to serve another guest.

"Cheers," Veronica said, clinking her glass to mine. "To the next one."

"To the next one."

"What's after this?"

"Well, we…"

"No, I mean after this is all done. Once Hunter has his prizes, and you're back in Boston."

"I don't know," I said. "I guess I'll be preparing for the new semester."

"Is it tough?"

"Teaching?"

"No," Veronica said. "Having to return to a tweed jacket and the students after being out here with the world at your fingertips will be the hard part."

"I guess it is," I told her. "But I need a balance. I like having a home base, and I enjoy teaching… even if some of the kids are annoying."

"I can only imagine."

"Did you go to college?" I asked. I knew next to nothing about the woman beside me, except that she was a daring pilot and didn't seem afraid of anything.

"Sure did. Art history degree from Columbia." She averted her gaze, sipping her beer as she looked at the TV screen behind the bar. It was a local news program.

"Art history. Not what I would have expected."

"I know… but that was kind of the point. My parents always wanted me to do something big with my life, and to them that meant becoming a lawyer, or maybe a journalist for one of the big guys. After high school, instead of going to post-secondary straightaway, I left on a whim, not telling them where I was going. I ended up in Europe and spent the next nine months moving from one city to the next, visiting their museums, seeing exhibits, drinking wine, and eating like a queen." She smirked, the action so natural on her.

"Sounds like you brought Daddy's credit card," I said, and she stiffened.

"My stepfather is a good man. He paid for me to do it, under the stipulation I'd come home to Manhattan and enroll at Columbia like he had. Seemed like a good deal. After witnessing so many wonderful things in Europe, art history made sense to me. He took it as an insult initially, but we're good. It was a long time ago."

"Did you ever use it?" I asked.

"The degree? Nah. But I can tell you the difference between Monet's brushstrokes in the *Garden at Sainte-Andresse* and in *Water Lilies*. I ended up with a guy that owned a mechanic shop on Long Island, and worked on city truck engines for a year before deciding that joining the Air Force was a good way to see the world."

She was full of surprises. "I assume that's where you learned to fly?"

"Yep. Spent a few years pulling soldiers from danger, but left and decided to work for a tour company in Hawaii. Flew the same route off Maui for three years, and as beautiful as it is, you can only make that trip so many times without it losing the luster."

"That's when you started this rich-kid company?"

"Social media made it possible, and once I had some socialite in Greece sharing the experience with the rest of her friends, it took off."

I glanced at the TV and saw three blurry shapes in a dark backdrop. "Is that…"

"You guys have to see this!" Marcus' voice carried

loudly across the bar, and everyone turned to watch as my friend dashed past the hostess and landed at the bar beside Veronica. His laptop was open, and he pressed play on a paused video.

"We can make out three objects presently, and scientists are predicting there might be more. It seems as though the mysterious shapes are attached to one another and are separating as they travel across our solar system. Some are claiming it's the end of days, others are hailing this as a miracle, but the scientific community is still urging everyone to be calm until more details can be determined," the serious newscaster said. A banner rolled along the bottom of the screen: *Doomsday or Deliverance?*

"Three of them," I whispered. "Where are they?"

Marcus tapped the mouse, and another screen opened with their predicted trajectory. They were slender and dark, like slivers of rock barreling past Pluto and onward. There were dates along the line heading for Earth, and it showed them nearing Uranus' orbit. "If they continue at this pace, we can expect arrival within three months."

"Three months. That's not a lot of time." I took a long pull from my glass and waved the bartender over, getting another round, and one for Marcus.

"And that's if they don't change speed again," Marcus reminded me. He pressed play, and the broadcast cut to a woman questioning an elderly lady on the street in Chicago.

"This is our punishment. We've filled this world with war and greed. Guns and hatred, and we're being judged for it," the interviewee spat out.

"You think this is God's will?" The journalist jabbed the microphone at the frantic lady.

"I don't know about all that, but I for one welcome whoever is coming for us." The screen flicked, and it showed the same interviewer talking to a man in a suit.

"What do you think of the Objects?" The Objects. That was the title given by the media. It was as good a moniker as any, I supposed.

"What are you talking about?" The guy held his coffee in one hand, a leather satchel draped over his shoulder.

"The mysterious asteroids heading for Earth," she informed him.

"I don't know what you're saying. I'm more into the Cubs and my work. I'll let the nerds watch the meteors or whatever." He walked off, whistling for a taxi.

"As you can see, Bob, there are a variety of reactions to the news of these Objects, but I have a feeling that as word spreads, things will change shortly."

The image returned to Bob at the anchor desk, and he looked afraid. *"Yasmine, I think you're correct. There are already talks of protests and marches in New York, Paris, London, Moscow, and right here in Chicago this weekend."*

Marcus closed the laptop, and I realized the bartender had already exchanged my empty glass for a full one. I took a sip.

"This is messed up," Marcus said. "What if the Believers are right?"

I had a hard time accepting that. "The governments must know what they're doing."

"You've seen evidence to the contrary over the years, haven't you?"

"Maybe Hunter has a contact in the—"

"In the what?" The billionaire had sneaked up behind us so quietly, no one even noticed. "Military? Homeland? Attorney's office? Take your pick, I know someone, but what would you have me do? Walk in and tell them aliens are coming, and I might have the only lead on how we can prevent our utter destruction?"

I almost dropped my beer but recovered. "Wait. What

did you just say?"

He pulled at a stool to my left, and I slid over, making room. "Why else are we doing this, Rex?"

"I thought you wanted to find this Bridge."

"The whole purpose is to make contact. It always has been," Hunter said.

"With whom?" Veronica asked.

"We don't know, but Hardy had countless theories. He anticipated that we'd been visited by otherworldly beings thousands of years ago. They left us the means to the Bridge, spread apart by such distance that it would be next to impossible to gather them all unless we had the technology, which would indicate a certain intelligence level."

"Classic concept," I said. "It makes sense. Only from what I read in my father's journals, they were each located by ancient civilizations, and almost all of them were revered at some point as artifacts from the stars to the locals."

Hunter's hand gripped my wrist at the mention of the journal. "You have his books?"

"I do. At home," I lied. I'd actually brought them with me, but I didn't want to let him know that. He'd take them, and I'd lose the connection to my father I'd only just found.

"What do they say?"

"They're short accounts of him and Clayton obtaining each Token."

"This is unbelievable. I funded him for years, and he wouldn't so much as..." Hunter peered at Veronica. "This is important, Rex. I don't know how much you've told our team, but I have a feeling that activating the Bridge is more imperative now than ever. The arrival of the Objects is like a ticking time bomb, and I fear that we'll be destroyed, should we fail." Hunter waved down the bartender and ordered Scotch. Neat. A double.

I cleared my throat. "I haven't told her much, Hunter, but I guess she's invested now."

His drink came, and he raised the glass. "To new friends."

"To new friends," Veronica said, but her face was whiter than before. The conversation had obviously affected her, and Marcus was tapping his foot on the barstool, his hands fiddling with his beer.

"We're going to be fine. We have four more stops, and then your guys will decipher the last location," I told Hunter, but he didn't appear to agree.

"Rex, I have some bad news on that…"

Marcus' phone beeped, and he cut Hunter off. "Uhm, bad news."

"What is it?" I asked, looking across the bar at him.

"I set an alert for local news near the town and airport in Madagascar." Marcus rotated the phone, and I recited the translation.

"*Three local men found dead.*" I read the rest, seeing a brief mention of Haja and Hasin, along with a picture of a third. "That was the man who led us to them at the airport."

"They know what we have," Hunter said, downing the Scotch with a tilt of his wrist. "If our guides overheard anything, you can be assured that the Believers know it."

I tried to remember what we'd said in front of the two men. "I think we're safe."

Marcus nodded. "Us too. We didn't tell Haja anything while you guys were at Tsingy."

"The Believers will have something to go by. And Hasin saw the Token, right?"

"He did," I admitted, "but what—"

"They'll double their efforts. Triple. He'll want to see this through," Hunter growled.

"Who? Who is *he?*"

"The leader. I don't know who's in charge any longer, only that he goes by Sovereign." Hunter said a few words in Japanese, and the bartender returned with the bottle. He left it without another word.

"I can't believe they're dead," Veronica whispered.

"Who's dead?" Tripp asked as he arrived. I'd noticed him sitting in the bar for the last ten minutes since Hunter arrived, probably trying to determine if there was anyone suspicious in the vicinity. That he was here talking to us meant he felt we were in the clear.

Marcus informed the ex-SEAL of our African guides' fate, and he flopped on the stool. "Can't say they were great people, poaching snakes, lizards, and lemurs as they did, but I wouldn't wish that on anyone. Especially knowing the cult would have interrogated them first."

I tried not to picture our Madagascar guides tied up at gunpoint. "What do you know about the Believers?" I asked him.

"Only what Hunter's told me. But from his description, they have powerful allies, and that means they've likely recruited people in my line of work. I've probably met some of them," he said.

"What's next?" Veronica asked.

"We move quickly. Faster than we wanted to. Because we must remain one step ahead of them. They won't know where we're going…" Hunter's words drifted off.

"They seemed to when we went searching for Castro," Marcus muttered.

"Astute point, son. Keep communication to a minimum. Don't tell anyone where you are, or why. No chatting to friends at home or trying to date while you're in Japan, no snooping on your ex-wife's Christmas plans. We have to stick together and find the last Tokens." Hunter said this softly, but his words held serious weight.

"We don't have the sixth, do we? We can't determine the coordinates," I said.

Hunter took another drink and passed the bottle across toward Tripp. Veronica grabbed it on the way and splashed some into her empty beer glass. "No. My team cannot determine the location. They think it's in North America, but can't be sure."

"So why do we bother?" Marcus asked.

"Because the Believers might have it already. We can't trust the Tokens in the wild. We must contain them, thus controlling the Bridge," Hunter said.

There was a certain logic to it, but my shoulders slumped at the connotations. If I couldn't secure all six Tokens, we had no means to access the Bridge.

6

"*A*re you certain you've managed to block the GPS?" Tripp asked Marcus.

"Definitely. It's not overly complicated," the younger man told him. "No one will know where we took this baby."

Veronica sat in the tour helicopter's pilot seat, and Hunter had chosen the one beside her. The rest of us cramped into the bench in the back, with Marcus taking the middle. "This is almost the same model as the ones I flew in Maui," she said. "Simple, simple."

She went over a checklist, her lips moving as soundless words emerged, and soon we were given clearance through the radio. Hunter spoke Japanese to the man on the radio, and Veronica lifted us from the concrete pad. There was room for a dozen other helicopters, with a few of them already departed for an aerial tour of Fuji and the surrounding area. This was big business, and another copter checking out the sites wasn't conspicuous in the least. My head was foggy from the late-night beers, but mostly from the stress of our revelation at the bar.

It was a clear morning, a contradiction to the crisp evening with light snowfall the night before. The sky was a brilliant blue, and I did my best to spot a single cloud, but failed. Mount Fuji stood straight ahead, a giant and picturesque reminder of how insignificant we were as humans.

Veronica took us on the normal path, heading around the city and toward Fuji. Below, lines of tour buses and private cars drove for the summit, and I spotted hikers moving for the base of the mountain as we veered off, heading west.

Veronica lowered, and I heard her voice through the headset. "Always wanted to see the Shiraito Falls."

They were spectacular, dozens of waterfalls dropping like silk into a crystal lake.

"If we're done ogling the sites, do you think we could move on to the target?" Tripp asked, making Veronica crane her neck to frown at the man behind Hunter.

"Smell the roses, Tripp."

We continued on, the journey taking a short time. The ground was snow-covered the farther north we traveled, and I stared out the window, seeing Fuji in the east, the presence of the mountain a constant in this region.

"I've rented the entire facility for the day," Hunter told us.

His money was good for a lot of things, including feigning private functions at places like the ice caves. Veronica found a safe spot to land, just on the outer edge of the empty parking lot. The entire complex was surrounded by thick forest, and I saw a single car in the lot near the entrance to the tunnels.

A woman ran toward us, her hair flying wildly in the wind. Veronica powered off the helicopter, and we exited, Hunter walking to the frenzied lady. She waved her arms around, obviously not thrilled with our choice of transportation. I couldn't hear their conversation, but eventually, she nodded before leaving in her car.

The blades slowed, and soon we were surrounded by a crisp silence. "Lava tubes? Dirk had some imagination," Tripp said.

"You're certain we're alone?" I asked Hunter.

"You'd be surprised how difficult it was to convince them to shut this down on such short notice." He smiled despite his complaints. "But it's done. Come. Destiny awaits."

The entrance was marked at the edge of the forest, dipping below a yard of earth. Tree roots broke through the ceiling, and I glanced up as we descended a handful of steps, gripping bamboo railing to steady myself. Veronica was hurrying, and Marcus chased after her.

I took a moment before entering to double check the GPS and saw the indicator close by. The coordinates were specific, but we'd still have some work to do to locate the Token once inside.

"Are you coming?" Hunter asked, and I looked around, realizing the others were long gone.

"Sure."

"Is there something on your mind?" he asked. It was strange seeing Hunter in jeans and an orange puffy jacket. He wore earmuffs, his hands adorned with thin leather gloves.

"There's a lot on my mind, but we'll have time to discuss that after we secure this Token." I patted him on the back and walked inside, careful on the wooden planks. It was quiet in the ice tube's entrance, eerily so, and Tripp was distributing hard hats. He was the only one of us to carry a pack, and I could guess what was inside it.

"Everyone stay safe. The ceilings are short, and it'll get chilly inside," Tripp said. "We don't have far to walk. These old lava tubes were created by Fuji a long time ago."

"This seems too busy a tourist location to leave one of the Tokens," Veronica said.

I didn't have the heart to mention where we were off to next. She probably wouldn't believe me. Hunter took the lead, ducking under a low-lying cavern opening, and we started down the manmade walkways. It was musty, and Marcus sneezed a couple of times. The sound was muted in the dense cavern. Metal railing lined the center of the passageway as we rounded a bend, and my helmet struck the rock.

Marcus laughed, but the distraction caused him to do the same, which made him laugh even louder.

"I'm glad this is amusing to you," Hunter said. "We're on the precipice of finding the second Token, and yet you're able to express your mirth."

For a second, I thought he was reprimanding Marcus, but his smile was genuine. He looked younger today and appeared happy to be part of the team as we explored the lava tubes. We continued on, and the air grew colder with each passing minute.

"The ice," Veronica said, pointing to the right, and I saw it. Thick frozen walls rose along the cavern stone, and the facility had placed fences around it, running the entire length of this passageway to prevent patrons from touching it. Lights shone from the ground every few yards, guiding the path.

We kept moving, but I stopped as I glanced at the GPS. We'd been inside for only a few minutes, but I noticed we were already heading in the wrong direction. "Guys. It's the other way."

"There is no other way, Rex." Tripp leaned over me, trying to see the device. "See?" He tapped the screen and then jabbed a finger at the wall behind us. "There's no route through."

Marcus had a flashlight and exited the trail, climbing past the fence. "Careful," I warned him, but he was already heading away from our group. With a sigh, I followed him.

"Just what I thought. There's an opening," he called

from around a corner.

"Stay where you are. We're coming." Water dripped from above, down my helmet and in front of my face. The ice was thicker, with long icicles stretching from floor to rocky ceiling, making them eight feet high as we arrived at Marcus' side. I checked the GPS and saw it was close, maybe three hundred yards in this direction.

"It's on the other side of here." Coordinates were only accurate to a certain distance, but it was clear the Token had to be across the tunnel. Unfortunately, our journey was blocked by thick pieces of ice.

Tripp set his pack down with a thump and unzipped it.

"Did you bring a hair dryer?" Veronica asked him, but he didn't reply. He pulled two ice picks out and tossed one my way. He handed Veronica a fine-toothed saw and assessed the obstruction before us.

"They're going to freak out when they encounter the damage," Marcus mumbled.

"Not if we're careful. They won't even notice until far later, and by then, we'll be gone," Hunter said as he set a gloved hand on the fourth icicle in. "This one. It'll give us space to slip through while still blocking the others, unless they walk all the way past the fence to look for damage." He glanced about, shining a light toward the fence we'd sneaked through. "Something tells me this area doesn't see a lot of foot traffic."

Tripp started at the top, swinging his pickaxe with surprising accuracy. It dug in, and he struck it a few more times before stepping aside. "You want to give it a go, Walker?"

I rolled my shoulders and swung, the pick slipping off target and striking the wrong icicle. I didn't let it dissuade me and tried again, this time sending a chunk of ice free. Once I built up a sweat, he took over, and in a few minutes, we had the top and bottom of the giant ice crystal severed. Veronica used the saw to finish the job, acting more delicately for the finishing touches, and it fell to the rocky ground, crashing into three large sections.

Marcus shone his light through, and his eyes lit up. "We did it." He was the first in, sliding between the remaining lengths of frozen water, and I slipped in after him. The room was cold, and my breath shot out in hurried misty puffs. His beam hit, the light reflecting wildly off the sheer formations. The Token was in here somewhere.

The room was small with all of us pressed inside, and Veronica stood close, her hips touching mine. "Where is it?"

It had been left here intentionally to be unearthed by the right person. That meant there had to be a sign, a label of sorts. The first one had been secured under a tree, growing where it shouldn't have been, so I sought an indicator similar in nature. I scoured the floor, with ice crystals over the rough tube surface, but found nothing.

I looked up, peering at the ceiling. It only took a few moments to see the etching, high enough to avoid being frozen and covered. It was directly above another corridor, one almost invisible until you were at the right angle. The mark was an ancient Mayan emblem, and I smiled, imagining Clayton or my father sketching the picture and handing it to Luis to use when he ditched the Token.

I was the first one through, the stone passageway pushing tight against my ribcage as I pressed between the walls, breaking free after an agonizing moment. My helmet's light guided me in the dark space, and I saw that the crevasse ran for another fifty yards or so, narrowly descending at every footstep.

"Stay back if you're claustrophobic," I called to the others, and no one else joined me.

It was so cold, ice crystals had formed along the rocky ceiling. The passage slimmed even more, and I sank to my knees, crawling over the stone floor for the end of the tunnel. By the time I reached the finishing point, my teeth chattered and my fingertips were numb.

"Where are you?" I asked out loud, but the Token didn't answer. My light illuminated the cramped area, but there was little more than lava rock coated in a layer of ice.

Perhaps I'd missed a marking somewhere, a tunnel I hadn't seen on the way inside. I retraced my steps, slowly and surely, until I returned to the start. Marcus' flashlight shone in my eyes, and I shielded them. "Tripp, pass me the ice pick."

"Did you find it?" Hunter's eyes were huge, his breathing labored.

"Not yet, but it has to be there. Probably buried in years of ice." That had to be it.

Veronica didn't look so confident as she rubbed her arms with gloved hands, shifting on her feet to stay warm.

"I'll be right back." I glanced at the tunnel again, not wanting to revisit the confined cold walls. But I did it, moving faster the second trip.

With as much mobility as I could muster, I hacked at the ice, pieces flying at my face. I kept hitting the surface, eventually making an indent. Sweat escaped my chilled body while I struck the ice, damned if I was going to leave these lava tubes without the second Token.

I heard Marcus calling for me, asking if I was okay, and I shouted with labored breaths that I was fine. Just a few more minutes.

The ice continued to separate as my arms grew tired. I ceased, letting the pick fall from my grip, and I stretched my fingers, leaning into the wall.

And I saw it.

The familiar hexagonal shape beckoned me from under a thin clear layer, and I laughed, the cackle of a madman nearing the cusp of his sanity. With a frenzied effort, I broke it free and slipped my glove off, wanting to feel the cold alien metal on my fingers.

We had the second Token.

---

*H*ours later, I was still shaking with a blend of excitement and trepidation. Our trip to Japan had been faster and more efficient than any of us had assumed. Hunter demanded we pack our things and head to the airport, before anyone caught wind of what the purpose of the ice tubes visit had been.

The Believers could be anywhere, and it was obvious Tripp was on edge since Marcus had advised us about Haja and Hasin's murders. Guilt had a funny way of surfacing. I'd dissociated myself from their deaths for the last day, but as we boarded the private jet, the pressure built, and I wondered how many more allies would fall prey to the cult's obsession before we'd completed our search for the Tokens.

"Everything good?" Marcus asked, taking the seat across from me. A private charter was so far removed from the regular coach flights and connectors we were used to, but Marcus acted like this was an everyday occurrence.

I peered behind me as the flight attendant chatted with Veronica near the cockpit doors. "Any word on the Objects?"

His computer was already out of his bag, and he opened the laptop. I watched Veronica as he checked his favorite sources, and smiled as she conversed with the

Japanese woman in English.

"Nothing to speak of, but we may encounter some issues in Paris," he said.

"Protests?" I asked.

"Looks like some group is rallying people into a frenzy, and the church is admonishing their claims. From the posts I've seen, things are about to get dicey." He turned the computer around and set on the table between us, positioning the screen so we could both view it.

The video followed a small group of people, holding signs, and walking toward Avenue des Champs-Elysées. They repeatedly chanted in French, and I attempted to decipher the phrase. "I think they're saying 'Come and save us.' These people hope aliens are heading for Earth?"

"You know the type. They're probably blowing off steam, desperate for a movement to stand behind. I dated a girl in college… she was always trying to drag me to some stupid event or another. Mostly it was a bunch of lonely kids using random causes to meet people. This is probably like that. See… wine bottles, lots of laughing." Marcus indicated another group joining up with our protesters.

"It's not like they have any foundation for a viable protest," I said.

"Don't they?" Hunter asked, appearing from nowhere.

"Not really. What good is jabbing placards into the air?" I waited for his response. Hunter took a seat at a couch between us, and the motion appeared to pain him.

"Rex, it's always them versus oppression. The youth against war, famine, the royals, the government. Throughout time, there have been anti-establishment factions, and nothing's changed. People do things differently in Western cultures, but as we've seen in our own country in recent years, no one is willing to stand by quietly while they feel a disservice is occurring.

"These Parisians want their voices heard, and it likely has naught to do with the mysterious Objects. Not directly. The Objects give them a reason to gather, their own deep-rooted issues the cause for protest, even if they don't know it."

"Subconscious protest?" Marcus queried, a smirk on his face.

"Of sorts," Hunter said. "This is peaceful." We watched the video, finding the group had increased to well past a hundred people. Some were laughing, others dancing and stalking the famous avenue, surrounded by glitzy storefronts. Men in expensive suits and manicured beards watched the procession from the sidelines; women in exquisite dresses cringed at the youthful mob storming their streets. "Do you see how they always go to the wealthy areas, knowing that they will undoubtedly receive media coverage? They also want the rich to take notice, to see that they exist. They want the government to remember that they pay taxes, that they have pulses and value to society."

I laughed as Veronica arrived with Tripp in tow. "What's so funny?"

"We're getting a lesson in civil rights by Hunter Madison in a private jet, en route to Paris from Japan. If that isn't a punchline to a bad joke, I don't know what is," I told her.

"Heed my warning, Rex. Paris may be calm at the moment, along with the rest of the cities around the world, but when these Objects are closer to our humble little planet, the story will progress from a walk in the park to a hike into hell." Hunter squinted as the lights dimmed inside the cabin.

Marcus closed the laptop, and we settled into the most comfortable airline seats I'd ever encountered and waited for takeoff. The flight was long and I, for one, was ready for some sleep.

"Any luck decoding the final location?" I asked Hunter quietly.

His eyes were closed, and I saw his lip flinch at my question. "Let's worry about locating the Tokens we know of, and deal with that another day."

He'd already suggested that the sixth would go unfound, but I was beginning to understand Hunter better. If he had the Case and five Tokens, nothing in this world would prevent him from solving the last piece of the puzzle.

I took the cue as we lifted from the airport runway and started our journey to the third Token in Paris, France.

7

*P*aris was one of my favorite cities, but I'd only visited it twice, and the second trip had been a quick stop. My mother had brought us when we were teenagers, telling my sister and me that we needed to experience culture, something more diverse than the bedroom community outside of Boston.

My mother was a shrewd woman with an English degree and an insane work ethic. She was always busy with a book in her hand, or working on a crossword puzzle in the years after my father vanished. The way Beverly described her was far different than my memories. Bev had been eight when Dad left, and I was three years younger.

Her perspective of things was always opposite of mine. She recalled the last time Dad was home with resentment. She'd overheard our parents fighting, arguing in their bedroom, and even swore Mom threw a vase at him, breaking their armoire mirror—whereas I remembered him picking me up, taking a break from loading a suitcase into his truck. He'd rubbed my head, mussing my hair, and crouched down, slipping his watch off. In retrospect, the most valuable gift of my life had probably been nothing more than an afterthought. I don't know what our conversation had been like, but I'd seen him drive away, pulling from the house, waving as he took off. Mom had been nowhere in sight, but Bev was gazing from the living room window.

She'd had tears in her eyes.

Bev had told me her viewpoint one day when I'd been around fifteen and was pining after his adventurous ways. She sat me on the deck and spoke in hushed tones, hoping Mom wouldn't overhear our conversation. I learned about Mom's secret worry that her husband had been stepping out, not just on her, but on his family.

She talked about that day and their fighting, reminding me he'd never truly been there for us. Her words were sharp-edged, and the manner in which she'd spoken of our father had hurt me deeply. I'd shouted at her, knocking my chair over as I dashed down the deck steps and onto my bike. I'd ridden out to Sleepy Grove Cemetery, and that was where they'd found me hours later, crying near Dad's gravestone.

I had no doubt everything she said was true. Dirk Walker had been a selfish man. A terrible father, and an even worse spouse, but despite all of that, I still longed to discover what had happened thirty-six years ago. I had the urge to explain to Beverly why her father had done what he'd done, and felt a sharp pang that my mother was gone.

Being in Paris brought it all back. The smells were the same as that trip when I'd finished the eleventh grade and Bev was done with her sophomore year at college. The temperatures were far cooler as I stared up at the majestic Eiffel Tower, the entire structure lit up. Paris had an air of excitement, and not just because it was days away from Christmas.

It was obvious there was a sense of unease in the people, but most appeared to believe the scientific community, as well as the government officials urging the population not to panic. The gatherings from the other day had ended without violence, yet Hunter was confident things would escalate eventually.

The hotel was a couple of city blocks away, and Tripp had suggested we stay in the confines and safety of the rooms, but I needed to stretch my legs.

I'd walked this very street with my mother, her forcing me to apply the French she'd insisted I learn throughout school, and it came in handy. I stopped at a café, rain dripping from the umbrella I rested on my shoulder. We'd come to this exact café, though the name on the awning might have been different twenty-something years ago.

It was dark outside, but the café was in full hustle behind clear glass windows. I watched as couples ate, smiling and laughing, waiters pouring rich wines and after-dinner cappuccinos.

Veronica bumped into me. "Are you going to go in or watch the happy people all night?"

"What are you doing? I thought Tripp put us under quarantine," I joked.

"Must have had the same idea as you." She looked up at the Eiffel tower, her eyes reflecting the million lights.

"Are you hungry?"

"I could eat." She smiled, and something my mother said to me on our first visit entered my mind.

Paris is romantic. You'll see that there are few places with such whimsy and possibilities. Everything feels different here. The wine is sweeter, the coffee richer. The food creamier. The love... Her hands had dropped by her sides. It was at that moment I'd first seen my mother for the sad shell of a woman she'd become.

Veronica waited at the entrance, and the maître d' plucked two leatherbound menus, motioning for us to enter. The lights were dim, the scent of roasted lamb and white sauces tantalizing as we wound our way past dining duos and groups of friends and family out celebrating a wonderful night in Paris.

He offered to take our coats, and I draped mine across the back of my chair. Veronica did the same with hers, and I couldn't help but stare. She wore a black dress, the neckline far more plunging than her usual practical blouses and travel gear.

"See something you like?" she asked coquettishly.

"I… I didn't—" I started to stammer. "You look lovely."

"One of my favorite designers is close to the hotel, so I figured I might as well indulge. It's not often I get to spend a night in the center of Paris, especially not so close to Christmas. And if the world is really going to end, why can't we enjoy our time here?"

"How do you usually celebrate the holidays?" I asked, not wanting to address her dire statement.

"Manhattan, if I'm around. I have a little sister. After my mom remarried, they had a kid. She's ten years younger, but of course, as things go, she's married with a girl of her own now." Veronica moved out of a server's way while he poured a glass of water.

"Tell me about it. Beverly's older, but she was always destined for a family. Here I am, closing on forty, and I've never felt farther from having my own family. I think I've missed the window." I didn't often let things out like this, but she was so easy to talk with.

"I doubt that, Rex. Yours just hasn't opened yet." She ordered the wine, and I let her choose, admiring how down to earth she was in the field; yet here she was, looking every bit the part of a socialite. "Don't tell Hunter, but he's buying."

"And this year? You weren't going home?"

"Wasn't planning on it. It's been more difficult every holiday season. Visiting New York with the snow and giant Christmas tree, and everyone skating in the park. I don't think I could handle it."

"My sister's kids are great and all, but the thought of sitting with a cup of coffee, watching them open a present only to drop it two minutes later and stare at a screen, is beyond me. Once every couple of years." The wine was delicious, and we ordered appetizers, duck foie gras, and a single quail pie, with crust so flaky, it melted in my mouth.

Veronica seemed distracted, fidgeting after the taster plates were cleared. "Something on your mind?" I asked.

She took a big drink from her wine glass and poured herself another round. "Rex, if I tell you a secret, will you promise to not to spread it around?"

When someone asks you that, there's only one option. "Of course. Mum's the word."

"I didn't happen to stumble upon you guys in Sydney," she admitted, a slight flush finding her cheeks. She took another sip and sat back, swirling her wine while avoiding eye contact with me.

I shifted in my seat, unable to stop the next question. "Are you with the Believers?" I said it quietly and stared at her, searching for a tell. It would make sense, with them so close to our trail.

She gasped, finally meeting my gaze. "Rex," she hissed, "how can you ask that? No. Truthfully, I've heard of them before, but only because of my similar interests."

"In cults?" I asked while the server brought our mains. Suddenly, I wasn't hungry, and I shoved it aside while the pollack dripping in sauce slid in front of me.

"The unknown. Aliens. Stuff Hunter Madison is pre-occupied with."

I sighed, finally understanding. "You wanted to meet him. Then you heard him mention a pilot and took your shot. Very admirable."

"What else was I supposed to do? Ask to see his

collection? Invite myself to his mansion?" She chuckled and poked a fork at her risotto, piercing a chanterelle mushroom. "I was the geekiest kid. *X-Files* posters on the walls, shelves lined with books about the solar system. I wanted so badly to believe there was more than what we saw each day. I was desperate for answers. When we moved to the city, I was so angry that my mother could take me away from my home."

I ate a bite of my dinner. "What made you upset?"

"A telescope." She stopped, chewing small bites of her food. She held an empty fork, and her eyes filled with tears. "Can you think of a more pathetic reason to be sad? A little girl crying because her telescope wouldn't work among the bright uptown lights of Manhattan. It wasn't that I had to leave all my friends behind or that I missed my bedroom. I pouted for months." A tear rolled free, but she didn't wipe at it.

I glanced at my watch, feeling a bond growing between us. "It was a gift?"

Her smile was so sudden, it almost didn't seem real. "How did you guess that?"

"Why else would you be so sad? How old were you?"

"Four when he gave it to me. It's the first birthday I can remember, but that might be because I've looked at the old photos my mom took a thousand times over." She fiddled with her designer clutch and pulled out a simple wallet hiding in the fancy red leather bag. She unfolded a picture, her thumb across the man's face. But there was Veronica, so young, her hair bright blonde. She was standing beside a telescope, and not a cheap department store version. This was the real deal. "It was the last birthday before he left."

I took a drink of my wine, trying to hide the creeping emotions of my own loss at her words.

"I still have it."

"The telescope?"

"Yes. It was one of the reasons I stayed in Maui for so long."

"It had nothing to do with white beaches or the lush tropical topiary?" I asked.

"Okay, that may have played a role. Rex, you're easy to talk to. I didn't know what to expect."

"You never did explain how you recognized me," I fished.

"Rexford Walker, son of renowned treasure hunter Dirk Walker. Anyone who's followed our illustrious billionaire's obsession knows of your dad, and subsequently, about you," she said.

The idea that anyone had interest in me was surprising. "I doubt that. It's not like my dad and Hunter's dealings were publicized."

"They're accessible if you know where to search." She drained her glass. "What do you say we go for a walk? Clear our heads."

I'd had enough French cuisine for a night and abandoned half of the fish on the plate. Veronica dropped a few bills on the table, and I smiled at the generous tip Hunter was leaving the staff.

With our jackets pulled tight, we grabbed our umbrellas, finding that the clouds remained, but the rain had ended. We chatted about inconsequential things as we walked down the cobblestone sidewalks, pausing to peer into storefronts, and ordered espressos.

It was late when we stopped, and I hailed a taxi to shuttle us to the hotel. I saw Marcus in the lobby, his chin drooped to his chest while he sat in an oversized chair. His computer was open, and I closed it, tapping him on the shoulder.

"Rex," he said. "What time is it?"

"Almost midnight. Where are the others?" I scanned the lobby, peering at the bar.

"Upstairs. Tripp didn't think Hunter should show his face. Too many pictures being taken around us." Marcus wiped his chin and stared at Veronica. "Were you guys…"

"We were both out and happened to bump into…" Veronica started to say, but stopped as Marcus rolled his eyes.

"Sure. How about we cut the—" My phone vibrated, and I heard the other various notifications beep on Marcus' and Veronica's too. We each checked our devices, reading what I assumed was the same message.

Tripp – *Get to Hunter's room. Number 913. Now.*

"He's giving us orders?" Veronica huffed.

"Must be important." I had visions of Hunter sprawled out on his bed, dead from his illness. "Has Hunter told any of you what he's suffering from?" We moved toward the elevators.

"Nope. I've tried to bring it up like you asked, but he isn't willing to share," Marcus told me.

"Cancer. Lymphoma, but they caught it quickly eight years ago. He fought it, and everything seemed to be in the clear—until a few months ago," Veronica said.

The elevators chimed, and the doors slowly opened. These old hotel elevators were usually cramped, and while I appreciated the quaintness and original aspects they offered, I always felt claustrophobic riding in them with other people.

"Where did you hear that?" Marcus asked.

"Like I was telling Rex tonight, I've been a long-time follower of all things Hunter."

"But my research didn't result with any hits about cancer," Marcus said.

"You need to do it the old-fashioned way. Like talk to

his in-house physician." She grinned as the doors opened on the ninth floor.

"No way. You spoke to his doctor?" Marcus held his arm out, letting us pass by him and enter the hallway.

She whispered the response. "His former doctor. And his old groundskeeper, and his chef."

"How did you find them?" I asked her.

"I learned who his accountant was and… made an appointment with him. You'd really be surprised by how trusting those spreadsheet types are. He went to get me a cup of coffee, and I snapped a few photos of an old personal payment schedule of Hunter's." She left us to ourselves, and Marcus stood frozen, his jaw dropped.

"We have to keep an eye on her," I told him.

He nudged me with an elbow. "I can see you've been doing a good job of that."

I ignored him, and we stopped at Hunter's suite. It took up an entire quarter of the floor, the door the only one in this corner of the hotel, and Veronica glanced at me before knocking.

Tripp answered a few seconds later, waving us inside.

"What is it? Have they tracked us?" I asked, observing Hunter's pale face at the kitchen island.

"No, but we have a problem," Tripp said. "Hunter, you want to fill them in?"

"The next Token… we won't be off to Hawaii as planned," Hunter said.

"Why not?" I asked, navigating past the room service dolly, which was stacked with empty gold-plated trays. Marcus found some untouched pastries and grabbed one, shoving it in his mouth.

"My tech team has a program running, constantly scouring the web for any shapes and items that meet our criteria for the Tokens. Now that we have the measurements from the first couple samples, they've made a hit." Hunter's voice was labored, and he took a drink of water.

Marcus plopped into the chair beside Hunter. "You've located a Token?"

"We have. In the wild."

Tripp brought over a tablet, resting it on its stand as he scrolled through a few images. "This man discovered it while hiking through Ni'ihau." It showed a fit man of about thirty-five standing on a boat, shirtless. Tripp scanned to the next picture and used his fingers to zoom on the tablet. "There's the Token."

I stared, unbelieving. "Are you certain?"

Tripp went to the next image, and it began playing as a video. The rest of the boat vanished, leaving the Token, which rotated, yellow lines encompassing the piece. Hunter jabbed a finger at it. "A software program has determined the size is precisely that of your first two samples. This is a Token, and he was at the exact location of its hiding spot earlier this year. Someone beat us to it."

"Who is he? Does he know what he has?" Veronica asked.

"Not as far as we can tell. He's probably using it as a paperweight. We must travel to Los Angeles as soon as we've recovered the Token hidden in Paris," Hunter exclaimed.

"He's a film executive. Works for one of the big guys and lives in Silver Lake." Tripp switched to a map of the area, the satellite image zooming onto a house with a long driveway and a kidney-shaped pool in the backyard.

"What's the plan?" Marcus asked. "Go in all covert style, masked up with guns?"

Tripp's arms were crossed, and he smiled as if that would make his day.

"Nothing of the sort. We've established that Cal Harken is holding a Christmas soiree at his house in three days time. What he doesn't know is that Frank Winkle and his lovely wife, Chantelle, have been added to the guest list as executives of the up-and-coming production company, Park Place Movies." Hunter's eyes twinkled.

"Who the hell is Frank Winkle?" Marcus asked.

"I am," I told him. "And I suppose my wife will be played by the flawless Veronica Jones?"

She rolled her eyes at my comment. "Hunter, couldn't you have made me the executive instead? And Rex my bumbling assistant?"

Hunter lost his smile. "I don't care how you get that Token; just do it. It wasn't easy to fabricate my fledgling fake movie business in order to garner an invitation. So you'll go to that party, drink a cocktail, and steal the damned Token from this Harken fellow before we depart to our final destination."

"And where is that?" Veronica asked bravely.

Hunter glanced at me, but I shook my head. "You'll learn soon enough," I said firmly. "In the meantime, we have a plan. But first, we'll scout the location in the morning."

Tripp tapped Marcus on the shoulder. "Okay, kid, give it up."

"Marcus, show them." I'd kept the details close to our chests, but we were mere hours from traveling onto the streets to search for the Parisian Token.

Marcus used the tablet, pausing before he finished adding the coordinates into the mapping system. "This is encrypted, right? No one can access anything?"

"Tight as can be," Tripp answered.

Marcus finished, and the map zoomed to a spot in the center of the second arrondissement. The Louvre was only a few blocks from there, but the location didn't seem right. It took us to a simple street with nothing notable around it. We'd obsessed over this before we'd left home, but Marcus seemed sure we'd find a secret marking to identify where Luis had hidden the Token when we searched the region.

"This is it?" Veronica asked.

"That's what we have. We'll know more when we see it tomorrow." I yawned and checked the time. "Or today."

"Everyone to bed. We'll convene at eight in the morning," Hunter said.

I stopped by the exit and faced Hunter and Tripp. "I think you should stay here tomorrow, Hunter. Your face is too recognizable. If anyone sees you waltzing around with me in Paris, we'll be ambushed in minutes."

He pursed his lips and stroked his white beard before responding, "What do you think, Tripp?"

"He's right. We'll do it." Tripp seemed hesitant. "You'll linger inside this room, and don't answer the door for anyone."

"I am not a—a child," Hunter stammered. "I can handle my own affairs."

"You've seen what the Believers can do. You hired me for protection, and I'm suggesting you listen to my advice. I've dealt with far worse than a fanatical cult."

I watched the exchange with interest and appreciated the manner in which Tripp handled his employer.

"Fine. Get to bed."

As I walked to the elevator, it felt like eight AM would come far too quickly.

8

*M*arcus walked across the street, rain pouring off his umbrella. "This sucks."

It was a miserable morning, doubled in its effects by our moods. We'd scoured the street for an hour already, finding no discernable markings or hints of the Token's location.

"The coordinates are only an approximation. Plus, these buildings are renovated. It could have been moved during a remodel," Tripp said, kicking at a bike fence. We were half a block from a café, and the smells of espresso and breakfast pastries wafted over despite the downpour. "Maybe we should go inside, regroup," he suggested.

"Fine by me," Marcus said. He walked quickly, his soggy shoes squelching with each step.

I started after them and checked to see if Veronica was following. "You coming?"

The rain fell harder, battering my clear umbrella, and a gust of wind nearly tore it from my grip. "Veronica!" I shouted, but she didn't acknowledge me. I stopped at her side, trying to see what she was staring at.

Water drifted across the one-way street, and I reached for her as a car drove by, not slowing as it splashed us, soaking me from head to toe. "What a jerk!"

Rain rolled down Veronica's face, and she smiled despite being bathed in water. "I think I know where it is."

"The Token? Where?" I asked.

Her finger pointed to the sewer drain along the sidewalk.

"In the sewers?"

"Why not? The coordinates show the position, not the depth." She beamed at the revelation, and I pulled her into a hug.

Someone honked at us, and I grabbed her hand, directing her to the sidewalk. "You did it. Now we just need to figure out how we access them."

The café was a warm respite from the morning storm, and we joined Marcus and Tripp in a booth closest to the kitchen. Their jackets dripped on the floor, hung from another table's chairs, and we added ours to the pile.

"I say we ask to speak to the building manager. They might have…" Tripp stopped as he looked up at us. "What has you so happy?"

"Veronica thinks the Token is in the sewers," I said.

"And that makes you pleased?" Marcus asked. "Way I see it, we can't go into the sewers in the middle of a rainstorm, not to mention in the heart of a city like Paris. There has to be some…"

"Bring up the map. See what can be done," I told Marcus, and he took out his computer.

I headed to the till, ordering four hot drinks and an assortment of pastries. By the time I returned, Marcus' expression was grave. "The sewer is there, but…"

"But what?" I asked, sliding the tray to the center of the table.

"Have you ever heard of the Catacombs?"

"Sure, the *Catacombes de Paris*. Pretty famous tourist spot," I said. My mother hadn't allowed us to visit them on our trip, despite my incessant begging. "They're intricate, with tunnels and caverns spreading out under the city. Many are unmarked and blocked off from public use, but they're down there." I plopped into the seat beside Marcus and saw the map of known tunnels, with the city map overlapping.

"And you're suggesting there's a section of the catacombs underneath our coordinates?" Tripp sat across from us with his hands wrapped around the warmth of a coffee cup.

"It appears so, but it's not part of the publicized network," Marcus said.

"How do we access it?" Veronica asked.

"No clue. I doubt that kind of information is easily available online."

Marcus began to search, but there was a glint of curiosity in Veronica's eyes. I could see the wheels spinning. "What is it?"

She blew on her drink, sipping it before responding. "One of my clients mentioned coming to Paris. He hired some locals to escort him into the catacombs. He filmed the whole thing. I guess there's like a whole world under Paris. They once found a cavern with a bar and movie theater in an abandoned region. It's also super dangerous."

"Collapses?" It was something we were used to in the archaeology field. Everything was always underground, and years of weather and water tended to make things unsteady.

"Those are a possibility, but also people. My client was fine, though, and he had a great time."

"Can you speak to him? See where he obtained the tour guide?" I asked.

"Hunter said no outside contact," Tripp barked.

"He also wants the Token, doesn't he? I'll send him a message." Veronica's phone was in her hand a split second later, her fingers moving quickly over the screen. "Done."

I didn't like the idea of waiting around. "Now what?"

Her phone beeped. "These kids love texting." She tapped it and read the message while we all waited impatiently.

"What does it say?" Tripp asked.

"I guess they call them cataphiles. People who enter illegally and hold parties, or just graffiti inside the caverns. He met one at a nightclub. A place called Charme."

"Nightclub? We don't have that kind of time," I said, not thrilled with delaying this mission any longer.

"Unless you have a better plan, we head to Charme and ask for Juliette tonight."

"And if she's not there?" Tripp asked.

"Then we find another way."

————————

*T*he music was far too loud, and I felt like one of the oldest people there. The truth was, even as a college student, I'd hated going to late-night bars. I'd always preferred the quiet, comfortable pub-style establishments, with the sound of pool balls clacking and darts being thrown into colorful boards.

Marcus walked with a cocky gait, and Tripp loomed behind me like a stone wall. His gaze darted around, and I was almost surprised the big man at the doors let us in at all. Veronica had mentioned her wealthy client, and the man softened, opening the velvet rope for us.

The joint was packed, and I guessed most of the young people were done with school for the semester—or maybe it was always like this in the heart of Paris at midnight.

Kids with glowing makeup pressed past me, aiming for the dancefloor, and I searched for a place to talk to a bartender. I noticed a bar behind a growing line of patrons, and moved for it.

"*Veuillez m'excuser. Urgence*," I lied to them, pretending to have an emergency, and a few people let me by until I was at the front of the line. The bar was busy, and two men prepared complicated drinks with a kind of casual ease that told me they weren't in a hurry to get things done.

I spoke in French and waved the closest bartender down.

"What'll it be?" he asked without making eye contact.

"I'm looking for a girl. Juliette. You know her?"

"I know a lot of girls. And a few Juliettes."

I reached into my pocket and slipped out fifty euros. I passed it to him across the bar, and he finally glanced up, the bill disappearing as quickly as it came. He didn't say another word, just pointed to the stair leading above the bar.

I nodded, and saw Veronica near the dancefloor. "I think I found her!" I shouted, and she came along, leaving Tripp with Marcus.

The pumping music got quieter as we ascended the stairs, and a group of twenty-year-olds hung out on a few leather couches, a bottle of liquor centering the table and a lot of empty shot glasses sprawled out.

I walked up to them, scanning the group, but it was Veronica who seemed to know how to introduce herself. She changed her entire persona, her hips moving to one side, her foot stance shifting. "Juliette?" she asked, her voice light and airy.

A couple of guys glanced at a purple-haired pixie cut, and we had our target. I spoke French again. "Juliette, we'd like to discuss something with you."

She slinked away from the men, moving from the couches. "Are you American?" Her voice was throaty, her English fairly smooth. I caught the eye of one of the guys, and he frowned at me before returning to his quiet conversation.

"We are. We're looking for a guide," Veronica answered.

"Are you? I don't do that kind of thing anymore," she said, and turned her back on us.

"Wait. Juliette, we'll pay," I said, loud enough for her to hear me over the music blasting below us.

She paused. "I have money."

Veronica had already asked her contact what he'd paid Juliette for the tour, and it was substantially less than what we were about to offer. "Three thousand euros."

She stiffened, and even though she was facing the other direction, I could sense the smile building on her face. Before I had to do any more convincing, she spun on her Converse heel, jutting her hand out. "Deal."

---

*T*he streets were almost silent, or as quiet as they could be in a city like Paris. No matter the hour, there would always be the ringing of a distant siren carrying across the vacated cobblestone roadways. We'd explained our destination to Juliette, and demanded she stay off her phone for the duration of the journey, which she'd hesitantly accepted.

Tripp held on to her phone, and I was almost surprised someone would concede the lifeline and walk into the underground with four strangers like this, but our guide seemed unperturbed by any of it. I suspected Veronica's presence gave us a credibility we wouldn't have had otherwise, and I was once again glad for her company on the team.

"We cannot enter near the destination, but I think we

can find it below," she assured us in English.

The area was rougher here, and I was happy the rain had ceased as we strolled down the road, hugging the old stone building's wall as we crept to the church. It stood like a Gothic monster in the night. I had no illusions that the building wasn't spectacular in the sunlight, but everything turned sinister as the dark night sky cast its shadow across Paris.

Footsteps in an alley drew my attention, and I hurried forward as I saw a man shuffling toward us. He mumbled in French, and we continued with Tripp in the rear, covering us. The streetlights were few and far between as we wound around the church, and finally, we broke from the protection of the narrow street into a courtyard. A statue rose from the ground, a plaque attached, probably describing the saint's significance and what year it had been erected.

The church had a central spire, with two more rounded on either side. The symmetry was beautiful, and even well past midnight, there were lights emerging from the front doors.

Tires squealed behind us, and a black car skidded to a halt at a red light. It was the only vehicle on the street, and it drove off in a hurry when the lights changed. The entire operation was filled with tension, which was why I preferred to do these things in the daytime.

But Juliette claimed there would be no eyes on us as we entered the catacomb tunnels from beneath this church. We took her word for it and walked as a group around the courtyard, to the rear of the building. I spotted a man smoking near a side entrance, his foot planted to hold the door open, and the burning cigarette spun from his hand, hissing in a puddle of water. Then he was gone.

The back of the church was nearly as well-maintained

as the front, and Juliette moved with grace for a secondary building. The doors were high and metallic, gates with a chain and padlock wrapped around the handles.

"How do we get inside?" Marcus asked as he tested the gate. The chains rattled loudly.

Juliette shook her head in annoyance and slid bolt cutters from her pink backpack. She winked at him as the padlock fell into her palm. "Leave it to the pros."

And we were in. "What is this place?"

"Lots of the old churches had crypts hundreds of years ago. Don't mind the bodies," she said with a grin, and we began to descend wide stone stairs.

The air cooled the lower we went, and the floor leveled out. The walls were dark gray, and the main room was lined with a series of carved stone pillars, reaching up to a domed ceiling. Juliette didn't leave us time to explore as she hurried across the floor, ignoring the heavy blocks that would be stone coffins. Some of them had markings, carvings at the fronts; others had effigies sculpted on top of their casket lids.

"This place is creepy," Marcus said softly, making our guide laugh.

"If this scares you, you might want to stay above ground," she said. The room ended, and we walked through an arched doorway, which took us down another flight of steps. We repeated this process a few more times, and I noticed how Marcus stayed in the middle of the pack as we went.

Tripp and I held flashlights, and Juliette kept hers on as she finally stopped. "This is where the crypt exits into the tunnels. There are a handful of skeletons, but we'll pass a major burial site eventually. Should be able to cross over to your location shortly after."

"Skeletons," Marcus whispered.

We exited the relative safety of the church grounds, and I instantly felt a chill. The ground was dirt, the walls narrow and confining. I touched the passageway, remembering the images I'd seen of the catacombs, with skulls and bones rising from the floor to ceiling. This was a different area, clearly, because it was nothing but stone and dirt.

"Which way?" Tripp asked, shining his flashlight left, then right.

Juliette walked past him, leading right. "Follow me."

Veronica caught my arm, and I waited while Marcus and Tripp continued. "Do you think we'll find it?"

"The Token?"

She nodded.

"Yes, I do," I told her.

"Not this one. I mean the sixth," she whispered.

The rest of our group was gaining distance, and I didn't like the idea of lagging behind in the catacombs. "Time will tell, but I think we have a shot."

"How? If we don't have the coordinates…"

"It seems to me Hunter has some serious detection systems in place. He found one of the Tokens from some movie producer's online photos. If the last Token is out there, he'll make sure we track it." My flashlight flickered, and I banged it against my palm. The beam shone brighter.

I tried to be positive about it. "Either way, you get paid, right?"

"Will it matter if these Objects are coming to destroy us?" Veronica asked.

"I guess you're right." I didn't want to think about that, not with so much riding on what happened in the next hour or two.

It was musky, and I found myself struggling to make a clean inhale. The corridors changed, the ground growing more even, the wall texture smoothing as we rounded a bend, and I saw our first skull. It was on the floor, fallen from its position. Marcus crouched near it, poking his finger into the eye socket. He fell back as a rat the size of a raccoon emerged from the jaw, scurrying across our path.

"What the hell!" Marcus shouted. "As if a skull wasn't bad enough." He bounded up, dusting his pants off. There were dozens more, the walls stacked high with various bones. "Whoever did this had to have long-lasting psychological effects."

"They didn't have a choice. The city cemeteries were too full, and storms were threatening the city's structure. The only way to ensure Paris didn't sink into the earth was to support it and bring the skeletal remains underground." Juliette's voice was haunting. Her eyes seemed yellow in this light, almost like a wolf caught staring from the forest.

I gawked at the remains, trying to imagine that these had once been people like me. They'd had lives, and families. They'd loved and felt pain. Now they were bricks in a wall.

"It's not far," Juliette said.

Tripp grunted, taking the lead in front of the rest of us. The corridors narrowed again, and we had to duck repeatedly, a handful of bones scattered here and there.

"Is this public?" I asked our guide.

"Not here. There's another tunnel this connects to. Right now, we're running parallel with it until it joins in a type of hub. Only we're lower, so it's easy to evade any patrols."

"Do they really patrol it?" Tripp reached into his jacket, and for the first time tonight, I wondered if he was packing. We had gone back to the hotel after the nightclub, and he'd spent a few minutes in the suite.

"Mostly investigate reports. Don't worry. This corridor

isn't on their list," she said with confidence.

Her steps were light, and her pace had picked up. Did she want to get this over with, or was it something else? I checked the GPS and saw we were half a mile away from the Token's predicted location. We passed a half-dozen doorways along this confined corridor, and Juliette slowed at each, almost as if she was expecting a skeleton to pop out and scare her.

"Does anyone ever go missing?" Marcus asked, breaking the silence.

"All the time," Juliette said. "Why else do you think people call the place the gates to hell?"

"I dunno. Maybe because of the millions of skeletons," Marcus muttered.

I held my GPS and saw we were shifting in the opposite direction to our target. I said as much to Juliette, but she only grinned at me as my flashlight cast over her. "There is no such thing as a direct route in the catacombs."

I don't know who noticed first. I saw the shadows lift from the wall, falling just short of my beam as Juliette slowed. Then I heard the voices. Laughter. A man speaking French, and the cigarette smell.

"What the hell have you done?" Tripp asked, and Juliette shrugged.

Footsteps echoed from the corridor behind us, and I turned around, shining my light in that direction. Two men approached, the ones she'd been with at the nightclub. Veronica was at my side, Marcus near Tripp, forming a circle.

"You're not really Juliette, are you?" I asked, feeling a fool for ever trusting the bartender and her word for it.

"Juliette is gone, but you'd be amazed at how many people show up at Charme seeking her out," the imposter said. Her accent miraculously vanished, and I heard a hint of Dublin in her tone.

A hulking bald man with a leather jacket appeared from the direction ahead of us, a cigarette still in his lips. A short woman with close-cropped hair and a neck tattoo stood defiantly near him, her gaze flicking between the four of us.

"What do you want?" I asked, trying to keep control of my voice.

"Usually your money, but I have a feeling there's another reason you've come. Maybe a treasure. Maybe a missing person. And if you're willing to give me three thousand euros for a simple tour, you must have a friend with deep pockets," Juliette said.

"You're mistaken. We just need to—"

I silenced Veronica by setting a hand on her arm. "We may as well tell them the truth." I didn't want this to turn violent. Tripp looked relaxed, and he hadn't spoken yet. This told me he was eager for action. He was probably harnessing his strength, ready to spring like a coiled snake. "We've been hired by a movie company to scout a location for a new flick. The government is dropping all kinds of red tape, and it was suggested this destination might be a safe spot to film a few scenes."

Juliette stepped back, her head tilting slightly as she listened.

"There could be more than ten thousand in it for you if you think you could get us in for at least three days without being seen. We'll have some gear, maybe these… fine people can help us carry it," I said, standing taller and adding in my cultured accent, trying to convey affluence and importance.

One of the guys behind me pulled a knife and mumbled something in French. "*Raconter des salades.*" He didn't believe us.

We'd given Juliette half the payment already, and the

rest was inside my jacket pocket. She'd seen it, and she walked forward, her sneakers quiet on the stone floor. She smiled at me and shoved her hand into my jacket, pulling the bills out. She handed them to the other woman, and leather coat pulled a gun.

I barely saw Tripp move. He rushed away and his arm flung out, striking the bulky man in the face. He spun, elbowing the guy's gut, making him keel over. The man with the knife lunged in, and I bolted at him, shoving him aside. Marcus was in his path, and the blade sliced my friend, who staggered back, striking the wall, knocking bones loose.

Veronica was already moving, grabbing hold of Juliette. The girl was slight, but she was fast. Her arm cracked against Veronica's face, and everyone halted at the sound of a gun firing.

Tripp held the big man's gun and pointed it at the ceiling, and motioned at Juliette, then the guy who'd cut Marcus. "Drop the knife." When nothing happened, Tripp aimed the gun at the perpetrator. "Drop the weapon!" His voice boomed in the corridor, falling flat against the dense space.

The blade fell to the ground, and I went for it, picking it up. The handle was warm and damp with sweat.

"What do we do with them?" I asked. The five thieves were in a line, with the four of us facing their group.

"I know what I'd like to do with them. Think anyone would miss these pieces of crap?" Tripp asked.

"We're not killing them," I told him.

"Are there more of you hiding down here?" Tripp asked them.

Marcus held his arm to his chest, his eyes closed. "You okay?" I whispered.

"Yeah, just a scrape. Nothing serious," he replied, and I nodded gratefully.

"It's only us," Juliette assured Tripp. She stared at the gun.

"What would have happened if we didn't pay you? How many bodies have you dragged and stowed in these tunnels?" Tripp stepped closer, and she pressed against a pile of bones.

"None. We don't kill anyone. We scare them."

"Here's what'll happen. Your friends are going to scatter, and you'll bring us in as promised. Then you'll leave, and all five of you will forget you ever saw us. Understood?" Tripp kept his voice level.

Juliette didn't move. Tripp fired the gun, a skull exploding from the impact. Juliette screamed and slammed her hands to her ears. The big guy started forward, but Tripp quickly aimed at him. "I'm not messing around. My boss tells me to leave you alive, and I'll do it, assuming you don't test my patience."

I almost smirked at him referring to me as his boss, but not quite. Things were still extremely tense in the catacomb's corridor.

"*Oui.*" The guy who'd brandished the knife was the first to depart. The other two men were right after, and the girl shrugged and apologized as she took off, leaving Juliette the only one of their gang left.

"Nice friends. They were quick to abandon you," Tripp muttered. "Come on. Take us the rest of the way, and you'll live to see another sunrise."

It turned out we were only a twenty-minute walk from the GPS coordinates Luis had left on the inside of the Caracas airport locker. Juliette clearly understood the layout of the catacombs, and we lowered another two flights of stairs, crossing under a bridge overhead before the path ended. Marcus' knife wound appeared to be superficial, and we tore a piece of Tripp's shirt off, tying it around his forearm.

"Is this a joke? Another deceit?" Tripp asked her, the gun ever-present in his grip.

"No. The corridors have secret passageways," she said, appearing to vanish. As I advanced closer, I saw the illusion for what it was. The wall looked the same as the opening, and we entered another hall. This one was colder yet, with water streaming from the ceiling. I thought about the street we'd been at in the early hours of this day, with the constant rainfall. This would be directly below that location, but perhaps a few stories under.

There were no skeletons here, just mud and slippery rocks and rats. I wondered what Luis had thought as he strode these hallways thirty-something years ago, trying to hide one of the Tokens. Had he seen my father using the Bridge? Was that why he was so adamant on burying them?

"Juliette, you were never here. Got it?" I asked.

She glanced at Tripp, and then to the gun.

"Lots of places to hide a body, pal. We don't have to let her go," Tripp said, and I hoped he was only trying to scare the woman.

"I won't tell anyone. I have no reason to."

"You might want to rethink your choices in friends. And maybe select a new career path," Veronica said. The other woman had already run off with the second half of her payment, and I decided this scammer might consider it hush money.

"Take the cash and leave," I ordered her.

She didn't need to be told twice, and I watched her dart through the doorway, hearing her shoes rush across the stone floor.

"Marcus, you're tracking our path?" I asked, and my sidekick nodded as he pulled out his phone with his uninjured arm.

"Got it here. We're good to escape."

"That just leaves the reason for this whole mess." Tripp shoved the gun into his belt, and we proceeded forward.

"I'm impressed," I told him.

"What? Back there? It was nothing."

"If you say so." I peered to the walls, then the ceiling, searching for any markings.

And there it was. A jaguar claw, like the symbols under the causeway at El Mirador. It was carved into the bumpy partition, pieces of dark stone chipped away to form the emblem. Water dripped over it, and I followed the flow, finding it creeping behind a stack of skull-sized stones. "Give me a hand with these."

Marcus bent over and, despite the cut, used both hands as we attempted to relocate the pile, which appeared to be supporting the wall. Structurally, I doubted it was, and imagined Luis here, rolling the stones into a neat line, then placing more on top. It looked purposeful.

With all four of us on the case, the removal was quick, and soon the dirty sack's corner stuck up from the mud. Without a second thought, I dug with my bare hands, freeing the bag. I grinned at the others, Tripp's flashlight illuminating the sack as it spun in my grip. I passed it to Veronica, and with a flick of my blade, I cut the bottom out, letting the Token fall into my palm: a half moon over a spoon shape.

"Let's leave," Veronica whispered.

They exited the room, and I waited, using a rock to bash the etching Luis had carved from existence. When the claw was gone, I grabbed the flashlight on the floor and splashed after my team.

The third Token was in my pocket.

9

*T*wo more days. Time was strange when you traveled around the world in such a short period. I struggled to remember what day of the week it was as I stared at the vast ocean from the window. Hunter had a property in Malibu, but he didn't dare use it.

"And why can't we hide at your mansion?" Marcus asked him.

"Because they're watching it. Waiting for us to screw up," Hunter said. He was clearly exhausted after the last week or so, and I wondered how he was coping.

Francois, his serving man, stepped into the room, holding a cell phone. "Sir, the doctor is here."

"Yes. Yes. Let him in. Do you mind if I have some privacy?" Hunter pointed to the living room's exit.

This might not have been his mansion, but it was a large rental with five bedrooms and an infinity pool, complete with a theater room and games area. Marcus was the first to stand, and I glanced at the bandage on his arm. It was healing up nicely, and I'd already apologized for my part in the injury.

I hadn't seen Veronica yet today, but there she was, outside on the deck, lying in the sun. While this was cold for most of the locals, it was far warmer than we were used to, and she soaked up the rays, wearing a tank top and tights.

"I should be the one to get the Token," Tripp muttered, leaning against the glass railing to stare at the splashing waves.

"You have the grace of a black bear," Veronica said without opening her eyes. "Old Rexy can really ham it up when he needs to, can't you? Harvard-educated."

"You don't live in Boston and mingle with the stiffs Rex does without picking up a few things," Marcus said with a laugh.

"I'll be watching," Tripp finally said.

The wind picked up, and water sprayed my face as I made my way beside the ex-SEAL. "You can sound really creepy, you know that?"

"Keep it together, Rex. Tonight is important. It's not like barreling into the stone forest or smashing an icicle. This is covert business, and you can't break character for a moment." Tripp was tense about something, but I didn't know what.

"Why are you suddenly so invested in this trip?" I glanced at the living room to find Francois gazing at me. He closed the blinds with a snap, but not before I saw the doctor at Hunter's side.

"I was hired to watch over the team and protect Hunter Madison. But the longer I'm around all this, the more I'm believing what he's spouting." Tripp took a seat beside the pool, between Marcus and Veronica.

"You think the Objects are coming to destroy us?" Marcus asked him.

"I don't know about that, but it's possible the Believers do, and they're fanatical. Deadly. I've seen proof. From what Hunter has compiled, they're so deeply rooted across the world that we could be in some serious trouble when they decide to flip the switch." Tripp's jaw clenched. He hadn't shaved since the beginning of the journey, and he was starting to appear feral.

"Flip what switch?" Veronica sat up, rubbing her bare arms as the clouds rolled in, obscuring the warmth of the sun.

"Hunter suggested they have members in high places. Once the Objects arrive, he's positive they'll enact a protocol. Self-serving, of course. If the cult is here to welcome our destruction, that means chaos for the human race." Tripp nervously tapped his foot as he watched the pool.

"Damn. If Hunter's right, what control do we have over any of that? The Tokens will offer no power against zealous government officials," Marcus advised.

"No, but if there is a Bridge, maybe our answers lie within it," I whispered, peeking toward the living room again.

"No one's really explained what that means. What does Hunter expect to unearth across this Bridge?" Veronica slipped a hoodie on and began pacing the poolside.

"I think he expects help." They all looked at me as I said it.

She continued the inquiry. "Help? From whom?"

I shrugged. "Damned if I know. There was a reason my father was so invested. We've been trying to determine what Hardy was referring to in his journal, but it's a bunch of scribbled madness."

"You have Brian Hardy's journal?" Veronica asked.

Had I even told her who Hardy was? I tried to scan our interactions but failed to recall. "Sure we do. Marcus is trying to decipher it, but so far, nothing."

"Have you shown Hunter?" Tripp was back on his feet. Everyone was exhibiting far too much pent-up energy.

"No, we haven't. We were keeping it to ourselves," Marcus told them.

"Why?" Veronica barked. "Aren't we on the same team?"

I walked over to her, grabbing her by the hands. "He has a lot of secrets, and he's been candid about his associations with the cult. If we want to see this through, we need each other, but he'll cut our throats as soon as he gets what he wants."

Tripp was there, shoving me. "If you have a journal he should see, show him."

I stood my ground. "Tripp, back off."

"Enough, boys." Veronica came between us. "I do agree with Tripp, though."

"About what? Showing Hunter the book?"

"Rex, they may be right," Marcus said. "There's a reason this language is getting zero hits on the server. Because it doesn't exist online."

At first, we'd assumed it was a cipher, created by Hardy to keep the book a secret, but now, after listening to them, it was possible it was something else. "It's written in the alien tongue." I remembered hearing *Across This Great Nation* with Bill McReary while he interviewed the woman claiming to have been in the Believers cult.

Tripp grimaced, but Veronica appeared excited. I looked at Marcus and nodded. "Bring the book."

———————

*B*y the time Hunter emerged from his bedroom, it had been dark for two hours. Despite our insistence that we had something the man needed to see, Francois wouldn't permit his disturbance, so we ordered in dinner and waited, not so patiently.

Veronica wore a slim dress, her heels strewn beside the

door. I wore a custom-tailored suit Hunter ordered, which had only involved taking measurements with Marcus' help. It had arrived hours later, fitting like a glove. The midnight-blue material felt too flashy for my usual tastes, but that was what Cal Harken expected from his guest list.

Veronica was a knockout with her blonde hair pinned up. She'd spent an hour in the master bathroom, using an assortment of blow dryers and curling irons. I hardly recognized our team member as she came downstairs, but she could probably say the same about me.

"What is it you need to discuss?" Hunter asked as he walked out of his room and down the hall.

"We have to leave soon, but Marcus and I wanted to… there's a bit of information we didn't disclose earlier," I admitted to him.

After his rest, Hunter seemed renewed, but he was frowning, likely upset about his meeting with the doctor. We were in the living room, with Francois disappearing down the hall.

Hunter rapped his knuckles on the wall. "Get on with it, Rexford!"

Marcus held the journal we'd discovered at Hardy's condo and jumped up, handing it to Hunter.

"What's this?" The old man's question didn't need answering as he turned the pages. His knees buckled, and he caught himself on the back of Tripp's chair. The military man hopped up, guiding Hunter into the seat. "How did you—"

I walked closer, my palms rubbing together nervously. "Is that what we think it is?"

"This is his theory on the Bridge. Or better so, the Sovereign's theory. Written in the Unknowns' language."

"The Unknowns?" The word sounded sharp on Veronica's tongue.

"That's what the Believers call their saviors. The race they believed once lived here. Settle in, everyone," Hunter said.

I glanced at my watch. It didn't match my suit, but there was no way I was parting with it. I never did. "We're going to be late."

"Rex, no one arrives at these shindigs on schedule. You'll be fine," he told me.

I sat on the couch beside Veronica, and Hunter snapped his fingers twice. Francois appeared, crossing behind us to retrieve a bottle from the bar. "Are you sure you should be drinking?"

"Rex, you'll need one to hear what I have to say." Hunter accepted the outstretched glass from his serving man, and Francois set the bottle and other glasses on the table, indicating that we could pour our own. Tripp did the honors, distributing the drinks.

"We've been moving so fast, and I haven't been as clear-minded as I'd like. But it's time to spill the proverbial beans, as it were." Hunter sipped his drink, and I did the same. My hand trembled slightly as I lowered the glass. "These are the facts as I know them. The Believers suggest a race was here long before humans. They aren't certain whether we originated from their stock, but many treat this like gospel. There are sub-segments of their cult, with a multi-faceted ranking system."

"They all agree that the Unknowns arrived ages ago, when the face of the planet was far different than it is today. It's suggested they created the spark of life and left us to develop, with plans to return one day."

"Why leave and return? What do they want to accomplish?" Marcus asked him.

"I'll tell you it is not philanthropic. They say the Unknowns want slaves, beings to control, and that is why they exist. The Believers want to be the middlemen in the transaction. They think their group will act as an intermediary, and while the Unknowns pillage our planet, they'll be rewarded for the ease with which the matter occurs."

I finished the drink, setting my glass down. It slipped off the table and landed on the hardwood, nearly shattering. "Sorry."

Hunter just kept talking. "There was no indication of how they would come back to Earth, or when, but it was obvious they were anticipating it over the last few decades. It began with this…" He tapped the book. "Hardy knows their language, but I'm rusty. It was never something I considered factual. To me, they were making it up, a design to sound advanced to the newer acolytes. It'll take me some time to determine what the journal says, but I will. And we'll be steps ahead."

I picked up the glass, refilling it. "And you think it all points to the Bridge?"

"Hardy learned about it from somewhere, and it wasn't the Believers. He picked up a trail, probably left by various truth-seekers in the generations leading up to your father's discovery of the ancient Tokens." Hunter was flushed, and he leaned into the couch, cheeks puffing out.

"There were other people searching for the Tokens?" Veronica had been quiet, but it was evident the wheels were spinning. Her gaze danced between me and Hunter.

"Dirk claims there were clues about their locations, dating back as far as ancient Egypt. He thinks the first appearance of a Token was in Karnak among artifacts on a shrine to the god Amun. They would have been unaware of its function, but the mere fact that it was there indicated that someone from long before had kept it as a prize.

"It's likely the Tokens would have passed hands countless times across the ages. Wars, vanishing civilizations, advancing technologies pushing out old beliefs. Dirk and Clayton had a knack for following leads, so once their noses were on the trail, they hunted each of the Tokens down like bloodhounds looking for a possum on their farm." Hunter stared at his glass, rotating it in his fingers.

"They thought it would work?" Veronica asked him. "Clayton, and Rex's dad. They trusted the Bridge was real?"

"I had many discussions with Dirk about it. Clayton was more reserved. He preferred to stay in Dirk's shadow, and that seemed to suit them both fine."

"Did my dad believe he was going to use the Bridge?" The breath caught in my throat while I waited for a response.

"No, not at first. But he saw it as an opportunity to do what he loved and make money in the process. He was a treasure hunter, a real-life adventurer. He was initially going to do as our contract stipulated: locate the Case and Tokens, and hand them over. But Dirk changed in those years. He had a family and, from what I gathered, had an altercation with someone in the cult. He cut me off shortly after, despite my demands that what he held was my property. I thought he'd come to his senses, and before he departed on that last trip to Portugal, he assured me that I could join them. He thanked me for my patience and funding, and apologized for his actions." Hunter smiled as he recalled the conversation.

"But something happened," I whispered.

"I suppose so. Dirk and Clayton fled, and from what we can gather, they had hired this porter of theirs to disperse the Tokens in some very difficult locations," Hunter said.

"And what's your theory for this?" Tripp hadn't touched his drink; he swirled it in the glass.

"Dirk was caught up in it. He needed to see the Bridge for himself. And if it was real, he wanted to hide it from the world so no one could find out what the other side held. If he'd left the Case as-is, I predict he could have returned to Earth."

I was thrumming with energy and glanced at the time. We were already thirty minutes late for the party.

Tripp finally drained his bourbon and frowned. "I've heard some wacky stories this month, but there's something you seem to be discounting."

"What's that, Tripp?" Hunter asked.

"These Believers… I think they tracked Dirk and this other guy's movements to Portugal. They found them with the Case and shot them, burying the bodies where no one ever located them."

I pictured my dad standing in a cavern with the starlight pouring through the open-air porthole to the sky. I closed my eyes, imagining two men dressed in black, entering with guns raised: before any discussion erupts, they fire, killing Clayton and my father. The Case clinks to the stone floor.

"That can't be. Why do we hold the Case? How did Luis have the Tokens?" I stood abruptly and headed for the door.

"Maybe Luis was in on it. One of the Believers?" Tripp suggested.

"No way," Marcus interjected. "We were down there in Venezuela. If the Believers knew about him and the Case, don't you think they'd have a better hiding spot than a pond inside a mine shaft?"

Hunter slapped the arm of the couch and grinned at me. "We're not finding our answers tonight, but with any luck, you'll locate the fourth Token. You two know what is needed, and don't forget to cover your tracks."

Veronica was at the door in seconds, with her

shoulders bare, and she grabbed a shawl from a hook near the exit. Francois abruptly entered from the front of the house, surprising both of us.

"This way." He'd put on a tuxedo, and he indicated we were to join him in the black Mercedes idling near the doors.

"At least we can ride in style," Veronica said, striding elegantly for the parked car.

Cal Harken's house was subtle from the driveway. Lush landscaping hid most of its front, and it was only when we entered the doors that we saw the expert craftmanship. This was the house of a young movie executive trying to break through in the competitive and nepotistic film industry.

Francois drove away in the car, leaving us stranded. He'd assured us he'd be close, and to text him the moment we needed to flee. We'd scouted three rendezvous points, varying from the front drive to the street behind the house to the gas station down the hillside, in case we were caught and had to make a dubious escape.

A young man in a tuxedo asked if we wanted to check any coats, and we turned him down, entering the foyer, which led to a large group of guests mingling. Many of them seemed to know each other, talking confidently and casually about politics or some movie they were trying to break ground on.

These houses were older, with low ceilings and compartmentalized rooms, making the place feel crowded. "Remind me why Hunter didn't just call Cal and propose to buy the thing?"

It was a good question, and Hunter had his reasons. "How was he going to start that conversation? I was stalking the internet when I saw the hexagonal shape in the background of your shirtless photo?"

"You're kind of sassy, aren't you?" Veronica slid her arm through mine and kissed my cheek lightly. "Just play nice, hubby, and we'll be out of here in no time."

Most of the people were talking in the living room, which opened up to unfolded patio dividers. Christmas music played in the backyard, and red and green lights were draped around the entire deck. The view was astonishing, with the classic hill views you could only manage in California. Most of the guests were middle-aged or older, with a few younger ones spread out, talking loudly with one another. I spotted a man eagerly discussing his newest film project with a clearly disinterested man. His companion was knocking them back, with four empty martini glasses piled up on the patio table.

"Do you see him?" I whispered.

"Not yet. Wait, that's his wife."

I followed her gaze to where Mrs. Sarah Harken was smiling at the couple in front of her. She was probably only thirty, with curled dark hair dusting her shoulders. She seemed to catch us staring and excused herself, coming to greet us. We'd descended the deck steps onto a wonderful courtyard. A wood-burning fireplace sat in a stone wall, and guests milled about, some choosing to sit by the warmth.

"Have you decided on a drink yet? Henry makes the best Old-Fashioneds," she said amiably. She walked us to the bar and kept talking. "I'm Sarah, Cal's wife. I assume you know Cal?"

"Not yet, but that's the purpose of the invitation, I think. My company has interest in working with Cal on a top-secret project, and we're all very excited about it," I said, mimicking the tones I'd heard on the pass through the house. Everyone had unbridled enthusiasm for the craft, their voices hitting octaves usually reserved for the theater.

Sarah perked up at this, and I had a feeling this house, the affluent neighborhood, and the fancy cars were something they'd stretched their budget to afford. "I didn't catch your names."

"Frank Winkle, and my better half, Chantelle," I said, putting Veronica on display. She gave a brief curtsy motion, which wasn't fully possible with the tight dress she adorned.

"Nice to meet you. What'll you have?" she asked.

The bar was built into the courtyard, and the man behind it waited for our orders. Veronica asked for red wine for both of us, and he nodded, pouring from a dark bottle.

"Is Cal close by? I'd love to put a face to the name." I peered around the yard, searching for him.

"He's here. You never know with him. He's always talking business with someone." Sarah seemed to catch herself oversharing and smiled again. "I'll let him know you're looking for him." She waved at two newcomers and grinned apologetically. "I have to go, but hopefully, we can connect later."

"Thank you for coming to say hi. And you have a lovely home," Veronica told her.

"Thanks, Chantelle." And she was off.

"Nice work," I mumbled. "Let's get inside and see where his study is."

Her heels clipped across the square and we returned up the stairs, me ducking to avoid the hanging lights near the top. I said hello to a few people, chatting with an older man about the beautiful out-of-season weather like I belonged, and finally returned into the house. Most had ventured outside, and I heard Sarah's voice trying to gather everyone's attention.

"I think the hosts are trying to move us to the courtyard," I told the few people in the living room, and they grabbed their finger-food plates and glasses, almost leaving us alone in the house.

"Nice work," Veronica said, kicking off her shoes. "I hate these things." She left them at the end of the hallway and padded for the bedrooms. It was a ranch house, and I stopped near the bathroom, hearing the toilet flush. The door sprang open, and instead of looking like snoops, I pretended not to see the woman as I kissed Veronica. She pressed against a bedroom door and let out a groan as we made out.

A few seconds later, she pulled away. "I think she's gone," Veronica panted.

I smiled, dabbing my lips with a sleeve. "I'm sorry. I panicked."

"I'm not complaining." She turned and tested the handle. It unlatched, and she entered the space. It was a guest room. I scanned the furniture. A twin bed with far too many pillows. An antique dresser with a vase of flowers and a candle. A closet. I went for it, opening the doors to find quilts and more cushions.

"Not here."

We exited into the hallway. The master would be through the end door, so we tried the next one, finding it open as well. "Cal's study," I said as we entered.

Framed photos neatly covered the entire wall, and showcasing Cal posed with numerous movie stars, some hot newcomers, others Oscar winners, but I ignored them all as I went to the desk. A laptop sat unopened beside a banker's lamp, and I flicked it on.

"If I was a unique metal souvenir from Hawaii, where would I be?" I asked out loud.

"He probably wanted to stick it on the mantel, but from the first encounter with his wife, she doesn't seem the type to have things out of place. Especially during a party." Veronica quietly sifted through his drawers, and we found the lower right one locked. The rest were stuffed with take-out menus, notes on napkins, and nothing remotely interesting.

I grabbed the utility knife from my pocket and sprang it open, making quick work of the cheap security system. The results were confusing. Inside were handcuffs, a necktie, and various contraptions I didn't picture his put-together wife, Sarah, partaking in.

"There it is," Veronica whispered, indicating beyond a clear bottle.

"Grab it," I told her as I watched the door.

"No, you—" Footsteps cut her off.

I snaked my hand into the drawer, clutching the Token before sliding it shut. Veronica was already searching for a hiding spot and opened the closet doors. I sprinted in behind her and struggled to pull the second panel shut as the study's entrance opened up.

"What are you doing?" a woman's voice asked.

"What do you mean? I'm making some alone time," Cal Harken said. I saw his face through the slats in the closet. The woman was most assuredly not his wife, and I judged her to be a good fifteen years younger than him: a young starlet looking for her first big break.

"Sarah's here, Cal." The girl put her hand on his chest, and he grabbed her wrist.

"I don't care. She's preoccupied with her little party." He kissed the girl too roughly for my liking. I could smell the booze on him from here and saw Veronica tense as the

Nathan Hystad

young woman struggled to break his grip.

"Cal, not now. You have a house full of—"

"Listen, Brittany," he said.

She slapped him, stopping his train of thought. "It's Brettanie, and I'm leaving."

His palm slammed the study door closed, and the girl gasped.

I was about to burst from the closet when Veronica beat me to it. She crossed the room with three quick steps and grabbed Cal by the collar, tossing him to the side. He hit a bookshelf and fell to the floor, his face shifting from shock to anger in a flash.

Cal tried getting to his feet, but I was on him, shoving him with my shoe's heel. "Not today, buddy. Here's what's going to happen. Brettanie leaves, and you'll go enjoy the party. You didn't see us, and you'll never touch her again." I pointed at the girl, who was wiping her wet cheeks.

"Who the hell do you think—"

I opened the study door. "Sarah! Would someone find the hostess, I think she might…"

"Okay. Okay!" he hissed. "Just get the hell out of here. All of you."

I smiled, making sure the girl went first, and we left abruptly, leaving Cal to recover inside. The Token was in my suit jacket pocket, and I could feel the metal shape pressing against my chest right where my tattoo was.

"Who are you?" Brettanie asked, her fake eyelashes fluttering.

"We're your guardian angels, so take this as a sign from heaven. This world isn't for you, sweetie," Veronica said in her best motherly voice.

The girl nodded, gathered her stuff from the valet at the door, and disappeared down the drive.

"We should leave," I said. The living room was half-full again, with guests tiring of Sarah's speech, and some-one had moved Veronica's heels.

"Rex. Time to go." Her voice was small, and I glanced up, seeing recognition in one man's eyes. His suit was dark gray, his hair styled lavishly, but it was the same guy, the one from the black BMW in Boston. I'd only spotted him through tinted windows, but it was him.

"Damn it." I turned, trying to be casual as I pulled my phone out. I texted Francois the number 2.

Veronica was out the door, barefoot, and I slipped the attendant fifty bucks. "Anyone comes after us, stall them."

He looked at me, then at the money, and nodded with a smirk on his face. And we were off.

Ten cars were tightly parked on the front drive, and we broke onto the street at a full run. It was dark, with the moon high in the sky. A pair of headlights shone onto the street, and tires squealed as Francois raced toward the house.

Behind us, I heard the commotion as the attendant earned his cash. The Believer fell, tripped up, and a woman tried helping him to his feet. He slapped at her arm and pulled a gun.

"Stop!" he shouted as the Mercedes skidded to a halt. We started climbing into the back seat, and the passenger window opened.

I heard the gunshots before I saw the 9MM in Francois' grip, and he pulled the trigger twice. The Believer fell to the ground before he had a chance to retaliate. I stared at his lifeless body, his own gun lying a short distance from his unmoving hand.

The car sped forward, tearing through the neighbor-hood, and after a few detours through side streets and around precarious corners, Francois slowed, pulling the car behind a grocery store. "No surveillance here," he said casually, and exited the car.

"You killed a man," I said, trailing after Hunter Madison's resourceful employee.

"Yes, I did. Would you prefer I let him shoot you?" He pressed a key fob, and another car four down beeped as the headlights blinked. "Move."

It was an older entry-level model, and we didn't hesitate. Veronica took the front seat, as if being closer to Francois and his gun would be useful. Sirens finally sounded, and we waited while two police cars sped past the parking lot before he fired the engine up.

"Did you get it?" he asked finally.

My heart raced in my chest. "We did."

"Good. Mr. Madison will be pleased."

10

*T*he living room seemed smaller as I paced around it, my hands unable to relax. "This isn't good. Your henchman killed that guy, right in front of witnesses," I blurted. Francois had dropped us at the hotel before speeding off in the borrowed sedan.

"Do you think so little of our operations, Rexford?" Hunter sat on the couch, eyeing me cautiously.

"What the hell is that supposed to mean?"

Marcus and Tripp were quiet as they eavesdropped from a distance, neither willing to exit the kitchen.

"It means everything is taken care of."

"Go on. Talk us through it, Hunter," I urged.

"Fine. The Mercedes was bought by Francois from a chop shop, the plates lifted a few hours ago. The sedan is a burner car, already heading under an overpass farther down the Five. The four houses nearest Cal Harken's home were using the same surveillance security company, and I've paid to have the footage deleted due to a software glitch." Hunter looked pleased with himself.

"What about us? Our faces?" Veronica asked.

"You hardly resembled Veronica Jones and Rex Walker, did you? You were Frank and Chantelle Winkle, working for Park Place Movies—which, you will find, no longer exists in any capacity." Hunter went to stand, and groaned as he began to walk. "If you'll excuse me, I need sleep." He stopped near the hallway, turning slowly. "Before I go, can I see it?"

I reached into my breast pocket and pulled the Token out. I rotated it and stared at the engraved symbol. It looked like the letter R, but upside down, with a wave that could be a simplistic bird above it. "This is it. The fourth Token."

Veronica grabbed it from me, walking it over to Hunter. "I hope this is worth killing a man over."

Hunter smiled, just enough to show part of his teeth. "My dear, when we have all six, you will see. And we'll learn how important this genuinely is. And that man is a Believer. By your description, he's one of the Sovereign's most trusted hitmen. You say he's the same man that had been trailing you?"

"That was him," I reassured Hunter.

"Then more will come. When word hits the Sovereign that his sidekick is gone, he'll retaliate."

"How did they know about the party? What aren't you telling us?" Tripp asked from the kitchen, breaking his silence. Hunter was starting to lose control, and the trust of his group.

"I can't know everything. I set these precautions in place because I don't want anyone to calculate our steps, but they have a knack for predicting our movements. It could be—"

"Don't say it," I muttered.

"The cult leaders have always suggested there might be advantages to attuning."

Marcus walked out, holding a cup of coffee. "You're not saying these weirdos are seeing the future, are you?"

"No. Nothing of the sort." Hunter rotated the Token and kept looking at it as he spoke. "Attuning is mostly a meditation, an art they plan on using to connect with the

Unknowns. If you ask me, they're full of it, but they did predict the arrival of the Objects, so who knows for sure?"

I crossed the living room, not willing to leave the Token in Hunter's possession. I had the rest in my bag, as was part of the arrangement. He frowned with his fingers latched around it, and finally returned it to my palm. His hand trembled as he passed it to me. I almost expected him to call the Token his "precious" and scurry down the hall.

"What do we do?" Marcus asked.

"We keep on," Hunter said. "Get some rest and leave in five hours. Everything has been arranged, and Veronica, I'll need you to pilot the jet. I'm afraid that with Christmas in two days, finding someone to shuttle us to Punta Arenas was impossible."

He walked off, reaching out to balance himself as he ventured toward his room.

Veronica leaned against the back of the couch. "Punta Arenas?"

Marcus nodded, bringing out his phone. "Rex, can we tell them? If we can't trust Tripp and Ronnie, then who's left?"

I almost didn't grasp who he was talking about, but he'd shortened her name. "Go ahead. We'll be there soon."

Marcus indicated a spot on his map. "There."

"Where the hell is that?" Tripp asked, squinting to see. Marcus zoomed out, and the location became obvious. "Antarctica! We're going to search for a Token in the South Pole?"

"That's about the gist of it," I said, grinning.

"Spending Christmas at the South Pole. You do realize that's the wrong end of the world, right? Santa's workshop is at the other Pole," Veronica quipped.

Jokes were good. It meant she wasn't freaking out from tonight, and the last thing we needed was our pilot losing grip with our final destination in hand.

"Everyone fine with this? I know we've come far, but if anyone wants to back out now, I won't hold it against you," I told them.

Tripp's arms crossed over his chest, and he lowered his chin. "Hunter will be pissed, though. From the looks of things, you don't want to end up on his bad side. I suspect he'd dispose of us without a second thought—not that I'd let him."

I contemplated the casual manner in which Francois had disposed of the armed cultist, and shook my head. "I suppose you're right. See you in a few hours."

Tripp and Veronica walked off without another word, and Marcus hung back with me.

"Rex, this is getting heated. What's going to happen when we find the fifth Token? Can we go home?" he asked, and for the first time, I wondered at that very answer.

"I don't see why not," I lied. Hunter wouldn't hurt us. I was almost sure of it.

"What about texting? I want to talk to my mom and dad. Tell them Merry Christmas before we're down south with no connection," he said.

Hunter had ordered us to refrain from any contact with home, but I didn't see the harm in it. Plus, I wanted to let Bev know that I was okay too. "Go for it. Just be quick about it."

He smiled and wandered off for his room. I sighed, checking the clock. Two in the morning. I used the washroom, enjoying the normality of washing my face and brushing my teeth, and ended up in my room ten minutes later with my cell phone in my hand.

I checked my email, finding a backlog of messages: some from Jessica, others from Richard, students, old friends and colleagues, and a string of unanswered texts from Bev. I hadn't been reading them because I was trying to focus on the Tokens, but I clicked the latest.

Beverly – *Rex, I'm really beginning to worry. I've heard from Richard Klein, Dad's old associate, and he's concerned you're into something dangerous. Call me!*

I read a few more and witnessed the growing anxiety creeping into her messages.

Rex – *Hey, sis. Sorry I've been incommunicado. Don't mind Richard. He's been acting peculiar. I'm fine. I'm almost out of cell range, so you and the kids have a very Merry Christmas. I'll be home before New Year's, and I'll come visit as soon as I'm close.*

I read the text and wondered about committing to a timeline. It would be fine. Once we found Token number five, I'd demand Hunter bring us home, at least until we figured out the next move.

It was past five in the morning for Bev, and I didn't expect her to read the text for a couple of hours yet. Instead of going to sleep, I went to my browser, reading headlines. The phone showed me some big news from the last places I'd visited, and I scrolled over talk about protests in Paris and an emerging alien watch in Sydney. The image displayed a group of people, half of them with aluminum foil wrapped around their heads. I was about to shut the phone off when I saw a caption describing a fire in New York.

I clicked it and almost dropped the cell. There had been a fire in the building across from the Museum of Natural History. It had started on the ninth floor, and half of the residents were affected.

Brian Hardy had lived on that story. The Believers had gotten to him.

Before I could tell Marcus, Tripp was calling through my door. "Boss man says we're moving." He banged on it twice, and I heard him shout the same message into Veronica's room, adjacent to mine.

———————

We landed bleary-eyed and beat. The trip had taken longer than we'd hoped, with delays at every corner. Landing in southern Chile had been simple, but departing in the smaller commissioned plane for our final destination in Antarctica had proven more difficult.

A storm hit, a deluge so heavy, Hunter had to bribe someone to eventually let Veronica take off. The subsequent flight had been shaky, but our team member proved how valuable she was, unflinching in the face of danger. I, on the other hand, was white-knuckled and silently praying to anyone that would listen for most of the flight.

"Where is this place?" Tripp asked as he stared into the white expanse through his tiny window.

"Private research base. Their funding recently ended, and everyone vacated a week ago," Hunter advised him.

"Convenient," I mumbled.

"Very." Hunter had a way of getting what he wanted. Whose pockets did one line to evacuate a small research facility in the middle of the South Pole?

The base was visible from the landing stretch, which was thankfully clear of piled snow. Considering the barren landscape, the landing had been smooth and effortless compared with the rest of the flight.

Veronica shut the engines off, and we opened the door after donning our parkas, boots, gloves and hats. It was cold outside. Not just cold, but freezing beyond anything I'd ever imagined. The base was only a few hundred yards from the plane, but in this temperature, it seemed like a deadly distance.

"This isn't natural!" Marcus called as he jogged for the research camp.

It looked cold and lifeless on stilts in the snow. The lights were all off, and snow drifted along the outer edge, coming almost as high as a window. The complex was larger than I'd expected, with a main building and three smaller portable units. We made for the primary research facility, my eyelashes already frozen, and Hunter stopped at the entrance. There was a keypad with ten digits, and he blankly stared at them for a moment.

"Don't you have the code?" Marcus asked, and Hunter waved him away.

"Quiet. I didn't keep notes. I didn't want anyone to find the information," he said.

The cold was already seeping into my bones, and I wiggled my toes inside the boots while I flexed my hands. Hunter tried a four-digit code, but nothing happened.

"Come on, Hunter," Tripp said. "You must have remembered it."

"Yes, I'm afraid my medication…" He turned, peering past me at the sun, which didn't set this time of year at the South Pole. It reflected brightly off the pristine snow. He whispered to himself, and we tried to give him space. I was already considering how we could break into one of the portables using what we had on us. Hunter finally returned to the lock, and with a smile of triumph, it clicked after receiving the proper code. "I knew I'd have it. Just took a moment to thaw out my brain."

We hustled inside, and it was far warmer, though nowhere near comfortable. It was clearly insulated, but when I tried to turn the lights on, they remained powered off.

"Do you have a manual?" I asked Hunter.

Marcus set his pack down and stomped through the

front entrance. "The maintenance room should be over here."

"I'll see if I can help." Veronica dropped her bag and followed Marcus. She used to be a mechanic, and I suspected that would help today.

The office was clean, with three long desks lining the far wall. Five swivel chairs sat empty, two of them facing the exit. A series of screens had been left behind, and a couple of keyboards lingered on the desks. Behind them were bookshelves, full of hardcover textbooks and research material.

The windows were tall, showcasing a beautiful bay a short distance from the facility. Before I'd had a chance to investigate any other rooms, the lights flickered on, then off, and stayed on a moment later.

Marcus let out a cheer from somewhere, and I heard Veronica laughing. Radiators clinked near me, and I smiled as heat emitted from the pipes. It was probably a good thing the research team had recently departed the facility.

Various Christmas decorations were up, with a miniature tree decorated near the living room. It was plugged in, and the moment the power was on, it started blinking white lights. They hadn't planned on leaving for home until Hunter had pulled some strings.

Marcus and Veronica entered, my sidekick looking far too pleased with himself. "Told you I could do stuff."

"I never doubted you. Not for a second."

We explored the base, finding two rooms with bunks: four beds in one, two in the other. Hunter and Tripp claimed the smaller, and Marcus called dibs on the top bunk over mine. Veronica smiled as she removed her oversized winter gear. I wore jeans with long underwear beneath, and a thick sweatshirt, while Marcus rifled through his bag to grab a hoodie. We were all going to be wearing multiple layers to stay as warm as we could.

"Still cold in here, no matter how high you crank it," he said, donning the warm fleece layer.

"Rex, can I speak to you for a moment?" Veronica asked, and Marcus slinked from the room, asking where the food was.

"What's up?" I asked.

"I…" She sat on the bottom bunk, stretching her legs as she regarded me with bright blue eyes.

"Go on. You have something to say."

"I haven't told you everything." Her hair was in a top bun, and pieces of it stuck out the sides, a wayward strand falling over her forehead.

"That's not surprising. I haven't told you everything either," I said, trying to make this easier on her. She was struggling to reveal a secret to me. "Wait. You're not going to tell me you're the Sovereign, are you?" I laughed, but Veronica didn't smile. This was serious.

"Nothing like that. Honestly, I've heard of the Believers, but they always seemed like phantoms. Not real."

"Then what?"

She swallowed, and I sat beside her, taking her hand. It was cold, but she didn't try to pull away. "I didn't know when to say it, because Hunter would have…"

"Come out here!" Tripp's voice carried from the living room, but I stayed put.

"What are you trying to tell me?" I asked.

Veronica looked at the exit. "It's not like I wanted…"

"Now!" Tripp's voice was louder.

"We'll talk later, okay?" Veronica stood, dashing out of the bunk room.

I followed, finding Tripp holding a satellite phone. "They're here."

"Who is?" I asked.

Hunter's eyes were wide. "They've found us. Despite our precautions, they followed us!"

"Wait, what are you saying?" I ran to the windows, searching for signs of someone in the blustery cold outside.

"Not yet, but my contact at the airport says the plane departed five minutes ago. The Believers are coming for us. They must know we're about to get the fifth Token, and they're making their move. This confirms my suspicion that they have the sixth already. I predicted they'd come for the Tokens when we returned to the US mainland, but they're losing patience," Hunter exclaimed.

Tripp's pack rested on the couch, and he unzipped it, pulling the M4A1 from inside. "We need to go now," he said.

"Where?" Marcus asked.

"To the Token. There's a chance we can recover it and leave before they land," Tripp said.

"No way. We've barely slept, Veronica has been awake for two days, and we haven't even checked to see if the vehicle is fueled up," I reminded everyone.

Veronica nodded once. "I can do it. You take the transport, grab the Token, and I'll bring the plane."

"Where are you going to land it? We haven't planned for the terrain," I said.

"I'll find a spot close enough to you. Don't worry about that. Hunter, you can stay with me," she told him.

Her expression from the bedroom had etched into my mind, and I feared betrayal from her. We'd spent a lot of time together over the last ten days or so, but she remained a stranger. She'd admitted to tracking Madison to Sydney, and God knew what she was trying to tell me just now. "I don't think it's a good idea."

"Too bad, Walker. It's the only one that has us leaving alive and with the Token. Hunter, you good with helping

Veronica?" Tripp asked our benefactor.

"I suppose I'll have to be. I won't be much use to you out there." He gawked at the exit, and I sighed.

Marcus ran for the bunk rooms, complaining about not eating as he gathered our things. When he returned, Marcus gave Hunter the destination on a tablet, and the old man clutched it like a lifeline. We dressed as quickly as we could, adding layers for the cold, and less than an hour after arriving at the research facility, we were leaving.

Once everyone was bundled up, we departed, Hunter moving for the plane. Veronica stopped and grabbed my arm while Marcus and Tripp ran for the garage.

"I'm sorry, Rex. I really am. If we make it through, I promise to tell you everything."

The air bit my nose, and I scrunched up my face while returning the scarf over it. "How can I trust you're on our side?"

"Have faith." She shifted closer and touched her forehead to mine, passing me a handheld radio before running for the airplane.

I heard the vehicle's engine turn on as I entered the garage, and grinned at the sight of the six-wheeled transport van. The tires were huge, with thick treads, and Tripp stood on the step up near the driver's seat. He passed each of us handguns, the same ones we'd taken out in Madagascar, and I shoved mine into my parka's pocket. I had the Tokens on me, and feeling the weight of the four otherworldly hexagons centered me despite our situation.

The Believers were coming for us.

The clock was ticking.

11

The Token's GPS coordinates were set thirty-seven miles from the research facility, which wouldn't have been much of an issue if there were roads. I wondered if this was what it felt like to traverse the surface of Mars in a dune buggy. It would be similar, with the exception that every direction was buried in ice and snow. I couldn't see any hint of vegetation as we drove inland away from the cove, and finally, the ground leveled out, with fewer jutting ranges blocking the wind from buffeting the vehicle.

I was in the passenger seat, with Tripp navigating the beast of a vehicle. The windshield stretched wide, giving us a good view as we drove across the snow-draped expanse. He went slowly, careful not to hit any rocks or jagged chunks of frozen earth. Ice formed along the corners of the glass, stretching like ghostly fingers trying to interlock.

"This thing could use some better suspension," Marcus complained from the back. He sat in the middle of the bench seat, not wearing a seatbelt.

"We're lucky no one took the keys, or we'd be screwed," I reminded him. The heater was on max, and still the windows were continually attempting to freeze up. We'd had some cold winters at home, but nothing had come remotely close to this.

Marcus leaned forward, his head sticking between Tripp and me. "You really think Veronica's going to be able to land?"

"If anyone can do it, it's her. I've seen some daring flying before, but I think that woman may take the cake," Tripp said. His praise for Veronica somehow made me proud, as if I had anything to do with her skills.

"She's downright crazy," Marcus muttered. "I thought we were goners, coming to Antarctica."

The van jostled, and Tripp threw on the brakes, sliding sideways in a fishtail before he gave it a little gas and recovered. The entire area sloped heavily, and he went with the grain until it leveled again. I checked the GPS and asked him to adjust the trajectory slightly.

"Tripp, you have a unique perspective. Why did they choose to attack now?" I glanced at the man driving, and he peered over, his brow set into a frown.

"Couple reasons. They do have one of the Tokens, as Hunter suggests, and they want to complete the task. What better way than to wait and have us do their dirty work?"

"So they know what we've been up to, and are anticipating our actions. Makes sense. If I wanted the Tokens and had no information to go by, I'd do the same," I said, and something clicked. "It's just like what you did to me."

"I already apologized for that."

"Are you sure we can trust you, Tripp?" Marcus asked, addressing the elephant in the driver's seat. "Or is it Hunter feeding them the info?"

"Don't worry. If you think this is me playing you guys, it isn't. I started this mission as a hired gun, but I've done work for Hunter in the past. I know full well he may be a little fanatical, but he's not stupid. He's as lucid as they come, and I've never seen him so worked up as I have these past two weeks. If you're asking if Hunter is legit, I'd put my money on it. If I still gambled."

"Why'd you stop?" I asked.

"I prefer a sure bet."

"Meaning you wait until someone else determines the winner, and…"

"Not like that. Hunter's a lot of things, but I don't think he's with the Believers. If he was, why all the pretenses?"

"Good point," Marcus said. "It would have been much simpler to kill us, take the coordinates, and send his minions to gather them up."

I grabbed a bottle of water from the bag at my feet and drank, suddenly feeling a thirst I couldn't quench. I passed it on and sank into my seat. "Even if we gather these five Tokens, what good does it do? We have the Case, but not the final piece."

"Hunter will track it. He always gets what he wants," Tripp grunted.

"He didn't thirty-five years ago, when Dirk took the Bridge without him," I reminded the ex-SEAL.

"Sure, and that's driven him harder. Any idea why Dirk left his sugar daddy behind?" Tripp stared at me, his gloves gripping the steering wheel tightly.

"Not the slightest."

"I bet someone convinced him Hunter was dangerous," Marcus said.

"Who?"

Marcus shrugged and settled into his seat. "Beats me."

"How much farther?" Tripp tapped the navigation screen, which was blank. I used my handheld and checked.

"Two miles." Wind shook the van again, and I gaped out the window to see a rocky blockade ahead. "We'll have to go around."

"Which direction?" Tripp started moving right, and I didn't stop him.

"I think this'll work." The engine struggled at the

incline, and we slid before the tires caught.

Tripp drove cautiously, and we finally rounded the rocky hills. He smiled and pushed the gas pedal as the landscape opened up. The sky was cyanic blue; pure white wisps of clouds floated in gentle layers in front of the glowing sun. It was peaceful, despite the harsh climate.

"I think we're in…" Tripp stopped mid-sentence as the van tilted at a sharp angle and stopped with a loud clunk. He attempted to steer out, pressing the gas again, but the tires didn't catch. "Damn it. We're hung up."

None of us had seen the hole, which had been half-covered by snow drifts, catching the van.

"This is just great," I said sarcastically. "We're half a mile from the Token." I pointed to the window. The Token seemed like it would be in the middle of an open field, flat and devoid of anything.

"As good a place to hide it as any. Nothing around here. No markers. Nobody would ever stumble upon it," Tripp mumbled. "I have no idea how long we can make it out there before we freeze our asses off."

"Hunter set us up for the weather." I patted the jacket, insulated with the best goose down money could buy along with the four layers underneath. My hat was wool, and I pulled it lower onto my forehead. My boots were lined and stiff, and I had on thermal socks underneath. Tripp fiddled with the fleece lining on his parka and flexed his fingers.

"It's going to be cold, and this wind is no joke. We stay together. I'll leave the car running. Veronica will be close." Tripp started for the exit, and I grabbed his arm.

"Hold up." I removed the radio from the console and tested it. "Veronica, come in. Hunter, do you read?"

It crackled, and we sat in silence for an excruciating ten seconds before I heard her voice. "Rex, what's the ETA?"

"We ran into an issue with the vehicle, but we're a half

mile from the objective. We're targeting it now," I informed her.

"Twenty minutes?" Veronica asked after I didn't really give her a direct timeline.

"Normally, I'd say yes, but… make it thirty." I looked at Marcus, who was shoving the water bottle into his pack.

"Roger. How is the terrain?"

"Flat, but could be some hidden dangers, not to mention the ice. Might be tough."

Tripp snatched the radio from my hand. "Veronica, Tripp here. Come in from the north. Wind is trouble, and that will give you the best cover and allow you to ride it, not fight it," he said.

"Roger."

And it was set. Marcus was the first one out, and I went next, instantly feeling the bite of the wind. I wrapped the scarf tighter and started forward. White flakes kicked up the moment I walked past the modified van, and Tripp was shouting curses as we strode in the direction of the Token.

Normally, a half-mile would take a couple of minutes at a jog, but we were walking into the wind, with a foot and a half of snow around our boots. Each step was a struggle, but we went on, determined to find the Token before Veronica arrived. I didn't expect it would be straightforward to land or take off from these plains, but I kept my worry to myself.

Marcus was the fastest of us, trudging through the elements like he'd done this a million times. Once again, I was impressed by his resilience and determination. The last Token. It was challenging to believe we'd only learned of those coordinates a few weeks ago, and here we were, seeking our last one.

I continued on, my eyes aching under the goggles. I squinted, almost keeping them closed, and tried to think about Beverly and Fred at home with the kids, warm in our childhood home with the Christmas tree lights on and the smell of a turkey baking in the oven.

Then I remembered hearing about Haja and Hasin, and the fire at Brian Hardy's condo in New York, as well as Castro's place. I'd been so stupid. If the Believers knew about me, they were definitely aware of my sister. I'd left her alone and vulnerable without a second thought.

I needed to warn her. To tell her to get to somewhere safe. Was it Christmas Day, or was that tomorrow? With the constant sunlight and the relentless traveling, I'd lost track of time.

"How much farther?" Tripp pulled me closer, his voice dying in the wind.

I pulled out the GPS device, but it fell to the snow. I plunged my glove in after it, wiping the flakes off the screen, finding it dark. "It's broken!"

Marcus had stopped farther ahead, hands on his hips as he waited, and Tripp plucked the tool from me. He rotated it, checking the underside, and hit it against his palm. The lights returned, and I could tell he smiled by the crinkling of skin around his eyes. He shoved it to me, and I signaled ahead. "Almost there. Marcus, a hundred yards that way!"

I returned it to my pocket and continued to think about Bev and her family. If anything happened to them… What about Marcus' parents in Florida? How deep would these Believers cut to obtain what they were after?

Marcus ran as the sound of the plane's engines echoed over the field of ice. We'd risen in elevation slightly, and the snow thinned, making the walk easier.

Veronica and Hunter had arrived, and that meant we needed to hurry. I imagined our pursuers were close, and I fully expected the cultists to be armed and prepared to leave our frozen corpses in the middle of nowhere Antarctica.

I stopped to check the GPS, and this was as accurate a location as we had. "It's here. Somewhere."

The ground was rocky, with ice chunks settled between any raised earth, and I spotted the bag sticking up from the shallow ice. "I got it!"

The plane flew low, the sound loud as I kneeled at the piece of burlap reaching for the sky. It was stuck, but Marcus already had something pulled from his pack. It was a slim pickaxe, one he'd found hanging in the garage. I took it, hacking at the frozen ground, trying to avoid the rocks as best I could.

"Rex." Tripp's voice was distant, and I glanced at him. "We have a problem."

Not the words you wanted to hear in a situation like this. My entire body was cold, the horrific weather creeping past the protection of my many layers. I shifted on my knees and kept chipping away with the hand-held tool.

"Rex, I said we have a problem!" He loomed over me, and I stared a short distance north, where Veronica was landing. The plane kicked up clouds of snow as it skidded to the ground.

"What is it?" I finally asked.

Tripp had his M4A1 out, his eye pressed to the scope. "Hurry. That's not Veronica!"

I understood what he meant when I saw the shape of the plane and the fact that it was far larger than ours, with a different logo on the side. This wasn't our friends; it was the Believers coming to steal the Tokens.

I scrambled with the pick, my heart beating so hard, I barely heard the pair of them shouting at me.

"Faster!" Marcus yelled. He had a gun in his grip, his huge mitten dangling from a string on his jacket.

I worked the ice and tugged at the sack with my other hand, banging tirelessly until I could pull it free. At some point, I must have torn the bag with the sharp edge, and the Token slipped out, falling to the rocks. I grabbed it without looking and shoved it away, safely beside the other four.

We'd done the work, and now the cult was here to claim the prizes. I hated them with a passion, this group of devotees who claimed to await the Unknowns' arrival. They'd lurked in the shadows for decades. Watching. Waiting.

But none of that mattered today. The Believers were here, and they wanted what I had resting inside my jacket. And they would stop at nothing to return to their Sovereign with the Tokens. But… the Case was with Hunter and Veronica on the plane, and I took a minor bit of solace in that.

"There are three of them," Tripp told us. Even from this far, I could spot their dark outlines against the white backdrop. "Can't recognize them with their ski masks on, but they're armed."

"What do we do?" Marcus' voice shook.

Their plane began to roll over the snow-covered ground, turning before halting. This meant the pilot was still on the vessel, making four of them.

"Three against four. I can handle those odds," Tripp said. "Time to hustle."

It was too cold to be exposed for much longer, and I noticed that he was heading for the van. I really had no clue what a military-trained killer like Tripp Davis would do in this scenario, but I never in a million years expected him to run. We trailed after him as he dashed across the field. My lungs burned with the cold, each breath growing more and more painful. Marcus had slowed down too, his eyelashes caked in ice. Air escaped the mouth hole of his balaclava in a haze, and I nodded, trying to send him non-verbal support. When I saw our abandoned vehicle again, still billowing exhaust from the tailpipe, I realized Tripp did indeed have a plan—not that I'd doubted him.

The others were probably five minutes behind us, and I was grateful for the respite. "Climb inside," Tripp said. "You have two minutes to warm up."

I didn't hesitate, opening the rear door for Marcus. I shoved in behind him and remembered we had a radio. It was toasty inside, and I unwrapped my scarf and lowered the protective neck shielding from my jacket. "Veronica! The Believers are here! They found us. We're at the van."

I paused, hearing something outside. Tripp was fiddling with the gas cap.

It was Hunter's voice that carried through the speaker. "Did you retrieve the Token?"

That was the only thing that mattered to him. "I have it."

"We're going to land. You'll need the backup," Veronica said, and I heard Hunter protesting beside her.

I shoved the radio into my parka, and Tripp knocked on the window. "Time's up!"

Marcus stared at me with fear painted on his face. "What the hell, Rex?" He still had the gun in his hand. "I can't do this."

"Sure you can. You remember what I taught you at the range." I hated using the cliché, but it was all that came to mind as I exited the vehicle. "It's us or them. I'm not dying today." I took the other P226 and dropped my mitten, gripping the metal tight with the insulated glove underneath.

Tripp splashed a bottle of liquid across the vehicle, and I smelled the gasoline as we approached the cover of the ridge we'd driven around a half hour ago. Where he'd sourced a tube to start the siphoning remained a mystery.

We pressed our backs to the cold rock, and Tripp chuckled as the three Believers entered our line of sight. They moved like soldiers, cautiously resting their semi-automatics on their chests as they checked out the vehicle. They were close enough that I could hear their voices but not make out the words. I stared at the trio wearing matching black jackets, possibly obscuring Kevlar vests. Their faces were indistinguishable with the dark masks, but they looked confident as the lead soldier opened the driver's door and turned the vehicle off.

Tripp grunted, aiming his rifle toward the group. "Ready?" he asked.

"For what?" Marcus asked.

"When it blows, we hit them. Got it?"

"Not really," I murmured.

"Follow my lead. Point and shoot. They won't expect this to work." Tripp began firing, but not at the soldiers. The bullets struck the side of the modified van, and the men tried to dash away. One of them slipped, falling a few feet from the vehicle.

Tripp's plan didn't seem to work, and I noticed the cultist relax slightly as he growled a laugh in defiance. My ally fired again, and the tank exploded. The concussion was so loud, rushing toward us with the wind, and I barely saw Tripp leave our side. The nearest man was on the ground, unmoving, and Tripp fired at the other two. I joined him, trying not to stumble on the rocky ground as I held the gun up, crossing the open space.

His assault rifle barked out bullets, and I fired at the man on the right, seeing Tripp's target was the adjacent soldier.

I missed the first three shots, and it gave my target enough time to return fire. I ducked, sliding on the snow as I fell. Tripp was still running, and I rolled around, taking aim again. I was facing the man, thirty yards away, and he was a much bigger bullseye than me.

His fire shot the ground a yard in front of me in a burst, and I stopped pulling the trigger, hoping he thought he'd hit me. I glanced to see Tripp's target fall to the ground, a red spray misting the snow around him.

"Drop it!" Tripp called. The guy who'd just been trying to kill me spun to face Tripp, and he snarled a remark I couldn't hear. "I said drop it!"

Another plane's engines roared from above, and I took a second to peer at the sky. It was Hunter and Veronica.

Marcus arrived behind me, holding the gun as I'd taught him. "You okay?" he asked.

"I'm fine."

Tripp was still yelling, but the man was unrelenting. Tripp jogged in the opposite direction, leaving us in the open. I took aim at the man's chest, trying to compensate for the wind and distance, but really, it was dumb luck that made the second tap of the trigger strike home. The man's gun went off as his other hand flung to his neck.

Marcus screamed as an errant bullet hit him, and I jumped to my feet, knocking my friend to the ground. The firing ceased, and I peeked to see the Believer drop his gun; blood soaked his hand as he pressed it to his collar.

Tripp was on him, kicking the weapon away and kneeling at the guy's shoulders. He shook the man as he interrogated him, but the man's chin lolled to the side. He was dead.

Marcus was hit, his leg bleeding at the thigh, and I wrapped my arm under his, helping him stay upright. He muttered and swore a few times, his thick layers of clothing blocking my view of the wound. "He shot me!" Marcus shrieked, and laughed, a hair-raising cackle.

"You're going to be fine, Marcus. Look, Veronica landed." I pointed to the plane directing toward us. In all the excitement, I'd forgotten about the pilot of the other plane. I grabbed for my radio and tried to use it. Nothing. Then I spotted the hole in my pocket and inhaled the scent of burning electronics. "He shot me too." Saved by a radio. I dropped it. "Tripp, we need to warn them. There's still another…"

The gunshot rang out loudly, causing us all to spin around. The van still burned, and the cultist we'd assumed had been killed in the initial explosion was on his feet, stalking us with an assault rifle raised.

I quickly stole a glance at our airplane and saw the figure creeping up behind it. "Veronica!" I called, but they were too far away, the wind coming from the opposite direction.

"Drop your weapons," the man near us said gruffly. He was limping, and a section of his jacket was singed. Despite the circumstances, my body was telling me I couldn't last in this cold for much longer. My breaths were labored, my feet and fingers numb. My friends didn't look any better than I felt.

"Why would we do that?" Tripp asked.

"We can all leave here alive," the guy said, and I thought his voice sounded recognizable. "My companion will be bringing your friends over, and we'll make this trade."

I saw Veronica and Hunter being ordered out of their plane by the fourth Believer, and hoped our pilot wouldn't do anything rash. These guys meant business, and we'd already killed two of their allies. The fact that I'd shot and killed a man didn't quite register in my brain. I was too cold, too concerned for my friends.

"We're not giving you the Tokens," I told him.

He hobbled closer, his gun unwavering in his grip. "I think you are."

We stood in a stalemate as Hunter Madison and Veronica arrived a few minutes later. She offered me an apologetic glance, but Hunter's eyes were wild as he surveyed the damage. Our gazes locked for an instant, and he finally spoke.

"You can have the Tokens," Hunter said.

The two remaining cult members went to stand near one another, with Hunter and Veronica still under the gun. "Good. Then we'll let you live." I struggled to recall the voice.

Hunter seemed to clue in. He turned to face the man and slapped his own palms on his thighs. "Francois! How dare you betray me!"

And it all suddenly made sense. The fact that the Believers always seemed to know where we were, or perhaps where we'd been. Francois must have been in contact with Hunter, and he was working for the Believers.

"You're surprised? I never was much of an actor." Francois peeled his mask off; his normally slicked dark hair was messy and clotted with sweat despite the freezing cold.

"Twenty years. You've worked for me for two damned decades, and now you're screwing me over," Hunter muttered. "Did they pay you off?"

Francois laughed loudly. "You think I've been bribed? I've been with them this entire time. Did you trust the Believers would let you escape and not keep tabs on you? They knew this day would come. That your obsession would lead them to the Bridge."

"Even if you take the Tokens, you won't have the Bridge," Hunter said. "You don't know the location. Not to mention the sixth Token."

Francois' composure fractured for a moment, but he

regained it. "That is all irrelevant, Hunter. You see… we only need to prevent you from accessing the Bridge. The Unknowns cannot be stopped, not with the Bridge sealed. But you were never a Believer, not in your heart. You were more interested in the theory of aliens than in our Unknowns. Tell me I'm wrong."

Hunter obliged and shook his head.

"That's your downfall. If you really understood what was about to happen, you'd have spent your life devoted to attuning and preparing for their return. The seas will boil, the people chosen for servitude. The skies will rain fire, and you, Hunter, will miss out on all of it."

Francois lifted his gun and fired at Hunter. The old billionaire was killed instantly.

My breath caught, and Veronica screamed, a curt noise to match the ferocity of the freezing wind. "Sorry. I couldn't let him live. Orders from the top." Francois actually smiled, and my stomach twisted at the sight.

The Believer behind Veronica shoved her forward, and she almost stumbled on Hunter's dead body. Tripp took the opportunity as the enemy soldier lowered his guard to catch her. Tripp shot him between the eyes.

Veronica fell to the ground, and Francois roared.

The servant angled his rifle up, aiming at Tripp as a report sounded from beside me. Francois was calm, peaceful even, before toppling over face-first into the snow. Marcus let the gun fall from his hand, his eyes barely visible through his frozen lashes.

"Hunter!" Veronica was at the old man's side, rolling him onto his back. I ran to them while Tripp ensured the others were indeed dead. Marcus didn't move.

"Veronica, he's gone." I tried to pull her away, but she reached into his jacket. Her gloves wrapped around a chain, and she tore it free.

"He told me to take this if anything happened to him. I can't believe he's gone." She cried, tears instantly freezing under her eyes.

"Come on. We have to reach the plane!" I helped her up and took one last look at Hunter Madison. He'd been so excited for this adventure. He'd spent decades searching for the Bridge, and my father had abandoned him all that time ago. He'd beaten cancer once, but the illness had a way of returning with a vengeance. He didn't deserve to go out like this. No one did.

"Rex, give me a hand with them." Tripp had started dragging the dead cult members toward the fire of the burning vehicle.

"Why?"

"Burn the evidence. We don't want anyone to know we were here," he said as he dragged Francois through the snow, leaving a streak of pale pink behind him.

"Veronica, help Marcus onboard. We'll be right there." She stood holding a small thumb drive on the golden chain and stared at it. I put my hand on her shoulder and pointed to the waiting airplane.

She nodded, and they took off, stumbling for the warmth of the idle plane. Tripp and I did our best to haul the bodies into the fire, and at last we hovered over Hunter.

"What about him?" I asked.

Tripp rubbed at his nose with his parka sleeve. "I don't know. I hate to be insensitive, but we can't take him home with us. We're going to have enough questions as it is."

I couldn't bring myself to burn him, so we lifted him away from the bloodshed and covered him as best we could. Tripp started away, muttering under his breath as he clutched his weapon to his chest, and I knelt next to Hunter.

He was just a mound of flakes, but I spoke out loud.

"I'm sorry this was your fate, Hunter. I know what this means to you. I will find the Bridge. Mark my word. I'll finish what you started, I promise you. Your life work won't be wasted by these bastards."

My toes ached, a dull throbbing in the bones of my feet, and every extremity burned with cold. It was time to leave the South Pole behind. I slowly rose and moved as quickly as I could for the waiting airplane.

We had the Case and five Tokens, but it felt like we were missing far too much to continue.

PART III
THE BRIDGE

1

December 28th, 2025

The last three days were a blur, but my toes were finally starting to feel normal again. Beverly's car pulled into the grocery store parking lot, and I stretched my hood over my head, stalking toward her as she exited the vehicle.

She let out a yelp as I arrived, her hands protectively moving onto her handbag as if I was a purse snatcher.

"It's me, Bev," I whispered.

"Rex? What the hell are you doing? I haven't heard from you for days, and…"

I grabbed her wrist and squeezed harder than I'd intended. "Your life is in danger. You have to call Fred. Tell him to meet us with the kids at the truck stop twenty minutes east of town. You know the one, with the cartoon fried egg sign?"

"I know it… what's going on?" Bev acted petrified, and I didn't blame her one bit.

"I'll tell you when we're gone." I looked around, wondering if we were being watched. "Have you noticed anyone following you? Parked outside your house?"

"No, Rex. Please, you're scaring me. Fred can't just leave—"

"Bev, listen to me," I said, holding her hands. "Trust me on this. I'm into some dangerous business, and they know who you are. These guys… they killed Hunter."

"Hunter?" Her eyes jumped open. "Madison? The rich guy Dad used to work for?"

"Shhhhh. Sis, bring the family and meet me at the truck stop. If you have to go home to convince Fred, do so physically, in case they're listening to your phone too. On that note, ditch the phone and tell Fred the same thing."

"What's this all about?" she asked.

"The Bridge. It's where they went."

"Not that again. Dad's gone, Rex."

I forced a smile. "Dad is gone, but the Bridge is real. You've seen the Objects, right?"

"The asteroids?" she asked.

"Right. It's all connected." I didn't have time for this, but I realized how insane it sounded as the words escaped my lips. "I know what you're thinking, Beverly, but it's real. Just pack them up and be there in an hour."

To her credit, she didn't freak out, which was better than I would have done if our roles were reversed. She climbed into the car and rolled the window down. "Rex, you won't let anything happen to my kids, will you?"

That was my sister and her big heart. She was always worried about everyone else before herself. "No, Bev. I won't."

She drove off, and I returned to my rental car.

"Good news. Passports are done," Marcus said from his makeshift workstation in the back seat. "We can pick them up in Boston."

"You know, I'm glad you kept some unsavory friends from college, buddy," I told him. "How's the leg?"

He shrugged ambiguously. "Fine. Stitches tickle a bit."

Lucky for him, the gunshot had grazed his leg, resulting in Tripp giving him a handful of sutures on the flight to Chile. It could have been far worse.

"Let's tell Veronica we're coming," I said as I backed out of the parking spot.

"Done."

The streets were busy in my hometown, with most of the residents still off for the holiday season. The restaurants and malls looked hectic, and I drove by them with little interest as we hit the interstate. The truck stop came quickly, and I took the turnoff, slowing as I skidded on the gravel lot.

"Do you mind checking the radio?" Marcus asked, and I tapped it on. We had a few minutes to spare, and I was tired of hearing myself overthink our plan.

"Bill, you don't think we're supposed to believe these Objects, as everyone is calling them, are actually stopping at Earth, do you?" a deep-voiced man asked across the radio waves.

"Carl, I'm only reiterating what I've heard. More and more members of the scientific community are beginning to ascertain just that. The Objects have not only changed trajectory twice so far, but their speed is no longer constant. What do you think that means?" Bill McReary asked.

"They did move close enough to Saturn to be affected by the gravitational pull of that planet, not to mention the smaller forces of the moons," Carl told him.

"You're both crazy. How in God's green Earth do we even know they are real? Have you seen the things people are doing with CGI these days? This is another conspiracy to distract us from what's really going on down here," a different man said.

"And what's that, anonymous caller?" Bill asked with a snicker.

"Our guns. The government wants our guns, and if you ask the

right people, they're after our firstborns too."

"Firstborns? I think you've called into the wrong show. Rumpelstiltskin isn't in today," Bill joked, and I turned the radio off.

"What'd you do that for?" Marcus asked.

"These wackos' theories aren't going to help us," I said. The window was open, letting in cool air. I pushed on the mirror, adjusting it. A minivan was directly behind us, a hundred yards away, and the car was running with the lights off. A trail of exhaust floated from the rear. I tried to see who was inside, and for a second, it was Francois, his menacing eyes piercing into the reflection. Then the door opened and a woman walked out, shouting at a little boy to hurry up. I was starting to lose it, to see things that weren't really there. I had to assume the Believers were around every corner, or they'd catch up to me.

A knock rapped on the passenger door, and I pulled the gun from under my seat.

"Relax, Rex," Veronica said as she opened it. Her hair was cut shorter, dyed a dark brown. Her eyes were a penetrating bright blue as she stared at me. "Tripp's waiting inside. Care to join us?" Her voice held a sharp edge to it.

Marcus had already determined there was no CCTV here, and that was why we'd chosen the discreet meeting location. Plus, with lots of truckers coming in and out, as well as penny-pinching travelers during the holiday season, no one would notice our group.

"Tell your contact we'll be there in two hours, Marcus." I climbed out, depositing the rental's keys in my pocket. I pulled a Red Sox hat on and saw my reflection in the gas station window. My beard was coming in, and with the dark bags under my eyes, the plaid jacket and the baseball cap, I didn't even recognize myself.

The door chimes rang as we entered the diner, but no one turned to see who was there.

"Sit anywhere you like," a red-headed waitress called from behind the counter. She was hastily refilling two truckers' cups, and we joined Tripp in a corner booth that would accommodate a party of ten. It smelled like every diner in the state: a mixture of stale coffee and hash browns.

Tripp could have been a stranger. His head was trimmed into a buzz cut, his face bare as an egg. With a leather jacket and jeans on, he looked nothing like the military man I'd come to know.

Marcus kept his own cap low as he sat, scooting over to Tripp's side. He'd chosen to grow a goatee and wore a plaid jacket similar to mine, completing his disguise. Veronica waited and went beside Marcus. I took the other end, constantly scouting the entrance for any sign of Bev.

"Coffees," I said, and the waitress flipped our white china cups, splashing thick brew into them.

"Anything else?" she asked.

"I'll take a burger. Fries." Marcus slid a menu at her and shrugged. "What? A guy's got to eat."

I was still a mess, not ready for a meal until Bev and her family were safe. I couldn't let anything happen to them or to these three people. Hunter's death clung to me like a bad cologne.

The chime rang again, and Bev was there, Fred taking the lead the moment he saw me. I stood, confronting his angry posture. "Fred, before you say anything—"

His fists were clenched, his eyes burning. "What have you done?" He spoke quietly despite his mood, and I motioned for them to have a seat.

The kids stayed behind Bev, who seemed far more exhausted than she had in the grocery store parking lot. Edith held Carson's hand, and their eyes were puffy, as if they'd just been crying.

"Fred, we'll talk about it when we get to the safehouse. Do the kids need anything to eat?" I asked my sister.

Fred poked me in the chest. Hard. "Where are we supposed to go?"

I looked around. We were garnering some attention. "Seriously, we can't talk here. Trust me, Fred. I'm only doing what's necessary for you and the family."

He glanced at my team and nodded slowly. "Fine. But this isn't over. Where are we going?"

I leaned in, whispering an address. He scrambled for a piece of paper and a pen, but I shook my head. "Memorize it. Marcus?"

Marcus stood, handing Fred a burner phone. "Use the map on this. There's one number saved on there, and it's mine. Text if there's any issues. We'll be at the house in an hour and a half."

Fred sighed and took the offering, shoving it in his jeans pocket. He no longer appeared upset, just afraid. "Are we going to be okay?"

I set a hand on his shoulder, giving it a light squeeze. "I think so."

The waitress came, dropping the one plate to the table with a clatter, and Marcus smiled apologetically at her. "Can I get this to go?"

———————

*W*e were ten minutes late, and by the time we arrived at the destination, we had a folder full of fake passports and a few other pieces of identification. Marcus hadn't been kidding when he'd said his acquaintance was the real deal. I only hoped they worked when we used them at the airport.

I opened one, seeing Edith's face. It was a good thing Bev was one of those mothers that insisted on posting every life event on social media, because we'd had a lot of options. This one showed the girl with no smile, cropped from a school picture the previous fall.

This region of Boston wasn't on my radar, but it was beautiful. To our left was the Massachusetts Bay, and to the right, I spotted a lone lighthouse, standing tall and white, matching the snow on the shore.

"How many places did Hunter own?" Marcus asked.

"No idea." The memory stick he carried hadn't contained much, but it had supplied this address and a five-digit code, as well as a farewell message from Hunter himself. I closed my eyes, picturing the speech he'd given us.

His expression had been cheerful, and I couldn't pinpoint when he'd filmed it. He'd fussed with the angle of the camera a bit before settling on one that made his chin look too big and his eyes distant. From the background, I guessed it had been inside the Parisian hotel, perhaps even on the night we'd ventured out in search of the third Token.

"Rexford, if you're watching this, something dire has happened to me. To be honest with you, since the moment I saw you in the alley behind Hardy's place in New York, I feel like each day has been a blessing. My life was due to come to an end eventually, and I'd been feeling that more and more lately. I am not well. The doctors have given me months, so if your heart is heavy over this outcome, rest assured it was inevitable.

"I suppose death is with every one of us, and I've lived a good life. Better than most, I like to think, even with my obsession looming over me with every step I took." Hunter smiled as his hand slipped from the frame, returning with a glass of wine. It was three-quarters full, and he sniffed it before taking a sip. *"Don't live with regrets, Rex. Drink the best wines. Find love. Start*

a family, because even though we die alone, it doesn't mean we should live alone."

I'd teared up the first time we'd watched this. The two of us were more similar than I'd understood, and I heard the truth behind his advice. Now, as I sat parked beside the gate's keypad, the memory only firmed my resolve.

"Are we going in?" Marcus asked. He was beside me, and he looked concerned. "Do you remember the code?"

"I remember it." I pressed the buttons and the gate buzzed, swinging inward.

The house was more subdued than his East Hampton mansion, but it was still sprawling, laid out in a ranch style facing the ocean. My sister's car sat beside Tripp's borrowed truck, and the lights at the entrance were on. I parked beside them and stepped out, breathing the salty air from the water only a hundred yards past the house.

As I threw Hunter's pack over my shoulders, I pictured the rest of the message. Hunter leaned toward the camera, his neatly-trimmed beard filling the screen. *"You'll find what you need where I've sent you. It's the best I can do,"* he whispered, glancing around the room. *"Rex, finish this, and if you find Dirk, tell him I understand why he left me behind."*

I thought about this as I approached the house. Beverly's shadow met me at the door, and Marcus walked past her with a quiet greeting. "I appreciate you bringing us to your dead billionaire friend's house, Rex, but you need to tell us the truth." Fred joined her, and I stepped inside, seeing the kids in the living room playing a card game with Veronica. They were laughing, a joyful sound to break the tension.

Kids were resilient, and they didn't understand or grasp the severity of our situation. "Can we talk outside?" I asked. I let go of my pack and left my shoes on as I strode through the place. It was warm and inviting. A fire crackled in the woodburning hearth, and Tripp knelt at it, feeding the flames another log.

This house was far different, a style I hadn't expected from Hunter. But he was a man full of surprises.

I glanced at the edge of the kitchen, to where a fully stocked bar sat. "I think you might want a drink for this."

Fred nodded, taking my cue, and he went over, pouring bourbon from a crystal decanter. I was grateful for his heavy hand as I led the pair to the balcony outside. A gas heater had already been turned on, and Bev wore a jacket, standing beside the hissing warmth.

"Okay, I know it was a jerk move, ambushing you at the grocery store," I admitted. The water crashed against the shore, and I stared at the waves as the sun descended in the west.

"You scared the daylights out of me. Can you imagine what it was like going home to Fred? Telling him we had to leave? And the neighbors took in Roger for us, but I don't know how long they'll keep him." The words poured out of her lips, and she took a drink with a shaky hand. A few drops slid off the glass and landed on the gray deck.

"Rex, this better be good. Tell us why we're here." Fred was far calmer than my sister, and I appreciated it. He'd be able to protect her if necessary. I could see it in his eyes.

So I went into it. I told them about the clue on Clayton's gravestone, and my subsequent trip to Venezuela to gather the Case. Bev started to cry when I described the coordinates we found in the airport, and Fred was done with his drink by the time I explained finding Castro's house burned to the ground in the outback.

The sun had fully set, leaving the evening air crisp and humid. The moon was large, reflecting angrily off the tumultuous ocean waves as I described the next five stops. When I got to the Believers and our showdown in the

South Pole, Fred was pacing the patio, running his hands through his hair.

"Rex, you're saying they know who we are? Why would that matter? We haven't done anything!" His voice was loud, and even though I didn't expect the cult to be nearby, I still pressed a finger to my lips.

"That won't matter. I'm beginning to understand how they operate. I have something they want; they'll use anything possible to get my attention. And that means you." I pointed at Bev. She was all out of tears, and I saw the fighting spirit in her eyes as she watched me.

"Maybe Richard can help," she said.

"Richard?"

"Klein. He's been texting me. Said if I saw you, to let you know he has something you'll want to see." Bev pulled out her phone and passed it to me.

"I thought I said to ditch these." I quickly turned off the location and data service. I glanced at Fred, and he shrugged.

"Left mine at home, like you said."

I scrolled her recent texts. Richard's name was third from the top, and I read them.

Richard – *Beverly, you need to take this seriously. Rex might be in some real danger. If you see him, tell him I have something imperative to his venture. Don't delay.*

I scanned it twice and turned the phone off, tossing it over the deck toward the rocky beach. The text was from yesterday.

"Where are we going?" Beverly asked me.

"Portugal," I said.

"Why?"

"That's where the Bridge entrance is. We're hoping to learn the location in this house. Hunter's message said we'd find what we'd need here." I glanced inside, seeing my niece and nephew had convinced Marcus to join their card game.

"Anyone want another drink?" Fred asked, and I declined. He took Bev's glass and brought it inside with him.

Beverly appeared deflated. "I can't bring the family to Portugal. We have school in a week, and Fred has the company…"

"We don't have a choice, Bev. This is important, and until we can figure out a way to convince the Believers that you're not on the playing field, it's the only solution I could think of."

"And how do we do that?"

"I'm working on it. We don't even have the last Token, so I don't know that it matters." The weight of the last few weeks bore down on me, and I watched my sister, wondering what I'd been thinking by dragging her into this.

Beverly's posture snapped straighter, and she grabbed my hands. "These Tokens. You didn't say what they looked like."

I scowled as I retrieved them from my jacket pocket. I hadn't let them out of my sight, not for a moment. All five of them were quite heavy together, and I slid the top one off, handing her the hexagonal alien metal piece.

It slipped from her fingers, and she quickly grabbed it from the bleached boards underfoot. "You have to be kidding me. And you need six of these to make this… Case thingy work?"

"That's what we're after."

She paled and turned away, heading through the doors. "Give me a minute."

Fred stopped her, but she shook him off, rushing to the kitchen island to snatch her purse. She took a wrapped gift out of it and returned with the slow walk of someone trudging to death row. Tripp and Veronica noticed something was off, and they both rose, coming closer to Fred. I walked inside, closing the patio doors, and saw my sister was crying.

"What is it?" I asked. She didn't speak, just handed the present to me. My name was written on a little sticker with a cartoon reindeer on it. The wrapping was quality, red and green plaid inlaid with gold flecks. Bev had added a cloth ribbon. She always had been good at this kind of thing.

"This was for you. Dad gave it to me when I was a little girl. Well, he sent it to me."

My heart fluttered.

"You had the watch, and when Dad vanished, I was so jealous that he'd given you a reminder of him, and not me. I was his princess, but he gave you a final present. I wanted that connection to him." Her eyes were flooded with tears, and they streamed down her cheeks. Fred was immediately there, wrapping an arm around her waist.

"What's in the box?" My vision blurred, white spots dancing around my periphery. Hunter's living room had soft leather furniture, and I stumbled toward the rear of the couch.

"He sent it to me, Rex. He loved me and wanted to offer something from his last dig. That's what I thought all these years."

"Why didn't you tell us you had this? Where was it postmarked from?" I asked.

"Paris, which didn't make sense. Until tonight."

It did to me. Luis would have mailed the Token to Beverly from one of the drops he was sent on. But the main question was why he'd couriered it in the first place.

I plucked at the ribbon, untying it. The paper came off in a hurry, with no thoughts of salvaging the wrapping as our mother used to do. The wooden box was stylish, dark and hearty, which reminded me of the African blackwood in Hunter's study. I hadn't noticed the others piling around, and when I peered up, the entire team was there, waiting from a few steps away. Veronica had tears in her eyes, but Tripp only crossed his arms, jaw clenched. Marcus was smiling, his fist near his chest in anticipation.

The lid was hinged, and I lifted it open. The sixth Token was inside, and I made a noise, a mixture of agony and unabashed joy.

"I kept it with me for the first year, in my backpack, under my pillow, hoping it would connect me to Dad. But after a while, I started to forget him. What he looked like, his smell, the roughness of his palms as he held my hand taking me to the playground. And just like any young girl, I forgot about the gift. I stowed it away in my closet, under piles of dolls, toy oven accessories, and eventually teen magazines and make-up cases.

"When I saw you at Thanksgiving, so adamant on finding his trail again, it made me think of what he'd sent me thirty-five years ago. And I had the box made up with the intention of giving it to you on Christmas morning. I imagined your delight at obtaining it, a connection to Dirk Walker. And then you told me you couldn't join us. Richard's texts, and the college president's calls..."

"What did you say?" I stared at the Token. The symbol was familiar, drawn in the borders of my dad's journals. It looked like a tree on fire, with the leaves each a flame. "Jessica?"

"She called me a couple of times, asking after you. I think she got your number from Richard, but..."

I had the entire collection of Tokens. "What did she say?"

"She was wondering if I knew where you'd gone. She had some things to discuss, but you weren't answering her texts, calls, or emails, and she was beginning to worry."

That didn't matter. Only the Token she'd given me was important.

"Rex, we did it." Marcus bumped shoulders with me, and I let him pick up the final Token.

It couldn't be real. None of it. The last few weeks had been a dream. Hunter was dead, and we were so close. But we still lacked the exact location of the Bridge's cavern.

"Where's the information Hunter left us?" I asked.

Tripp nodded toward the hallway. "In the study."

"Good." I took the Token from Marcus' palm and added it to the pile of five. A spark carried through my body, making my toes and fingertips tingle, but it could have been the minor frostbite reminding me of the cold I'd endured a couple days prior.

"There's something else," Veronica said. She departed from the room, and returned with Hardy's journal in her hands. She passed it to me, and I studied the pages. It had been written in the Believers' alien language, and Hunter had begun to decipher it. There were notes in the corners, sections highlighted and transcribed.

"Did you read it?" I asked.

"Haven't had an opportunity. We just remembered it," she said defensively.

"This changes everything, doesn't it?" Tripp walked closer, and I handed the journal to him.

"We stick to the plan. Head to Portugal, as he suggested. We'll make our base at his property there and see if we can find the coordinates for this cavern. Estrelas." I whispered the last word.

"What are you doing?" Marcus asked. "You have that gleam in your eyes."

"I'm going to see an old friend." I had my jacket on, and I hesitantly passed Marcus the Tokens. "Watch these for me."

"You're not leaving alone," Tripp said, reaching for his own jacket near the exit.

I stopped him from putting it on. "No way. You're staying with my sister and her family. Richard's my friend." I questioned my trust in the man, with his recent actions. Sending Beverly cryptic messages saying he could help me. If he knew anything in regard to my father's disappearance, why had he never shared the details with me before?

"I'll join you," Veronica said, and she was out the door faster than I could deny her. To be honest, it was a relief.

"Don't go unarmed," Tripp said, and I nodded, knowing there was a gun under my seat in the rental. He tossed me my keys from the island, and I glanced at Beverly.

There was one more thing I had to know. "Did the Token come with a note?"

Bev wiped away her tears and smiled at my question. "I'll never forget it. *Be the light that shines like a star. I love you, Beverly Jane Walker.*"

The words from my father echoed in my head. "He adored you," I told her, and turned to Tripp. "Find out what the journal says, and whatever breadcrumbs Madison left behind. I want to be off first thing in the morning."

Marcus nodded to me, and I glanced at the stack of Tokens in his grip. I hated to leave them but didn't want to risk bringing the entire collection into the open.

"Who is this guy?" Veronica asked as we climbed into the rental.

"A friend of my dad's. He's been... a mentor to me," I said, and drove past the gate, heading for Boston.

2

Richard's street was quiet. Most of the houses still had their decorations up, seeming quite festive with the snow blanketing their yards and Christmas trees lit inside spacious bay windows. I preferred not to be seen but didn't have time to waste. With our modified appearances and an unfamiliar vehicle, we could play acquaintances showing up for an evening cocktail, though I was dressed more like a maintenance worker than a contemporary of Richard Klein.

His driveway was empty, and I pulled into it, hopping out. I remembered Tripp's warning and took the gun from under my seat, checking that the safety was on, and shoved it into my pants under my jacket. I felt too light without the weight of the Tokens, but they were safe with Marcus.

Veronica stared at the house, and I noticed the Christmas lights weren't turned on. It looked like the home was empty. I walked around the house, using the rear entrance again, and knocked loudly. When no one answered, I rang the bell.

Finally, the lights flicked to life, and I heard footsteps as the door opened. Richard looked tired and possibly drunk.

"Rex! Come inside, it's freezing out there," he said.

"If you think this is cold…" I didn't finish. I went first, scoping out the interior, and only then did I step aside to permit Veronica entrance.

"Where have you been? I've tried calling you."

I appraised his disheveled appearance and struggled to understand why he was so unlike the usual version of himself. "What happened to you?"

He stared at the ground. "Janelle left."

"Really?" I asked. Was this what he'd wanted to talk about? I found myself relaxing as we entered the home, and suddenly, I felt foolish for carrying a gun.

"She went after Christmas, to her sister's in Rhode Island. Said she needed space, but we both knew this was coming for some time."

"I'm sorry." I patted his arm, and he ran a hand over his face. He smelled like an ashtray, and I caught a whiff of whiskey. "Are you holding up okay?"

Richard's gaze shifted to Veronica, and he straightened up. "Who's this lovely lady?"

"Veronica," I told him.

"Are you two…?" Richard asked. The question seemed so out of the norm for my mentor that it caught me off-guard.

"Do you need me to call anyone? Have you eaten?" I went farther into his house, and saw the lights were mostly off. A few dishes sat in the sink, but otherwise, it looked commonplace.

"I could use a drink," he said, moving toward his bar. I glanced at the living room and hit the light switch. A man stood across the room, watching us. I recognized him from the party, and my gaze instantly ran to the cuff of his shirt, where I'd seen the Believers' tattoo that night.

"What have you done?" My words were a sharp whisper.

Richard poured himself a drink, spilling more than landed in the glass. "You have to understand. They took my family, Rex. Janelle and the kids… if I cooperate, they'll be safely returned. It was you or them, and frankly, an easy choice. You don't listen to me. You haven't taken my advice or stopped these foolish trips you keep making. Your father is dead, and these bastards aren't to be trifled with." He took a long drink and slammed the glass onto a bookshelf. Veronica had stayed frozen, nearly making me forget she was with me.

"Mr. Walker, I think you have something that belongs to us," the bald man said. He held a gun, and it wasn't pointed at me. It was aimed directly at Veronica.

"I'm afraid I don't know what you're talking about," I said glibly.

"Don't mess with me, Walker. We're aware you have the Bridge. You'll hand it over this instant, or she dies." He said it with little inflection. His gaze was harsh, and his expression all business.

I glanced at Richard, but he was looking away, unable to bring himself to witness our deaths. "You don't work for them?"

"I hadn't heard of them until your father brought me in. Even then, I only met a Believer a couple of months ago. Whatever you did down in Guatemala really sparked their interest. They came the next week, threatening me. I went to the police; can you believe it? Whoever these guys are, they have the department on the take. I was ushered out so quickly... I thought about contacting the FBI, but…" Richard gazed at the bald man and shook his head. "They had my number. Told me to play ball or they'd kill my son Henry first." He picked up a picture frame of a family trip to Yosemite. I remembered him telling me how much fun they'd had on the vacation.

The report of the gunshot surprised me, and I jumped as Richard clutched his stomach. The gun fired again, striking him in the chest, and he tried speaking. Blood gurgled out as he slumped to the hardwood.

"Mr. Walker, I'm losing patience. Where is the Bridge?" the man asked as the back door opened. It sounded like two more people entered, but I didn't check to confirm. Veronica reached out, taking my hand, and I squeezed it, wishing I could reassure her, but I sensed our finality. The Believers wouldn't give up, not with the Objects' imminent arrival to Earth. Their entire organization would be activated, with a lot of their efforts centered on making sure the Bridge wasn't used. That was what this was all about. I was desperate, so I did the only thing I thought that might work.

"It's not here," I said. "We split them up. Veronica's hidden hers, and I stowed the rest." It was a bold lie, one that would probably be easy to see through, but could they take the chance?

The bald cult member finally broke his stoic expression and marched toward me. His hand struck out, slapping me across the cheek. "Where are they?" He pointed the gun at me, shaking slightly.

"I told you, they're not…" He hit me again, this time with the gun in his grip. I fell back, pain erupting in my cheek.

"Stop it!" Veronica shouted, and he turned his attention to her.

"What do we have here? I liked you better blonde." He traced a finger along her jawline, and I heard a woman chuckle from behind me. It took all my strength not to deck the guy, but I felt the guns aimed at us from beyond the living room. I chanced a peek and remembered their positions. The woman wore a brown leather jacket, and she chewed gum loudly. The other man was tall, a long beard draping over his sweater. He wore a necklace, and for a second, I thought it held a cross, but it was a symbol: the three-pointed star.

"Get your hands off me," Veronica spat, and the guy clutched her chin with his meaty digits.

"Don't worry, honey. You're not my type." He winked at me. "You'll tell me where the Bridge is, or you'll die. Here, beside your good friend Klein. He was only too happy to sell you down the river, Walker. It was almost like he'd been waiting for an excuse to screw you."

I knew he was just trying to rattle me, but it made me gape at Richard's dead body. Whatever he'd done, he hadn't deserved this death.

The doorbell rang.

"Who the hell is that?" Baldy barked.

"I dunno," the woman said, gum smacking.

"Go check!" he shouted.

"Who is it?" I heard her ask from the other room. "Sorry, we're not interest—"

A thump.

"Dammit. Gord, go see what that's about," Baldy said, and Gord walked away.

The wall rattled, then glass shattered. I took my chance.

My hand reached for the gun, pulling it free from my lower back, and I clicked the safety off instinctively. Baldy tried to lunge for Veronica, but she was already moving. Her fist connected with his stomach, and he gasped but didn't fold over. His gun fired before mine, and for a second, I thought Veronica was struck. Her eyes were wide, her pupils dilated, and I pulled the trigger, hitting the target from six yards away.

One. Two. The bullets penetrated his chest, and he dropped his gun.

I started to turn around, but I felt woozy, my vision blurring. We needed to help whoever had come to the door. My fingers were numb, and I felt the weight of the gun slip from them as I staggered toward the kitchen.

"Rex, stop moving!" Veronica called, and I saw Gord on the floor, face-down in a pool of blood. Just past him was the woman, her gum fallen out. Her dead eyes stared at me.

"Good thing I showed up." I heard Tripp's voice but saw my father walking to me. He wore beige cargo pants with leather boots, and a hat to protect his face from the sun. He crouched and whispered something faintly. *Be the light that shines like a star.* His mouth didn't move, and then he was gone, replaced with Tripp's form.

I pressed my hand to my stomach, only to find it soaked in blood.

I'd been shot.

---

*I*t was dark. I realized my eyelids were shut.

Beep. Beep. Beep. Hospital machines chimed in a consistent fashion.

I tried to open my eyes, but they were so dry. I managed to croak out a query while blinking roughly. "Where am I?"

"He's coming to," Marcus said.

Bev was near the bed, holding my hand, and I smiled at her. "Thanks for the Christmas present. It'll look good on my..." I was nauseous, and I quickly understood what it was. Drugs. The IV was taped into my arm, and I glanced at the saline bag, with medication attachments labeled in indistinct writing.

"You were shot, Rex." Beverly's voice was warm. "But you're going to be okay."

"Do we have them?" I didn't have to explain myself. My own words were slurry, sloppy from the drugs and dry throat.

"Don't worry about that. You have to—" Bev moved as I tried to sit up.

The room was private, and I saw it was just the three of us. "Marcus, are we safe?"

He shrugged. "I doubt it, but what were we going to do? Tripp has the… things. Wait until you see what our old friend left us."

"The kids are okay?" I asked Bev. Obviously, they were, or she wouldn't be here with me.

"They're fine."

And my injury finally returned to the conversation. "How bad is it?"

"Lost some blood, but nothing major was hit, somehow. It passed through you, but the police are trying to…"

Panic kicked in, and I tried to think clearly. Everything was muddled. "Marcus, tell Tripp we need to leave. Bev, find out where they keep the patches. Pills too." I pointed to my stomach. "We can't stay."

"Rex, you're nuts. You got out of surgery this morning. You're staying overnight, and we'll—"

"What? Go home? Bev, listen to me. The police are in on it. Richard went to the cops, and they ignored him. The Believers are deep into everything."

"We can't just leave," Bev said.

"When was the nurse last here?" I asked.

"Twenty minutes ago," Marcus said.

"Don't let them know I was awake. I need a day, that's it." The drugs made my eyelids heavy. "We'll wait until morning. After the first rounds, we'll make our move. Pull the damned fire alarm, for all I care. That'll occupy the police." I assumed they were waiting to speak to me, since I'd been shot.

Marcus checked out the door's small window. "Fine. Bev, stay with him. He'll need your assistance to escape. Follow the blue lines when you leave. That'll take you to the elevator. We're on the third floor." Marcus had his phone out, and he was checking it intensely. "Go through the hall on this level. That area has a small library, so there'll be fewer watching eyes. Act as if you're a patient out for a stroll. Rehab or whatever."

I laughed, the movement making my wound pulse. "How did you come up with that so quickly?"

"Watched a lot of bad hospital dramas when I was in college. Almost every third episode had someone escaping," he mumbled. "This is your destination." He showed Bev the map. "Find the parkade. We'll come back first thing. Five AM. We'll be at the doors in the van. Use the burner to text us when you're in range. We'll pull the alarm."

Bev looked ready to argue, but her shoulders rolled forward and she sat beside me. "Fine."

Marcus smiled. "Glad you're okay, Rex."

"What about flying? How am I going to get on a plane like this?" I asked.

"I forgot. You don't know yet. We're not flying commercial, or private."

"What do you mean?" I asked.

"You'll see." Then he was off.

My eyes closed, and I grabbed Bev's hand. "Have them remove the catheter too, would you?"

"I'll make sure." I heard her sit in the chair as I drifted off into sedation.

"Rex, you have to be losing it if you think it's a good idea to escape the hospital," Bev whispered as the nurse left.

"Bev, Richard's dead. We just killed three Believers." I lifted a hand and tested my trigger finger. I'd killed two men in the span of a few days. I felt much better today and was glad they'd decreased the drug dosage they'd given me.

"Fine. But when we're done with this, we're contacting the authorities." She glanced at the door and smoothed a wrinkle on the shirt. "I'll see if I can find you a robe or something less conspicuous. Don't go anywhere."

She opened the door, and I spotted a police officer across the hall. He stared at his cell phone and gazed up when Beverly departed. I snapped my eyes closed and heard her muffled reply to him asking if I was awake. "Not yet," she said.

I managed to turn the drip of sedatives off, and when Beverly came in with a buff trench coat draped over her arm, I started to climb from the bed. The IV came out easily enough, but the machines started to beep as I removed the finger sensor.

"Now," I said, and Bev texted Marcus.

A moment later, the fire alarm rang out. My feet were bare, my knees wobbly as I swung off the bed. Bev was there to catch me, and I steadied myself as she helped me with the jacket. She had her purse strap around her body, and I glanced at it, seeing medical supplies stuffed inside.

We moved to the room's doorway, and I pushed it open. The cops were jogging down the hallway, and a few nurses were talking to security, trying to determine if they should be evacuating the patients in recovery.

"Help me out," I whispered, and we departed quickly. Beverly had her arm around me, and I attempted to walk as normally as I could, following the blue line on the floor as Marcus had instructed until we spotted the unoccupied wheelchair. To our advantage, no one seemed to notice us as we rolled through the halls.

I gritted my teeth, grimacing in pain as we went, and Bev hit the elevators. People were leaving the library, and Bev hastily pressed the "Door Close" button as a group began to approach.

The doors shut right in time, and we started descending, until we stopped at P1.

A firefighter was in our way, talking with a man in a blue jumpsuit, and we shuffled around them with a soft "Excuse me" from my sister.

They didn't pay us any mind, and I was about to ask Bev for the cell phone when the van honked from our right. The tires screeched as it rounded a corner sharply and skidded to a halt. The side door slid wide, and Marcus was there with Veronica, helping me into the vehicle. Bev rolled the wheelchair away, abandoning it. I fell into the seat as Beverly jumped in behind me, and she slammed the door shut as Tripp raced forward.

Lucky for us, the gates were open wide, but a line-up of early evacuees waited in front of our van. It took five anxious minutes to leave, and my stomach protested at the movement. The drugs were still working their magic, and I dreaded coming down from the painkillers, but knew my sister well enough to know she kept over-the-counter stuff on her at all times.

The sun was beginning to rise as we exited the hospital grounds, driving for the freeway. "Where are we going?" I asked, seeing we'd missed the exit to Hunter's cove house.

"To Portugal," Tripp said from the driver's seat.

I closed my eyes, hearing the kids behind me asking their dad if Uncle Rex was going to be okay. Then I fell asleep.

3

*W*hen I came to, it was much brighter, and I glanced at the sky, finding the sun hadn't shifted much. I hadn't been out for long. Bev was beside me, her head rested on my shoulder. She snored softly, and I hated to wake her.

"Tripp, are we almost there?" I had to use the bathroom, and I was extremely thirsty. "Any water around?"

Marcus was in the front passenger seat, and he opened a fresh bottle, passing it to me. "Just a few more minutes."

I was about to ask where but looked out the window to see high fences along open fields. A distant sign indicated we were nearing an army base. "What are we doing here?"

"I'm calling in a favor," Tripp said, smirking at me in the mirror.

"Can we trust them?" I asked.

"This guy owes me. Big time. Trust me when I say he's no Believer." The road was gravel, and the rocks grumbled under us as we slowed near the front gates. An officer with a tablet stood near the entrance, and he marched up to Tripp.

"We need to see Colonel Jerkins," Tripp said.

"You're not on the list," the officer said.

"Tell Jerkins that Davis is here. He's expecting us," Tripp's voice was different, more clipped and authoritative. I expected he'd used that when talking to subordinates during his entire military career.

The man walked away, and I opened my jacket to find my wound had bled through the hospital gown. Bev was awake, and she gasped at the sight. "Tripp, Rex needs help."

The officer opened the gate with the press of a button and climbed into a Jeep, waving Tripp forward. We followed him through the base, which was quiet at the moment. A lot of people would be at home with their families if they weren't overseas. A large spruce tree was decorated for the holidays, and we drove toward the main structure, a boxy building with bland paint colors.

The Jeep stopped, and the man hopped out, indicating we take a parking stall. Tripp parked there and stepped out first, talking to the young officer. He nodded and took off as an older, broad-shouldered black man targeted Tripp. For a second, it seemed like the man was about to punch Tripp; then his face broke into a huge smile, and they hugged. Colonel Jerkins wore his uniform and looked imposing in it.

Five minutes later, we were inside the building, Edith and Carson staying with their mom and dad in the foyer.

I started down the hall with the others, but Tripp slowed, coming to my side. He grabbed for my arm. "They have a doctor on site. He's going to patch you up again, and then you can join us."

I slapped his hand away. "Damn it, Tripp. I'm not missing this meeting."

Tripp lowered his voice. "Rex, you were shot. You need attention. We won't do anything until you join us, okay?"

I relented as his tone softened. "Fine. Can you find me something to wear?" My feet were still bare, my legs only shielded to my lower thighs by the trench.

"No problem." Tripp waved the young officer closer and barked a command at him. The guy looked ready to salute him but stopped short, saying he'd locate some things in my size and bring them to medical.

"Tripp, I thought you were a Navy SEAL. Why does an army colonel owe you?" I asked.

"Maybe when this is done with, I'll answer that," he said with a laugh.

———————

*T*he sun was high in the sky, reflecting off the snow-draped field. My wound had been cleaned and disinfected, and the doctor ensured I left with enough antibiotics and painkillers to fend off a zombie apocalypse. The airplane was huge, with vast space to carry an assortment of military personnel inside; only today, it was transporting a handful of civilians across the Atlantic Ocean.

The seats were combined into benches along the outer walls, facing a middle row. Carson raced past us, running through the airplane with a huge smile on his face.

"I have to ask why I'm lending you this, Tripp," Colonel Jerkins said before stepping foot on the plane.

"No you don't, sir," Tripp said resolutely.

"Do you have any idea the paperwork this'll take?" Jerkins frowned, looking at me, then at Veronica and Marcus. "Tell me there's nothing dangerous on board." His gaze drifted to the bags Marcus lowered to the floor. Inside was the Case, but I'd reclaimed the Tokens. They were in my borrowed jacket's pockets, three in each front fold. My hands were wrapped around them tightly as the colonel stared at me.

"We're in some trouble, Colonel. Serious business

involving the Objects," Tripp said.

Jerkins' eyes blinked wider as he pointed to the ceiling. "Those? How is this group tangled in anything involving the asteroids? Better yet, don't tell me. Consider our affiliation concluded, Tripp. I owed you, and this is my repayment. I'll have the pilot return through Britain like you asked, but I have no idea who'd be able to track you through this undocumented trip. You'll land at Lajes Field in the islands, and I've arranged for a civilian plane to be at your disposal from there."

"These guys are tricky. They always seem to be one step ahead." Tripp glanced toward the cockpit. "You trust the pilot?"

"He's coming in for this mission on my personal request. We're skeleton at the moment," Jerkins said.

"I take it I'll be flying from the island to Porto?" Veronica seemed pleased with the idea. I'd never seen someone so delighted to be in control of a winged vehicle.

"We have an Air Force veteran?"

She saluted and smiled. "First Lieutenant Jones, sir. I could take …"

"Not this time, I'm afraid. Captain Berkowitz will arrive shortly." Jerkins turned for the exit, and stopped near Tripp. "Son, would you like to keep the kids and their parents at the base?"

I thought about it and glanced at Beverly. It would be safer with them, but I couldn't trust that the Believers weren't integrated into the Army. I was taking a flier on the fact that Jerkins wasn't involved in the slightest.

"Thanks for the offer, but we're traveling together," Fred told him. "We're not letting Rex go into this alone, and if things are as dangerous as he thinks, I don't want to put the kids in jeopardy. Or Beverly."

And it was settled.

"Have it your way." Colonel Jerkins appeared on the verge of saying one last comment but disembarked instead.

A half hour later, the captain arrived with a carafe of coffee and some paper cups. He wore street clothes and apologized for the delay. We strapped in, and a handful of minutes later were taking off. I peered out the window, seeing Boston to the south, and soon, there was nothing but ocean below us.

I was beat, and my stomach ached, but the drugs dulled the pain. Marcus sipped a coffee and pulled out his laptop, and Tripp unclasped his belt, reaching into his pack. I glanced over the middle row to see Fred, Bev, and the kids sleeping. I hated having to bring them with us but didn't feel like we had much of a choice. If I left them, they might share Richard Klein's fate, and I couldn't let that happen.

"How you feeling, Rex?" Marcus asked.

"Like someone shot me in the gut," I said. I tugged the sweater up and peered at the wound. White dots floated in my vision again, but the bandage was clean.

"You're lucky to be alive," Veronica said, her voice chastising me.

"Like I wanted this," I muttered. "Tripp, if I haven't said it enough… thank you."

"Think nothing of it. Just doing my job." Tripp had Hunter's journal in his hand, and he rifled through the pages.

"Where are we? I've been so out of it. What did Hunter leave us at the house?" I sipped my coffee, hoping the jolt of caffeine would help me focus through the muddle of drugs in my body.

Marcus answered. "Hunter told us to fly to Porto. Wine country in Portugal. Looks incredible. He owns a place there, off the record, so no one should be aware it exists. He's paid some locals to maintain it for a couple of decades and hasn't shown his face there for the entire time."

"He was playing a patient game," Tripp said.

"I wish he was alive to see the Tokens together," Veronica whispered.

"What else? Do we have the location of the Bridge entrance?" I was more curious about that than anything.

Tripp bobbed his head: not quite a no, not quite a yes. "Sort of. He described it but failed to leave coordinates. He really didn't want the cultists to find it."

"How do we track the cavern?" I asked.

"It's clear it's within twenty miles of his house. He says as much. We just need to use his clues to locate it from there." Marcus brought up a map, showing the location of the home.

"Are those satellite images?" I asked, seeing the grids and intense detail. This was no web browser software at work.

"Apparently, Tripp still has access," Marcus said. "I think we've partnered with a real live secret agent man."

Tripp grunted but didn't deny anything. "Glad to help."

"What does his description say?"

Veronica laughed, a bright sound over the plane's humming engines. "*Where the water flows, the pathway glows. Seek a star's flight on a cloudy night.*"

"What the hell is that supposed to mean?" I was tired of the games. "Can't someone for once tell us a fact? Like, it's located two-point three kilometers northwest of my house. Can't miss it. Valley with a giant waterfall. A tree that looks like a bird."

"Then where's the fun?" Marcus asked.

"Fun? This stopped being fun the moment someone died. Marcus, you were slashed with a knife in the catacombs, and we've both been shot."

"Don't forget you were clipped in the face with a gun," Veronica reminded me.

My hand went to my cheek, and I felt the puffy skin. "With the gaping hole in my stomach, I'd almost forgotten about that."

She watched me from across the seats, next to Tripp, and I grinned back. We'd faced the barrel of the Believers' gun and had somehow lived to tell the tale. That was something that would bond us forever, or as long as we lived— which, considering the dire circumstances we were under, might only be days.

"Let's break that down, Marcus. What do you see with water in the area?" I asked.

"The most obvious is the Douro River, but it's twenty-two miles at the closest juncture of his property. According to his message, that makes it improbable."

"Maybe he was mistaken. Maybe he measured it differently," I suggested.

"Have you known Hunter Madison to screw something up?"

Marcus made a good point, but I had one counter to that. "Francois. He had a Believer working beside him for years. That's a pretty big mistake." I didn't take solace in that fact.

"How was he to know? It's easy to trust someone once they've built that relationship. I don't blame him in the least. Plus, these cultists are organized. They know exactly what they're doing." Veronica removed her straps and stepped by Marcus, peering at the laptop's satellite image.

"Okay, take out the river. What else?" I watched as Marcus zoomed in, using the program to create four quadrants originating from Hunter's property. They formed a circle, with twenty miles as the farthest reach on any edge.

His place was north of the city of Porto, quite remote, with no apparent neighbors for a few miles. From this vantage point, it appeared like he owned a vineyard, with rows of grapes lining the fields and valleys behind the home. It was classic Hunter.

"The mountains aren't huge, but over here"—Marcus directed his finger to the top right quadrant—"there's a small lake, and if you look, it runs downward toward this valley."

"*Where the water flows, the pathway glows.* What is this pathway, and why would it glow?" I pondered the riddle left by the dead billionaire.

"There have to be markings. Like, Hunter made a trail." Marcus tilted his head to the side, raising his eyebrows.

"Could be. But what about *Seek a star's flight on a cloudy night?* How do you see a star on a cloudy night?" Veronica asked, but none of us had the answer.

"Save that. I think you're onto something with the location in the mountains. We know it's a cavern, which means peaks or a hilly range." We continued to scour the images and pinpointed another four locations that might work for his puzzle.

"There's more," Tripp said once Marcus finally closed his laptop. I saw my sister was still asleep, with the kids lying sideways on the seats. Fred's eyes were open, but he was just gazing toward the bathroom.

"What is it?" I glanced at the journal in his hands. Marcus and I had pilfered it from Brian Hardy's place, and now he was dead.

"Hunter had been in the midst of translating the book." Tripp handed it to me, and I curiously scanned the pages.

I saw the symbols for the Tokens etched into the

margins, and finally clued in. "He's been working on their positioning. I've been so caught up in getting the Tokens, I hadn't considered utilizing them in any particular order."

I glanced at the bag across the seats, and Tripp dove into it, pulling the Case free. It felt smaller than when I'd pulled it out of the mine's underground lake, and I reached for it, the black metal cold in my grip.

The others sat around expectantly, and I appeased them by taking the Tokens out. Six Tokens, six slots.

The first had the half moon over a spoon, and I peered at Hunter's drawing. It slid it into place, and I checked the next in order. The upside down R with a bird above it was subsequent, and I set it as Hunter had translated, sideways to the right of the first Token.

The third choice was the Token we'd gathered in the stone forest. Three rings, each smaller inside the other. This one was tough to determine which direction to place it, until I noticed the miniscule line etched at the bottom. Hunter's drawing showed it facing up, and I copied that position as I slid the metal hexagon home.

The last piece was the one Beverly had given me, wrapped for a Christmas gift. I still couldn't believe she'd had it all those years, a present from my father from beyond the grave. If Dirk Walker hadn't wanted to be found, why had Dad gifted a Token to his daughter? I supposed I'd never learn the truth, but the fact of the matter was, we'd acquired the six Tokens, and that was what counted.

I couldn't shake the feeling of hurt, or favoritism, that came with bestowing such a powerful gift. I looked at my watch, the leather straps cracked, the face worn. I wound it on instinct and sneered as it ticked the seconds away.

"Rex, are you going to finish?" Veronica asked. She climbed around Marcus and sat once again. Her foot tapped nervously as I continued.

The Token depicted a tree with burning leaves, and I clicked it into the proper spot, rotating the Case in my hands as I grabbed the fifth piece. The image was disturbing in some off-putting way. It resembled eyes, almond-shaped, in a circle. Lines like sunlight stretched from the round center. It went on the top of the Case. Then there was only one remaining.

"Should we really be doing this now?" Marcus asked.

"You might be right." I stared at the last Token, discovered in Antarctica. It depicted a shooting star.

"Maybe you should. Just to see." Fred was behind me, and I looked back to see Bev and the kids there too, my sister holding their hands.

"No. It might not be safe," I decided. From what I knew, the Case only worked in the cavern, but I was guessing by the conjecture and hypothesis of two dead men. No one could be certain.

As I started to set the Case into the pack, the pilot advised us we were in range of the island's landing field. The sky was dark, and I saw lightning flash through the window. We were almost at Portugal, the last stop in our adventure.

Unless it worked. Then we had one more to go.

Across the Bridge.

4

*T*he sun hid behind clouds as we drove toward Hunter's vineyard. Porto was a beautiful city, but I scarcely took notice as exhaustion overtook me. I'd somehow slept on the plane between the landing field and Porto, despite the fact that Veronica had to fly us through yet another storm.

The kids had been petrified, but Fred kept them close, humming a tune to them in an effort to remain calm. Beverly was as scared as them, but I was useless after taking another pill for the pain. Each jostle of turbulence sent a shot of agony through me. But sleep came, and I didn't wake until we'd landed in the airport near the city.

Tripp handled the local customs agent paperwork with surprising expedience, and then we were off, renting a huge passenger van and a Jeep. Veronica took the Jeep with Marcus, and the rest of us were piled in with Tripp at the helm.

"This friend of yours must have been quite the character," Fred said. "I can't imagine owning a plot of land like this."

The gates were high, and I spotted cameras at either end, sensing our motion as we neared. Tripp used a code given by Hunter, and they opened. The driveway went on for a mile, and it was paved the entire distance. My injury was grateful for it.

"What day is it?" I asked.

For a second, no one answered. "December thirty-first," Bev finally said. "New Year's Eve."

I felt like I was missing a few days. Portugal was gorgeous in the morning light, and the grass here was coated in a fine dew. Hunter's house was perched on a hill, with the drive over the last ten minutes a constant but patient climb. Once we drove up to it, I could see the valley beyond, and it took my breath away. Endless rows of vineyard spread out. The ground was terraced across the hillside, giving it an even more distinct appeal. Beyond the hills sat a calm lake, and I swore there were swans swimming in it.

The home itself was magnificent. Classic Portuguese styling gave it a two-story colonial appearance, the top floor with eight windows facing the driveway. I imagined the rear of the house would showcase views for miles.

"This is cool," Carson said, dashing from the van. Fred followed the kids as he hauled their luggage in two hands.

"Don't go too far!" Beverly called, but neither of her children listened.

"Sorry about all this, sis," I told her.

"It's not really your fault, is it?" She stuck her arm through mine, helping me walk the incline toward the front doors.

A woman opened them, her smile friendly and welcoming. She rolled a suitcase out and handed Tripp a set of keys.

"Thank you," Tripp said, but she didn't reply, just walked away, not making eye contact. She'd likely been paid to leave when Tripp sent the message, using Hunter's firm instructions. The woman walked to a red hatchback and drove off.

We had the estate to ourselves.

Veronica and Marcus parked as close as they could to

the front steps, and my sidekick hopped out, his computer bag slung over his shoulder. "This again? I know we're in some sticky situations, but at least we get to chill in style."

We filed into the home, and I instantly saw the view through the house. The layout allowed for a straight sight line to the vineyard in the valley, and I plodded across the terrazzo tile directly to the deck. The home was built into the top of the hill, and the patio was braced on the decline, making it seem like you were floating above the vale.

And the words echoed in my mind. *Seek a star's flight on a cloudy night.* I knew what it meant. With a renewed sense of urgency, I stared at the land. Hunter had purchased this vineyard, a piece of property that must have cost ten million dollars, not including the upkeep, just to be close to the Bridge's portal. He'd wanted to see the Bridge so badly, and my father had cut him out. Hardy also wanted to go, but in the end, it had only been Clayton Belvedere and Dirk Walker to make the trek across the stars.

I turned and watched the rest of the team inside. Veronica grinned as she talked to Marcus and Tripp. The tough guy's chin was once again covered in rough stubble, and he frowned as she spoke. I'd watched him dispatch a few Believers so far, and he'd done it with such casual regard. I still hadn't truly let myself come to terms with the two men I'd murdered. I'd built a barrier, a brick wall around my emotions, to carry on. The cultists were wrong, at least from my perspective. From their depiction, they were doing what they were taught was necessary to hail the salvation from the Unknowns.

Regardless of who was evil or just, I was alive, and it was thanks to Tripp. The Believers shouldn't have been aware of this home, and it gave me a sliver of hope and peace. We had the Tokens, the Case, and hopefully soon, the location of the cavern.

Estrelas. The stars. We were so close.

I heard the kids laughing from another room and looked down the hallway. The living room was furnished nicely, with expensive hand-crafted wooden-framed couches and ornate coffee tables. The entire floor was the same tile, and I noticed a huge fireplace with a thick mantel across the space.

"We should get moving, check the location you marked first," I told Marcus, and my hand tried to rest on the couch top. I was woozy, and it missed, sending me sprawling ahead. Veronica half-caught me as I struck the ground.

"After you rest, Rex," Tripp said. My stomach throbbed, and my mind spun as they directed me toward a first-floor bedroom. I tried to argue with them, but the words wouldn't come with clarity. In the end, I stopped fighting and lay on the bed, fully clothed.

Marcus returned a minute later with a vial of pills and a glass of water. "Sorry, Rex, but you have to heal up first. We'll wait as long as we have to, right, guys?" he asked the others.

I closed my eyes after swallowing the pill, letting the soft pillow cradle my head. They muttered their agreement, and I was out, sleeping like a baby.

———————

*T*he music was familiar, a song from my childhood, and I let the words wash over me. I opened my eyes and almost expected my mother to be at my bedside. The light was on, but dim on the nightstand, and she kept singing. Only this wasn't me at six with the chicken pox, and that wasn't my mom; it was my sister.

"Rex, are you feeling better?" she asked. It was obvious she'd been crying, her eyes red and swollen.

I sat up, noticing an improvement. My brain didn't feel like it was being squished in a vise, and my stomach pain was just a dull ache. "Yes, thanks. How long was I sleeping?"

"It's evening. Six hours or so," she said, and I tried getting up.

"Six hours! Couldn't someone have woken me?" I was furious we'd wasted a whole day already.

"Rex, calm down. It's not all up to you, okay?"

"Where are they?" I asked, slowly swinging my legs from the bed. Bev watched me with sadness on her face.

"They went out and haven't returned. Tripp gave Fred a gun," she said.

Fred with a gun. Something that I had a hard time picturing, but at least he was willing to protect his family. He was twice the father mine had ever been. He worked hard, ran a business, and came home every night, eating dinner with his children. He was a real father.

I didn't know where the pent-up anger at my dad stemmed from. Usually, it didn't bother me so much, especially knowing what I did now about the Bridge and the Believers. But where had he ended up? Why hadn't he let Hunter and Hardy go instead? Both Clayton and Dirk left families behind.

I walked to the bedroom exit and heard a television playing.

"You're not going to leave us too, are you?" The question was so simple, yet years of torment were layered into it.

"What?" I asked, facing Beverly. She sat on an uncomfortable chair, a bunched-up tissue in her hand.

"You won't take off like Dad, will you? What are we

supposed to do if you vanish like he did? Do we just live out our days in this vineyard?" she asked.

"I… I don't know." Was that even an option? "What do you want me to do?"

"Can't we just give them this box thing?" Bev stood, crossing the room in a few quick steps. "Hand it over and make a deal? We have nothing to do with these people, they have nothing to do with us." She slapped her palms together, like she was dusting them off.

"It's not that simple." Could I do that? I had a feeling the Believers would entertain that deal. I could leave with everyone, return home to Boston, and pretend this hadn't happened. I wouldn't have to worry about being killed in a shootout, or dying as I attempted to cross into the Bridge.

Hunter and Hardy would reprimand me for even considering this as an option, but look where their participation in this adventure had gotten them. Hunter in a shallow grave at the South Pole, and Hardy engulfed in flames.

I didn't want to end up like them, but even if I knew how to contact the Believers, how would I be able to trust they'd stick to their side of the bargain? They'd probably take the Case and Tokens and kill us without a second thought. No loose ends.

"Rex, tell me you're contemplating what I'm suggesting."

The door opened from down the hall, and I heard the voices of my friends as they entered the home. "I better check on them." Bev appeared crestfallen, and I hugged her, careful not to press my stomach anywhere near her. She let out a drastic sob and melted into my shoulder.

"I know you won't stop until you find this Bridge, but just be careful. Dad is gone. Mom is dead. And I can't stand the thought of losing you too," she said softly.

I didn't reply as I walked away, moving for the sound

of Marcus' voice. He paused while taking his jacket off, and he wore a black t-shirt again, with the outline of a wine bottle on it. "Rex. You're up. Feeling okay?"

"Some minor improvements. Where have you guys been?" I saw the bags of groceries, and some from a clothing store, and relaxed. They'd been shopping.

"What did you get?" Edith asked, running up to Veronica.

Veronica reached for a bag and dumped the contents on the coffee table in the living room. "A few outfits for you." Edith squealed in delight, but Carson looked less than pleased at being given new jeans and a sweatshirt.

Tripp brought the last of the groceries in, setting the brown paper bags on the kitchen counters, and I was almost pleased to see Hunter had kept the place practically original. The appliances were from the eighties but remained in pristine condition.

"Would you like to help make dinner?" Tripp asked me, and I laughed, trying to picture the tough guy wearing an apron and taste-testing a bisque.

I put some vegetables into the fridge crisper. "You've been gone a while."

"Okay, Rex. We didn't wait for you, but we've managed to count three of the five locations on Marcus' map out of the running," Tripp admitted.

Part of me was furious they'd proceeded without me, but I was also relieved. I would have done the same thing in their shoes. "You didn't bring the Case, did you?" I asked.

"No. Marcus put that under your bed."

I glanced at my bedroom door. "Good. What's the plan?"

"The plan? We have dinner, then we check out the last two locations. Marcus had an idea, so we bought something in town, along with flashlights and various supplies," Tripp said.

Tonight. We were going to try to track our final destination after dinner. My stomach growled at the thought of eating, but it also flopped nervously at the idea of finishing this mission. "What are we making?"

He shrugged and laughed. "The same thing I always eat before rushing into the enemy's lair. Spaghetti."

"It's also probably the only thing you know how to make," Marcus shouted from the living room. He was playing with the remote control, and I heard a newscaster speaking in English. A British news program was on, and I walked toward the TV as they mentioned the Objects.

"Turn it up." Veronica stood near the fireplace, which Fred was feeding logs to, and we all gawked at the image on the screen.

The Objects were coming.

"This image is the clearest we have yet, and many are speculating that they are indeed spacecraft. See the way the lines are rounded, not jagged? Some claim they are too smooth to be natural, and from what we can discern, they're each the same length." The woman spoke slowly, her accent heavy. *"There are three of them, but the center one is wider. This suggests there may be more than three, and as many as five separate Objects. We received the images an hour ago, and watch parties are forming around the world. US representatives are questioning China, wondering if this was a secret project returning from the depths of our solar system. As of now, there has been no reply from China on the queries."*

I stared at the Objects. The picture wasn't very clear, the edges blurred, but the shapes were distinctive.

"This is definitely aliens," Marcus said quietly.

"We don't know that," Fred responded.

"Sure we do. I mean, what the hell else is riding in like this? It's all true. We have to stop them." Marcus sighed.

"And you think playing with a Rubik's Cube in a cave is going to do that? What do you expect to find in there?" Fred asked. So far, he hadn't been overly vocal about what we were doing, but he was growing a voice after spending time with us.

"We aren't positive, but Hunter was confident there was something on the other side to help us, or some*one*. Traveling through the Bridge is the only solution." We still had Hardy's journal, but Hunter hadn't gotten far enough in his translation.

"And the Believers want these aliens in the Objects to return? Then what?" Fred crossed his arms.

"Your guess is as good as mine. They think the Unknowns are coming home, and that people will be irrelevant to them. The aliens will scourge us from the planet, making room for themselves," I said, repeating what Hunter had told us. "But for some reason, the cult thinks the beings will connect to them. Attune."

"You don't think it's possible?" Bev joined the conversation. The kids stared at the TV with wide eyes, Carson looking uneasy about the whole scenario.

"We can't be certain until we activate the Bridge. It's the one thing I can control. And the fact that the Believers are willing to kill for it means that it's important." The screen changed, showing a protest in London, with thousands of people walking across Tower Bridge.

"What do you think they look like?" Veronica had stayed quiet beside me, and her voice was small and distant. I recalled she'd had something to tell me back in Antarctica but still hadn't shared it with me.

"Who?" Tripp asked.

"The Unknowns. If they really are from Earth and were here before us, what do you look like?"

"Who the hell cares? I hope we don't ever see them."

Tripp grabbed the remote from Marcus and turned the blaring speakers down. "Let's focus on our task. Which, at this moment, is making dinner. We can worry about the rest of it when we're full. Deal?"

Veronica sat in a chair, placing her elbows on her knees as she watched the TV with Marcus and my family. I followed Tripp into the kitchen as he turned on a gas burner on the stove. "Why do you care about this?"

It was a simple question, and he stopped what he was doing. "Hunter did pay me up front, if that's what you're wondering. He also left a pile of cash for us to use, so we have some serious funding to carry us forward." He grabbed a saucepan and set it on the flame. "But I've never abandoned a mission worth winning, and I'm not about to start today. Plus, someone has to watch out for you three, and your sister's family."

I smiled, patting him on the back. "Thanks for sticking around." We got to work; something so mundane as cooking a meal with my new friend was just what I needed to ease the dread at what we were about to attempt later that night.

5

*T*he clouds had rolled in late in the afternoon, according to Veronica, and tonight they covered the entire region. A light drizzle fell against the van's windshield as we drove up the steep incline toward our destination. I had the Case in my lap in the front passenger seat, unwilling to set the last Token in its proper position until we were in the appropriate cavern. Hunter had spoken of a podium, a stone dais directly beneath an opening in the cavity, and I pictured myself placing the metal box onto it before pressing the final hexagon into the cube.

"This is it," Tripp said, pulling over. "Road ends where the streams intersect, and there's a pathway leading into the mountains."

They weren't really mountains, at least not compared to the great ranges like the Himalayas, Rockies, or Andes, but they were tall, rising high into the sky. The clouds were low, creating a dense fog. It was chilly, and I zipped my navy-blue jacket up. I was glad I hadn't shaved in some time, and I scratched at the beard.

Marcus tossed a backpack at me, and I caught it, depositing the Case inside. I closed the bag and slung it over my shoulders, not wanting to carry any more weight than this. My stomach felt okay, but it was a far cry from healed.

"Where the water flows, the pathway glows." Veronica gripped a flashlight, and she passed one to me too. "Let's see what we can find."

Insects chirped their nightly songs, and I heard a few birds call out as we walked along the stream. The trees were lush and green, giving off a fragrant scent. It was full of life here, as good a location as any to hide the Bridge.

Even if someone happened across the entrance to the cavern, they would think nothing of the strange setup, not ever imagining it might hold the entrance to another world inside, because you needed the Case and Tokens to access it.

"My father and Clayton walked this very path thirty-five years ago. With this exact cube in their hands."

"If this is the right spot," Veronica chimed in.

Her comment was astute. Nothing here shouted "alien world entrance" to me.

The path wasn't wide, and Marcus ran ahead, pulling an item from his bag. He turned it on, and the trail lit up in a blue glow.

"You bought a black light?" I thought it was a good idea.

"I figured Hunter might have marked it off with something only a black light would pick up." Marcus aimed it at the ground for a few steps, then at the tree trunks along the trail's edge. So far, nothing was out of the ordinary.

The stream ran away from the top of the hill, and the fog grew thicker with each passing minute. My side burned with effort, and I peeked behind us, but Tripp was out of sight. He carried a handgun, and I really hoped we didn't run into any tourists out for a late-night hike. We'd look like quite the quartet.

The path narrowed again, and we walked in single file toward the cliffside. The sound of the stream grew more distant as we moved away from it. This didn't feel right. I couldn't explain it, but as soon as we broke from the forest into a clearing near the fog-covered peaks, I knew it.

"Hunter said *Seek a star's flight on a cloudy night*. It's cloudy. It's night." I peered up, but there was no sign of the sky through the pea soup. "No stars. We're in the wrong spot."

The echo of an engine carried through the valley up to my ears, and I looked around. Tripp finally caught up, and he seemed worried. "Is that what it sounds like?"

"That's a helicopter. I don't think any moonlight tours were planned. Especially in this fog," Veronica said.

The light shone from behind us, and for a second, I thought it might be the Bridge, finding us instead of the other way around, but the wind that blustered around the rocky clearing told me otherwise.

"We have to go," Tripp said, but two soldiers emerged from the pathway twenty feet from him. They were tricky to discern in the fog, the bright spotlight of the helicopter adding to the hazy effect.

The rush of the wind finally cleared the low-lying cloud from the vicinity as the helicopter landed, and the two armed soldiers wearing black uniforms walked closer, guns aimed at the four of us. Their faces were obscured with masks, and they meant business.

They motioned with their guns. "Stay put!" one barked over the noise of the helicopter.

It was easier to see with the mist scattered by the rotors. Marcus backed up, raising his hands. The black light shone into the sky.

"What do we do, Rex?" Veronica asked, her voice muddled with fear.

This was the third time in a week we'd faced the Believers, and I was growing sick and tired of it. We were so close, and here they were again, jamming guns in our direction.

"I'll tell you what we're going to do!" The voice was confident, but somehow recognizable.

The rotors slowed, and out walked a man. Someone struggled behind him, and I saw another Believer soldier holding a woman inside the helicopter. It was Beverly.

My entire body clenched, like a snake about to strike. That was my sister. "Why is she here?" I shouted, and suddenly, the mountaintop grew silent. With the chopper off, the fog began again, but not as thickly as before.

"Rex, it's…"

"Fred." I said the name with disdain, my lips sticking together as they went dry. I charged toward him, uncaring about the guns pointing at me.

"Rex, hand the Bridge over—"

I punched him in the face as hard as I could. My fist stung, but the pain scarcely registered. "What have you done? Where are the kids?"

A solider stepped between us, and Fred shoved the man aside. "The kids? *My* kids are fine, Rex. They're at the lovely little retreat you booked, sleeping it off until we retrieve them."

I stared at the man, blood dripping from his nose. He appeared so different in this light. "Why, Fred? Why the Believers?" I wanted to buy some time. Tripp's gun had vanished, telling me he'd concealed it when the soldiers had arrived. He was full of tricks. He was either guns blazing or quiet as a mouse, lingering like a shadow.

"Why? Why is it okay for millions of people to have faith in their god, but when we're absolutely confident the Unknowns exist and are coming home, it's insane? We're a cult. A group of fanatics." He wiped his upper lip, then broke into a smile. "Too bad you won't see what's to come, Rexford. When the world learns how deep the Believers go, there will be no turning back.

"We're everywhere. We control governments, stock markets, and corporations. The Believers are the Earth's only hope, Rex. That's what you should understand. When the Unknowns come"—he tapped his watch—"and they're on the way. They will destroy us unless the Believers are present to greet them. Can't your doctorate brain comprehend this?" Fred had a gun in his hand, and he tapped it to his temple.

I peered past him at the helicopter. The pilot held Bev, and she was crying with heavy racking sobs. Her husband wasn't who she'd thought he was, and her world was devastated. "Why the charade?"

"I was told to position myself close to the family. The famous Dirk Walker's kids. At first I thought about working at your school, becoming friends with you, but I hated the idea of teaching this generation of youth with their fragile egos and self-righteous opinions of everything." He pointed at Marcus, who was protectively standing beside Veronica. "I happened to meet Beverly one day at her workplace. I asked her to coffee, and a year later, we were engaged. Can you imagine? True love." He laughed, a delirious sound that cut short in the thickening fog.

"You son of a bitch," I said, moving for Fred again, but his gun lowered as the laughing ceased.

"One more move and you're dead." He said it flatly, without emotion, and it was obvious he wasn't lying.

"What's the plan? You take the Case and then what?" I asked.

He motioned to the helicopter, and one of the soldiers ran to it, patting a crate. "We send a surprise to the other side." Judging by the markings on the surfaces, it was a high-tech bomb, maybe a thermonuclear device. I cringed at the implications. He was banking on the Bridge working, and planned to send a nuclear bomb through the portal.

"Who's across the Bridge?" Fred and the Believers probably didn't know for sure, but I had to ask.

"Someone you don't want to meet," he said with so much self-assurance, I found myself trusting his word on it.

"Jerry, prepare the device. We're going in," Fred called to his soldier.

The only problem was, this wasn't the entrance to the Bridge. He'd followed us to the wrong location. It gave us an opportunity, albeit a slim one.

"Why don't you go scope it out, Fred? Let us help you. If what you say is true, I won't fight you on this. I've been tricked by Hunter Madison. He lied about everything." I hoped my acting classes from the ninth grade were paying off.

Fred stared at me, walking closer. "Cliff, go up the path. Check if there's an entrance nearby."

The soldier nearest Tripp jogged off, gun barrel bobbing as his helmet's light guided his path toward the mountain peak. He was quickly swallowed in the fog.

We didn't have long. Once Cliff realized there was no cavern, he'd return, and we'd be in trouble. I nudged Marcus with my elbow, and he must have sent a signal to Tripp behind him.

It was three against four, five if you counted my sister, but they were each armed.

Beverly shouted at Fred, cursing him for what he'd done to her and the kids, and he started to turn. I took the chance.

I barreled into Fred and heard the gunshots behind me as Tripp fired at Jerry near the helicopter. Fred's gun fell to the rocks, and my own wound stretched, a pain tearing through my stomach. I scrambled over him, but Marcus was there, snatching the weapon. Tripp had a handle on

Jerry, who was crumpled to the ground, dead eyes watching the clouds.

Fred spun on his back, and he jabbed a punch into my gut, sending me reeling. I gasped as the air shot from my lungs. I squinted through the blackness and heard muffled shouts.

"Marcus, now!" Veronica shouted, and I opened my eyes to see my sidekick standing over Fred.

The gun lowered. He couldn't do it.

"I'm sorry, Rex," he said. For a second, I thought Marcus was telling me he was with Fred. A Believer. Then I understood. He'd already killed someone, and he couldn't do it like this. Point blank with the man staring him in the eye.

Tripp shoved Marcus out of his way and hauled Fred to his feet. He pressed his pistol against Fred's temple, using the man as a shield while walking toward the helicopter and the last remaining soldier in the clearing. "Hand her over or your boss gets it!"

The soldier helped Beverly out and removed his mask. His frame was massive, and he was older, maybe mid-sixties, with gray hair and white stubble. "Kill him. If you don't, I will," the guy said, releasing Beverly. For a moment, she just stood there, tears streaming down her face, and then she ran past Fred and to the spot where I lay on the rocks.

Tripp still had Fred, and Beverly's husband fought to escape. Tripp clubbed him over the skull, sending him to the trail. "Let's see it, then," Tripp said.

The big soldier pulled a gun, but instead of pointing it at Fred or us, he aimed toward the cliffs. He ran off, and half a minute later, we heard three gunshots. He came back, dragging Cliff's body with him. He dropped the Believer soldier and shoved his gun in its holster.

"Who are you?" I asked as Veronica assisted me to my feet. The gunshot wound was reopened, bleeding through my shirt and into my jacket.

"A friend." His voice was gravelly.

"What the hell are you doing, Saul?" Fred asked with a laugh. "You're all going to die! They won't stop until you're gone and the Bridge is closed forever. The Unknowns are coming! Then you'll see!" He clawed his way to his feet, dashing toward the crate in the rear of the helicopter.

Tripp and Saul raised their guns at the same moment, but it was another gun that fired, hitting Fred in the back. He slid forward on the stones, his breaths coming ragged. Beverly walked toward him, the gun taken from Marcus in her grip. "I like to think I'm a reasonable woman, but what you did was unforgivable. Our children, Fred… What were you going to do with them?"

He managed to roll over, blood spilling from his lips. "I love them, Bev. I love you too. It would make sense when the Unknowns came. I wanted to save you…"

More tears spilled from her eyes, and she shook her head. "You aren't my husband." She walked away, leaving him sputtering, and a minute later, his chest stopped moving.

"We need to go," Saul said. "I take it you realized this isn't the Bridge entrance?"

I nodded, hardly able to stand. Veronica was there to brace me as we rushed for the helicopter.

Tripp aimed at Saul. "We can't trust this guy. Who the hell's to say he's not the Sovereign?"

"Thank you for helping us," I whispered to Saul.

"No problem, kid. I only wish I could have exposed my presence to you sooner. I was deep undercover," he told me.

"But Tripp's right. How can you prove your story?" I

asked.

Saul unbuttoned his shirt, pulling it apart. The tattoo on his chest stared back at me. I unzipped my jacket and tugged my shirt open too. They matched.

Beverly gasped. "That's what Dad had, isn't it?"

"It is," I said. "And Hardy told us there were four of you with them. Clayton Belvedere, Dirk Walker, Brian Hardy, and…"

"Saul Goldstein." He stuck his hand out. It was like shaking hands with a stone. "When we learned what the Believers were doing, I went in. Haven't broken character for almost four decades."

"The tattoo. It looks like a P over a T. What does it mean?" Veronica asked.

Saul smiled, the expression frightening on the tough older man. "*Promissa terra*. The promised land."

6

*W*e ultimately discovered a flat spot to land near the Bridge's cavern. It was higher in elevation, and the low-lying clouds were below us as we descended to the narrow landing strip.

"Have the Believers sent reinforcements?" Tripp asked Saul, but the other man shook his head.

"The Sovereign didn't believe Fred was ready, but they figured a nuke and three of the best soldiers would do the trick if he did find the Bridge. Only I selected the soldiers, and they were greener than spring grass," Saul said.

We landed, with Beverly managing to keep it together despite everything that had just occurred. Her children were at the house, and they'd be safer there for a few hours.

She cleaned my wound, with Veronica reapplying a bandage and wrapping gauze around my torso. I popped a painkiller, chugging some water, and hoped I'd have enough strength to finish what we'd started.

It was well past midnight, and I glanced behind me at the crate, cringing at the thought of sitting so close to a nuke. Tripp was the first to dash from the helicopter.

"Rex, who do you want to enter with you?" he asked, leaving it up to me.

I glanced around the group, scanning from face to face.

Marcus was the first to speak. "I'll stay here, Rex. If you're trapped on the other side, I'll use the Case to bring you home."

Tripp nodded. "I should stay too. On the off chance more of the Believers come."

I assumed he also didn't completely trust this newly-admitted turncoat, but there was something about Saul that I instantly respected.

"I'll go," Veronica said. "I want to see what's across this Bridge as much as anyone."

And it was settled. Beverly stayed at the helicopter, her hands clasped tightly together. "I'll be okay. With any luck, I'll be right back." I placed a palm on her stacked grip. "I'm sorry about everything."

She didn't respond. The shock was sinking in.

I peered around the area, and despite the adrenaline racing through me, I admired the view. The ocean was twenty or so miles away, but we could see the stars reflecting from it as the clouds parted under us. There were a few sparse trees, but mostly rock at this high point in the hillsides.

Marcus used his black light again, scouring the rocky area, and called me over. An arrow was drawn, pointing to a spot in the cliffside. "This is it! Hunter did mark it for us."

Thousands of stars gleamed above us. I'd seen a lot of night skies in the middle of nowhere, far from the light pollution of a populated metropolis, but this was special. I was drawn to it. Hunter's riddle described it well. *Where the water flows, the pathway glows. Seek a star's flight on a cloudy night.* I listened, catching the sound of the trickling water running along the fissure at the base of the peak.

The moon was a half-crescent, reminding me of one of the Tokens, and I basked in the radiance for a moment. Veronica helped me as we walked for the rocky hillside, and Marcus located another arrow. We amended our direction, and when we were twenty feet from the entrance, it jumped out at us.

I slowed and Tripp dropped the bag, pulling the Case out.

Saul walked toward me, but Tripp stepped in his path. "I don't think so."

"I just want to see it again. It's been years," he said.

"Why didn't my dad ever mention you in any of his journals?" I asked.

"We had the idea to send me to the Believers. It was tougher than you'd think to breach, but I did it." His chest puffed up a bit at his self-praise. "Did you ever see Dirk mention an 'S' in his excerpts?"

I thought about it, and did recall him referencing someone named S on occasion. "I think so."

"That was me. He couldn't know who would end up with the journals, after all, and I didn't want to be detected by the Believers," Saul told me.

I had the Case in my hands, with the solo Token in my pocket. I showed Saul, and he let out a high whistle. "Your father would be proud of you, kid."

"It's been a while since anyone's called me 'kid'," I advised him.

"Get to be my age and see what I've seen, even your elders seem like kids. Well, on with it. Don't forget this." Saul pulled a gun, flipping it around deftly, and passed it to me.

"What do you think we're going to find?" I asked him.

"We never did figure that out. We could only hope"—he patted his chest over the tattoo—"that it led to the promised land."

"Let's do this, Rex." Veronica took my hand and walked with me. The air was thin, and with my reinjured bullet wound, I was struggling to stand properly. I fought the urge to bend over protectively and kept my spine straight, limping for the cavern entrance.

We paused before ambling in, and Veronica smiled at me. "I never told you my secret."

It seemed like an odd time to bring it up. "Can you wait until after we find out if we're alone in the universe?"

We stood a foot apart, and I felt the stares from everyone on my back. "It can wait."

"Would you two hurry up?" Tripp called from behind us.

I'd forgotten anyone was watching and stepped into the room. Our flashlights shone around, discovering etchings on the walls and unlit torches set into metal holders. "Anyone have a lighter?" I asked, and Saul jogged over, passing me one. His eyes were huge as he stared past me.

"Stay here," I warned him, and Veronica and I walked through the cavern, lighting the four torches. They lit easily, and soon the room was inviting in its orange glow. "Look." I pointed at a life-size carving of an alien being on the cave's wall beside Veronica.

"My dad stood here. He held this." I lifted the Case. "He saw this depiction." The figure was human-like, resembling many ancient cultures' take on a god from the stars. Elongated forehead, stretched limbs.

This was all I'd ever wanted, to end up where my father had disappeared. Now I was attempting to travel to the same place. Would I share his fate? "You should go," I whispered to Veronica as I hesitantly stepped up to the stone podium. The surface was flat and polished, and I drew my gaze upward to the opening in the cavern ceiling. The stars shone brightly above.

"You know I can't," she said.

"Why?" I didn't quite understand why someone who'd just started this adventure a few weeks ago would be so invested in the Bridge. "It's not worth your life."

"Is it worth yours?"

I didn't answer and set the Case on the table. The Token fell from my weakened grip, clattering to the ground. Veronica retrieved it, returning the hexagon to me. "Do you think this was what it was like for them?"

"Dirk and Clay?"

She nodded.

"I don't know. I can only imagine it was similar." I glanced upwards again. "Are you ready?" The room was stuffy, and wind howled from above us, sending a light layer of dust across the table.

She picked up a bag of supplies and draped it on her shoulder. If we were heading somewhere far away, we'd brought provisions. Suddenly, I felt like a fool. What if the Bridge brought us to space, and we died in the terrible freezing vacuum? What if we couldn't breathe the air on the other world? What if the Case did nothing, and we'd been chasing our imaginations?

"I'm ready," she finally said, and I judged she was running through her own series of reservations.

The last Token slid into its designated holder, and I released the Case as the corners began to burn brightly. Wind circled around us, and Veronica cried out, her hair flying over her face. I grabbed for her hand, squeezing it tight as the torches extinguished, temporarily leaving us in the dark, until blue light filled the entire cavern and I shouted, a desperate shriek of anticipation.

Veronica looked up, tears on her cheeks, and I followed her stare. The stars were different through the opening. A tunnel raced downwards from some distant point, and the room went black again.

"Veronica?" Our flashlights were off, the torches out, and the blue light had dissipated. I couldn't see a thing.

We were still clutching hands. "I'm here."

I felt for the lighter and flicked the gear, a butane flame bounding to life. Two men stood across the podium, gaping at us with wild eyes.

"You did it," one of them said. "You brought us home!"

"Who the hell are you?" I asked, but Veronica was already moving from them. She grabbed a torch and tossed it to me, while aiming her gun in the newcomers' direction. I lit the tip, a sulfur smell catching my nostrils, and held the bright wooden stick out, trying to garner a better view.

"You found a way to bring us back," the other man said, his voice practically a whimper. They were dressed in ill-fitting robes, and the one man was mostly bald, with cracked glasses placed precariously on his nose. Their faces were shrouded in shadows, and the taller man reached for the Case.

"How did you find it? I made sure no one would," he whispered.

"Back away!" I had the gun aimed between them, the effort making my stomach hurt fiercely.

His hair was matted, long and curled at the ends. Dark brown eyes glanced up at me, and even though there were more lines on his face, and he was a good twenty pounds lighter than any pictures I had, his identity was obvious.

"It's impossible." I walked around the stone stand, using it to keep my balance. The wound was aggravated, and I stuck a hand to it, pressing tightly. My vision was distorted, blood seeping through my fingers. I stumbled, and the man caught me.

"Who are you?" he asked, and I heard a voice from my past.

I was four years old, wearing a birthday hat and sitting at the table, waiting for Mom to bring the cake in. A scattering of friends sat around me, and Beverly saw Dad first. She started to get up, but Mom shut the door. She was yelling. Dad hadn't been around for weeks, perhaps months, and Mom had told me earlier that he wasn't coming for my fourth birthday party.

After a few minutes of shouting, he walked into the dining room with a small gift, wrapped with a section of the newspaper and an elastic band. *This is for you, son,* he'd said, and I'd dug into it, finding a multi-knife, the kind a kid that age should never have. I jumped from my seat, clinging to his waist, and I remembered seeing my mom's expression. A mixture of sadness and relief.

"I'm your son." And I passed out.

7

I only recalled sections of our return trek to Madison's vineyard.

"Are you sure we can go back there?" It was Tripp, and I scarcely heard him over the whir of the rotors.

A gruff voice answered, and I kept my eyes closed. I didn't have the strength to open them. "Fred had no access to the network. The moment you arrived, I cut the communication ties from his end."

"Impressive." This from Marcus.

"Is he going to be okay?" the voice that haunted me asked.

"He has to be," Veronica said. There was a tinge of sadness to her voice, a heaviness I'd never heard before. But it was gone with everything else as the darkness overtook me again.

I woke in a bed, with sunlight peeking through the drawn drapes.

Images flashed in my mind: of the Tokens, the Case, the blue light cascading from the stars, and lastly, of the two figures that had emerged in the cavern. It was impossible. Clearly, I was delusional, likely feverishly dreaming in the hospital bed in Boston. I fumbled for a call cord but didn't find one.

"Good, you're awake," someone said.

The drapes were pulled aside, sending motes of dust into the beam of sunlight. He wore the same robe and walked across the room from the chair he'd been sleeping in.

"Dad," I muttered. My lips were dry, and he passed me a glass of water.

"I don't know how this came to be, but I'm so grateful." He sat on the bed, his weight tugging at the blankets. He must have noticed, because he loosened the covers off my stomach. "You were in rough shape, Rex. These people… they really care about you."

I nodded, unable to find my voice.

"I know you have a lot of questions, and I'll do my best to answer them, but bear with me. I've been somewhere else, not sure I'd ever get home. Things haven't been easy on Clayton and me."

The other man. Clayton Belvedere. It was so obvious.

"I… never gave up on you," I whispered.

He clutched my hand, and for a second, I was that little boy at my birthday again. "Thank you, son."

"How… you're not much older than me," I told him. It was true. He could have been my brother, or a young uncle at the very least. Fifty, tops.

"The Bridge… it defies a lot of what we assumed," he said.

"I don't understand," I admitted. My head felt clearer, and I took another sip of water, letting it ease my throat.

"Neither do I, but we'll figure it out together. I hear they're on the way," he said.

"Who? The Unknowns?"

"They *are* known, Rex. They are very known. But we'll get to that later. You need to rest. Are you hungry?"

I sat up, cringing as I propped the pillow behind me. "You owe me this. I've spent my entire life searching for your ghost, and you show up and say we'll talk about it later? No. Give me answers. Where the hell were you? Why did you leave? How come you hid the Tokens?" The questions flew out of me, and he nodded. His body looked calm, but his eyes were restless.

"Let's find you some food. Clayton and his kid should be there when we talk. Beverly too." He smiled. "I can't believe your mother is gone."

I'd missed something, and circled back. "Clayton and his kid? Who…"

And it hit me as I recalled a distant memory. The wisp of a blonde girl. Those same striking blue eyes. "Veronica… is Ronnie Belvedere!"

"She didn't tell you?" Dirk asked.

"Help me up," I said. It was entirely strange, giving my absent father orders, but it felt right at this moment.

A pair of gray sweatpants sat folded on the dresser, and he assisted me while I slid them on, sitting at the end of the bed. I snatched a bathrobe and wrapped it protectively around myself.

With the door open, I heard something I didn't expect. Laughter. Music. The scent of bacon and eggs.

We walked toward the kitchen, and Marcus held up a champagne flute with orange juice in it. "Rex!" He jogged over, handing the glass off to me. "This one is just a splash of the good stuff. Your pills…"

"What… what are we celebrating?" I asked, trying to make sense of the picture. Beverly had her kids pulled tight, their expressions grim. Her husband had died. I'd almost forgotten. Veronica and Clayton sat on the couch, near the crackling fireplace. She stared at me as we approached, and everyone went silent.

Except Marcus. "It's New Year's Day. Since we missed out on the eve, we thought it might be a good way to ring in the new year. With some tunes, and food…"

I wasn't keen on celebrating. I stared at Veronica, and her expression said it all. A silent *I'm sorry. I had to do it.*

Saul was in the kitchen, working at the huge gas range, and he nodded to me.

"Since we're in this together, Dirk Walker is about to regale us with his story," I said. "Dad, we've been to hell and back, and I can only assume that's likewise for you. We're here to stand against these Believers and stop whatever is coming. Tell us what you know, and don't keep anything out."

"Rex, can I have a minute?" Veronica asked, and everyone turned to stare at her. After my speech, no one had expected the interjection.

I glanced at her father, who appeared to have showered and trimmed his hair. We walked to the fireplace and turned from the others.

"Who wants another drink?" Marcus asked, and they started talking amongst themselves.

"I'm so sorry for not telling you," she said.

"Why didn't you say something?"

She brushed at a strand of dyed hair covering her eyes and sighed. "I assumed Hunter would freak out if he knew who I really was. He was so paranoid. I'd heard from second-hand sources that he blamed my father for being cut out, and I couldn't risk him learning the truth. I had to find the Bridge, Rex. You understand."

"You could have told me."

"I tried in Antarctica, and then everything turned into a nightmare."

"We've had other instances alone," I reminded her, trying not to let her omission of truth affect me so much.

"When? We haven't exactly been sitting around the breakfast nook playing cribbage and sipping tea, have we?"

I stepped closer, and our noses almost touched. "You don't get to talk to me like that. You were the one lying, not me. I've been nothing but truthful."

"Maybe, and that's fair. But look what we accomplished. We've brought our fathers home. Shouldn't that be sufficient?" She took my hand, and I didn't fight it. I had no energy for squabbles. Veronica was probably right about Hunter. He had been erratic, but I did feel like his passion had come from a good place.

"No more of that. We have to trust one another."

She blinked rapidly and bent in, kissing my cheek. Her lips tilted toward my ear. "Something's wrong with him. I don't know if that's my father." The words were so subtle, I wondered if I'd misheard her; then she was gone, returned to Clayton's side, grabbing another mimosa from Marcus.

I watched my friend interact with everyone. He was making jokes and cheering the kids up. They wouldn't know what happened to their father, and I wasn't sure how Beverly was going to explain it, but I would be there for them. Carson and Edith needed that. I'd grown up without a father, and I'd make sure they had someone in their corner for years to come.

"Food's up, Rex." Saul waved at me from the kitchen, and Marcus dashed to the counter, relaying the plate as I sat on the couch opposite Ronnie and her dad. *Ronnie*. Marcus had called her that once on our trip, and now I felt foolish for not having picked up on it then.

Beverly made the kids settle in the smaller living space and turned the TV on quietly before coming back. She sat next to our father, and to my surprise, Beverly leaned in, resting her head on his shoulder like no time had separated them for the last three-plus decades. I still couldn't believe Fred had been with the Believers.

Saul washed up and grabbed a cup of coffee, finishing off the group, and stood behind a couch with Tripp.

And Dirk Walker began. "The Bridge was an idea. A theory Hardy had heard of years before Clay or I finished high school. He was an interesting man—brilliant, really. There was a hypothesis of ancient beings on Earth. The Believers, whom I've been told you had a run-in with, worshiped a race they call the Unknowns. They feel that these aliens weren't technically aliens, but the original inhabitants of Earth. They speculate they weren't evolved from microorganisms; rather, they flew here on interstellar vessels.

"The Unknowns lived on our planet for countless years, far before dinosaurs, or anything else we've managed to dig up. It's thought they dismantled their cities before leaving, but before they went, they left the spark of life they knew would one day create us. Homo sapiens. The Believers, in all their rhetoric, think we've reached our precipice as a species. Some think we've passed it, and our decline is imminent."

I swallowed a few bites of my eggs and peered around the room, seeing everyone was as enthralled with my father's storytelling as I was. Saul nodded along, which was proof in itself, considering he'd secretly been among them for decades.

"By learning their language, the cult thinks they can attune and merge with the aliens' minds upon arrival. Hardy dismissed this, along with many of their ideologies, but he did agree about our creators, and the fact that they'll return.

"There is evidence of them coming to check on our progress throughout the ages, most recently in a community in what we now know as the remote Canadian tundra. The entire village was wiped from the face of the planet, leaving the military to construct an elaborate environmental hoax." Dirk Walker paused and took a sip from his wine flute. "Hardy imagines this was to test their concepts. If they deemed them worthy, they would send a contingent."

"What do they want?" Tripp asked.

"We can't be certain, but Hardy thought they wanted workers. There's no empirical evidence of this," my father replied. "But it's what the Believers built their religion on."

"A god that created us… aliens. This is messed up," Marcus mumbled.

"And where does the Bridge come into this?" I managed to ask.

"That was all Hardy. He studied every single culture he could, dating back as far as the Stone Age. Eventually, he made the connections: mentions of the hexagonal shapes, though they were never described so similarly. Unfamiliar black substance. Six sides. Flat stones. Then the markings.

"There were six in total, or so he thought. Six Tokens, as he called them. He determined there had to be a correlation, a link between the items, since they were from so many different ages and spread apart across our globe. And he found it."

Veronica cleared her throat and said the words. "The Case."

"Yes. The Case would hold the Tokens, and he imagined that linking them simultaneously would create a portal to another world. A design left for mankind to prevent their creators from destroying them."

"But who would bother to do something like that? Why didn't they just stop in and say, 'look at us, we're going to stop an invasion'?" Beverly said.

"How do you assume that would go? Plus, this was before we became a global community," I said, and my dad nodded in agreement.

"Rex is right. When they visited, we were fledging societies, with no contact with one another. They knew the

Unknowns, as you called them, wouldn't return until humanity was far more advanced. Which meant they'd have the ability to find the Bridge pieces and use it."

"And you did. You both did." Veronica smiled at her father, and I noted how quiet he'd remained this whole time.

"So where's our help? Tell us about the Bridge," I urged him.

Suddenly, Dirk looked less of my childhood hero and more of an aging stranger. "We departed under great duress, Rex and Beverly. I didn't want to leave you two or your mother, but we'd heard rumors of the Believers' redeemers returning. Now I suspect they were just that: lies perpetuated to provoke us to find the Bridge and lead the Believers to it. Only they never did track us."

"Is that why you cut Hunter Madison out?" Veronica asked.

"He had too many ties to the cult. He promised he'd severed them, but I couldn't…"

"What about Hardy? He told me you were brothers. That you were supposed to bring him too," I said, remembering the doddering old man.

"Brian Hardy wouldn't come. We tried. He said he might be needed here," Dirk said.

"Well, they're both dead. At the hands of the ones you put Saul's life into." I was angry for a multitude of reasons but was quickly realizing that my father had been trying to save the world. It did little to ease the decades of unanswered questions.

Dirk and Clayton watched one another as I told them, and Clayton finally spoke. "We must return to the Bridge."

My father squinted, his lips pressing together hastily. "Clay, remember yourself."

I saw something pass between them, an invisible

understanding.

"Why?" I pressed. "What's there?"

"Time is different. We found a city, empty. We could breathe, and there were food sources, water wells, but we were alone. Hardy was certain we'd find our salvation. The Promised Land. *Promissa Terra.* But he was wrong. They were gone. We think the Unknowns are to blame," he told us.

"We're doomed. The Unknowns are coming, and we have no defense," Tripp grunted.

"That's not quite true. They left something else behind: a seventh Token. And we know where the Case is."

"Where?" I asked, my blood thumping through my veins.

"In Rimia."

"What's Rimia? Is that where the Bridge leads?"

Clayton nodded. "That's the planet, or the city. We aren't sure. We didn't venture far. Dirk made us return to the other end of the Bridge each night. Plus, leaving was… not safe."

"You thought these beings who created the Tokens would be there to help you, right? That's why you had Luis disperse the Tokens around the world?" I asked.

"Yes. You know about Luis?" Clayton asked.

"We uncovered his trail on your gravestone. The coordinates to the mine in Venezuela," I said.

Dirk went rigid. "Clay, you did that?"

Clay coughed and slid his broken glasses up his nose. "I had to, Dirk, and for good reason. You two were so sure help would be across, but I was more pragmatic. On the chance we traveled the Bridge and couldn't return, I wanted someone to find the trail. I didn't think it would take so many years."

"And, Dad, you sent Beverly the Token," I said.

It was Clayton's turn to get upset. "And after all the chiding you gave me about wanting to set up a contingency plan, you went and sent one to your daughter?"

My father held his daughter's hand. "They needed to know it wasn't them. It was something bigger."

"Well, we do now. But the question is, what's next?" I set my half-empty plate on the coffee table and waited for the answer.

"We locate the seventh Token and carry it across the Bridge. There, we'll revive a second Bridge, one that will lead us to the only people who can save us from the incoming Objects." Dirk spoke with passion and enthusiasm, and despite everything that had just happened, I was optimistic.

"Where is this mysterious Token?" Veronica asked.

"We don't know," Clayton confessed.

Dirk Walker had returned, the Objects were two months from arriving at Earth, and we had no means to stop them from invading. With the Believers after us every step of the way, I didn't expect the next part of our adventure to go any smoother than the first had.

Veronica met my gaze. Marcus already had his computer out, asking for any details on this seventh Token, and Tripp and Saul were quietly discussing provisions.

The team was assembled, and my father leaned over, whispering to me.

"It'll all make sense soon enough, Rexford."

I nodded, but his cryptic words only added to the mystery.

Epilogue

Dirk Walker listened from his bedroom and waited until the entire house had retreated into late-night silence. The mansion had plenty of rooms to seek shelter in. He adjusted the pajamas, sliding into a pair of old slippers that were slightly too large for his feet.

He crept to the door, slowly opening it to keep it from squeaking. His steps were light as he shuffled through the hallway. Someone coughed, and he froze, waiting to see if there was movement following it. Nothing.

Thirty-five years. How had time gone so far here, while by their judgment, they'd passed eight Earth years on Rimia? While it didn't seem fair, he could understand to an extent. Brian had warned them that time dilation might be a possibility, but he'd never expected to be stuck across the Bridge for any considerable length.

His children were an oddity to him. He'd been gone so much during their first few years, and today they were grown, almost as old as he was. But he still felt a bond with each of them that couldn't be broken. It was difficult to explain, even to himself.

The loss of Rebecca was tough, a sting he hadn't anticipated. They'd once been in love. Real, passionate exuberance, which had dwindled to companionship with marriage and children and his obsession with the Bridge. She'd never understood him, nor had he comprehended her. By the end, they were as alien to one another as the beings destined for Earth.

Marcus had shown Dirk images of the Objects, and seeing the aliens' ships was bizarre. Hunter and Brian had been so sure they were coming, but Dirk and Clayton hadn't been as confident, though they'd left on the Bridge just the same. Their period in Rimia had been far from a waste.

They could save Earth.

Dirk walked to his son's room and opened the door. Rex was sleeping soundly, his medication strong enough to knock out an elephant for a few hours. The Case was under his bed, in the original burlap sack. Dirk crouched on the floor, slipping the device out, and he opened it, setting a hand on the Tokens inside.

Anticipation burned through him as he slid it back under the bed. He stood beside Rex and smiled. He'd grown up to be a spitting image of Dirk. He hoped Rex and his sister would understand everything in the long run.

He left the room, moving farther into the house. The patio doors were locked, and he flipped the switch before stepping out into the chilly night air. The sky was clear, and he walked over to the edge of the deck. The moonlight cast its serene glow across the sweeping vineyard, crossing the entire valley's many hills and mounds.

His gaze drifted to the stars. "I'll be back. I just have to do something first."

His thoughts drifted to the incoming ships, and he sighed. This should have been a heroic return, but it was filled with regrets and sadness.

Dirk returned to the living room and saw the man on the couch. "Tripp, I'm sorry if I woke you," he said quietly.

The man had a killer's stare. "I don't sleep much."

Dirk didn't engage and softly plodded his way to bed

before closing the door and locking it.

He'd seen too much across the Bridge. They couldn't know it all yet. But one day soon, it would be revealed. It was imperative that they locate the last Token. He wished Hardy was alive, because he was the only person Dirk knew that might be able to discover its location.

Sleep found Dirk Walker, and for the first time since he'd vanished from Earth, he didn't dream.

The End
Lost Contact (The Bridge Sequence Book One)

Continue the mystery with
Lost Time (The Bridge Sequence Book Two)

ABOUT THE AUTHOR

Nathan Hystad is an author from Sherwood Park, Alberta, Canada. His books include The Event, Final Days, and Lost Contact.

Keep up to date with his new releases by signing up for his newsletter at www.nathanhystad.com

Printed in Great Britain
by Amazon